AWAKEN

DESCEND INTO DARKNESS

L.G. BENITO

Instagram & TikTok: @LGBenitoAuthor

Edition Three
First edition April 2022

Cover, Typography and Interior Design by *Natalia Junqueira*
Developmental & Line Edit by *Warren Layberry*
Proofreads by *Joe Pierson* & *April Kelly*
Map by *Kate Korsak*

ISBN 978-1-7378068-1-3 (paperback)
ISBN 978-1-7378068-6-8 (hardcover)
ISBN 978-1-7378068-2-0 (ebook)

www.mikaplum.com

DISCLAIMER

Before proceeding, note that some readers will find actions taken by characters and scenes describing the severe, graphic injuries in this story disturbing.

The human body is resilient; unless the brain or spine are *severely* injured, a body can continue to function anywhere from a few minutes to several hours after being mauled or damaged, depending on what organ was hurt, total blood loss, and willpower of the wounded person. Examples of this can be seen in survivors of vehicular crashes, industrial accidents, animal attacks, terrorist/violent acts, and injuries of war.

War, combat, anger, and trauma trigger innermost thoughts of unleashing pain on the enemy. Torture methods employed by the Ancient Romans, destruction caused by the Mongols, and depravity of the Japanese Empire are a few examples of the evil that armies are willing to commit when unrestrained by rules of war.

Today, most militaries follow the law of armed conflict, but we keep seeing the willingness of humans to commit atrocities on their foes. Terrorist armies make public displays of torture, execute their captives, and sacrifice women and children in bombings. Criminal organizations record beheadings, live amputations, and rapes of their rivals. Homegrown attackers plan and execute mass murder on children, adults, and the elderly for publicized infamy.

One can only imagine how atrocious battles involving swords, axes, and maces were, how captives and citizens on the losing side of a battle were treated, and the willingness of warfighters to unleash evil onto their opponents. The violent, explosive, vengeful, and sometimes secret and life-changing wickedness that humans have employed when on death's ground have been present from the beginning of history and to the present day.

Remember: you believe the cause you fight for is virtuous, but so does your enemy. In the end, everyone thinks themselves the good one.

This book will expose the reader to scenes showing graphic violence and gore.

This book will NOT expose the reader to scenes containing sexual assault or torture, but such actions will be mentioned.

REGION CONTINE

<- REGION OF VELONDE

ADVENTURER'S PASS

COUNTY OF
VICQUA

THE

GRAND
WATERFALL

FARMLANDS

MARKET 135

CITY OF
DI'ABRIBEL

TOWN
YEVEI

REGION OF IMBRIS

CELESTE
OF IRSTIA

PALADIN
OUTPOST

TOWN OF
TRIUMPH

T FOREST

WARRIOR'S
EDGE

BRIA

PEAK'S
LAKE

TOWN OF
REACH

N

Name	Type	Control	Symbol
vita	life	life and health	angel wing
mori	death	death and afterlife	vertical rectangle
lux	light	light and intelligence	five-point star
aevum	time	time and memories	hourglass
tenebris	darkness	darkness and emotions	black moon
ignis	fire	fire and corruption	ember
ventus	wind	wind and electricity	three silver strands
terra	earth	earth, animals, disease	sprout
aqua	water	water and righteousness	water droplet

Deity	Mastery Hair Color	Title
Angelis (f)	golden-blonde	healer
Gral (m)	ash black	necromancer
Rend (m)	platinum blonde	paladin
Baigh (m)	aevum mastery is impossible	-
Nessa (f)	jet black	witch
Liranda (f)	burgundy	sorcerer
Dwin (m)	silver	wizard
Mooredoth (m)	khaki	shaman
Kymarinou (m)	baby blue	druid

PROLOGUE

The sight of him sent an unexpected rush of adrenaline through her blood, making her thighs feel frail and rubbery. She stood on a patch of dry, yellow grass, her hand spread open on the rough bark of a tree, making sap stick to her finger. Brushing her chestnut-brown hair behind her ear, she focused on the boy yards in front of her.

The teenage boy, the one with the dark, sparkling blue eyes and wavy brown hair, held a large wooden stick in front of him. His lips moved as he whispered something under his breath. A brown glow appeared from his hand, telling the girl he was using a terra spell. He passed the glow through the top of the stick, using the element of earth to carve the object into a spear with three points. Satisfied with the sharpness, he smiled and submerged his new weapon into the flowing river. With a quick move of his shoulders, his bare arms extended in front of him, making the muscles flex and causing the twelve-year-old girl's mouth to drop. The boy pulled the stick from the water and held it up to the cloudy sky, reveling in his prize: a lone fish that flopped and rained glimmering drops of water onto his face. With a smile, he turned, looked toward the girl, and recoiled, dropping the stick when he saw her.

He let out a short scream, holding a hand over his racing heart. His other hand clasped a small mace that hung at his belt.

"What are you doing just standing there looking at me?" he exclaimed.

She ran forward, only a few steps before she realized her actions could be threatening, if not weird. She scratched the side of her head, trying to think of the right thing to say.

"I always see you fishing when I pass by. We go to school together."

His head tilted to the side, one of his eyebrows raised in question. Without looking away from her, he squatted and wrapped his fingers around the stick with the impaled fish.

Her voice shook, but she mustered the courage to continue talking.

"I am Mika Plum of Yevera." Not receiving the immediate response she expected, she curtsied. "What is your name?"

The boy's shoulders lowered, and the corner of his lips rose before he tilted his head back and laughed.

Mika stood straight with mouth and eyes wide. She covered her neck with her fingers and felt a rush of heat burst from her face. The cool air wasn't enough to prevent the embarrassing warmth from making her sweat.

He continued to laugh, and her heart sank.

After all these months, I decide to talk to him, she thought, *and he laughs.*

The boy straightened himself, pretending to wipe away at a tear. "I know you're from Yevera; we're *in* Yevera!"

Mika passed her finger across the top of her ear. "That's just how I introduce myself ..."

Anger was beginning to overtake embarrassment. *Stand your ground, stupid. Think of something witty. Mom said boys like witty.*

Nothing came to mind. The only thing she thought was to glare at the boy. He stood in front of her, still chuckling to himself. His flowing hair danced with the passing breeze, forcing little squints out of his glimmering blue eyes.

"Well, Mika Plum *of Yevera*, I am Page Briarhart! Of ..." He stopped, stared, then looked away in thought.

Mika took a step forward and smiled. She knew the boy wasn't from her town, so he would have a different response.

"Yeah?"

His eyes traveled to hers. "Page Briarhart ..." He dug the makeshift spear into the ground and placed a fist on his hip before puffing his chest. "... of Triumph!"

Mika hopped and widened her stance. "Hah!" She pointed her finger right at Page's face. "If you hadn't introduced yourself like that, I wouldn't have known you were from Triumph! It's always good to know where someone is from!"

Page rolled his eyes. He moved his lips, *blah, blah, blah.*

She put both fists on her hips and puffed her chest more than Page, mocking his stance.

"I won that one! Now," she said, brushing her hair behind her neck for dramatic effect, "you owe me dinner." She looked at the fish on the stick. "And I feel like eating fish."

Page's face straightened. He looked at the fish, still flopping in misery as the humans conversed, then narrowed his eyes. "Deal."

Mika's smile exploded, revealing her perfect, white teeth.

"You just gotta catch me first!" Page sprinted away, taking the fish with him, leaving a trail of dust for Mika to follow.

The girl watched Page run farther and farther away. He looked back, revealing a big, arrogant smile. She shook her head and took a deep breath.

He doesn't know I'm the fastest girl in Yevera ...

Starting at a walk, Mika picked up her pace, gaining speed every other step until she was at a full sprint. The wind whistled past her ears and washed into her eyes, forcing them to excrete tears. She swung her arms with force, blading her hands open to help cut through the air. She straightened herself to allow her lungs to expand, breathing in cadence with every other right step. Only the toes of her boots made contact with the ground.

Hearing her approach, Page turned and flinched when he saw her just behind him. He misplaced a foot and tripped, causing him to tumble to the ground and drop his spear.

He crawled to his knees, gripping a scraped elbow. Mika's shadow made him look up at her. She raised the fish to his face.

Mika smiled. "Dinner, please."

1. MIKA

Two years had passed since that cool and breezy afternoon. Mika and Page, now in a loving relationship, spent almost every day together. Page had grown accustomed to Mika's aggressive personality, and Mika accepted the fact that Page wouldn't kiss her until they married.

The evening wind blew past Mika, making her hair drift in front of her eyes. The season of growth was in full swing, but the air at the top of the mountain was cool. She ran on the narrow mountain trail behind Page. After the two years of running with him, she learned Page ran best when she was running behind him. No excuses for him to slow down.

Page carried a backpack and wore a thick shirt, loose trousers, and comfortable boots that kicked up dirt with every step. Page veered off the trail and onto a rocky path. He told Mika there was a shortcut to the top of Mount Cabria. Looking back to make sure Mika was still following caused him to misplace his step and almost fall when a rock shifted beneath his feet. He caught himself and held his arms out for balance.

With wide eyes and heavy breathing, he looked at Mika. "Are you okay?"

The fourteen-year-old girl slowed to a walk and rolled her eyes. "You're the one who almost fell, Page." Mika wasn't tired; she took a deep breath that made her heartrate slow.

"Hey, just making sure." Page adjusted his backpack. "I know you'd die if I got hurt."

Mika's lips puckered when she tried to hide her smile. She rolled her eyes and shook her head.

"I'm not tired, Mika. I'm just pretending." Page closed his mouth and breathed through his nose. Mika would have believed him had it not been for the throbbing vein on his forehead.

"Then please ..." Mika hopped in place and braced herself to take off in a sprint. "Move faster. My walk is the same speed as your run."

Page mocked, "*My walk is the same speed as your run.*" He turned around and ran off at a pace similar to Mika's light jog.

It was a few more hops over rocks and trudges through grass until he slowed to a walk. A set of large boulders blocked their path with no way to go around them without falling off the edge of the mountain. Resting for a brief moment, Page jumped on a boulder, reached as high as he could, and pulled himself up, wagging his legs to help him pull himself over.

Page lay on his stomach and reached down, smiling. "Grab on, Mika!"

Mika shook her head. "Who do you think I am? Move out of the way!" Mika sprinted toward the boulder and kicked herself up, grabbing on to the top. With a light kick of her leg, she hurdled over.

Page panted with his arms on his hips. He stared at Mika.

Mika held her chin high. The sun was behind her head, making her silhouette shine as if she were a mighty empress.

Page grabbed her head and shook it with playful energy. "One day, you're going to need my help, and I'm gonna ask, *who do you think I am?*"

"You can fight; I can run. Perfect couple." Mika stuck her tongue out and crossed her eyes.

"Come on." Page let go and waved her to follow. "We're almost there."

Mika followed on the rocky trail with a smile on her face, looking down every few steps to make sure she didn't roll her ankle on a loose stone. When Page placed his arm across Mika's chest, she looked up to see the view of Celeste from the top of Mount Cabria. Placing her hand on the tree next to her, she leaned over the edge of the mountain with an open mouth, taking in the sight of the distant forests, mountains, grasslands, hills. The sunset that painted the sky with an orange and purple brush made the scene unforgettable.

Celeste is beautiful, she thought, taking in the wonderful sight of the small region known for its stunning skies, constant wind, and natural wonders.

Page stuck a finger in Mika's gaping mouth, bringing her back to reality.

Mika coughed. "Page!"

Page ran off laughing, forcing Mika into a chase.

"Get back here, you little—"

Her foot slipped.

Falling face first, she sank into a puddle of cold, thick, brown mud. With arms shaking from sheer anger, Mika pushed herself to her knees, feeling the mud drip from her face and splash into the puddle. Her clothes felt heavier because of the clinging mud.

Mika wiped her raging eyes. With eyebrows furrowed so much she could see them, she looked at Page. Had Page been within arm's reach, she would have killed him.

Page was yards away; holding his stomach with one hand, he pointed at Mika with the other. His laughing was inaudible past the strange whispers that came to Mika when she was angry.

Mud seeped between Mika's fingers when she clenched onto a handful of the stuff. She took a deep breath and exhaled as she threw it at Page's head. His face straightened, and too late he tried to duck. The wad of mud hit him full in the mouth, and he stumbled and fell on his butt. Now it was Mika who laughed.

Her laugh grew and grew, becoming hysterical when she saw Page spit out the mud, his face wrenched in disgust. Page stood and took off after Mika.

Mika sloshed her feet until she was out of the mud. She ran from Page, outdistancing him in seconds. She looked back with a smile covered in mud, and she turned to run faster, but the combination of the day's hike, the high altitude, and the need for food ended the pursuit within moments.

Page rested his hands on his hips and looked up toward the darkening orange-and-purple sky to better open his throat and feed more air into his lungs.

"I'll keep up with you one of these days," he huffed.

Mika approached, exhaling a deep breath. She fixed her hair behind her ear.

"Be more confident, Page! You have to say," –and here she deepened her voice and bobbed her head from side to side– *"I'll pass you one of these days. Maybe once I stop playing jokes on Mika will I be able to."*

Page laughed and took off his backpack, tossing it next to a tree. He stepped to Mika and locked eyes with her. "No."

Mika couldn't stop herself from shaking. Was she shaking from the cold, the hardening mud that clung from her clothes, or because Page was standing so close in front of her?

Mika lowered her head and gazed up at Page, who stood just a few inches taller than she.

Page began cleaning off the mud from her face. His gentle wipes brought happiness to her cheeks, warmth to her heart, and safety to her soul. He wiped the mud from her forehead, her ears, and then her chin. His dark-blue eyes gazed into Mika's, and he gave a genuine, gentle smile. Mika looked down, hiding her now-rosy cheeks and wide smile that revealed her teeth.

"What will happen once I pass you?" Page's voice was smooth. Never before had she heard his voice like that.

Mika straightened her face and looked up, allowing Page to finish cleaning her face.

"I, uh ... I will let you kiss me."

Page's eyes widened for a moment. He tilted Mika's chin so that her lips were closer to his. He grazed her hair. His hand caressed the back of her neck.

"You'd let me kiss you," he whispered, "even if I never pass you."

Page was right, and she knew it. And he *wanted* to kiss her, didn't he? He would break his promise of waiting until marriage, right? *Right?*

Mika closed her eyes and inched closer to Page, exhaling an erotic breath.

"Then kiss me ..."

Mika stood with her eyes closed, waiting for Page to kiss her. It was the perfect moment: the soft breeze that carried a cold nip brushed her cheeks. The multicolored sunset would reflect off Page's skin and into her big, beautiful eyes when she opened them. The scent of sweat and mud made the moment unrepeatable, further telling her that this, *this* was the moment she and Page were meant to kiss. She felt his hand slide onto her sternum, then felt herself being walked back. Mika opened her eyes to see Page's arm extended to her.

Page's lips curved into a smile, revealing his teeth. "Too bad I haven't passed you yet!"

Page burst out in laughter when he saw Mika's face turn redder than a burning piece of steel removed from a fiery furnace.

"Page!" Mika clenched her fists. "One day you're going to make me so mad, I am going to *kill* you!"

Page held up his hands when Mika wrapped her fingers around his throat. He remained motionless, knowing if he didn't fight back, Mika would stop her attack.

Mika's raging eyes looked into his, to his hands, then back to his eyes, somehow begging for him to fight her so she could kill him. When he didn't move, Mika released his neck and began to circle him like a werewolf waiting for the slightest moment of weakness, the slightest moment of fear, to pounce.

Stop calling her crazy, he thought to himself.

The girl continued circling him.

An angry exhale told him Mika's anger was at a decline. She stormed to the edge of the mountain, sat, and took a deep, deep breath.

Page reached for his backpack, made sure she was out of earshot, and began unpacking his supplies. "She's crazy!"

Mika watched the sun set behind the mountains far to the northwest, days away at Adventurer's Pass.

Why am I like this? He was only joking. Mika wondered why Page wanted to wait to kiss her. He'd expressed his attraction to her, ignored the other girls in town, bought her gifts. Mika shook her head and squinted at the thought. She didn't want to wait until marriage. She wanted him now.

Too embarrassed and ashamed to approach him, she stole glances at Page. He worked, adjusted his hair, bent down, lifted things. Mika looked in his direction, lost in thought.

He's been with me through the fits of anger and understands them, but what if he gets tired of them? I'm going to lose him.

Page stretched his back. When he caught Mika staring, he stretched and flexed his arms. "Too easy."

Mika rolled her eyes and smiled. She looked at the scenery in front of her to let Page continue his work.

Page finished just before the stars appeared in the heavens above the couple. Bright moonlight kept the area well lit.

"Like I said, too easy." Page walked up to Mika, wiping his hands on his clothes.

Looking back, Mika saw the tent sitting erect with two sleeping bags in front of it. "We're ... sleeping *outside* the tent?"

Page offered her a hand and pulled her up. "Do you wanna see something cool?"

"I do."

"Terra!" said Page, extending his open palm to the tent.

Within seconds of shouting the name of earth magic, large rocks rose from the ground and congregated feet away from Page's hand. Page closed his eyes; evidence of strain and focus appearing on his eyebrows. With a twitch of his finger, the rocks surrounded the tent, encasing it in a protective wall of stone.

"Very neat." Mika tried her best to seem intrigued. Magic didn't interest her; she would rather learn about technological advances, science, and her favorite thing—the human body. She wanted to practice healing, but not with magic. She wanted to heal with the use of objects, vegetation, and technology.

"I'm just putting some protection in case of ..." –Page raised his hands above his head– "werewolves!" He growled at Mika.

"Oooh!" Mika covered her mouth with her fingers, looked at the black sky, then placed her palms over her heart. "So scary!"

Page grabbed her hand and guided her to the tent.

"Page, there are so many things more interesting than magic. Look." She raised her hand to the sky littered with stars and two moons, one much larger than the other. "Scholars say the stars are actually suns that are far, far away. *Massive* balls of *fire* hanging from the distant heavens." She looked at Page.

Page had his eyes closed and pretended to be asleep.

Her angry exhale forced him to open his eyes. "All right! All right!" He wrapped his arms around Mika and continued their walk to the tent. "I'll let you teach me about science and machinery and *technology*, but you have to practice magic with me."

Mika stopped and looked at Page. His eyes looked back at her with a wide, hopeful gaze. Since it would make Page happy, she agreed to learn magic with him.

Page grabbed her hand and guided her to the sleeping bags. Mika slid into her bag until it covered her up to her eyes. She waited for Page to enter his then scooted herself closer until they lay side by side, touching each other, the sleeping bags an annoying barrier between them.

Mika shrank further into her bag. "I'm sorry I get so angry."

Page lay on his side and faced Mika, but he didn't speak.

"I don't know what happens, it's so overwhelming. Sometimes, I hear little voices, little whispers ... I can't figure out what they're saying, but I know I have to stop when I hear them." Mika swallowed; her voice shook, and she closed her eyes. "I know they're trying to tell me very, very bad things."

The thought of what the whispers told Mika made Page's heart quicken. Page held Mika closer and laid her head on his chest. He didn't know how to respond, so he said something that would make her happy.

"You're the best thing that's happened to me, Mika."

Mika's heart might have burst. She snuggled closer to Page, resting her head on his chest, and they both looked up at the bright, glimmering stars. Mika recognized thirteen constellations. Page caressed Mika's hair, but to him, the stars looked like distant lanterns placed in random spots above him. He found it hard to believe that stars were distant suns.

"Tell me a story," Mika said.

He told Mika a story about a massive, muscular man, Orlan, on his quest of revenge after finding his village destroyed, his wife murdered. Orlan's valiant defeat was followed by an appearance of his wife in the afterlife. She begged him to forgive his enemies, so they could live in peace together. In the end, Orlan agreed, and he and his wife set off into their forever home in the realm that supposedly followed this one.

Page remained quiet, waiting for Mika's response to his impromptu story.

Mika looked at the stars, soothed by the story's happy conclusion. "I love your stories." Mika drifted to sleep with a smile on her face.

At that moment, Page decided he would one day marry Mika, the young, adventurous, patriotic girl who had no interest in magic and was slightly—no, not slightly, *definitely*—crazy. He had reached the age of sixteen, the legal age to marry. Mika had a year and a half left until she could marry. His thoughts raced with ways to propose before he started hating himself for not kissing her. His grandfather wouldn't have found out ... right? Before long, he too fell asleep.

*　　*　　*　　*　　*

The jog down from Mount Cabria was much easier than the ascent. By the time they reached the bottom, Mika and Page weren't out of breath like the first few hours of the previous day. Passing the all-too-familiar sign that read MT. CABRIA TRAIL III, they jogged at an easy pace on the road back home. Page told jokes that made Mika laugh. She did her best not to jump onto Page and hold him the rest of the way. Just after the morning ended, the teenagers reached the wooden walls of Yevera, ran past the open gates, and waved at the soldiers near the entrance. With a goodbye hug, they planned to meet in front of their school the following day. Page waved and walked away. Mika took off at a run through the gravel roads.

Yevera was a medium-sized town known for its lumber production and fierce, tenacious warriors. The small, gravel roads were littered with exercise stations at every corner, encouraging the citizens to stay strong and agile. Since the town's wooden homes and businesses sat on quarter-acre lots, everyone grew their own fruits and vegetables. With a river running through the town, Yevera could sustain itself without the help of the other, larger cities in Celeste. Still, Yevera traded with every city in the region and, despite the recent war, the neighboring region of Imbris.

Mika's boots kicked gravel up as she ran. She caught a glimpse of Yevera's flag: a black battle-axe in front of a crimson square. The flag swayed with the wind from the top of the single-story house that Mika called home. Mika remembered the day she bought the flag and, full of joy and courage, climbed her roof and hung it from a protruding pole.

Mika's patriotic thoughts escaped her mind when she blew through the doors of her home. To the left was the kitchen, and straight ahead was the hallway that led to her room, then her mother's room. Taking a deep breath, she sprang to her mom's room, diving onto the bed.

"Hi, Mom!"

Her mother, Cynthia, was reading a book on the bed. Ambushed by Mika, Cynthia was startled and held the book over her face. When she realized there was no danger, she relished the hug her only daughter gave her.

Cynthia placed the book under the bed, then looked at Mika. "You … stink," she said, only half joking.

"I know!" Mika laughed and rolled onto her back, dancing her feet left and right on the bed.

"Tell me how it went," Cynthia teased her daughter. "How was the date?"

Mika stopped, rolled her head to the side, and looked into Cynthia's green eyes. "Mom … I am … in *love!*"

"In love?"

Mika stood on her elbow and inched her face closer to Cynthia. "I asked him to kiss me, but he didn't."

"Well, that's outrageous! Why didn't he kiss you?" Cynthia mirrored her daughter's pose.

"Because he's a brat, Mom!" Mika's eyes widened so much it concerned her mother. "Can I marry him?"

Cynthia laughed. "Oh, Mika …" She closed her gentle eyes and shook her head. "You're almost an adult. You don't need my permission to—"

Mika squealed. She was on all fours, eyes wide, too wide, with her face inches from Cynthia's. "Mom, are you serious? I can marry him?"

Cynthia chuckled, sat up, and brushed Mika's hair behind her ear. "We can discuss this over lunch." Cynthia pinched her daughter's cheek. "But please, get off the bed with your dirty clothes!"

"What's for lunch?" Mika hopped off and watched her mom stretch before getting off the bed.

Cynthia appeared to study something imaginary in front of her. "Lentils, eggs, veggies, and …" She hesitated and looked at Mika. "Chicken?"

Mika's shoulders dropped. "Mom …"

"Rolo is getting old, Mika." Cynthia's voice was smooth, but it carried a motherly sternness. "We *must* put his body to use. It's what he's here for."

Mika nodded in agreement, yet she still felt sad. Mika adored all the animals, and she hated culling her own. "I'd rather kill hundreds of people than kill an animal."

Cynthia's mouth wrenched in worry, revealing her clenched teeth. "Mika!" She placed a hand on her daughter's shoulder. "You mustn't say that."

"But I *want* to kill someone!" Mika's eyes were trained on her mother's. "I feel like I *need* to! I want them to burn!"

Cynthia rubbed the back of her neck. She shouldn't discourage this mentality from a soldier in training. She knew Mika would one day be a ruthless killer, but she hoped her killings would be just and not for self-pleasure.

"Understood, Mika, but the only dying today will come from Rolo's sacrifice."

Mika's shoulders dropped, her gaze followed, and Cynthia led the way through the room and into the hallway. Cynthia wrapped an arm around Mika's shoulder, and they both made their way to the backyard.

Outside, Mika threw seeds out to the chickens, who stepped closer and closer to her. The oldest rooster, Rolo, wobbled over and began to eat. Mika grabbed Rolo and embraced him before walking back to Cynthia.

Cynthia leaned against the wooden rail on the porch. Her wavy, shoulder-length, golden-blonde hair told the world her mother had reached complete and utter understanding and mastery of vita magic, the magic of life and health. Because of this, the magic manifested itself in her hair, creating the golden-blonde tint and forcing all who did not know her name to refer to her as *Healer*. Her secondary mastery of mori magic, the magic of death and the afterlife, manifested itself within the golden-blonde, creating ash-black lowlights. The hair, Mika thought, went well with her mother's piercing green eyes.

They knelt in front of each other, with Rolo set between them. Cynthia called to Mika to say a prayer.

"Angelis, deity of life and health, thank you for Rolo's sacrifice, which allows us to continue living healthy and strong lives for you."

Cynthia's hand glowed a gentle ash black. She hovered it over Rolo and, using mori magic, touched the rooster's head. Rolo lowered his head onto Mika's arm and closed his eyes. Giving a last breath, the rooster expelled a bright-green mist that flowed toward Cynthia and seeped into her chest. The rooster's life essence had left its body, and now, Rolo's happiest memories were forever tucked away into Cynthia's mind. Mika looked at Rolo, saddened by his passing.

"Why don't you go shower? I'll prepare the food." Mika's mother slid her arms under Rolo and took him from Mika.

Looking up, Mika could see a gentle smile on her mother's face. The girl rose and nodded. She hugged Cynthia and placed her head on Rolo, Mika's way of saying goodbye. Yeveran homes did not have showers, so Mika grabbed clean clothes, walked out of her house and, before setting off in a run, she was greeted by Andellia, her neighbor and a classmate of hers.

Andellia's extreme intellect was matched only by her extreme shyness. She spoke in a low, soft voice. "Hi, Mika."

Mika ran up to her brunette friend and hugged her.

Andellia didn't hug back, but she placed her head on Mika's shoulder. "I read about a new plant that can help with skin irritation." Andellia pulled away and looked at Mika's boots. "Would you like to find some with me?"

"Of course! Let's do it tomorrow." Mika exhaled and widened her eyes. "I'm so tired!"

Andellia looked at Mika's eyes. Mika had always kept her word; if Mika said she would do something, nothing would stop her from doing so. Andellia nodded and thanked her.

Mika headed toward the showers and zoomed through the streets, running in a straight line without moving for anybody. The townsfolk knew to move out of the way of one of the best runners in Yevera. Because of her nimble body, small stature, amazing stamina, and inability to fight hand-to-hand, she was placed in scout and assassin training the year prior.

"Run faster, Mika Plum!" a man yelled with a smile on his face.

Mika panted and waved. "I'm too tired!"

She vaulted over a small stone wall and slid to a stop at the end of a short line to the showers. There were three people ahead of her.

She caught a glimpse of several guards escorting shackled prisoners to the rear area of the showers. Yevera had refused an aqueduct connection from the neighboring city of Di'Abribel, arguing that Di'Abribel wanted further influence on Yevera and Celeste as a whole. Because of this, prisoners were taught aqua magic to provide water for the town, in addition to transporting water from the river. These prisoners would provide a constant flow of water for the showering Yeverans.

A hilt from the guard's sword to a prisoner's head snapped Mika from her thoughts. These prisoners were once Imbric soldiers, and to Mika, all prisoners should be tortured and killed for raising weapons against Yevera. She didn't want anything to do with the prisoners, so she decided that today, and for the next few days, she wouldn't use the showers. Instead, she would bathe at the river. She took a step back, bumping into someone behind her.

Embarrassing heat flashed across her face. She lowered her head out of respect for her mathematics instructor.

"Sorry, Mrs. Trowill."

Mrs. Trowill was reading a slim brown book. She looked at Mika, then continued reading. "Be more aware, Plum. You may proceed."

Mika scurried in the direction of the river, following it miles downstream so no one who used the water was infected with her grime.

After folding her dirty clothes into a neat pile, Mika submerged herself into the river, watching little bubbles rise from her nose, bursting into freedom once they reached the surface. She saw two bubbles rising at the same pace but separated. Those two bubbles came closer until they touched side by side. Mika reached for the two bubbles, but they managed to move away in unison, slithering toward the surface and toward freedom.

That's me and Page, she thought, remembering her night at the top of the mountain.

Her lungs began to beg for air. Her chest compressed. Mika let out the remaining air, causing her to sink into the deep river. The jagged rocks at the bottom poked her toes and tumbled away, allowing her to feel the slimy riverbed.

She bent her knees, placed her palms together above her head, and shot upward, taking a deep breath the second she felt the hot breeze kiss her nose. She wiped the water from her eyes and whispered to herself, "Just like the bubbles," giggling at the analogy she had come up with.

She bathed herself. Once she finished, she dove under the water again, this time spinning in circles, pretending she was a siren, the strange female creatures that turn into humans once their bodies leave the water. According to traders and adventurers, the sirens had been seen swimming in Peak's Lake. She was determined to see a siren one day, but not with Page. What if the sirens seduced Page and took him from her? Although Mika told herself that wouldn't happen, it worried her.

I'll go with Mom.

Mika got dressed in clean clothes—a comfortable, white, long-sleeved shirt and breathable, brown pants bloused into her boots. Her boots were dyed bright red, so that Page could see her when she ran ahead of him in their adventures.

"I'll dye them brown when you finally beat me at a race!" She remembered shouting at the end of a trip to Vicqua.

Without energy, Mika decided to walk, admiring the wonderful hills in northern Yevera.

Wooden walls danced up and down the hills. The walls were a recent addition. Mika remembered the speed with which they were built—completed in almost a month. Magicians, soldiers, and builders from Di'Abribel and the town of Reach helped with the walls. Yeverans provided food and housing for the volunteers. The elders didn't protest this type of assistance.

The walls were built to protect the town from the army of necromancers, humans who specialized in mori and tenebris—the magic of death and darkness. The army of necromancers, like most warriors, were trying to take over the region of Celeste to please Gral, the deity of death, and Nessa, the deity of darkness. Once taking over Celeste, necromancers would use it as a base of operations to control the whole of the continent, since they had flanking bases at both the southern and western shores of Irstia.

Nessa had no continents under her rule, and if they could convert the continent under her powers, the necromancers would gain everlasting treasures in the afterlife. Because of their affinity with tenebris and mori, that army was able to navigate and live off the Lost Forest in the northern reaches of Celeste. Neutral parties said Celeste would be an easy target since the region was divided and the rulers of each town and city only cared about their own territory.

Although the stories scared a lot of her peers, Mika didn't care or worry; Yevera was the home of the most skilled warriors in Irstia. She knew they would defeat the necromancers if they tried anything stupid, especially with the new walls and help from Reach and Di'Abribel.

She looked to the sky. The gray clouds warmed her heart because, if rain came, her mother would make steaming-hot tea, and both of them would relax and read together. Mika smiled when she remembered the smell of rain.

Lost in thought, Mika continued to walk, thinking of Page, Cynthia, marriage, school, traveling … and didn't notice the black balls shooting up to the sky, exploding in silence above Yevera, releasing a black blanket that stretched below the clouds. The black fog thickened and began to cover the sun, darkening everything underneath its massive, mysterious black color.

Mika's legs stopped moving. She turned her head one way, then turned her body when she looked the other way before looking toward the sun, which shone a dulling yellow behind the black blanket. The birds stopped chirping, and the bugs stopped buzzing. Yevera began fading. The last thing Mika saw was the dull sun that flickered away, surrounding the teenager in complete darkness.

Her dirty clothes thudded to the ground. She listened but only heard her short, choppy breathing and the fabric of her clothes, which shifted with her moving diaphragm. Her eyes were wide open, scanning back and forth, looking for any sign of light in the deep darkness. Maybe she was dreaming? To see if she was in a dream, she pinched her nose and tried to blow out some air, causing her ears to fill with pressure.

She wasn't in a dream, otherwise she would be able to blow the air out.

I'm blind, she thought, rubbing at her eyes, applying pressure, then opening them.

Nothing.

She slid onto her butt, placed her head on her knees, and whimpered.

"I'm blind." Mika began to cry. What did she do to deserve this? Was it something in the water? Did she insult a deity by accident? Did her eyes just stop working? She hugged her legs.

She didn't want to move. She didn't want to get lost. She knew her mother would notice if she did not come home. Her mom would look for her … right? A kind fisherman or huntsman would see her in distress and ask if she needs help. Page would sense that she was in danger! Or maybe she would be found by dogs, bears, or worse, tortured then devoured by werewolves. Her breathing quickened as panic set in. She began to tremble. She let go of her legs and rubbed her arms in fear.

She looked up but saw nothing. "Help me!" she cried, and her voice cracked. "I can't see!"

Mika placed her head between her knees and forced her eyes shut. Minutes turned into hours before she looked up again. Her eyes swollen from crying, she strained to see in front of her. She wiped her blurry, teary eyes and noticed a deep orange glow miles ahead of her, like a lone star shining in the night sky. The glow danced in intensity, up and down, back and forth, forcing a relieved, yet desperate chuckle out of Mika.

I'm not blind. I'm not blind!

She sniffled and knuckled away snot and tears before jumping to her feet. She walked toward the glow, trying to figure out what the mysterious color was.

Her pace quickened into a jog, then into a sprint. Her controlled breathing and the thudding of her bright-red boots were the only sounds in the air the moment she realized Yevera was being consumed by fire.

2. YEVERA

Mika hurried to the dancing flames in her town. What could have caused the fire? Why were the flames so big? How had the town been consumed? What was with the black blanket that covered the sun? She slowed her pace when a man's scream was followed by a shriek of pain. She caught her breath when she slowed, inhaling the sweet smell of burning wood, hearing the roars of the fire in the distance.

"What's happening?" she whispered.

Her eyes widened. In the distance, she caught a glimpse of her neighbor, Jack, helping a woman walk away from the burning town. Mika ran to the couple.

The woman clenched her mouth and limped; her leg was covered in blood and had a makeshift tourniquet tied to the top of her thigh. The woman moved her hand, revealing a swollen cheek and a broken jaw that hung open. The woman was Jack's new girlfriend from Vicqua, and stress didn't allow Mika to remember the woman's name.

Mika felt around the woman's head then stomach for injuries. She wiped blood away from the leg and made sure the tourniquet application was correct. "What's going on?" she said, helping support the woman.

"Plum," Jack panted and wiped sweat from his brow, "I need you to heal her leg."

"I don't know vita." Mika felt useless. She should've paid more attention to her mother's magic lessons; Mika knew how to heal, but not with magic. From Jack's facial expressions, she could feel him judging her incompetence.

"What's going on?" Mika repeated.

He adjusted the woman's arm around his shoulder. She tried to speak, but the damage to her jaw didn't allow her to. Jack continued walking. "Let's go, Plum, out of the darkness."

Mika looked at her burning town; the flames grew with every passing second. Where was her mother? Where was Page? Where were all her friends and fellow townsfolk?

"What's going on, Jack? Aren't you going back for the others?"

Jack continued walking. "I'd rather live a coward than die an idiot, Plum."

Mika let go of the woman and watched the couple limp away.

With a pumping heart, Mika dug her boot into the ground, flexed her thigh, and propelled herself toward the fire.

I'm coming, Mom. I'm coming, Page. Please be safe.

The smell of roasted meat became infused with the smell of burning wood. She got closer and closer to the burning buildings. Soon, the crackling from the structures and the swooshing roars of fire surrounded her. She took a final dash forward and crashed her back against the first flameless building she came up on. The sound of shattering glass prevented her from catching her breath.

"It's coming through the window!"

She recognized the voice—Susan, the owner of her favorite tea shop.

Her gut told her to run away, to run back to the river, run and catch up with Jack, run to Di'Abribel or Reach, somewhere other than here, but the need to protect her mother and her friends forced her to stay with her back pressed against the wall. Her heart pumped with such force that she could feel it pulsating on her back. She forced her breathing to slow, and her heart calmed. She peeked around the corner. Her eyebrows dropped, her eyes widened, and her lips trembled into a curl.

Yeverans lay dead on the gravel streets, most missing limbs or cut in half at the torso, some with their heads several feet away. Charred bodies hung from the windows of burning buildings.

Realizing the scent of burning meat came from the bodies made her cover her mouth and close her eyes. She turned away from the carnage and tried to exhale, but a roar of swooshing fire made her duck. A shout escaped her mouth.

When the deafening roar waned, she took a breath and peeked out again.

There was a woman hanging from the building in front of her; drops of blood fell from her face and splashed onto a pool of blood underneath. She noticed the only source of light was from the buildings that were set on fire. How did the buildings catch fire in the first place? Her eyes made a slow travel to the black blanket that covered the sky.

They set the buildings on fire to be able to see in the darkness.

A walking figure caught her eye and interrupted her thoughts. It was humanoid, but thinner and taller than the tallest man she had ever seen. Its flesh was a shiny black, reflecting the orange flames from around it. Instead of arms and legs, it had sharp, razorlike swords. Its movements were choppy; the legs dug and thudded into the gravel with every step.

The figure froze, lifeless like a doll, as it looked toward the heart of Yevera. Its head twisted, and it looked at Mika.

Mika snapped her head around the corner, her heart pounding. She covered her mouth to hide her surprised yelp. She closed her eyes and pressed away the fearful tears that gathered there.

It saw you. It saw you.

Ignoring her weak legs, shaking arms, and trembling lips, Mika opened her crying eyes and glanced around the corner. The monster had sneaked toward Mika and was now closer. It stopped, locked its pearly eyes with Mika's, and smiled, revealing skinny, pointed teeth.

Mika exploded into a run, and the thudding of the bladed legs followed. Turning the corner, Mika plowed into a wooden sign extending from the building; momentum sent her legs forward, and her head bounced on the cobblestone entry.

Vision faded to black. Coming back to a blurry reality, the world spun and stretched. Dots flickered.

She bit her lip and, placing a hand on her burning face, she used her opposite hand to sit up. The monster, several yards away, snapped its head left and right. When it sensed Mika's eyes, it turned to face her.

She flopped to the ground and held her breath, trying to hide the involuntary twitches of her muscles, hoping the monster wouldn't see her chest thumping with every heartbeat.

The monster's blades thudded closer.

Her heart throbbed, the vein on her neck pulsated with each pump of life, and her lungs begged for air. If she didn't move, her lungs would require a breath and betray her. If not her lungs, her heart would be heard over the screams and swooshing fire. If not her heart, sheer terror would force her to stand and run.

The thuds came closer, and Mika squeezed her eyelids harder, as if doing so would hide her from the monster. The pain in her lungs and face, the fear in her heart, were too much for her.

Mika's chest began to compress and decompress; her lungs were flexing, trying to push past the barrier she had created in her throat.

I can't. I can't. I can't, I can't, I can't!

"Matthew! Run!"

The rapid thuds of the monster's blades were inches from Mika's ears, but it began running away, toward the screams of a man in the distance.

Mika's eyes shot open. She puffed out the air in her lungs and inhaled a deep, painful breath that scratched the inside of her throat. She coughed into her hand to mask the sound. She wheezed another breath and cleaned the tears from her eyes. Without conscious thought, her hand traveled to her nose, and she felt tenderness and warm blood oozing from the impact. She placed a hand on her head to try and quell the feeling of her brain slamming against her skull.

Lying still, she looked into the lifeless eyes of an older man next to her, one of the town's woodworkers.

Everyone is dying ...

A lump formed in her throat. How many more of her townsfolk were dead? What about her friends? Page? Her mother? She pushed the thoughts away. She needed to focus. Mika sat up, and the world spun, making her sway side to side.

With no monster in sight and no thudding blades within earshot, she stood and fought through the concussion, ignoring the dizzying headache and her stumbling feet. Mika leaned on the wall until she caught her balance. She pinched her bloodied nose and continued home, coughing through the thickening smoke and ignoring the indescribable dread she felt every time she jumped over the cut-up bodies of her townsfolk.

*　*　*　*　*

Mika's home was engulfed in deep, red flames that burst out the windows like a demonic hand reaching to a pure and innocent child. When Mika ran through the open door, the suffocating heat filled her lungs. The deafening screams of the fire prevented her from hearing herself breathe. Despite the home being consumed by uncontrollable fire and choked with thick, black smoke, both parted away from her wherever she looked and wherever she moved.

She looked to the kitchen just to see the meal her mother was cooking. She looked under the table, failing to notice the overturned chairs. She went through the hallway and peeked into her room. Incinerated. She ran to her mother's room. There, she saw her gasping for air, holding her late husband's great sword with both hands. Too heavy for Cynthia, the blade of the great sword rested on the floor.

In front of her was a woman dressed in a black robe with a belt with two human skulls. Extending behind the woman in black were seven slithering black arms made of a black fog—ghasts. The fingers of the arms twisted and wrenched in unnatural movements. Her ear-length, jet-black hair and the symbols of a black moon and vertical rectangle on the woman's robes meant she was a necromancer, an adept of mori and tenebris. The necromancer's body was bladed to the side, and a taunting smile sat on her face.

A wall of ventus surrounded the two fighters. The magic of wind pushed away the smoke and fire.

"Vita!" Cynthia shouted, raising her palm to the sky. Her hand glowed a beautiful gold, and when she touched her chest, the gold radiated through her body, healing and closing the lacerations on her face, torso, and legs.

The necromancer laughed, revealing a short sword in her hand.

Letting out an exhausted cry, Cynthia swung the sword.

24

The necromancer dodged, and chips of wood flew to the ventus wall. A slash to Cynthia's face preceded a gash to the back of her knee.

Cynthia let out a cry and fell, grasping her cut leg.

Mika released a cry and ran to the necromancer with a fist behind her head.

"Mika, don't!"

The necromancer braced herself and swung a powerful kick into Mika's ribs.

Mika tumbled and crashed into the closet.

Cynthia shouted, "Ventus!" and doors of the closet shut. The bed slid across the room, striking the necromancer, and crashing into the doors of the closet, locking Mika in.

The necromancer slammed against the wall. Mika pushed on the door, allowing her to see through a crack.

"Mom, let me out!"

Mika watched as her mother swung the great sword into the necromancer's hip. The wall of ventus faded.

The necromancer screamed and swung her sword, hacking at the side of Cynthia's head. Once, twice, three times. Blood spurted onto the walls, sizzling away when it hit the flames.

Still holding her sword, Cynthia fell onto her back. She gurgled, "Vita," but extreme pain prevented her from using the magic. She inched away from the necromancer.

"Mom!" Mika shrieked. She tugged and pushed at the immovable doors. The flames burst and grew, sending violent pops that tore toward the two fighters.

The necromancer tossed her sword in the air, and a serpentine ghast grabbed it and threw it like a javelin at the defeated healer. The sword cut through Cynthia's throat and nailed her to the wooden floor.

Cynthia brought her hands toward the blade. Her eyes shut and her mouth opened to shout a scream that was prevented by the blade.

Limping to Cynthia, the necromancer handed one of the ghasts a dagger. One ghast grabbed Cynthia's head, as another pushed the sword further into the ground. The dagger's blade sank into Cynthia's chest once, twice, again, and again, and again; blood sizzled when it touched the flames on the ceiling.

25

"Mom!" Mika pulled, pushed, slammed her shoulder against the doors, kicked, punched, screamed; the doors would not move. She slid to her knees when she saw her mother go limp. Life essence did not escape her body.

The necromancer tilted her chin toward the ceiling, inhaled, but then coughed when the smoke filled her lungs.

The necromancer limped to the corpse, placed her foot on its forehead, and pulled the sword from the throat. She hobbled toward the door, passing the closet Mika was in.

Locking her eyes with Mika's, the necromancer's ghasts grasped the corners of the bed. The necromancer got on the bed and began striking the closet doors with the hilt of her sword. The strikes sent loud booms throughout the room, intensifying Mika's headache and making the flames explode with every strike.

Wounded and unable to move the doors, the necromancer stuck her blade through the opening. Mika squished herself in the corner, avoiding the blade by inches. With each scream from Mika, the flames inside the house grew larger, hotter, and the pops and roars became more aggressive. Mika thought the necromancer was controlling the flames, forcing the poor girl to cry, and wished she could wake up from this horrendous nightmare.

Wiping the sweat from her brow, the necromancer exhaled and bowed her head. She stepped down from the bed and shuffled away, as the ghasts behind her disappeared in a poof.

With a dry mouth, the necromancer looked at Mika. "Enjoy burning to death."

She forced a laugh that was followed by a groan and coughs. She staggered out of the bedroom, leaving Mika's spirit broken in the dark closet as it filled with black smoke.

Mika covered her eyes with her hands, grinding her teeth and holding herself back from collapsing in surrender. She wiped away her tears, sniffling and choking, and began pushing and pulling the doors, hoping they would open, but hope did not avail her. The bed was wedged against the wall, and the only way to push it away was from outside—and even then, it had proven too much for the necromancer to move. Through cries of despair and constant coughing,

Mika stuck a leg through the small opening. She squeezed her shoulder through and hung halfway out. The smoke seeped into her eyes, and they began filling with tears. Her coughing intensified. She lost oxygen. In a panic, she pulled herself back into the closet, fell to her knees, coughed, and gagged. The smoke made her eyes felt like needles poked her pupils.

"Angelis, please help me!" she cried out between coughs, praying to the deity of vita. "Please, Angelis!" Feeling the now-extreme temperatures, Mika took off her shirt. She lay on her stomach, looking out from under the bed at the lifeless body of her mother, now covered in flames.

The young woman realized she would never hear her mother's voice, eat her delicious food, watch her remarry, go to the graveyard to visit her father, or see the smile on her face when Mika grew into adulthood. Mika would never joke with her mom, drink tea with her, talk about boys, go on trips to Di'Abribel. Mika would never see her mother again. Mika would die in the same house as her mother.

She grieved when she remembered how much love and affection Cynthia had given her. She was never angry, never upset. She never judged, she never criticized, she never said anything mean. Never told her she couldn't do this or couldn't do that. Never told her she couldn't go see Page, never told her—

Page. Where is Page?

Was Page safe? Had he suffered the same fate as Cynthia? Had Page been killed by the monsters with bladed arms? Sadness turned into fiery determination. Mika stood and continued pummeling the closet door and kicking with full force until her knuckles bled. The heat zapped the little energy she had left, and she could feel sweat running down her back and sliding into her pants. Her broken nose sent her a jolt of pain when she wiped the sweat from her face.

"Aqua!" she screamed above the roars of fire.

Tiny orbs of moving water appeared at her fingertips. Mika moved her fingers closer together and concentrated on the image of water until water spurted from her fingers. She doused herself with the weak stream, trying to cool down before drinking the spurts of water. Images of Cynthia teaching her the spell flashed into her mind, but she pushed the thought away before she again fell into surrender. The smoke filled the closet.

Mika dropped to her knees and screamed through the opening.

"Let me out! Let me get out! Somebody, help me!"

As she struck the closet doors with her elbow, the flames grew with every strike, popping and sending swooshing roars in front of the opening.

The monsters are controlling the fire.

She needed to get out.

She looked at the bed and kicked at it through the gap between the doors. It wouldn't budge. She kicked at it with her heel, her anger growing with every strike, to the point she began hearing the small whispers. She knew the whispers were talking about her, but she couldn't understand what they were saying. Why couldn't she understand what the whispers that make people call her crazy were saying? The thought of being called crazy made her scream louder. Her screech made the flames reply with a violent roar; a roar so strong, so powerful, so explosive, it sent a beam crashing down onto the bed.

The fire on the beam spread through the bed and burned a bright blue that seemed to call to the flames from around the room. Every inch of fire in the house propagated to the bed. The fire exploded, sending a flame at Mika through the gap. She crashed her back onto the wall, her eyes wide, scared yet amazed.

The flames dispersed and continued ravaging the wood around the home. Mika blinked once. Twice. She moved her head to peek out of the opening before crawling forward. A pile of black, glowing ashes had replaced the bed.

She blinked, shook her head, and began to open the closet doors. She blew away parts of the ashes, then flung the doors open. The smoke was lower, forcing her to crawl toward her mother. Cynthia was being consumed by the fire, but when Mika approached, the flames slithered away, leaving the charred body of the mother alone with the daughter. The fire surrounded the two.

"Mom!" Mika screamed, tucking her mother's burnt hair behind her scorched ear.

Like they had always done with each other, Mika pinched Cynthia's cheek, but this time pulling parts of her mother's skin when she let go. Mika laid her head on Cynthia's forehead and cried. The feeling of her mother's flesh sticking to hers didn't matter. She clenched her fists around her dead mother's shoulders and, ignoring the burns on her hands, let out a cry of despair, angering the flames around her. They replied by roaring with such force, parts of the roof began to fall. Something deep inside Mika told her she needed to leave.

With a final squeeze to charred remains that had once been Cynthia Plum, Mika crawled out of her burning home with tears in her eyes, wishing she'd never gone to the river.

3. PROMISES

Scraping her belly on the ground, her clothes smoldering, Mika clawed her way out of the burning home. She closed her eyes to quell the feeling of nails scratching into her pupils. She sat on all fours and coughed up the smoke she had inhaled during her escape. The house shook behind her, and the fire roared. Looking back with watery eyes, she stood and dashed away, only to fall in pain, exhaustion, and grief. She rubbed her eyes, but the lingering smoke continued to cut at them like razor-sharp claws.

"Mika!" Page cried out in the distance. "Mika!"

Mika popped her head up and looked in the direction of Page's voice, straining to see past her watery vision. The blanket of darkness below the clouds was beginning to fade away, but the fires and smoke continued around the buildings, filling Yevera in an orange glow.

Page hurried toward Mika, half crouched, half running, keeping a wary eye open for danger. He slid to his knees, tearing his pants and cutting open his knee, and crashed into Mika, taking her in his arms and holding her with such strength it made it hard for her to catch her breath.

The impact made Mika feel like her brain rattled, but she ignored the pain, dug her face into Page's chest, and let out a howl.

"Cynthia ..." Page pushed Mika away. "I'll get her! I'll get her right now!"

Page lurched to his feet, but Mika grasped the mace at Page's belt. Page stopped and looked at Mika, lowering his shoulders when she shook and hung her head. He knelt beside her and put his arms around her once more as she wept.

He didn't know what to say. *It's okay?* It wasn't okay. None of what happened was okay. *I understand?* He didn't, he didn't know what was happening. *I'll make them pay?* He'd just seen a veteran fighter in plate armor cut clean in half.

Page kissed her forehead and spoke, holding his lips to her skin. "Let's find the others."

Before they walked off, a bright-green orb appeared above them. The life essence of all the dead slithered toward the orb. Accepting the essence, the orb grew above Yevera until it seemed to burst, then expelled all the essence to the north and northeast. Neither Page nor Mika knew the reason for the orb, but both knew they had to get to the town center.

To prevent Mika from walking through the town in her under-shirt, Page took off his shirt and gave it to her. Mika slipped into it, taking comfort in the musky smell of her man. She wiped off her tears and held Page's hand, following him to the town center. She didn't look down but didn't look straight ahead either. Instead, she looked up at the smoke-filled sky to prevent her eyes from seeing the carnage in the streets of her town.

Upon reaching the cobblestone streets nearing the town's center, Bronket—a Yeveran soldier in chainmail armor—ran up to them.

"Injuries?" he asked.

"Mika has injuries to her head and torso." Page looked at Mika, then at Bronket. "I think her head needs immediate healing."

Bronket whispered a darkness spell. "Tenebris."

His gaze went past Page as he used telepathy to speak with someone else. Then his eyes refocused on him.

"If she can walk, she needs to continue to the town center. A healer will tend to her injuries," he said. "But you, Page Briarhart, need to report to the east gate."

"The gate? What for?"

"You're being drafted into the Yeveran army." Bronket's words were quick. "Report to the east gate immediately."

31

"The Yeveran Army?"

Mika looked at him. "Page what's going—"

"I'm a builder, not a warrior! Look!" Page held his arms to the burning buildings, fallen statues, and destroyed roads. "I need to help rebuild this place!"

Mika turned to Bronket. She could see him using telepathy. A loud voice boomed behind Mika, causing her to flinch.

"Page Briarhart!"

Still holding Mika, Page turned around.

"You have been drafted into the Yeveran army!"

Sergeant Carr wore damaged steel armor and strode toward Page. Sergeant Carr was older and an inch shorter than Page. Several bruises, fresh cuts, and the dried sweat on his face told Mika he had been fighting for hours. His scruffy, graying beard and dark-brown hair showed he hadn't mastered any element of magic. Sergeant Carr was followed by two soldiers in chainmail, and the second he was within arm's reach of Page, Carr placed his hand on Page's shoulder, moving him back a couple of steps.

Carr continued, and Mika could smell the scent of alcohol coming from his breath. "Page, brother, cousin, Yeveran …" Carr shook his head. "Don't make this harder on Mika or yourself, man."

Carr's overfamiliarity and disregard for customs and traditions were ignored because of his fighting skills and leadership. His platoon of soldiers had never lost a battle.

Page's voice was calm; he was trying to sound nonconfrontational. "Sergeant, this is dragonshit. I'm not a fighter … and drafted? Drafted for what? I'm not even from here!"

Carr slid his hand up Page's neck and grasped the back of his skull. He pulled Page in.

"You've been living off our lands for years, Briarhart. You're from here." Carr locked eyes with Page, his lips wrenched, and his nostrils widened. "We're going to fuck these necromancers in their asses, impregnate their wives, and kill the children," Carr's voice was so slurred it was hard to make out what he was saying. "We're burning that fucking forest to the ground and shitting on the ashes."

Page squirmed and pushed the sergeant away.

"You're sick and demented! And no one has survived the Lost Forest!" Page pointed his finger at Carr. "You're going to die in there!"

Carr nodded. "You're right." He held his arm to Mika, who was too hurt, dazed, and sad to disobey. Carr sat her on the ground, opened his hand like a blade, and slapped Page in the face.

Page stumbled and fell to his knees. Carr grabbed Page by his armpits and lifted him to his feet, placing both of his hands on Page's shoulders. Then he started screaming, saliva flying from his mouth. "I never want to hear those words come from you again! We are soldiers of the Yeveran military, and nothing, *nothing,* will stop our success! We lost today because we were caught by surprise! We'd all be dead otherwise! Do you understand me?"

Since Page didn't reply, Carr punched him in the gut. "Do you understand me?"

With hands clasped on his gut, Page nodded. He locked his gaze with the sergeant.

Carr guided Page toward the east, complimenting him on how he handled the strike. They walked away, and Page pretended to listen to what Sergeant Carr was saying. The reality of the situation kicked in the moment Page began disappearing into the smoke.

Mika stood. "Page!"

Page looked back and stopped walking. He made his way to Mika, only to be yanked back by Carr. They exchanged a few words, and Page tried to pull away, pointing at Mika.

Carr's lips moved, and his fist tapped on Page's chest in rhythm of every syllable.

Page stepped back. Carr stepped to Page.

Page bladed his body; a muffled *"Fuck you, Carr!"* sailed into Mika's ears.

The sergeant latched onto Page's shoulders, and Page crashed his elbow into the man's face.

Fumbling backward, Carr couldn't stop Page from sprinting toward Mika. The other soldiers chased him, but their armor slowed their run. Mika held her arms open, and Page wrapped his arms around her. Page held the back of her head, wrapped his fingers within her hair, and kissed her.

She was overwhelmed, and for a moment the carnage around her faded. She was unaware of a soldier telling his comrades to give them a moment.

Page kissed me ... She wrapped her arms around Page and slid her hands over the top of his shoulders. *Page kissed me!*

Page pulled away and held his forehead to hers. "I'll come back for you," he whispered. "I promise I'll come back for you. No matter what happens, just wait for me."

"I'll wait for you," she whispered back. Tears touched her trembling lips.

Page gave Mika a peck and let go of her, turning to face Sergeant Carr.

Standing with a wide stance, crossed arms, and furrowed eyebrows that covered his eyes, Sergeant Carr did not look away from Page. Page kept his stare, and Carr's face relaxed before he laughed. "That what I like to see, boy!" Sergeant Carr applauded and hugged Page.

The new Yeveran soldier hung his arms to his side and didn't hug back.

"That's how we live, by fighting for our loved ones!" Sergeant Carr pushed Page away and bowed to Mika before turning his back on her. "You know, I'll make you pay for that hit, right?"

Page walked away with his new squad. "Prove it, Sarge."

Page slowed his pace, looked back, and held his arm out to Mika.

Mika returned the gesture and read his lips.

"I'll find you."

* * * * *

Mika followed the caravan of Yeveran survivors toward Di'Abribel, the largest city in the region of Celeste. Rale, a young healer with an old burn on his neck, held a golden glow of vita magic from his hand to Mika's head, clearing and healing her headache.

After almost an hour of constant healing, the golden glow flickered. "Concussion should be gone, but I've reached exhaustion before healing the bruises." Rale placed his hand on his forehead to ease his headache. "I need to rest."

Once a person reached a certain level of magical exhaustion, their head throbbed for hours. Further magic use could cause them to faint, sometimes falling unconscious for days. Someone could die of dehydration or the elements if they reached exhaustion and were left unattended. No one in the caravan had energy to carry Rale, so Mika understood that he needed to stop.

When the caravan reached the outskirts of Yevera, Mika was able to see the peaceful, purple glow of the sunset sky. The wind danced, helping birds fly with ease, and carrying the beautiful aroma of the wildflowers stuck between the swaying grass. Anger coursed through Mika's veins. This scene, she thought, shouldn't be this peaceful, not after what just happened.

Looking at the rolling hills in the distance, a paladin in white robes with golden embroidery walked past her. Mika turned her attention to the front, where paladins, adepts of lux and vita, light and life magic, and sworn enemies of the necromancers, were escorting the Yeveran refugees to Di'Abribel.

Paladins rushed from Di'Abribel the moment the black cloud became visible from the city. Armored paladins on horseback arrived within hours, but not fast enough to prevent the massacre. By the time Mika had spoken with Bronket and Carr, the first platoon of shock cavalry paladins had arrived.

The paladins answered questions about the necromancers. Necromancers had been at war with paladins since the dawn of time, fighting over contested territory in all continents of the world. The group of necromancers in Celeste had been sent by a regiment in the southern parts of Imbris after defeating the paladins there. Paladins were losing the war and had just a few heroes among them.

Axel, a paladin leader with the platinum-blond hair of a lux master and baby-blue highlights of secondary aqua mastery, rode on a wingless unicorn.

"The black creatures with bladed limbs are walkers." He spoke with a loud voice so everyone around him could hear. "Bodies are hard as dragonscale. Only way to defeat them is to destroy both of their eyes."

"Dear, they're so fast," said an older woman escorted on a horse. "How do we do that?"

Axel looked straight ahead. "Necromancers cover the sky with the blanket to block the sunlight, and at night, the moonlight. Walkers are sensitive to light. Once they see light, they become slower. The brighter the light, the slower they become."

Ignoring the conversation, Mika's ears were filled with the soft cries of women. The quiet ones were in shock, lost in thought and looking dead ahead or at the ground. Children complained about the long walk. The ones who saw the carnage cried for their lost parents, siblings, friends, pets. Some of the children, like the women, stared away into nothingness. The only teenage boys and men in the caravan were those with severe wounds, amputations, paralysis, or those who, because of their mental state, were deemed too weak to be of use in combat.

The rest had been drafted and were on their way to Warrior's Edge, a military training camp, with nothing but the clothes on their backs. At Warrior's Edge, they would train and gather forces from other cities and mount an attack on the Lost Forest. Many had tried entering, raiding, looting, or attacking the Lost Forest in the past, but no one had ever come out alive. Rumors suggested that the forest shifted on its own and consumed the bodies of those who fell within its boundaries.

Sadness filled Mika's heart, knowing Page and her townsmen were on their way to die.

"I'll come back for you. I promise I'll come back for you."

The words filled her heart with hope. Maybe this time it would be different, and the Lost Forest would be conquered. Necromancers would be no match against Yeverans, paladins, and other warriors.

Mika trudged behind the caravan. Looking down at her feet, she noticed her little red boots had turned black from ash and dirt. She began thinking of her mother and wondered what had become of her body. Mika imagined Cynthia walking next to her, healing all the injured townsfolk, telling them payment was not needed. A distant memory sparked in her mind.

When Mika was much younger, she watched her mom heal a battalion of soldiers after they returned from battle. The young girl watched her mother without blinking; Cynthia's tears dropped onto her patients. The injuries the men had sustained were gruesome: severed limbs, hanging flesh, spurting blood, missing organs. She didn't know weapons of war could cause so much damage to the human body and not kill them. Still, the biggest question in her mind was not the injuries, but why her mother was crying.

"How are they alive, Mommy?"

"Not now, baby." Her mother's voice shook. "I need to focus, okay?"

Mika was guided away by an elderly healer whose name she couldn't remember. "They're alive because Yeverans never, ever, ever give up."

Those words, and that woman, ignited the fire that was now Mika's relentless patriotism. It wasn't until years later that Mika realized her mother was crying because Mika's father had died in battle.

Tears began filling Mika's eyes at the memory of her beautiful, sweet, loving mother. What would've been the outcome had Mika just gone to the showers? Maybe they would have cooked together and seen the blanket. Maybe Mika and Cynthia could have teamed up against the necromancers, maybe they—

Distant, high-pitched whimpers broke Mika from her thoughts. She blinked, shook her head, and then scratched her nose. She looked ahead and noticed she had fallen to the rear of the caravan. The noise from the footsteps and conversations must've helped her hear the whimpers. She stopped moving to listen better. Another set of whimpers crept into her ears from behind a tree in the distance.

Mika, too tired to run, walked to the tree, hanging her shoulders and head on the way there. The whimpers became louder and louder until she placed her hands on the trunk and looked around it. A small puppy lay on the ground; its ribs were visible from beneath its black and tan fur. Its torso rose and lowered with every heave.

She recoiled at the sight of the thing.

People hated dogs. Though smarter than most animals, they weren't as elegant. Dogs were pests with little use; they ate their own feces, peed wherever they wanted, bred with their offspring, attacked children, and killed livestock. Dogs were such a problem in Di'Abribel, the citizens hunted them for sport and entertainment.

37

The hunting became so extreme, dogs were afraid of leaving their hiding spots, causing most to die of thirst and hunger. Mika, knowing how disgusting dogs were, took a step back, and her feet faced the caravan.

The puppy whimpered louder when it realized it would be left behind. A twitch of Mika's eyes told her she would regret leaving it.

Mika approached the sick puppy and knelt next to it, wincing when it looked at her with hopeful eyes.

"Where is your mother?" Her voice did not change in tone, and her eyebrows continued to show disgust.

The puppy licked its nose and heaved. It closed its eyes and reopened them to look at Mika.

Mika looked around for the puppy's mother, then back at the puppy. "I lost my mother too." The words made something in her mind click.

I lost my mother too ...

Reaching for the dog, Mika felt its dirty fur and ribs that reminded her of a xylophone. "I can be your new mother."

Mika picked up the puppy. Motivation caused energy to return, and she ran back to the caravan. When she reached the road, she stayed far behind so no one would question her about the new companion. Even after hours of walking, the puppy would not look away from Mika's eyes.

"I'll take care of you ... and I won't let anyone hurt you. I'll add you to my family and call you ... Addie." The puppy licked Mika's fingers, causing her to smile. "I promise I'll take care of you."

Thoughts of ways to nurse the sick puppy made the memories of Yevera blur and the long trek to Di'Abribel seem painless.

*   *   *   *   *

"Miss ..." A man in fancy silver clothes knelt in front of Mika when she passed through the gates of Di'Abribel. "What is your name?"

Mika held Addie close to her chest with both arms. She could feel his heavy breaths on her neck. "I am Mika Plum of Yevera."

The man smiled with gentle brown eyes. "Nice to meet you, Mika Plum. Are your parents around?" His bushy eyebrows curved upward.

Mika held the man's gaze. She looked at one eye, then the other, then back to the other before she looked down and pressed her face against Addie's ribs. There was a lump in her throat. "No."

The man sighed and placed his hand on Mika's shoulder. "I understand it's hard—"

"I don't want to cry." Mika couldn't control the high pitch in her voice or the shakiness of her throat. Her lips trembled when she opened her mouth to speak. "I don't want to cry." Still holding her face against Addie, her shoulders began to tremble.

"Here, here." The man brought Mika into his arms and hugged her. "It's okay to cry."

Being held, reassured, and given permission, she burst out in fits of crying. Uncontrollable, shaky cries that released all the built-up sadness she carried during her trek.

When she finished crying, the man let go, stood, and waved for someone in the distance.

Through her tears, Mika saw a younger man with the same type of clothes, a large hat, and an even larger book run toward them. The man squatted down, opened the torso-sized book, and placed it on his thighs before using terra from his finger to write. "Go ahead, David."

David spoke. "Here we have Mika Plum, teenager, and her wolf."

"Wolf? It looks more like–"

"Yes, Aiden, wolf." David's voice didn't change.

Aiden looked at Addie, sighed, and wrote in the book.

"Miss Plum has no family." David gave Mika a gentle smile. "Have the builders make a home for her at the expense of the city. The home will be paid for so long as Miss Plum can keep a steady job and she pays monthly taxes to the king."

Aiden wrote.

Mika stole glances at David, who pretended not to notice her stare. After a few minutes, Aiden closed the book and stood. He took a breath and nodded.

"Thank you, Aiden." David nodded back and watched Aiden run to another person who requested his services. He turned to Mika. "In a few months, you'll have a home. Builders have already been sent throughout."

"Thank you." Mika lowered her head in respect.

David knelt to Mika's height. "Your puppy will grow soon, and people will begin to hate him. Dogs aren't welcome here." He shook his head and looked at Addie.

Addie looked at David, his snout bent with each sniff.

"I don't know what the council will say about him, but you'll have a few months to figure it out." David looked at Mika and looked at her big brown eyes, waiting for a response.

Mika stared at David. What could she say? Mika's head dropped, for Addie's breathing had quickened. She looked at his closed eyes; his face was wrenched in pain. Addie would be a burden to her, for she wouldn't be able to do a lot with him around. She'd also have to keep him fed, train him, clean his feces, castrate him. It'd be so much easier just to leave him outside the walls as though she never knew him.

Mika looked at David.

"I'll get rid of him! I just want him." She extended Addie to David. "I just want him to heal! He won't be a bother, I promise!"

"Right on, girl. I trust you." He placed his hand on Mika's shoulder, squeezed it, and winked. "Go on now; there's warm food and cold drinks waiting at the plaza."

David walked away and talked to the Bonins, a family of Yeveran fishermen.

Mika adjusted Addie on her arms and turned toward the plaza. She squatted and held her forehead to Addie's face.

The long travel had caused the dog's life to seep into Mika's territorial personality. No one would hurt something she considered part of her circle. She looked around and made sure no one could hear her.

"Don't worry," she whispered. "They'll have to kill me before I get rid of you."

4. PROPOSAL

Although Mika had come to Di'Abribel a few times with Cynthia and once with Page to shop and sightsee, she felt as if Di'Abribel were a brand-new place. By law, all buildings were made of stone and painted light gray with red roofs. The flag of Di'Abribel—a vertical row of gold representing wealth, a vertical row of white representing health, and a silver horizontal strand representing ventus, the most prominent magic in the city—flew high atop the city walls. Prisoners cleaned the city in the morning and at night, keeping Di'Abribel pristine and beautiful.

Di'Abribeli citizens buzzed back and forth, going about their busy lives. Most seemed to ignore the Yeveran refugees who wandered the streets. What Mika loved most about Di'Abribel was the massive golden statue of Angelis at the center of the town. Her statue stood with her hands crossed in front of her pelvis, looking down with gentle eyes to the people below.

Sunlight beamed from the blue morning sky, reflecting a rainbow off the golden statue and into Mika's blinking eyes. Mika knelt at the base of the statue that rose above the buildings.

"Hello, Angelis." Mika held Addie across her chest. "I hope your day went well. It's been a week since I lost my mom, and I found out about your statue yesterday."

Movement caught her eye, so she closed them to concentrate.

"Mom always told me to pray more, so here I am. I ask that you keep Addie and me safe, so we may continue to pray and serve you. By vita, I praise your name and essence."

41

She looked up at the statue and leaned over to kiss the toe. With a shuffle of her legs, she stood and turned. Her heart skipped a beat and she recoiled when she saw a row of men and women with shaved heads, tattered leather garb, and chains around their legs standing in a line in front of her.

"You done, Miss?" A guard holding a whip approached her.

Mika glanced at the spiked mace hanging from his belt. "Yes, yes. I'm done."

The guard cracked his whip in the air. "Hurry up, you curs and bitches! I've got food waiting for me at home!" He turned to Mika and smiled. "Thank you."

Mika moved out of the way and watched the prisoners flinch at every move of the whip. They worked as a team and carried buckets to the statue of Angelis, cleaning the deity's figure with aqua, ventus, and terra.

"Do they clean the statue every day?" Mika asked.

She watched one of the prisoners use ventus to hover in the air and clean the upper parts of the monument.

"Every morning and every night. These useless fucking peasants." The guard looked at Mika up and down. "How old are you?"

Mika shrugged. She wanted to brush the hair behind her ear but didn't want to let go of Addie. "I'm almost fifteen."

The guard, realizing Mika wasn't as young as she looked, continued his foul language. "These useless fucking peasants need to repay society. They've broken the laws of Di'Abribel, especially this rapist cur."

He whipped the back of a man's knee. "Hurry up, rapist!"

He pointed his chin at a woman. "Child abuser." He pointed his chin at the man hovering around the statue. "A murderer." He pointed his chin at another woman, but Mika interrupted him.

"I'm devoted to Angelis. Can I help clean her statue?" She kissed Addie before looking at the guard. "I can come by once per week."

"You can do whatever you want, Miss." The guard cracked the whip in the air. "Just don't show compassion to the prisoners."

I'd have them killed if it was up to me, Mika thought, but she agreed to the terms.

After a day of exploring the city, she returned to the military barracks that had been turned into temporary dormitories for the Yeveran refugees.

She sat on the top bunk with Addie and ignored the low conversations that bounced off the plain gray walls. She hung her feet off the side of the bunk and looked at the bowl of thick chicken soup and vegetables. The same food they ate the day prior, and these, Mika knew, were leftovers. Mika moved the wooden spoon into her mouth, chewed the chicken, and swallowed the cold dish. She sighed and moved toward her pillow to give some to Addie.

"Eat, Addie." She moved the bowl close to his snout. When he moved away, she followed. "You need to eat. Please eat."

I can't believe the healers won't help me with him. Mika again cursed herself for not learning healing spells with her mom.

Mika stuck her fingers in the broth and pulled out a chunk of chicken. She put the chunk in her mouth, ground it into smaller pieces, opened Addie's jaw, and shoved the chunk deep into his mouth.

Addie tasted the chicken, chewed it, and swallowed. His weak, sick eyes widened, and he looked at Mika for more.

"You're dumb." Mika chewed another chunk before feeding it to Addie. When her sick puppy didn't want any more, she moved away from him and kicked her hanging feet back and forth.

She gazed at the fireplace in the distance, lost in thought. Although she wasn't close to the fire, she could hear its pops and crackles in her mind. The fire, she thought, was looking back at her. Calling her, asking her to approach. A child ran across the fire, then two others followed in a chase, breaking Mika from her reverie.

She blinked, shook her head, and scratched her nose before drinking the remaining soup. She climbed off and went back to the massive cauldron that held more soup. She served herself another bowl and returned to her bunk, covering her and her puppy underneath the blanket. She placed the bowl between her legs and looked at her rescued baby.

"Good, Addie." Mika passed her hands over Addie's snout and toward his head. Scratching the back of an ear made Mika giggle when Addie began to move his leg along with the scratches.

Addie licked the bowl clean, and then the two of them fell asleep under the blankets.

A knock on the bedframe woke her the next morning. Mika opened her eyes to see a young Di'Abribeli boy reaching up to the bed.

"Are you Mika Plum?" he whispered.

Mika rubbed away the sand in her sleepy eyes and looked at the boy.

"Yes." She covered her mouth but didn't close her eyes when she yawned. "I am Mika Plum of Yevera."

The boy handed her a letter with a red wax seal and walked away the moment Mika grabbed it.

Mika looked at the seal. The initials V.T. were in front of a floral pattern. Mika opened the letter and read:

Mika Plum,

I give my condolences for the tragedy that occurred in your amazing town of Yevera. Your warriors sacrificed themselves so that my son could return home from the battlefield during the Imbric War. My family and I will be forever indebted to yours.

It is my understanding that the council has offered you a free home in which you are to reside so long as you maintain a job and pay the king his fair share of taxes. We need another maid and would love to give you the opportunity to work for us at a rate of ten silver coins per day, double the average of the profession.

Should you wish to accept this offer, my wife and I, as well as our current maid, Janice, would like to meet with you over dinner at our home tonight.

We are located at 02 Amery Gardens, Academic District. Show this letter to any guard who asks for papers permitting travel. I've attached a map. Though outdated, I have faith your intellectual abilities will allow you to find your way with it.

With Respect and Honor,
Professor Verity Tovey

P.S. Leave early in the morning; the sun beats down on the city during this time of the year.

Unlike most maps, this map's text was oriented in a way that, when held, the front of the map was to the west instead of the north. In fact, the north arrow was not present, and the only reason Mika knew the orientation was because *Eastern Walls* was written next to the black line near the circled *Barracks*. Amery Gardens was on the northeastern side of the city. Mika folded the map so parts could be viewed without having to open the whole paper before tucking it back into the envelope.

She jumped out of bed and went about her morning hygiene routine, brushing her teeth and cleaning herself at the barracks bathhouse. She dressed in her best available attire: a wrinkled, light-red dress donated by a Di'Abribeli teenager, ankle-high boots, and an oversized yellow hat that she needed to adjust every few steps.

"You're leaving?" Andellia asked in her faint voice when Mika passed her bunk.

Mika faced Andellia so fast it caused her hat to fall over her eyes. "I didn't see you! Yes, I got offered a job!" Mika adjusted her hat and handed Andellia the letter.

Andellia read the letter in seconds. She handed the letter back to Mika, lay down, and covered herself with the blankets. Her voice was muffled. "Have fun."

Mika looked at Andellia's body under the blankets. She was good at reading emotions and moods and knew Andellia was upset. Mika was giving Addie more attention than she was giving her classmate. Adjusting her hat, Mika knelt next to Andellia and moved the blankets. She noticed tears glistening on Andellia's cheeks.

"I'll be back." Mika gave Andellia a hug. "We need to be adults now. I need this job to pay taxes so I can get the house and get out of here!" She pulled away from her friend and gave an optimistic smile when Andellia opened her eyes.

Andellia looked at Mika's big brown eyes, her perfect white teeth, then back at her eyes. Andellia sniffled so hard it turned into a snort. She turned away from Mika and spoke in her low, sad voice. "The letter said to leave early. Have fun."

Andellia yanked the blankets from Mika and covered herself. Mika saw Andellia's chest rise and rise underneath the blankets, then lower and keep lowering when she exhaled.

45

Mika's hat fell over her eyes when she stood. She adjusted it, leaned over, and kissed Andellia over the blankets where her head was. She continued to her bunk and held Addie in her arms.

"Walk?" she said.

Addie wagged his tail, happy to see the outside sky.

Mika walked out of the barracks and through the busy streets of Di'Abribel, stopping only to use her aqua spell for water and to read her map. Addie continued his whimpers, and Mika fought through carrying him, orienting herself, and adjusting her yellow hat. The only reason she didn't toss the hat was because it was providing her and Addie shade on their long trek through the scorching heat.

"Is that a *dog?*"

Mika turned to see a man with his mouth open in disgust, revealing his top teeth.

"No, he's a wolf cub. He was hurt in Yevera."

The man's eyes narrowed, and he leaned to the side. He looked at Mika. "Sure, he is." He gave Mika a long stare before he walked past her, trying to bump his shoulder into her.

Mika swallowed and shook her head, causing her hat to fall over her eyes and stop at her nose. For some reason, the small comments made her heart quicken. She adjusted her hat and pulled out her map, oriented herself thanks to the oval building next to the two houses, on a street with three roads, and then drew in the new building that had a peaked roof. She sighed, wiped the sweat from her face, and lathered it on her neck to cool down before she continued walking toward Amery Gardens.

Mika took off her oversized hat and wiped sweat from her brow when she reached the massive steel gates of Amery Gardens. When she placed the hat back on her head, a shiver ran down her spine when the sweat-soaked band touched her forehead.

The gates were intertwined with grassy vines that extended to both sides of the steel bars. Attached to the gate were flanking stone pillars, and green bushes created a wall that surrounded the outside gardens of the home. The home itself was three stories tall and longer than it was wide.

"You must be Miss Plum." A gentle voice with a slight tremble broke Mika from her thoughts. Just behind the gates stood a woman wearing a dirty outfit and gray hair in a tight bun.

Mika looked at the woman's clothes. *This must be Janice.*

Mika adjusted her hat and curtsied with one arm so that Addie didn't fall. "I am Mika Plum …" Her hat fell over her eyes and onto her nose. "—uh of Yevera." She stood and adjusted her hat.

Janice unlocked the gate. "I'm Janice."

The gates swung open without a creak, and Mika stepped through. Janice held a palm out.

"The Toveys aren't fond of dogs," Janice looked at Mika with tired eyes.

"He's a wolf; he just looks like a dog!"

Janice kept an unimpressed stare on Mika. "I'm a maid, not an idiot."

Mika's eye twitched; that's not what she meant to portray. She was about to apologize when Janice spoke.

"I have a place we can keep him."

Janice walked along the grass wall and into a shed a few yards away. The shed was the same color as all the houses in Di'Abribel: red roof, light-gray walls. Janice unlocked the door, and it squeaked open. Janice summoned an orb of lux, and the orb shone a bright white that created rainbows around it and chased off the darkness inside.

Mika followed, sneezing when she inhaled the dust.

"Stand here." Janice pointed next to her.

Mika obeyed, still sneezing into her forearm.

Janice held her palms out and whispered, "Ventus."

Wind rushed from outside and spun inside the shed with enough force to gather all the dust, but not strong enough to move the jars, pots, plates, and assortments that were spread throughout. Janice guided the wind with her hands, and all the dust concentrated in a single corner. With a quick sweep of her hands, the wind ran outside, carrying all the dust away with it.

Janice made the orb of lux float under the ceiling in the center of the shed. She reached into a chest and began digging through it, creating clattering noises that bounced off the walls and scared Addie.

Mika covered Addie's ears. "Where does the dust go?" She had to raise her voice.

The maid pulled out leather sheets with fur on them. She didn't respond to Mika. Instead, she began making a bed with the leather near a corner. When she finished, she placed objects around the bed, creating a small, makeshift box.

"You can place him here." Janice stood and walked to the door. "Hurry, please, we need to start dinner."

Trying to make a good impression, Mika hurried to the box and placed Addie on it, covering him with parts of the leather. "I'll be back soon."

When Mika stood and walked to the door, Addie began yelping and screaming for his mother. Mika ground her teeth, hoping he wouldn't alert the Tovey family of his presence. She stepped out with Janice, and the squeals and yelps became louder. Janice closed the door, locked the shed, and held her palms to the shed when she used a terra spell. The yelps and squeals became more and more muffled until they were inaudible.

"What did you do?" Mika looked at Janice with wide eyes.

Janice began walking to the house. "Surrounded the walls with sand."

Mika was astonished! She remembered Page using terra to protect a tent, but terra to hide sound? She looked at the shed and then back at Janice with an open mouth.

Feeling eyes on her, Janice looked at Mika. Her lip curved into a smile when Mika's hat fell over her eyes.

"In Yevera, we use magic for fighting, crafting, and healing," Mika said, adjusting her hat, "not stuff like that."

"Here in Di'Abribel—" Janice took Mika's hat from her head. She closed her eyes and whispered, *Terra*. "—magic is used in far more different ways." Janice placed the hat back on Mika's head.

Mika's eyes widened, her smile grew, and her shoulder rose when she realized the hat's band had been tightened, causing it to fit perfectly around her head.

"Do you know how to cook?" Janice adjusted her posture and walked with her hands in front of her pelvis.

Mika looked at Janice's hands but only imitated her posture. "Nope!"

"Good." Janice looked toward the house. "Means you won't have bad habits."

The afternoon was filled with a tour of the mansion. Janice explained what the Toveys were meticulous about and what they overlooked. The maid used combinations of ventus, terra, and aqua to clean the house.

"Can you teach me that?" Mika asked when they walked down the long hallway of the first floor. Janice had used the spell to move wind around again.

Janice gave Mika a gentle look. "Do you not know how magic works?"

Mika stayed quiet. Although her face kept pointing at Janice, her eyes moved away. Mika didn't want to admit that she always fell asleep or daydreamed during Basic Magic class. Mika knew magic had its use, but it just did not interest her.

"There's three ways to learn spells." Janice looked ahead and guided Mika into a dark room. Janice used an orb of lux, illuminating a storage room with rows of chests of different colors lined against the walls.

"This is a chest room. All the chests are infused with magic. On every floor, there is a room like it. What is put in a chest—" Janice placed a diamond coin from her pocket into the red chest, "—will appear in the same-colored chest on every floor until it is taken out."

Mika's interest in magic had been piqued. She watched Janice close the chest. "What are the different ways to learn magic? I only know how to use a stream of water." So as not to sway the conversation, Mika didn't tell Janice she learned the spell from her mother.

Janice recalled the orb of lux into her hand, and it dissipated, surrounding them in darkness. They walked out of the room and through the hallway.

"Someone teaches you the spell. Some people are so good at magic, they learn spells just to sell them."

They reached the stairs. "Then there are the deity statues." Janice stopped and shut her eyes; she leaned on the railing and whispered,

Vita. A golden glow appeared on her hand, and she hovered it over her knee. After a few seconds of healing whatever was wrong with her leg, they continued.

"When you kill a living being, you absorb parts of their soul, their life essence. In the realm of the deities, life essence is like diamonds. In exchange for it, they give you spells if you go through a deity statue." They reached the second floor. "The issue with that is the life essence you spend doesn't stay with you, and you need to gather more."

The pair walked down the hall and turned into a room. Janice lit it with a lux orb, showing a room with the same layout as the chest room from downstairs.

"Then there's the hard way. You teach yourself a spell." Janice opened the red chest and pulled out her diamond coin. She smiled when Mika's eyes widened.

"How do I teach *myself* a spell?"

Janice and Mika continued walking. "Delve into your mind, and think of a spell you want to learn. Unique feeling, hard to explain. Feels like you're pushing yourself through a wall. The less you understand the type of magic, the thicker the wall feels."

Mika looked at Janice. "Just like that?"

Janice looked at Mika then looked ahead. "Not easy. Takes a lot of practice. If you have absorbed life essence, it will make it easier to break down the wall. Knowing scholastics about the element will also help."

Mika remembered her mom absorbing Rolo's life essence, and the life essence orb that appeared above Yevera at the end of the fighting. *Seems easy enough.*

The two continued walking through the house until they reached the third floor. Then, they made their way downstairs, through a library, past a small dining room, and into the kitchen. Janice taught Mika how to cook baked rabbit, rice with vegetables, bread, creamy potato soup, and cocoa cookies.

There was no need for candles, Janice lit the dining room with lux orbs. They served Professor Verity and Madame Virgilia. The couple invited Mika and Janice to dine with them.

Professor Tovey had a respectful appearance and a receding hairline eating away at his ventus-mastery hair. He mostly spoke about his son, a dragon rider in the Kingdom of Caithiopo, continent of Azilia, east of Irstia. Madame Virgilia spoke a lot about politics and the deities. Her wild, bushy, dirty-blonde hair reminded Mika of the Velondian creatures known as lions.

Mika talked a lot about Yevera and its amazing warriors and what daily life was like. She included Page and Cynthia in every sentence. Although she felt an extreme urge to talk about her new dog, she knew she shouldn't mention him.

Janice didn't speak about herself, but she listened and asked questions when appropriate to carry on the conversation.

After the four finished eating, Janice and Mika stood, cleaned the table, served the couple wine, and washed the dishes. When they finished, they both approached the professor and the madame. Verity was resting his head on Virgilia's shoulder. Virgilia held on to Verity and rubbed his back. Janice stood with her hands clasped in front of her pelvis. Mika did the same.

"Anything else for the night, Madame?"

Virgilia shook her head and smiled. "No." Her voice needed to be cleared. When she did so, she continued with a whisper, "No. Thank you, Janice. Thank you, Mika."

Janice bowed. Mika curtsied.

"Anything else for the night, Professor?"

Verity used a tablecloth to wipe tears from his eyes. He blew his reddening nose, folded the cloth, and kissed his wife on the forehead. He sat straight and looked at the maids.

"Nothing else." He reached to his belt and pulled out a coin purse. He counted thirty silver coins and gave them to Janice. He counted ten and gave them to Mika.

He pays well!

"You two are welcome to enjoy some wine. Mika, you're welcome to take up quarters in our home until your house is built. I'd love to have you back the day after tomorrow, since we let Janice rest every ten days."

"I'll be back!" Mika's mood showed in her broad smile and closed eyes. Thinking of her pup, she had to decline her stay. "I'd like to stay at the barracks until I get my own house. I want to keep seeing my townsfolk, sir."

The Toveys scooted their chairs back and stood. "Understandable," said the professor. "Thank you for your services." The couple left the room with clasped hands.

Mika walked with Janice out of the mansion and into the moonless, starless night. Janice was upfront. "Leaving because of the dog?"

"I promised I would heal him." Mika wanted to be stern, but her voice was soft.

They reached the shed. Janice undid the terra magic, and to Mika's relief, there were no yelps coming from inside. Janice opened the door and illuminated the shed. The rank scent of feces slapped Mika in the face. Addie's wagging tail sent his sick diarrhea all over the walls and shelves.

"Oh, my goodness!" Mika shouted. "No! No!"

Addie had also urinated on himself. Mika rushed to hold his cold, feces-coated tail. She dug her nails into his ear in hopes that he'd stop making a mess. Addie's happy face began to wrench, his mouth released squeals of pain.

She pressed her eyes shut. She hadn't known how tired she was until she realized she had to clean his mess. It was the middle of the night, and she had to find her way back to the barracks, in the dark, with her stupid map. Stress began compressing into her head until Janice touched her shoulder.

"He's happy to see you."

Mika looked into Janice's sad eyes, then at Addie. He didn't look happy at that moment; he looked at her as if she was a predator about to rip his stomach open and eat him alive.

"Raising a puppy takes a lot of patience," said Janice. She slid her hand off Mika's shoulder and began cleaning the feces with aqua and terra. "Sternness and consistency work much better than anger and meanness. Go on home, Miss Plum. You have a long walk back."

Mika knelt next to Janice. "I can help! It's my fault ..."

Janice stopped and stood on her knees. "It will happen again, and you will clean it next time." She continued washing away the feces with aqua and placing it into a terra bin with ventus.

Mika sighed and thanked Janice. She cleaned off Addie's urine and feces-covered tail with aqua, cradled him, and walked into the dark night.

Sternness and consistency, not meanness.

* * * * *

Two months after she met Janice, Mika was able to leave Addie alone. He knew not to defecate or urinate if Mika wasn't around, especially if he was inside a crate. Mika had spent the last hour inside the hot waters of the bathhouse. Her skin was turning red from the heat of the water warmed in a large cauldron. Andellia had approached and asked to speak with her, so Mika dried herself with a towel and drained the water.

"What do you mean you're *leaving*?"

"Exactly that, Mika." Andellia's voice was, as always, soft.

Mika was too surprised to get dressed. She dropped her towel. "Where are you going? With who? Why?"

"It's *with whom*, not *with who*." Andellia looked at Mika with sad eyes and an open mouth. She closed her mouth; her eyes became alert when she saw Mika's eyes narrow. Dropped eyebrows and clenched fists on Mika showed her anger. Everyone in the barracks knew that angry Mika was a big, big problem.

"I'm, well ..." Andellia swallowed. "I'm going with the wives of the builders. They say the attack on the forest will fail and—"

"Don't say that!" Mika took a step forward.

"Mika!" Andellia matched her aggression. "Mika, I'm telling you what they're *saying*!"

Mika sighed and let Andellia continue.

"*They* say it will fail, and we'll be stuck in Di'Abribel forever, at the mercy of its people and its stupid government that hasn't done anything to prevent the necromancers from attacking!"

Andellia passed her hand through her boyish hair, her new style since the day Mika got a job as a maid. Andellia continued. "They're tired of the wars, of the fighting, the warrior and militaristic lifestyle. We're going to Sytu."

Sytu, the continent across the sea to the east, north of Azilia was, according to books and stories, the only continent where there was peace.

Andellia studied Mika's emotions. Anger and sadness showed on her face—each emotion tried to overtake the other in Andellia's crazy, aggressive *friend*. Andellia had been trying her hardest to make Mika think she liked her.

Mika shook her head. "Why didn't anyone ask me to go?" Mika's lips trembled, and her eyes felt heavier because of the forming tears.

"You were always working, always with the dog, always sleeping. We figured you had adopted Di'Abribeli customs, lost your Yeveran roots. We thought—"

"Are you fucking *serious*?" Mika's shout penetrated through the walls. She bit her bottom lip. Her nostrils widened and she dug her nails into Andellia's shoulders.

Andellia flinched and tried to back away, but Mika dug her nails deeper and pulled her closer.

"Just because I adapt to my surroundings doesn't mean I forget who I am! You think you're so smart and you can't figure *that* out?" Mika's angry outbursts caused her to sweep Andellia off her feet and slam her to the ground. She climbed atop her classmate and wrapped her hands around her neck.

Rushed whispers told her people were watching, but when she looked around, no one was there. She shifted her attention back to Andellia and applied slight pressure to Andellia's throat.

Mika's words contained a sinister hiss. "My roots are dug far deeper than any of yours! I know our men will win!" Mika banged Andellia's head against the floor. "They're Yeveran." She banged her head again. "Fucking…" she banged Andellia's head one last time. "—warriors!"

Mika got off her fellow classmate and pressed the sides of her head. "You've lost faith in Yevera; therefore, you are no longer my sister." Mika got dressed in an aggressive hurry and ordered Andellia to sit every time she began to stand. "Leave, and never set foot in Yevera's lands again."

To add insult to injury, Mika kicked Andellia on the chest before storming out, ignoring the greetings coming from the wives of the Yeveran builders. Sheer disgust filled Mika's mind. How could they expect failure from their husbands, brothers, and sons?

*   *   *   *   *

Dear Page,

I finally found a way to get letters to you! I'll be writing you every day until you go on your mission. I know you'll be fine; you're a strong and handsome man, and you are definitely a capable warrior. Maybe when this is over, you can teach me the moves you've learned? I miss combat classes. Too bad they didn't teach scouts how to fight head-to-head with their enemies. Specializing in ambushes and silent killing seems unfair!

These first few months in Di'Abribel have been hard. A lot of the people here are extremely rude and self-centered. Only a few are nice. Most people from Yevera have already left to other cities, regions, or continents. It seems like the Di'Abribeli are starting to get mad about us taking refuge here. They see us as a burden. What's worse, they told us that if we leave the gates, we can't come back into the city. No travel, no exploring, nothing. I've explored every inch of the city that I'm allowed to be in. They say if I don't have "papers," I can't go into some districts. Stupid, I know! Either way, I'm not leaving. I'm going to make a life for myself here, and you promised you'd come, so I'm holding you to that.

I miss you bunches, but I'm sure you miss me more, being there training hard and the like. I included some paper and a letter for you to write me back.

With love and kisses,
Mika Plum of Yevera

P.S. I had a lucid dream last night. I realized I was dreaming when you actually beat me at a race!! I grabbed you, and I flew up high, high, high into the heavens and into space until we landed on another planet, just you and me and a lot of weird animals that moved very slowly and clumsily on the big trees.

P.P.S. I can't wait for you to see the animal I've been taking care of!!!! I'll give you a hint: Addie's not a wolf (though I tell people he is)!

The letter was placed on the ground, and a rock was used to prevent the wind from stealing it. Another letter was read. This one was small

55

and, based on how it was folded, the reader could tell it was folded with anger and speed.

> Page,
>
> Addie ate my yellow hat.
>
> Sincerely,
> Future Dog Murderer Mika Plum of Yevera

The letter was placed underneath the rock. The next letter was thick and had a news article attached to it.

> YEVERAN WARRIORS AND TRIUMPHI PALADINS LAUNCH SURPRISE ATTACK ON THE LOST FOREST!
>
> Almost one year after the attack on Yevera, its fierce warriors have mustered, trained their forces, and rallied with paladins from Triumph in a surprise attack on the Lost Forest. Yesterday, just at the break of dawn, Yeveran archers launched flaming arrows into the forest. Although the fires were quelled with ease, infantry plummeted through the forest's tree line. While the Yeverans attacked from the south grasslands, paladins ambushed from the north after crossing the river. The battle continues as this is being written.

The article was placed above the letters on the floor. The letter read:

> Page!
>
> I just read on the Passing Wind that the raid on the forest began! You're in my prayers to Angelis. I KNOW you'll win, and when you do, you'll be hailed as a hero! I can't wait to see you! You'll probably get this once you get back to Warrior's Edge, but if not, someone will see that your name should be praised for ridding this monster that lives in our beautiful region!
>
> See you soon!
> Your girlfriend,
> Mika Plum of Yevera
>
> P.S. I hope it's you who kills the bitch with the short hair and belt of skulls.

The letter and article were placed in the same pile. The pages of the next letter were tear stained.

YEVERAN WARRIORS AND PALADINS DEFEATED AT THE BATTLE OF THE LOST FOREST.

For one long month, the warriors of Yevera and the paladins of Triumph fought the necromancers in the Lost Forest. Last night, a full retreat was ordered by the paladin general, who also assumed command of the Yeveran forces after Elder Kessap was slain. During the retreat, paladin forces were split from Yeveran forces, allowing the necromancers to annihilate the retreating Yeverans. A spokesperson from Triumph has informed that no Yeverans survived the battle, and all bodies have been dragged into the forest to allow the trees to recover.

The article continued, but it was torn—the attached letter read:

Page,

I don't know why I'm writing this, especially after all these months since it happened. I guess I'm just hoping, wishing, praying that the scribes got it all wrong, that maybe not all Yeverans died, that maybe the retreat was successful. Something deep inside me tells me you're okay, it tells me that you're doing fine, that you're happy... And I just wish I knew that was true. I'm so, so broken. I'm so alone. I'm so scared of what my life will be like by myself. I have no family, I have no friends, I have no one with me. I'm all alone... The Di'Abribeli council won't pay to rebuild Yevera. I don't know what to do. I wish I had a way to

The letter had a blotch of ink, but another paper continued where it had left off.

Everything hit me when I found out about the failure. I was feeling fine before that. I was feeling like it didn't happen, that after the attack, everything would return to normal... Now I know it's all real. Now I know it's all going to end in darkness...
I regret going to the river. I wish I'd died with my mom.

57

With a lot of love and a painful goodbye, I send this letter in your memory. I miss you, Page. I miss you so, so, so much.
Mika Plum of Yevera

P.S. Thank you for your sacrifice.

The letters were placed in a pile.

"Terra," the man said, and a small portion of snow, sand, and stone formed a small grave. With another call to the magic of earth, the papers were buried at the top of Mount Cabria, forever hiding the letters that made him feel the most emotion. The man turned around and began building a fire underneath the beautiful meteor shower above him.

Further away, Amirra pretended not to be cold, despite the freezing temperatures. She chopped several limbs off a tree, then trudged through the snow back to the campfire. Tossing the logs to the side, she plopped herself next to her partner and adjusted her platinum-blonde hair that told everyone she was a paladin.

She spoke with a strong and beautiful accent. "I cannot believe you made it to the top with only one arm!" She giggled, bumping her shoulder against his.

"Just goes to show," he said, returning the shoulder bump, "how strong I really am." A wink preceded a smile.

Amirra's face reddened, and she, too, smiled. She leaned back and felt him grab her hand. She refused to look at him, instead basking in the meteor shower of varying colors that fell from space. The spectacles of lights made her pupils dilate, more so because of her affinity to lux magic.

"Amirra..."

She felt the man's warm breath kiss her cheeks. She turned and faced him, revealing a big smile. "That is me!"

The man held out a gold box and opened it with a flick of his finger. Inside was a gorgeous diamond set in a gold ring that reflected the lights of the passing meteors. "Will you marry me?"

The woman recoiled, not from disgust but from surprise. She covered her mouth when she realized he was serious. He wasn't playing one of his dumb jokes. She looked at the ring, the box, then at her partner. Tears filled her light-blue eyes.

She grabbed the box, closed it, and set it next to the man's leg.

"Page!" She charged into him with a hug that knocked him onto his back. "Of course, I'll marry you!"

5. FLOWER

With eyes closed and ears perked, Mika, now nineteen, listened to the snips of the shears, the brushing of the hairdresser's hands on her hair, the footsteps of patrons walking about in the salon, and wind chimes singing along with the outside breeze. Her lips curled into a smile, one that overtook her cheeks and eyebrows. She took a breath, smelling the lavender throughout the shop. The moment she exhaled, she giggled.

"We are almost done." Sandra's voice always carried a hint of apathy, no matter what was said. "Do not open your eyes yet."

Mika whispered, "I can't wait." She bounced her leg on the chair. Her head moved along with the brushes. Her smile widened.

She remembered the day she met Sandra three years ago, a year after the Yeveran defeat in the Lost Forest.

"Your hair is so pretty," she'd said.

Sandra hadn't moved her head but looked at Mika with her soft eyes. "Stop by my salon. I can make yours look even prettier. Only single-story building, south of the west castle gates. Closed the third day of the week."

Sandra's voice rang in her ears. "Do not move a muscle. I will be back."

She heard Sandra's footsteps fade away. Mika had a hard time realizing that Sandra was a sweet person. Sandra never showed any emotion, she never laughed at Mika's jokes, never frowned when Mika said something mean, and never cried at Mika's sad stories.

60

Still, Mika enjoyed her company because something about Sandra reminded Mika of her mother. Maybe it was Sandra's age, her knowledge of teas, her love for books, her pretty nose, or her stunning olive-green eyes. It wasn't her hair, though, since Sandra's hair was silver, denoting her mastery of ventus.

Mika heard Sandra move in front of her. She felt a sharp object pass through her hair and brush her scalp, coming to a rest on top of her ear. The object curled itself along her ear and dangled next to her earlobe.

"Okay." Sandra moved to the side. "Open your eyes."

Mika obeyed, opening her eyes, and caught her reflection in the mirror. A fresh, dark-blue flower rested on the side of her head.

Mika squealed and shot up from her chair, placing her hands on the counter and leaning closer to the mirror, eyeing the flower. "It's so beautiful!"

Mouth open and eyes wide, she examined the flower. Five blue petals shaped like arrowheads extended from a lime-green pearl in the middle. Upon looking closer into the pearl, she felt a strange connection to it, like the pearl was the flower's eye, and the eye was looking right back at her.

Mika turned to Sandra. "I've never seen this type of flower before. It's—"

"That," said Sandra, crossing her arms, "is a dragon flower. Lime-green pearl means it came from a terra dragon. Dragons sprout them when they hatch from their eggs."

Sandra raised her eyebrows, shifting her gaze from Mika to the mirror.

"They are special. If you allow it to, it mirrors your emotions in its petals. Some say the dragon it sprouted from will feel every emotion the flower feels. Happy Mika, happy dragon. Depressed Mika, depressed dragon."

Turning back to the mirror, Mika took a step back to get a better view of her face and the flower. Locking her eyes on the flower's pearl, she reached up to touch it. The flower had a smooth, glassy texture, but it bent and moved with her touch. She gazed into the lime-green pearl and smiled, and the flower seemed to return her happiness by arching its petals back toward the stem, further revealing the pearl. Mika's eyes widened, and her mouth dropped. She snapped a surprised look at Sandra.

A regular person would have returned the smile, but Sandra's face was serious. "Grab the flower and look into the pearl. You will see something far more surprising."

When Mika's fingers gripped the flower's stem, the stem around her ear straightened so she could pull it out. She held the flower in front of her face and focused on the pearl. The lime-green pearl cleared, and Mika saw shining pillars illuminating the inside of a dark cave. Just in front of her view, Mika could see the large snout of a dragon. The dragon looked toward its tail, making Mika feel dizzy.

"I can see what the dragon sees?" Mika looked at Sandra with eyes too wide for Sandra to think she was normal.

Sandra nodded.

Mika gazed into the pearl again. The dragon moved his head, again making Mika dizzy. Mika looked at Sandra. "This is insane! This is so amazing!"

Sandra sighed. "What do you think of your hair?" Sandra faced the mirror.

Mika looked at herself in the mirror.

Chestnut-brown hair was styled into wavy curls, swirling down to the small of her back. Sunshine beamed through the window, radiating onto the smooth skin of her round face. Large eyes sat below her arched eyebrows, her pupils almost invisible inside of her cocoa-colored irises. Her button nose complemented her downward-turned lips which were curved upward into a smile, revealing her perfect teeth. The blue flower went well with her pink sundress.

Though Mika's looks weren't spectacular or close to anything someone would consider astonishing or beautiful, she had magnificent flowing hair and eyes that seemed to sparkle with every ray of light that bounced from them. Her average looks didn't intimidate men, prompting them to approach Mika and flirt with her often, therefore increasing Mika's confidence.

If only Mom could see me now.

"You have come here every ten days for three years." Sandra's voice boomed, breaking Mika from her thoughts. Mika blinked, shook her head, and scratched her nose, and Sandra knew this meant Mika had snapped back to the present moment.

"No need for payment this week. Although I appreciate your patronage, you need to invest your money in something better than your hair." Sandra played dumb; she knew Mika only came to Sandra for social interaction, since the Yeveran had no friends other than Janice.

Mika rolled her eyes and stuck her tongue out. "What would I invest in?"

"I am a coiffeuse," said Sandra, "not a merchant."

"How do I care for the flower?" Mika asked, noticing Sandra tapping her foot on the ground, anxious for Mika to depart. "And how old is it?"

Sandra sighed and crossed her arms. "Eight years. Ensure it does not get crushed. It will live forever otherwise."

Mika could see through Sandra's guise and knew Sandra was hiding her sweetness underneath her stern façade. She knew most people were the opposite of how they acted. Mika dashed toward Sandra and gave her a hug, resting her head on Sandra's shoulder. Caught off guard, Sandra held her arms out, reluctant to touch Mika.

"Thank you, *friend*!" Mika mocked.

Pushing open the wooden door, the hot afternoon air ambushed Mika, reminding her the season of growth was just around the corner. Mika despised the approaching season, when the heat was the highest; she was a girl who loved the cold from the season of endurance. She brushed her hair to the side, feeling the dragon flower.

The dragon flower.

Addie lay panting on the cobblestone street under the shade of the salon's roof. She knelt beside him. Although he was four years old, Mika considered Addie a puppy and her adopted son.

"Addie." She looked into the eyes of the dog. He had big, pointy ears. The top half of his coat was black, and the bottom half was tan, and his mean, yellow eyes made him look like the werewolves found in the Frozen Mountains of northern Irstia. Addie twirled in a circle, stood on his hind legs, and barked.

"No!" Mika said, pointing a finger. "Don't bark at me!"

Addie replied by closing his eyes and smiling, letting his tongue flop out of his mouth.

Mika shook her head and glared at Addie until his eyes widened and he closed his mouth.

"Let's go." She signaled for him to follow.

Addie had been obedient for the past couple of years, so Mika did not guide him with a leash. Addie heeled by her side and walked at the same pace she did. When Addie was not looking at objects, people, or passing birds, he would stare at Mika as if she were the most important thing in his life. Nonstop, obsessive, protective stares.

Mika had planned on returning home after her appointment with Sandra, but now, with the flower in her hair, she decided to walk around town, even visit the market and show everyone her rare gift. Her thoughts raced. How did Sandra come across such a unique item? Dragons are dangerous and territorial, and their scales are stronger than most objects in the world. Dragons shed their scales, and humans have been killed in trying to acquire them. The only people who have tamed dragons have been the Caithiopians. Did Sandra face a dragon once? Maybe she—

"No! Darling, no!" a woman cried out.

Mika shook her head, blinked, and scratched her nose. Next to her, Addie was being petted by a child. The woman's mother ran up, grabbed her daughter, and began to raise her arm to strike the animal.

Mika sprinted toward the woman.

"Hey!" She used her arms to shield Addie, retracting them when the woman's fingers slapped her bare skin.

Mika hissed in pain; her forearm was beginning to welt with three fingermarks.

Addie revealed his teeth when he snarled. Mika yanked him down by the collar. If Addie did something to a Di'Abribeli, he would be killed and Mika exiled.

"Are you insane?" The woman placed her child on the ground; spit flew into Mika's face when the woman screamed. "Who allowed you to let your pest loose?"

Mika pulled on the barking dog. After a reminding slap on the gut, Addie shut up and Mika ordered him to leave. She turned to the woman. "Your child approached *him*! Leash your child instead!"

The woman scoffed, looking Mika up and down, judging Mika's sundress, an attire used mostly by Yeverans.

"You Yeveran refugees have always been a burden on this lovely city." The woman's nostrils widened, and she stepped toward Mika before pushing her to the ground.

Addie stepped in between them and growled. Had Mika not trained him better, he'd be digging his teeth into the woman's neck.

The woman stopped, looked at the dog, and forced a laugh. She adjusted her elegant gown and grabbed her child.

"Who owns *dogs* anyways? Get yourself real animals instead of this disgusting ... thing. Better yet, leave this city so taxes go somewhere useful instead of being wasted on trash."

The woman walked past Mika, staring down the young lady.

With teary eyes and balled fists, Mika returned the stare until the woman looked away. She controlled her breathing. Everyone who saw the altercation continued walking, with none offering any sort of help. She stood and continued glaring. Addie had sat and was looking at Mika, ready for her to give a command.

Mika brushed herself off, adjusted her hair, and felt the dragon flower. The flower's petals spread out and the tips pointed forward, showing everyone Mika's feelings of anger. She snapped her fingers and pointed up the street toward the market, signaling to Addie where to go. She ignored the jeering comments and scornful looks from those who despised the refugees, especially the one who housed pests.

One day ...

She shook away the wrathful thoughts that flashed in her mind. Her flower agreed, relaxing its petals when the image of fires burning the people of Di'Abribel faded away.

*   *   *   *   *

Mika took the flower with her everywhere, only taking it off to bathe and sleep. She noticed people's eyes would always travel to the petals and pearl when she spoke. Some would start conversations with her, people she normally wouldn't be approached by.

"That flower is just as stunning as your eyes, young lady."

"By Rend! Where did you find that beautiful creature?"

"Miss, does your flower ever need watering?"

But the comment that ran through her head every time she wore the flower came from an old, frail lady with a cloudy eye.

"I hope you're staying happy. If you're happy, the dragon that flower belongs to will be happy ... And he won't know why ... but he'll be happy."

Mika pulled the flower from her hair. She placed it atop a small leather pillow on her nightstand. Mika rotated the pillow so that the pearl looked at her as she slept. From inside the pearl, she knew the dragon could see her too. The moment the thought crossed her mind, the flower's petals arched back toward the stem, fulling revealing the pearl in joy. Mika could tell that was the flower's way of smiling, the same way a human's lips arch back and reveal the teeth.

The flower and the dragon had seeped into Mika's personality. It was now part of her circle that she would protect with her life. No one would hurt her flower, and anyone who tried would die.

Addie rested his head on the nightstand. He smelled the flower, causing his nose to twitch with every inhale. He sat down, smiled at Mika, and closed his eyes. He let his tongue hang from the side of his mouth.

"We're going to go looking for the dragon one day, Addie."

He panted harder when he realized Mika was talking to him, much harder when she placed her hand on his head. He licked the coconut oil she used as moisturizer from her forearm.

"I just hope he's not as silly as you."

6. BOOKSTORE

Morning sunlight crept through Mika's open window, shining its warm, powerful rays onto her face, waking her from her deep, comfortable sleep. Though her eyes were closed, she squinted when the powerful light fell across her eyelids. The rays intensified, forcing her to groan and turn away from the window. She sighed and tried to go back to sleep. It was just a few moments before the feeling set in … the feeling of hungry eyes staring at her. Sensing the unbearable feeling of being watched, she opened her eyes to see a black, wet nose followed by yellow eyes and pointed dog ears. Addie opened his mouth into a smile and started to pant, his warm breath slapping Mika in the face.

"It's my day off, Addie!" Mika complained, pushing Addie's face out of hers. The Toveys, being amazing lords, gave Mika and Janice a full week's paid vacation.

At the sound of his name, Addie panted harder, stood, and licked Mika. His tongue hung from the side of his mouth. Mika closed her eyes and dragged her hand from her forehead down to her chin, pulling down her eyelids and lips, giving Addie a close-up look at the ugly sight. Mika threw the blankets off and sat up. She grabbed a silver brush beside her pillow and brushed her hair. Once she finished, she hopped off the bed, slipping into a pair of sandals that slapped at the wooden floor with every step. She brushed her teeth, using a mixture of coconut oil and salt, the coconut imported from the

Valentina Islands. She trudged to the kitchen but turned back for the dragon flower before going back to the kitchen.

Mika opened the food box, feeling the cold magic air escape from inside. The city of Di'Abribel taught every citizen a spell of combined ventus and aqua to create refrigeration for homes and food preservation. She grabbed two pieces of meat, tossing one to Addie. Addie looked at the slab and drooled.

Mika placed her slab on the counter. She went through the kitchen and opened the door to her backyard. Inhaling the cool morning air, she caught a whiff of food coming from the homes surrounding hers.

"Eat," she ordered, and Addie began to devour his food.

Her backyard wasn't big, but she made the most she could with it. On the left, she had a place where Addie would play and a spot where she dried her wet clothes. In the center was an unpleasant walkway made of soggy wood. To the right was Mika's small, yet prized, garden. She walked toward plants with light-green foliage and tall, bushy stems—angelwish berries. The name angelwish derived from their petals that looked like angel wings. When the temperature dropped, the petals came together and appeared to be hands making a wish, a wish for warmth. The berries were white, transparent ovals, just larger than strawberries, with a large, squishy, yellow seed on the inside.

Next to the angelwish were watermelons, potatoes, tomatoes, peppers, blueberries that were hanging on for dear life, and cateye fruit. Mika didn't like cateye fruit, but she liked the black stems, purple leaves, and the yellow line running down the black and squishy palm-sized fruit.

Mika pointed all her fingers at the plants. "Aqua," she whispered. Orbs of water appeared at her fingertips, ready for her command. Had she voiced the spell louder and with more authority, the element would have replied with more energy.

With slight concentration and some thought, she imagined water flowing from her fingertips. The orbs became a stream of water, though it wasn't the same strength Mika had imagined or needed.

"Aqua!" she shouted. The water replied, its stream becoming more powerful. She smiled. Just what she wanted.

She watered her garden until the plants dripped with water that glistened in the sunlight. Mika harvested the ripe fruits and vegetables, took them inside, and set them on the counter. She opened her window and did the same to the herbs, harvesting the best ones for her meal.

She sang and cooked, straining to remember last month's song from the amphitheater. The song was dedicated to the power of the two moons hovering above the horizon. She moved her head side to side, then her feet, until she was dancing along with her cooking. She pushed Addie away with her hips when he tried to sneak a bite of the fruit on the counter. Cutting at the vegetables, she cut and cut and cut until Addie barked at something outside, startling Mika, making her cut her finger.

"Shit!"

She dropped the knife and screamed at Addie, applying pressure to her bleeding finger. Mika clenched her fists and slammed them on the counter, rattling the knives and dishes, and shaking the walls. She breathed through her nose and glared at the dog.

Addie tucked his ears and lay on his side. Other than a few disciplining slaps to the face, she never abused her pet, but Addie knew not to make Mika angry. Addie feared Mika more than he adored her, so he would always obey her commands. When the mood passed, Mika approached him, apologizing for her outburst. She kissed his head and returned to her cooking, this time without the singing and dancing. The mood had been killed.

Addie stayed on the ground and kept his eyes wide on Mika.

Mika extinguished the flames underneath the hanging cauldron and served her food. She ate the meat and veggies, passing the fork into her mouth. Her other hand held a book titled *Warrior of the South.* Mika was a slow eater; she loved to savor every bite.

The sound of the church bell was followed by eight booms, signifying eight in the morning. She smiled and got to her feet. Devouring the last few bits of meat, she folded the corner page of the book and ran toward her room. She dressed herself in a long, light-pink dress with red embroidery; grabbed a couple of baskets; filled them with veggies, fruits, and herbs; kissed Addie goodbye; and burst out the door, pivoting toward the market.

The steps tapped on the cobblestone street. The tops of her brown boots had bits of water from Mika misting the produce with her magical aqua. The basket swung back and forth on her forearm like a swing hanging from a tree; she waved at the people who smiled and said hello, returning a smile with closed eyes and rising cheeks. It disgusted Mika seeing people treat her differently when she wore her fancier dresses and went about without Addie. She wasn't recognized as the *Yeveran with a dog.* She always remembered the faces of those who insulted her when she walked with Addie but were nice to her when her dog wasn't around.

I hope you feel your skin fall off as you burn to death, she thought to herself after smiling at those people. If it weren't for Sandra, Janice, and a few others, she would hate all Di'Abribelis.

She passed through the stores, looking into the glass windows, admiring the fancy clothes, the beautiful silverware, the comfortable furniture. She had reached the point where she could buy almost anything she wanted, but she always felt inclined to save all her coin. The only thing she would spend on would be travel or fares. If someone offered to take her on an adventure for a fee, she would, without a doubt, take it. The issue was being allowed entry back into Di'Abribel. What about the other towns and cities? What if they didn't allow entry despite having paid someone? She continued walking; the booms of the bell reached the ninth hour, and the sun was beginning to sizzle her skin. The market was so far from—

"Papers."

Mika stopped and looked forward. A guard in leather armor squared off in front of her, gripping his weapon with such force Mika thought he would crush the grip. In his other hand, he held a small booklet with a yellow string. The guard scanned Mika with wide eyes and peeked inside her baskets.

"Are you going to identify her?" an older guard cried out from behind him.

Flustered, the young guard held up his hand, dropping the book he was holding. He stepped back, looked at the book, and bent down to pick it up.

Mika felt a rush, her primal instinct telling her the threat she faced was in a vulnerable position, in a spot where she could sink a dagger into its spine. Still, Mika had no intent to harm the guard. She respected those who fought against the criminals in the city. Mika held back her laugh when the older guard sighed and tried to conceal his disappointment.

The young guard rose and placed his hand in front of Mika's face. "Aevum."

His big palm was motionless in front of Mika's face. The guard tilted his head and looked at Mika's big eyes. "Mika Plum, descendant of … Cynthia Plum. Born in Yevera? Allow me to see the papers permitting, uh," –he looked at his trainer– "permitting travel through this district."

"I don't have papers, but I'm on my way to the market to sell my harvest." Mika slid the basket from her forearm to her wrist and held it in front of the guard. "Would you like to try some angelwish berries?"

The guard didn't look convinced.

Mika continued, "I'm allowed passage to trade at the market, per the king's new policies." Mika lifted her basket higher.

The young guard looked at Mika's basket, back at Mika, then at his trainer.

"What now, rookie?" The trainer held his arms out to the side.

The rookie looked back at Mika. "Sorry, ma'am, I can't allow passage." He stepped toward Mika. "You'll be fined in accordance with—"

The trainer smacked the back of the rookie's head and yanked the trainee toward him.

"Have a good day, Miss Plum." He smiled at Mika. "Good luck with your sales." He bowed and moved himself and the rookie away from Mika's path.

Mika curtsied and kept walking, pressing her lips together, she tried to hide her smile when she heard the trainer scolding the trainee.

"… and you bend over to pick up your manual while you're in front of her? Are you fucking stupid?"

Mika walked past the long window of a bookstore. Bookstores were new to Di'Abribel thanks to an Imbric shaman. The shaman, an avid reader and writer, crafted a terra spell that allowed the user to write whatever they thought and whatever they read, in the same penmanship. That, along with him teaching the spell to everyone who would accept it, and people writing without need of quills, caused writers, scribes, and bookstores to spring up throughout Irstia. Irstia was now home to the largest writer's guild in the world.

Mika looked through the window at the displayed books, not once slowing her pace. In front of the books, she read the titles and authors. *Necromancers and Why They Want Celeste* by J. I. Loback. *Tales from The New Lands* by Erna Breaker. *Mastering the Bow and Arrow* by Master Archer Sigmond. *Does He Love You?* by Anayeli Rivera. *Blunt Weaponry and Tools: Beginner Lessons and Fundamentals* by Page Briarhart, *Hunting Dragons and Drakes …*

Mika stopped. She blinked several times, walked backward, and approached the window, her eyes locked on to a large book with a mace engraved into beautiful brown leather. A red string hung from its side, down to the paper that Mika read out loud.

"Blunt Weaponry and Tools. Beginner Lessons and Fundamentals by … Page Briarhart."

Mika burst through the door. Fixated on the book, she ignored the greetings from the store owner. Moving aside a chair, she reached over the counter and grabbed the book, sinking her shaking fingers into the soft leather. She flipped to the last page.

About the Author
Page Briarhart was born in the cold town of Triumph and raised in Yevera by his father and grandfather. Page survived the necromancer's raid on Yevera and was drafted into the military to counterattack the Lost Forest, where he became an expert blunt weapons handler. Page is now a master instructor in blunt weaponry and lives peacefully in—

The book hovered away from Mika's hands; her hands followed and reached.

The owner of the shop, a tall, older man with a long beard that had terra lowlights, took the book from her.

"This isn't a library!" he said. "Payment is required before you read, ma'am!" His high-pitched voice annoyed Mika.

Mika followed the attendant to the counter.

"How much for the book?" she asked, her words fast, choppy, and for some reason, out of breath.

The man curved his lips to a smile. "I can feel your lust for this book radiating through my store!" He tilted his head and spread his arms, revealing his palms. "One gold piece will—"

"One gold piece?"

"His books sell faster than your heartbeat, ma'am!"

"If that's so, how have I never heard of him as an author?" Mika challenged.

The man leaned closer. "His books sell faster than your heartbeat, ma'am!"

Bastard.

Mika placed her palms on the counter and leaned closer. "Could you hold it for me?" Her eyes were wide, and she didn't blink. "I can come back with one hundred silver coins."

"No, no, no!" The man wiggled his long, skinny, dislocated-looking finger at Mika. "I will not waste my time exchanging silver to gold. No!"

Mika began to speak, but she was interrupted.

"One gold coin or no sale! You have until dusk, ma'am!" He placed the book under the counter and pointed at the door for Mika to leave.

Mika's eyebrows almost came together when she glared at the man. She nodded and stomped out the door.

She had two options. The first was to go back home, count one hundred silver coins, carry them to the closest exchange point, then run back to the shop to buy the book. She would need to sneak past the patrols, since she wouldn't be allowed to pass through this district if she wasn't going to the market. If she avoided the guards, she might make it, but only if she changed to her walking gear and exerted herself the whole way.

73

Her other option was to continue to the market and make one hundred silver coins and take them to another merchant and pay ten extra silver coins to exchange the currency.

She looked through the window at the paper with Page's name just as the owner pulled it away, replacing it with a different book and a different paper. The store owner leaned over, glanced in the direction of the nearest church, and held his palm to his ear, pretending to listen for the bells to tell the time. He looked at Mika, then walked away. Mika caught her reflection in the glass, stared into her big brown eyes, and advanced in the direction of the market.

Mika set up her stand, placing her fruits and herbs together in such a way they complemented one another, convincing people to buy them together. The vegetables were separate, but she ensured her produce remained misted. The day started well; she made twenty-six silver coins within the first hour. When business slowed, she stood by her stall, shouting the name of her produce, trying to get the attention of the passing shoppers. To catch the attention of the more distracted ones, she offered free samples of the angelwish. By the thirteenth ring of the bells, Mika could see the decline in shoppers, and with thirty-one silver coins in her pouch, her hopes were bleak.

"This is angelwish?" a small, high-pitched voice with a strange accent asked.

No one was within view, prompting Mika to lean over the stall. She saw big, light-brown eyes looking up at her. Short, wild, curly hair was sat on top of an innocent young girl.

Mika looked back at the young girl, around for her parents, then back at the child. "Yes. Yes, it is."

The girl's eyes widened. "I like to buy some, please." The girl unclenched her fist and released a single coin. The gargantuan face of the Di'Abribeli king looked into Mika's eyes. The coin shone gold in the sunlight.

Mika placed her finger on the gold coin, covering the king's face. "Angelwish is only one sil—" Mika stopped and looked at the girl's squinting, smiling eyes.

"… is only one gold coin."

Mika slid the coin into her pouch. A huge smile appeared on her face, and her hands shook with excitement. She placed several clusters of angelwish into a bag made of cheap leather and, to prevent guilt from setting in, added a cateye fruit and some herbs.

The young girl skipped away toward her parents at an alcoholic-beverage stall a few yards across from Mika's. The girl held up her bag to a woman with beautiful, black, curly hair. The woman smiled and knelt in front of the girl. The woman congratulated the girl, then waved and smiled at Mika.

Mika raised her hand and smiled back, a painful smile. She reached into the coin pouch and pulled out the gold coin, stroking the smooth sides.

Mika imagined packing her stuff and sprinting to the bookstore. She could feel herself pushing open the door and mocking the owner by slamming the gold coin onto the counter.

"Here you go! And some cateye to remind you how dark your heart is! Now give me that book!"

The look on the owner would be priceless, and he wouldn't be shaking his disgusting finger at her again!

Mika reached for a basket and began placing the produce inside. One by one, she was careful not to ruin her fruit. She would celebrate her victory by eating all her harvest by herself at home. She grabbed a potato but caught a glimpse of the girl. Hands still on the rough vegetable, she watched the girl hopping in circles behind her mother and father. The girl reached into her bag and filled her mouth with a handful of angelwish. The girl savored the taste of the fruit.

Thoughts raced through Mika's mind. If Mika were the girl, how would she feel if someone scammed her out of ninety-nine silver coins? Would her parents be mad? How sad would Mika feel? What if the gold coin was being saved to buy something far more important? Mika knew it would change her trust in people for a long, long time. Was Mika like the people in Di'Abribel? Based on the accent, the girl wasn't a local; she didn't deserve Mika's malicious actions. But Page ... But the book! It says where Page lives! It says more about him! She needed to find out how he writes, how the words from his mind flow from his hand and onto the paper! Mika shook her head.

I'm more important than some hapless rugrat.

Mika placed the potato in her basket. She looked up and saw the girl studying the cateye fruit. The girl sensed eyes on her, prompting her to look at Mika. The girl waved her tiny hand at the person who scammed her.

Mika's eyebrows rose, and her lips lowered further than they naturally were. When Mika looked down, she sighed, and her shoulders lowered. She slid around her stall; the fruits tumbled when she dropped the basket. Mika jogged to the family.

"Excuse me! Excuse me!" When the family looked back, Mika waved her arm in the air. "Your daughter, I, she dropped this near my stall." Mika opened her sweaty, trembling hand, revealing the gold coin.

The woman's eyes widened before she scooped the coin from her palm. The woman looked young; her rosy cheeks made it seem like she wore blush, but Mika could tell the woman had no makeup on. Her dark, almost-black pupils looked back at Mika.

Although the woman had a smooth, tiny voice, she wasn't familiar with the language, making her hard to understand. "It is of kind you to return this!" The woman reached into her pouch and offered Mika five silver coins. "Please, for honesty to my person."

Mika scratched the back of her head. *I don't deserve this.* She closed the woman's fingers with both hands and shook her head. "No, thank you. I do not need it."

The child was eating angelwish from the bag, her mouth full; transparent fluid dripped from her lips and caught Mika's attention.

Mika smiled at the girl. *Sorry I called you a rugrat.*

The girl raised her hand and waved.

Mika glanced back at the mother, who was still holding out her silver coins. "No, really," said Mika, "she already paid."

"Your name," said the woman, her perfect, pearly-white teeth stunning Mika, "what it is?"

Mika shifted her attention and curtsied. "I am Mika Plum of Yevera. Nice to meet you."

"Yevera!" The woman lit up. She pointed at Mika and smiled. "Strong, strong warriors! Legends reach my land!"

Mika closed her eyes and nodded. "Yes, yes we are ... What is your name? Where are you from?"

"My name is Rosa. We are is travel from ..." she looked at her husband, or boyfriend perhaps, and motioned with her hands, trying to translate the proper words. "We are from Land New. Travel to East Celeste, to boat, to ocean, to Sytu. More calm, more peace."

Mika tried not to squint and roll her head in question when she tried to understand what Rosa was saying; it would be rude to do so. *Okay, they're from the New Lands and are traveling to Sytu.*

"This Antorio ..." Rosa held her arm to Antorio, an attractive, strong-jawed man with long hair. The man approached Rosa and interlaced his fingers with hers. "My lover!"

Mika curtsied.

Rosa held her hand out to the child. "This Lila. My ..." Rosa asked Lila a question in their language.

Lila hugged Rosa's leg. "Sister!"

"This Lila, my sister." She rubbed Lila's hair.

Mika smiled and curtsied. With a few more words, a few more gestures, and a few more hand movements, the conversation finished, and Mika returned to her workspace. She picked up the fruit that didn't touch the ground and placed it on the stall. Sad, but at the same time satisfied, she continued her best to make one hundred silver coins.

*   *   *   *   *

Mika was the last to leave the market. She packed the rest of her fruits and headed toward the sunset. Her shoulders hung low, and the pouch, which carried forty-six silver coins, slapped her leg with every other step. She passed the bookstore just in time to see the owner place Page's book on the shelf next to the window.

The man looked at Mika and held arms to his side, palms up to the sky. His body language was clear enough. *"What happened, ma'am?"*

Mika returned the gesture by shaking her head. The man shrugged his shoulders and made a half-frown, walking away to lock the door.

Mika caught her reflection in the mirror. She noticed her flower's petals had drooped, mirroring her feeling of sadness, only further plummeting her feelings. Mika looked at the paper bearing Page's name, then at the wooden board above. *New Releases.*

With sad eyes, she looked back at the cover of the book. The mace depicted looked like the one Page carried in Yevera. Moments passed until she squinted and elevated her shoulders, tilting her head to the side. She looked at the wooden board, at Page's name, then back at the book. Her eyes widened, and her heart skipped a beat. All day she was focused on making the gold coin; all day she was focused on selling her harvest; all day she was doing her best to achieve her goal, not letting her stop and think for a moment, but now, now, she was able to realize the one thing that mattered, and she said it with a whisper that escaped from the bottom of her throat. "Page is alive."

7. STONES

Lying on a comfortable, reclined chair in the salon, Mika looked at Sandra's face through watery eyes. She could see the hairdresser's lips pressed together in thought. A quick tweak of the outer corner of Mika's eyebrows sent a sting through her skin.

"How are you going to find him?" Sandra asked, cleaning off Mika's eyebrows from the tweezers.

Since Sandra stopped for a moment, Mika wiped the tears from her eyes. "He has to be somewhere close if the books are coming here, right?"

Sandra's silver hair was in a ponytail and dyed with white highlights. Perfect bangs swayed above her trimmed eyebrows. Black eyeliner and long lashes accentuated Sandra's narrow eyes. Mika didn't know what was more perfect: her smooth, rosy skin or her immaculate jawline. The hairdresser inched closer, squinted, and continued plucking.

Mika answered before Sandra could ask why she didn't return for the book. "I sneaked back to the store the day after, and the book had been sold!"

"If he is alive, would he not be looking for you?" Sandra tried to have sympathy in her voice, but it was hard for her to do so. She plucked away. "What if he forgot about you?"

Mika snapped, "He wouldn't." She pulled away and glared. "He probably doesn't have time to look for me."

Sandra glared back. Noticing Mika's anger, she calmed her face and raised her eyebrows to ease the mood. "Hon, he is writing books on how to be a fighter. He has plenty of time to look for you."

Mika scanned around for an answer. Sandra couldn't be right! She had to be wrong. Page wouldn't do that. Would he? Mika couldn't find a reason to disprove her hairdresser, but emotions overtook logic.

"He promised me he'd look for me. He's looking for me," Mika reassured herself. "He's looking for me."

Sandra's eyes narrowed. Mika's naivete was too much. "Mika," she said, her voice stern and direct, "he is not looking for you."

Mika jumped from the chair. "Do *not* say that!" Her voice could have shattered the windows.

Her outburst caused the shop to fall silent. Mika looked around. The patrons and other hairdressers stared at her. Some shook their heads; others covered their faces in embarrassment. Mika hung her head and placed her hands on her face, applying pressure to her eyes.

Why am I like this?

When the noises of the shop continued, she lowered her hands to her mouth and was met with Sandra's stare. Sandra had knuckles resting on her hips. Mika recognized the *are-you-done?* gesture, so she sighed and sat back down on the chair.

"I'm sorry," Mika whispered.

Sandra didn't reply. She kept working away at Mika's eyebrows in silence.

Mika began to think of what Sandra said, how Page wasn't looking for her, how he had enough time to be writing books on how to handle weaponry. He was a war veteran allied with paladins, meaning the paladins would pay for his housing, more so if he assisted with a daring attack against the necromancers. This meant he would have plenty of time to do what he pleased. Mika's mind took her back to the day when the smoke and fires from Yevera covered the sky, the moment Page kissed her and promised he'd be back for her no matter what happened.

And then told *her* to wait for *him*.

Mika was glad Sandra's plucking made her eyes water, for she didn't want Sandra to know she was crying, but her sniffles were quick to betray her. She closed her eyes and remembered Page slowing his pace, looking back, and mouthing the words *I'll find you.*

The plucking stopped, and Mika blinked her eyes open to wipe away the tears with her eyelids.

Sandra cleaned off her tools and placed them on the counter. "Come with me."

Sandra walked away, giving Mika full view of her ponytail, which swung from side to side like a pendulum with every step. Sandra disappeared past a red-and-gold curtain. The sound of a closing door followed.

Continuing to look in her direction, Mika refused to move. She had never seen Sandra, or any of her other workers, go past those blinds. She continued to wait, looked at herself in the mirror, at the reflection that showed someone looking back at her, then hopped out of the chair and walked to the curtain. She pulled the curtain to the side, opened the white door, and stepped into a candlelit room. Her jaw dropped when she stepped through the threshold.

The dancing flames of the candles gave only a temporary view of the walls, adorned with different types of weapons, emblems, jewels, maps, paintings, jars, and tools, spiking Mika's levels of anticipation and curiosity. Everything in the room had a placard with the item's name on it.

Rectangular tables were lined and pressed against the walls around the room. Maps and scrolls lay on some of the tables; others held larger, heavier weapons and items. The scrolls were written in ancient magic symbols that shimmered in a blinding blue color. Mika made her way around each table, studying the maps, recognizing several names of different cities, kingdoms, and empires.

Island of Dabria read a label atop one map. At the bottom: *Destroyed Prior to Arrival.* Mika walked to the next table.

"Sea of the Angels." Mika whispered the name on a map, marveling at the name. She read the footnotes: *Unable to navigate without Trident of Kymarinou.* Mika took a step back and wondered why the trident of the deity of aqua was needed to enter the Sea of Angels.

Trident of Kymarinou, Mika read on the wall, just below a baby-blue trident the length of her forearm. A medallion of the symbol of aqua, a water droplet, was engraved under the middle prong of the trident. Mika gasped and covered her mouth.

Sandra moved next to Mika. "I lost my whole team after acquiring that."

It took a few seconds for Mika to uncover her mouth. "Your whole team?" She looked at her friend.

"I used to …" Sandra closed her eyes, inhaled, and let out a long breath. "*We* used to be adventurers."

Mika wanted to speak, but she knew Sandra would continue, and after a pregnant pause that stretched for almost a minute, she did just that.

"Oniusus, Rachel, Jane, and myself. We adventured everywhere, past Velonde, beyond the Anngoran Sea, the Scorched Desert, and the New Lands the deities were expanding to the west."

From her studies, Mika remembered learning about the deity expansions. In a never-ending world, the creators added according to needs and wants of the people. They offered new adventure and discoveries to those brave enough to go into the unknown.

"What happened?" Mika asked, even though she knew the story wasn't going to end well.

Giving Mika a half-smile, Sandra shook her head and dismissed the question. "I know a way for you to find Page."

Mika inhaled to speak, but Sandra cut her off. "You have always longed for travel and adventure, have you not?" She kept her eyes on Mika and moved to a cabinet on the wall.

"Yes." Mika took a step toward Sandra. "I would if I could come back." There was hesitation in Mika's voice on her last sentence. "This is my home now."

Sandra opened the cabinet. Inside the cabinet was a gray stone, a crimson stone, and a brown stone.

Sandra grimaced, and Mika looked away, but not before her eyes fell upon a label below the pommel of a honey-colored sword: *Sword of Oniusus who died in the Scorching Desert.*

Stopping in front of the young woman, Sandra handed Mika the gray stone.

"What is it?" Mika looked at the stone but didn't accept it.

Sandra leaned on one leg. When she spoke, her voice was the same as it was when she'd given Mika the dragon flower, suggesting perhaps that Mika should accept the gift rather than ask about it.

"*This* is an adventurer's stone. It is the staple of anyone who has a strong desire for exploring." Sandra shifted her gaze to the stone.

"But I don't want to adventure," said Mika, looking up from the stone.

Her eyes widened in fear when she saw Sandra's usual, emotionless face churn in anger for a split second.

Although Sandra didn't show it, she was doing her best not to lash out at Mika. Sandra had to remind herself that Mika was only speaking through her heart and wasn't trying to be insulting.

"When this stone is active," Sandra said, "It will grant you passage throughout any district, city, region, and continent. That means you can pass through the gates of Di'Abribel and through the checkpoints and towns in Celeste to help you find Page and bring him home."

Mika's gaze dropped back to the stone in Sandra's hand.

"Really?" She took a step forward and held Sandra's hand with both of her own hands. "How do I use it?"

After sliding the stone into Mika's hands, Sandra brushed Mika's hair behind her shoulder.

"In the beginning times, humans were used as pawns of war by the deities. Proving ourselves by being relentless, courageous fighters, deities granted us some of their power, which we harness in our daily lives."

Sandra opened her palm and summoned a ball of aqua. The ball of water combined with ventus spun the aqua around Sandra's hand and created a whirlpool until she closed her palm.

"Humans have relished the use of magic, but advanced, arcane magic can only be learned with life essence."

Mika nodded. "But life essence can only be earned by killing."

"Not just any killing," Sandra said. "*Justified* killing. So, how does a person who builds grand monuments, raises cities, and creates massive bridges over continents learn the advanced magic to do so?"

Looking up to the ceiling didn't help Mika find an answer.

Sandra used ventus to call the brown stone on the cabinet to her hand.

"Builder's stone. The builder talks to the deities through the stone, giving a proposition for their plan. If accepted, the deities grant access to resources. The reward for completing the proposition is life essence, all without him having to kill a single being."

"Amazing," said Mika.

Sandra smiled. "So, how do you think a person who explores new places and creates maps, travels through the grueling seas, collects artifacts, and looks for their long-lost boyfriend learns advanced magic?"

Mika looked at the stone in her hands. She passed her thumbs through its pear-shaped edges and held it up to Sandra as her answer.

"Correct."

"Okay, what does this have to do with me finding Page?" Mika's words were fast. "Can't I just leave the city and live with him?"

"Slow down and think." Sandra used ventus to put the builder's stone back in the cabinet. "You need a way to get past the patrols. Though they are not as heavy in a divided region like Celeste, they do exist within the cities, suburbs, and markets. That is assuming Page is in Celeste and not Velonde or Imbris. You will not be allowed entry anywhere unless you have an adventurer's stone or documents permitting official travel."

Sandra allowed Mika time to digest the information, then answered the question forming in her mind.

"Because it works like a passport stamped by the deities," said Sandra, "no one will reject entry. Best of all, once you find Page, you will be able to learn an advanced spell or two." Sandra raised Mika's hands to her face, placing the stone within her view. "This will help you find Page."

Mika looked at the palm-sized gray stone, shaped like a pear rounded at the corners. On the face of the stone, near the top, was a blue swirl that extended down and around the face of the stone. In the center were nine carved insignia—two on the top, three in the middle, four at the bottom.

The top-left insignia was an extended angel wing. This was the insignia of Angelis, whose sphere of influence was vita, which is to say life and health. The wing was followed by a vertical rectangle. This was the insignia of Gral, whose sphere of influence was mori or death and the afterlife.

Furthest to the left of the center row was the insignia of a star with five points, the insignia of Rend, whose sphere was lux—light and intelligence. Next came the hourglass insignia of Baigh, whose sphere, aevum, was time and memories. To the right of the hourglass, the mysterious moon insignia of Nessa, whose sphere, tenebris, was darkness and emotions.

The last row started with the insignia of Liranda, an ember denoting the fire and corruption of ignis. The wind and electricity of ventus, commanded by Dwin, whose insignia was three wavy strands. The strands were followed by Mooredoth's sprout insignia representing terra, the sphere of earth, animals, and disease. Finally, the water-droplet insignia of Kymarinou, whose aqua sphere belonged to water and righteousness.

How do I use this? Mika shook the stone.

"Repeat after me," said Sandra. "I, Mika Plum of Yevera …"

Mika echoed her friend.

"Will begin an adventure to find Page Briarhart of Triumph. I do not know where Page is, and I am willing to reach him, despite my negligible survival, combat, and magic skills. To guarantee completion of this adventure, I offer …"

Mika's eyes went wide when she realized it was now down to her.

"What do I offer?" she whispered to Sandra.

Sandra looked at Mika but remained quiet. Only Mika could make this choice.

Mika panicked. "I offer all the money I have."

The swirl on the stone lit with a blue color, but it faded away.

"All deities refused your offer," said Sandra looking at Mika, then at the stone.

Mika's shoulders lowered, she felt defeated. "But why?"

"The greater the offer, the greater the chances of it being accepted, and more deities will follow because of the higher stakes. More deities, more essence at the end." Sandra raised the stone again. "Offer something more important."

Something more important? What could convince the deities that Mika would complete this adventure? What would they want to see her lose if she quit, if she decided she didn't want to see Page anymore? Mika looked around the room, looking around gave her the answer she needed, when she remembered the moment just before she saw Yevera on fire, when she thought she was blind.

"To guarantee my completion ..."

Mika's shaky exhale told Sandra she was afraid.

"I offer my eyesight."

Mika felt Sandra's fingers tighten at her offer. Still, Sandra didn't show emotion on her face.

They looked at the face of the stone. The swirl lit up, and the ventus symbol began to glow a beautiful silver. The colors of the rainbow radiated from the lux star. Mika's favorite symbol, Angelis's angel wing, shone a pure gold.

"They either believe in you or expect you to fail."

Sandra went to a table, picked up an object, then returned to Mika. She handed Mika a silver dagger and a hard, leather sheath.

"Although Celeste is not as dangerous as the New Lands, Velonde, or Azilia, there are still bad people and powerful creatures within and outside these walls."

Though the dagger was uncomfortable at the grip, Mika accepted it with a smile.

"Thank you, Sandra, I ..." Mika held back the urge to hug her. "I don't know what to say."

Mika strapped the sheath on her leg. She hopped, wiggled, and swung her leg, ensuring the sheath was tight enough but didn't constrict her movements. Having a dagger made her miss her training in Yevera, since daggers were the assigned weapons of Yeveran scouts and assassins.

Sandra touched her forehead with her fingertip and whispered a word. A thick silver drop appeared on her fingertip.

"Come here."

Mika approached and leaned forward. She felt the silver drop of ventus touch her forehead and sink into her skull. She felt wind pass through her cranium and into her brain. Learning the spell made her feel like she remembered a lost and distant memory, like a dream that began reconstructing itself at the smallest detail remembered from it. Her new spell had been engraved in her mind.

"The wind will come from Page's direction. The stronger the wind, the closer he is. Call upon Dwin and say Page's name."

"Ventus." She closed her eyes, imagining Page's face, trying to piece together what he looked like. "Page," she said.

A weak breeze caressed her skin from northeast.

"Where did the wind come from? How strong was the breeze?"

Sandra moved toward the painting of a walker. Its white eyes were one of the most prominent features, second to the orange flames in the background. On the table below the painting was a map of Celeste.

Mika described the wind, casting the spell several times to get the most accurate description. Sandra studied the map.

"He is in Triumph."

Leaning over the table, Mika looked at a beautiful, colorful map. On the northeasternmost corner, just before the ocean, and on the opposite side of Celeste, was the town of Triumph. Page's hometown. Between Triumph and Di'Abribel were towns, rivers, grasslands, hills, mountains, and the home base of the necromancer army in Celeste, the Lost Forest.

Mika flicked the leather on her dagger's sheath and looked at Sandra.

"I'm going to find him."

8. ESSENCE

Two days later, Mika rolled out of bed and slipped into gray pants. Feet walking on a cold floor that needed to be swept, she started her day when the sun first came through her open window. She buttoned a brown shirt, leaving the top two buttons undone before tying her hair in a ponytail that swung side to side like Sandra's did. She walked to the living room, let Addie out to the backyard, and returned to her room to place the dragon flower on her head. She looked in the mirror and watched the petals open to the sky to show her feelings of anticipation. Her heart was booming with excited anxiety. Sliding her feet into her calf-high black boots, she bent over to tie the laces. The second she finished, Addie burst into the room and attacked her face with his tongue.

"Thank you, thank you, thank—"

She latched on to Addie's mouth and forced it open, sniffing the inside before pushing him away.

"You ate shit again?"

Addie sat down, closed his eyes, and smiled. His eyes snapped open when he heard Mika growl, his ears pointed back when he saw her clenched fist. Mika leaned forward onto the balls of her foot.

Addie dashed out the room. Mika chased Addie into the backyard and along the fence.

"Addie!" Mika shouted, jumping over the mossy walkway.

Addie looked back with a smile and flapping tongue.

"Addie, when I catch you, I'm going to kill you!" Mika picked up her pace, and Addie accelerated to stay just out of reach. Her cold muscles began to cramp, and her lungs begged her to stop.

Mika quit, slowing to a stop and placing her hands on her head to further open her lungs. Addie continued running with his tongue flopping from the side of his mouth. He passed Mika twice, looking at her in hopes she would continue playing with him. He locked eyes with her, sprawling out his legs, ready to be chased again.

"No more!" Mika panted. Tightening her ponytail, she made her way to Addie.

Addie sprinted past Mika and began running the perimeter again.

Mika sighed. "Addie!"

Addie passed her.

"Addie!"

Just before he passed, Mika stepped in front of him and caught him by the hind legs, dragging him to a stop.

She grasped her way to his ears and brought him close. "Stop eating your shit."

Before she was able to kiss him, Addie perked his ears and pulled away at the sound of the word *eat*. Mika rolled her eyes and went inside. She fed Addie and fixed herself something to eat as well.

When they were done, both left the home. Mika with a backpack, her adventurer's stone, and her silver dagger strapped to her leg. To prevent another accident like the one with the child and the mother, she strapped a leash and collar around Addie's neck.

Traveling through the new parts of the city was nerve-wracking, but when asked for papers, she held out her adventurer's stone.

"I'm just buying supplies and equipment for my adventure."

The guard looked at the three shining symbols and moved out of Mika's way without another word.

Easy enough.

Continuing through the economic district, Mika reached a store that bore the name Shop of Adventure. She tied Addie's leash to the straps of a box and went inside. A small bell rang when she opened the door.

The attendant was nowhere in sight, so Mika browsed, overwhelmed at all the items available. Tents, sleeping bags, books, maps, packaged food, clothing, minor weapons, tools.

Mika walked to a large book with the word *Spells* on the front cover. She flipped through the pages to the vita section. Scrolling through the catalog of spells, she heard footsteps approaching.

"Would you like some help?" an athletic yet unattractive man asked.

"I'm new to adventuring; is this a good spell to learn?" Mika pointed to a vita spell that would strengthen her muscles and lungs. "Will this one let me to carry a heavy backpack easier?"

"Oh, no." Turning the pages to the aevum section, the attendant pointed to a spell worth four gold coins. "This one is so much better! You can carry more *and* for longer."

Mika read the description:

Cast on a closeable object to shrink items placed inside. Unusable on living beings.

Mika nodded and asked for help in picking equipment. The man told her no one would give her a ride because of her dog and that she would have to walk, so the man helped her pick a better backpack, a tent, sleeping bag, packaged food, and adventuring clothes. The man could tell she was uneasy about spending all the money, but he reassured her that adventurers who trade, along with traveling merchants, might be few and far between.

She paid, and the man held his finger to his forehead. A bubbly orb that shone with crystalline, changing colors appeared, and he pushed it into Mika's head. A portion of time seem to rush through her head, awakening the spell that would allow her to shrink items.

Using the spell on the new backpack, Mika placed all the items she bought inside. The second the items passed the opening, they shrank to the size of an apple.

Taking advantage of the stone, she kept walking and exploring the city. She made it to a section near the northwestern wall that had no homes or buildings. The paved road turned to dirt and led into an area filled with trees and grass.

An immaculate wooden sign with red letters read:

WOODS
DANGER: STAY ON TRAILS

Reading the sign, Mika wondered why it was dangerous to veer off the trails. Her mind wandered, thinking about how many trails there were and how far the woods went on for. She looked toward the sun and raised her arm toward the floating ball of fire. She extended her fingers between the sun and the mountains in the distance. Each finger meant fifteen minutes, and seven fingers separated the sun from the mountains, telling her she had about an hour and forty-five minutes before the sun disappeared behind the highest of the peaks. With that, she adjusted her clothes, tightened her backpack, and cracked her knees before setting off at a run past the sign that read:

WARNING!
DO NOT ENTER DURING EVENING HOURS

The woods felt cold in the season's heat. Branches of the thick trees waved above her, making it seem like they were trying to fly away with the sweeping breeze. Careless chirps from the birds hidden within the leaves filled her ears, almost hiding Addie's panting and the thuds of her footfalls on the dirt trail. Orange and green glowing orbs of fairies chased each other through the trees, resting on Mika's skin to hydrate with her sweat. Mika stood still when they did so, moving her face closer to the small orbs, trying to see what the fairies looked like inside of their bright lights. When her eyes began seeing the details inside the orbs, the fairies circled her head in a taunt and buzzed away. No human had ever seen inside a fairy orb.

A smile lit Mika's face. She felt so free! No people in her way, no Di'Abribelis giving her dirty looks, no need to stop for a guard asking for papers, and the sights, smells, chirps! The reptiles scurrying away, the birds gliding from above, fairies zooming past, Addie turning in circles at all the sights. She took a breath and picked up her pace.

The trail cut through a large field of green plants with soft, palm-sized petals. They moved away from Addie's steps, saving themselves from being crushed and telling Mika they had some sort of connection to that around them. Mika hopped to a stop and reached her hands to the plants; they moved toward her in return. The tiny hairs of the plants' petals felt wet, but when she looked at her hands, they were dry. Curiosity piqued, she inched her face closer, sticking her tongue out.

The plant reacted by yanking away in fear of being eaten.

Retracting her tongue back into her mouth, Mika kept her mouth open in amazement. She smiled and continued running on the trail. Mika noticed Addie's pace slowed, and she was having to pull at his collar for him to continue.

After running for almost an hour, the woods were darker; the sunlight struggled to penetrate the thickening foliage. Mika was breathing hard, and Addie couldn't keep up with her anymore. He looked at Mika. Through the corner of her eye, she looked at down at Addie smiling back at her with his tongue flopping up and down outside of his mouth. Thick, bubbly saliva hung around his lips and clung to the edge of his tongue. Mika's fingers were beginning to tingle from the cold, and her mouth was dry.

Slowing to a stop, Mika looked around with hands on her hips, panting, she tried to catch her breath. Her exhausted pup lay on the ground. She removed Addie's leash.

"Aqua," she said between breaths.

A stream of water came from her fingertips, and she held it to Addie. Her pup drank from the stream, and once he'd finished drinking, Mika drank, her face wrenched from tasting the slimy, putrid water that spewed from her fingers. The more she understood aqua magic, the better the water would taste, but for now, it tasted mossy and brackish. At least the flow was more powerful now than it was when she was a child.

Mika looked around, taking in the gloomy, peaceful woods. The sound of forest fauna surrounded her. Below her were white, capsule-like flowers surrounded by several different roses of varying colors. Her fatigue made her mind wander, bringing her brain to think of Sandra. How could Sandra have been an adventurer? She didn't seem strong or agile, just a beautiful woman with a rough, intelligent attitude. What about her team dying? That must have been tragic. Maybe that was the explanation for her stern attitude. Death made memories of Yevera creep into her mind.

Mika continued thinking, ignoring Addie's lick to her hand for more water.

She remembered her mother and tried to recall the sound of her voice. She remembered her mother's beautiful green eyes. Her grace and her willingness to help any sick, hurt, or dying person in Yevera. Staring off into the distant trees, memories of Page soon eclipsed the memories of her mother. A rush of emotions fluttered into her heart.

How was Page still alive? How had he survived the attack on the Lost Forest when the paper said no Yeveran survived? Since he was alive, why was he not looking for her? Maybe there was someone else named Page? That wasn't possible, since she pictured his face when she cast the ventus spell. So many questions. Her mind snapped back to reality when Addie sprang to his feet. Mika shook her head, her eyes fluttered, and she scratched her nose.

"What's wrong, Addie?"

A rabbit twitched its ears, catching Addie's attention, and he bolted toward it, barking. He'd never seen another creature like that before.

"Addie, stop!" she called, chasing after him.

He ignored her, jumping over a fallen log that Mika, in pursuit, tripped over.

She gripped her torn pants and bleeding shin with both hands. She clenched her teeth and looked at Addie. He continued into the foliage and disappeared behind the trees. Mika scrambled to her feet and trudged through the thick shrubs away from the trail.

Mika screeched his name, and the animals around the woods quieted at her voice.

"Addie!" She looked left, right, left. No Addie. Her voice trembled. "Addie!"

Mika's worry multiplied when she remembered the sign warning to stay on the trails. She slid to her knees and analyzed the ground, looking for pawprints in the dirt. Her breathing was fast, but not from running. She caught a pawprint, then another.

Mika sprinted behind the tracks, following until she stopped just before a stand of trees free of undergrowth, and there was Addie, growling between barks. The stand was bright, lit up by rays of sunlight. An elk and a deer looked at Mika, and a rabbit munched away at a piece of grass. There wasn't a care in the world in any of those animals.

In the sunshine, there was an array of tall flowers of assorted colors, much more vibrant than the flowers outside of the sunshine. Butterflies danced above the animals, seeming to mock the fireflies that stayed on the darker side. The elk and deer looked away from Mika and ate the grass. They lifted their heads and munched the food, looking at Mika and her pup before reaching down for another bite. Mika brushed away at her shin, cleaning off the blood from her hand on the dirt. She limped toward Addie and smacked him in the nose.

"Stop means *stop*."

Addie looked at her and lowered his ears. A sound Mika didn't hear forced Addie to turn to the sunshine. He growled again. Looking at the sky, Mika noticed the stars hung in place above her, yet the field where the animals stood was clear and visible. Mika shook her head.

I must be dreaming.

She plugged her nose and tried to blow out some air. Her ears filled with pressure, reassuring her she was awake.

Why didn't the animals run away? Why was Addie growling? Mika's eyes narrowed in suspicion. She stepped into the sunlight and felt like she passed through a wall of goo. A gentle heat radiated onto her face. Entering the sunlight made her feel calm, relaxed. The pain on her shin disappeared. Her shoulders lowered, and she smiled.

Mika walked toward the elk, extending her arm until she was able to pet it. The elk's groans echoed in the air, but he didn't move. Mika's smile grew and grew until she showed her teeth. She wrapped her hands around the elk's neck and pushed her face close to its rough, musky fur.

"I love you, dear elk. You're so tall and handsome." Her words echoed. The elk's fur scratched her cheek. "Dear elk ..." Mika chuckled. "Deer-elk ..." Still holding on to the elk, she burst out in a laugh that bounced around her mind and ears, causing explosions of colors to burst from outside the sunlight.

She moved toward the rabbit and knelt next to it, not noticing how slowly she was moving.

Wrapping her arm around the rabbit, she gazed off into the distance. "Hello … Mister Rabbit. Addie is so mean. He wanted to eat you!" She passed her hand from the animal's ears down to its fluffy tail. Their eyes met, and neither of them blinked as they stared into each other's soul. The rabbit's black eyes only moved to follow her swaying head.

In the distance, Mika heard muffled, familiar sounds. Part of her strained to discern the sounds, while another part of her told her to relax. Mika's head bobbed. Feeling extreme exhaustion, she brushed away the foliage and lay on the ground. The sounds became louder when a hand with long, pointy nails caressed her face. A figure knelt beside her; the weird sunlight covered its features, but it looked like a man with a large, round head.

"Hey." Mika chuckled. "Cuddles?" Mika laughed, and it grew until it became hysterical.

The man slid his arms under Mika's neck and held his calloused hands to her head. He clawed at Mika's face, dragging his sharp nails from her cheek down to her collarbone. Mika winced and turned her face from the pain, which disappeared within seconds. She noticed the rabbit had not moved from its spot; neither had the elk, nor the deer. Colorful explosions beyond the sunlight burst with every familiar sound that came from outside.

Celebratory magic … Yes, celebratory magic … That's the explanation for the explosions.

The man gripped Mika's jaw and sank his fingers into her skin. Trying to rid herself of the pain, she looked at the man. At the angle he lay, Mika could see the man's pure, black eyes. His blood-red pupils were dilated. Looking down at his mouth, she saw sharp, yellow teeth. She looked up and noticed the lack of a nose and sagging, pointed ears on the sides of the man's head.

This is a dream, Mika thought to herself. *A dream turning into a nightmare.*

Mika wiggled her hand up to her nose, pinched it and blew. Her ears filled with pressure. She rocked her head back and swallowed, relieving the pressure in her ears. She pinched and blew again, feeling the pressure in her ears again.

Not a dream. She studied the man, and that's when her mind began to clear.

The muffled noises became clearer, louder, like booms from a bell. The man caressed Mika's hair, lulling her to sleep, but the noises in the distance exploded in her head, preventing her from drifting to sleep. Mika felt as if the noises were calling to her. Focusing on the noises, they soon became distant barks. The barks became louder until she could hear growls preceding the barks.

Addie was going berserk, and his fury echoed through the woods. With blurry vision, Mika turned to look at Addie; he lunged forward with each bark, refusing to step out of the shadows and into the sunlight.

Mika turned to the elk and deer. The smell of rotten meat seeped into her nostrils when she saw the animals were nothing but piles of rotting flesh on the ground. The butterflies were flies that buzzed around the carcasses. The rabbit was nothing but a skull. No sounds of the woods were present, only the barking, the buzzing flies, and now, Mika's gasps.

She let out a scream upon seeing the man—no, not a man but a winged creature with orange skin, blood-red pupils, and long, pointy ears. An imp.

Mika shot to her feet, but the imp grabbed her arms and forced her down, releasing a demonic laugh when he choked her. Mika slapped away, trying to break free, causing Addie to leap onto the imp, knocking him off Mika but succumbing to the trance.

The imp stood up, kicked Addie, and turned to Mika, who was at a full sprint toward the imp. Crashing the dagger into the imp's ribs, both tumbled over Addie, and all three rolled out of the sunlight. Addie dove toward the imp, who leaped into the air. Wings extended, he fluttered to Mika, bear-hugged her, and set himself ablaze.

Mika let out an agonizing howl when the flames seared her skin. She dug a thumb into its eyeball, breaking free and running away, but falling to her knees from the nauseating burns. She sobbed and hunched over, feeling the forming blisters. A kick to the stomach forced her to the ground; dust rose when she fell.

She squirmed backward. "Somebody help me!"

The imp, wreathed in flames, slammed his feet onto her and laughed.

Mika wailed and thrashed. Smoke rose from her skin. She smelled burning clothes and seared flesh; heat radiated through her body.

Mika pointed her fingers at the imp. "Aqua!"

Her brain rattled; she wasn't focused. The imp's fire turned blue. Mika's screams drowned Addie's barking. Sneers of other imps came from the trees.

Whispers bounced in her mind before the fire's potency waned, allowing her to focus.

"Aqua!"

A surge of water shot out from Mika's fingertips, searing and evaporating when it cut through the flames.

"Aqua!" The stream became stronger, drenching the imp.

Its ignis weakened, Addie soared and clenched to its neck, forcing the imp onto his back. Addie ripped out its throat and crunched the imp's wounded ribs.

Sitting up, Mika held her wrist and sprinkled water on her burns. Addie's jaws ripped into the imp's flesh, and the violent snaps of his head jerked the imp's body from side to side. Wet gargles escaped the creature's mouth. Mighty jaws tore through skin, muscle, then crushed ribs. Green blood pooled under the imp.

The imp's spell of sunlight began to wane, and Mika realized Addie had risked his life by jumping into the sunlight to save her. Her breathing choppy and her legs shaking, she watched the carnage for a moment and then closed her eyes.

When the gargling stopped, Addie returned to Mika with green blood around his snout. He sat next to her and rubbed his head on her hand. Mika's fear dissipated. She opened her eyes and felt her dragon flower extend open. Its petals rested open and allowed looking into the pearl, showing her feelings of trust with Addie, the same way a person reveals their chest before they hug someone they trust. She hugged Addie and looked at the imp.

The imp lay lifeless, chunks from his face, neck, torso, and legs spread around him. Mika never knew a dog's teeth could cause so much damage. She rose to her feet, crept to the imp, and looked down into eyes that seemed to follow her.

Mika noticed she was still clinging on to her dagger, bringing back a distant memory. She was standing outside in undergarments, the harsh rain pelting her bare skin.

"Hold it!" the Yeveran lieutenant's screams seemed louder than the rumbling thunder.

Mika and her fellow students were lined side by side with their arms extended like a T. They all held wooden training swords in their hands. The freezing rain was making all of them tremble. Yeveran soldiers walked behind them, striking them in the legs and arms with wooden weapons at random intervals.

Thunder rolled away, and the lieutenant shouted, "Your weapon is your soul! Your weapon is your life! You only release it when it is sheathed!" A piercing smack was followed by the squeals of a boy. The lieutenant looked to make sure he still held on to his weapon before continuing. "A true Yeveran never drops their weapons!" His voice was stronger than the thunder. "It must be pried from their dead fingers by their brothers or sisters! Do you understand me?"

The kids replied in unison, "Yessir!"

"Do you understand me?" Now the lieutenant was in front of Mika.

"Yessir!" the children boomed.

Mika was struck in the arm. The penetrating cold made the strike feel like it pierced her flesh and cut open her muscle. She held her scream, grunting and closing her eyes just as a follow-up strike cut through the back of her bare knee.

"You dropping your weapon, Plum?" The lieutenant knelt to her level, his face inches from hers.

She rose, keeping one eye closed and blowing away the water on her lips. "Yeverans never quit."

The lieutenant smiled and walked away, laughing when a girl screamed after her strike.

They did that exercise every day after class on combat-training months, after every child was tired and weak from the day's training.

Mika sheathed her dagger before stretching her cramped fingers. At that moment, the imp exhaled its last breath. With its breath came the bright-green mist, its life essence. The imp's life essence entered Mika and Addie. Life essence felt delicious; the indescribable feeling she felt when it entered her body was soon replaced with the imp's happiest memories.

Through his eyes, she saw the imp approaching his mother somewhere in the dark woods. Then she saw the imp completing a sacrifice atop a large stone table surrounded by candles and white sigils. The imp sat on top of a teenage boy. With fiery thumbs, the imp pushed both boy's eyes into his skull, laughing when the boy screamed in pain.

The snapping of a branch forced Mika out of the last memory. She looked up and noticed the imps watching from the trees had moved closer. Some flew on wings; others crawled toward her.

Mika snapped her fingers at Addie, pointed toward the city, and set off in a painful sprint back toward Di'Abribel.

The guards sprang to their feet and brandished their weapons the second Mika burst through the door. One of them had red, watery eyes from being asleep.

"I've been attacked in the west woods!" Mika placed her hands on her head to help her breathe.

A guard scanned her and sheathed his weapons. "What happened?" He didn't sound concerned and grabbed a piece of Mika's singed clothes.

Mika was calm when she talked. "I was running on a trail in the west woods about an hour ago. I was attacked by an imp."

"An imp?" The drowsy guard snapped awake at the word.

The guard talking to Mika approached his partner. Mika could hear the whispers. "We took care of them months ago."

"Yeah … but the rounds … We haven't done the rounds."

The guard pinched the corner of his eyes. He made an inaudible response, followed by a deep sigh. He returned to Mika. "How many and where?"

Mika closed her eyes, piecing together everything she saw before Addie ran off. After a moment, she opened her eyes.

"White flowers that look like capsules and a lot of flowers of a lot of different colors. Less than a quarter mile off the trail there." She pointed in the direction they would take when they reached the flowers.

The guard closed his eyes and pressed his lips together. He swallowed.

"I killed one with my pup, but there were more."

The guard rubbed his palm to his forehead. "Thank you, ma'am, but uh" –he looked at the other guard, who nodded– "we need you" – he placed his hands on Mika's shoulder– "to keep this incident hush-hush, know what I mean? It's for the good of the city. No panic or worry, you know? Imp infestations are deadly, but we'll take care of 'em." He didn't let go of Mika's shoulder, waiting for her response.

Mika nodded. "I understand, but my injuries." She showed her burned wrist and lifted her shirt just past the sternum, showing white, bubbly blisters and red skin.

"How did you survive?" The guard waved to the other one, who approached. Both said "Vita," and began to heal her wounds. After several minutes, Mika's skin was back to normal, and she felt no pain.

"You're welcome to use the deity statues through that room if you need to expend the imp's essence." He pointed to a purple door behind the desk. "Your dog's welcome to join you. A … thank-you, for our little agreement." He turned to his partner. "I'll get the others."

Mika followed him out and brought her tired dog inside. She opened the purple door with the gold handle and entered a dark room lit by dim lights set at nine different man-sized statues. The statues were made in the likeness of the nine deities, humanoid with their one distinct physical trait. The statues stood in rows, in the same way as the adventurer's stone. Mika went to the statue of Angelis at the back row; her physical trait were the two angel wings on her back. Angelis stood with her eyes closed. She was smiling, her hands clasped together in front of her pelvis.

Mika admired the gentle face carved into the stone before touching it. When she touched, Mika was ambushed by magical runes floating around her, a couple cyan blue, most scarlet red. She focused on a random scarlet rune, and the scene around her changed.

People with severe injuries were littered on the ground in the middle of a grassy landscape; rain poured from above. Mika saw herself shout, her hands snapped to the heavens, and the falling rain began to glow a golden light. Everything the rain touched was healed before she appeared back in the dark room. The rune had shown her the spell she would learn if she expended the essence on it, a spell that would turn drops of water into drops of healing magic.

She looked at a different rune, seeing herself release a massive explosion of healing magic and another that showed her shooting healing arrows at people. A cyan rune showed her using a healing touch on herself.

She reached her hand to the healing rain rune. The life essence from the imp floated out of her hand and filled the rune, stopping less than an eighth of the way, telling her she needed more essence for that specific spell. Retracting her hand, the essence returned to Mika. After looking at several spells, she settled on the spell that allowed her to heal wounds on herself. The cyan rune exploded and, like a distant memory creeping back into her mind, Mika learned the spell.

Mika looked for Addie, who stared away at Mooredoth's statue. Mooredoth's physical trait was a horse tail near his tailbone.

Mika didn't know animals could use the statues, and she wondered at the boon Addie had received.

Animals like dogs couldn't learn spells, but they could use the statues. Addie chose to become smarter.

Mika left for her home to sleep for a couple of hours before the sunlight woke her up for her last day of work. She would be surprised to see the Toveys and Janice congratulating her on her new adventure with a farewell party and gifts.

*   *   *   *   *

Because of the fight—and now realizing the dangers she could face—Mika dedicated a few days to training, conditioning, and studying before departing on her adventure. She wasn't taught many fighting moves in Yevera because of her scouting role, but she remembered basics about fighting. Footwork, movement, fast strikes that were weak and slow strikes that were powerful. She practiced moves that used her natural agility to dash and jump. All her moves ended with a strike to the throat.

Mika knew her footwork was wrong because when she ended a move, she was off balance. Mika's fighting capabilities were poor, and she would lose a fight with any warrior who had received some sort of training. Despite this, in her mind, she felt confident and satisfied, thinking she knew what she was doing.

Mika was in the beginning stages of assassin training, yes, but a scout's main responsibility was reconnaissance, sabotage, and assassination. Likewise, she only learned about reconnaissance before Yevera was destroyed. One lesson about reconnaissance resonated in her mind: one taught by a slender instructor with a low voice that had a hiss after every sentence.

"Y'all ain't fighters. We don't train you to be bruised and beaten. We train you to stay low, quiet, stay quick, stay alive, kill in silence. Can't win a battle without intelligence, and y'all the intelligent ones. A fight come to you? Run. Your position compromised? Run. Only time you fight is when your partner can't run with you, but if he dead, you best be running, and you best be running fast."

Mika wondered what became of that instructor, whose name she couldn't recall. Did he follow his own advice and flee when the fighting broke out, or did he die against the necromancers?

The sunlight began sliding up her window, telling her it was time to go on a run. She grabbed all the gear she would take on her adventure and set off with Addie, arriving at the woods where she encountered the imp.

The woods split into three trails at the trailhead. She followed the same trail she had on her first visit. The roaring wind hid her heavy breaths as she zoomed past the cluster of fairies that danced in the same location, past the massive boulder that she missed on her first run, and past the flowers that moved to avoid being stepped on. She jumped over a fallen tree and pulled at Addie's leash when he caught a glimpse of a rabbit. She hopped to avoid stepping on a lizard that didn't scurry away before she slowed to a stop at the capsule-like flowers. She took a breath and faced the path off the trail.

After composing herself, she traced her steps as best she could, turning back when she didn't recognize something. After a few times of having to return to the trail, she stumbled upon the pile of deer and elk bones on the ground. No dreamy sunlight covered them this time, so she prowled to the location where she almost died. Her heartbeat quickened, she breathed louder, her legs were weak, and her shaky hand hovered over her dagger.

Kneeling next to the pile of bones, she saw traces of blood, both green and red.

Probably the guard patrols ... or a victim.

She looked around, trying to see if anyone had dropped equipment. Her ears perked at the sound of ruffling branches and grass. She was pulled off balance by Addie about to give chase. He had his snout pointed at the bones of the deer.

Addie squirmed out of his collar and dashed to the bones, snapping his teeth at something underneath. Brandishing her dagger, Mika sprinted to the bones, crushing them under her boot. A young imp was curled in a ball under the rubble and rising dust. The imp snarled at Mika, but his eyes showed nothing but fear.

Addie reached to bite its head, and the imp lurched away.

Mika kicked it.

The imp tumbled and rolled, releasing a cry.

Mika grabbed the imp by the neck and lifted him in the air. The imp kicked and scratched. Mika plunged it to the ground and squeezed. She held her dagger on the imp's abdomen, where its heart was.

The creature went limp and opened its mouth, eyes closed in defeat; the impling knew it would die. Mika inched her face closer and pressed her dagger against its abdomen. The imp replied by wrenching its face. She pressed her thumb onto its trachea, enough for the imp to stick its tongue out to breathe. Just as she was about to crush his neck and sink her weapon into its heart, Mika's furrowed eyebrows relaxed. She loosened her grip on its neck and pulled her dagger back. She shouted at Addie to shut up before releasing the imp's neck and standing up.

The imp held its neck and stared at Mika with wide eyes. It scrambled to its feet and, after a quick gaze at the dog, ran off. It stopped and it looked back at Mika, still holding its neck.

"Leave, you little shit!"

The little imp squirmed but continued staring at her.

Mika relaxed her face when the imp raised his hand and waved a gentle goodbye. Confused, Mika blinked a few times before raising her hand and waving back.

Sheathing her dagger, Mika made her way back onto the trail, looking back to see if the imp followed her. With no sign of it, she ran back to the city, unsure if her choice was the right one.

*   *   *   *   *

This time the deities met in the realm of aqua, Kymarinou's home. Water dropped from four pillars, one in each corner, creating a refreshing waterfall of purified water. The deities ate at a table with their feet submerged. Talk of the world filled the deities' discussion room that night. They wowed at interesting adventures, cheered at amazing feats during wars, marveled at beautiful creations from the builders, and analyzed settlements, cities, regions, and kingdoms. They celebrated another month of wonderful gifts and sacrifices their human creations had offered. They drank from diamond cups filled with mysterious beverages, and food from every part of the world lined the table.

Liranda, the deity of ignis, sat twirling her burgundy-red hair, bored with the discussions occupying the other deities. She rolled her eyes when Kymarinou told of a man's righteous deeds to his town. Liranda scoffed and shifted in her chair.

Liranda's physical trait was two black, pointed horns above her eyebrows. She caressed one of the horns and became lost in thought. When would she find more humans who did things to interest *her*? War existed, yes, but not the fun Liranda wanted. She wanted to see the depravity in humans. She wanted to cherish and celebrate the men who kidnapped and raped, the women who sold their children for alcohol and drugs, and youngsters who murdered and destroyed over small disagreements. She wanted to bathe herself in human evil and corruption. A boom of cheers broke her from her thoughts. She hated herself for giving humans without stones privacy, for she couldn't hunt for a corrupt human if they didn't pray to her.

"Liranda!" Dwin, the deity of ventus, called to her. "A human single-handedly defeated one of your imps!" Dwin's physical trait was hair that defied gravity.

Liranda faced him and took in the sight of his long, silver beard. "Go ahead, wind. Tell me *all* about it."

The deity of ignis sighed and rolled her eyes when Dwin began the story of a girl running in the Di'Abribeli woods. Once Dwin reached the part where the girl didn't die from being enflamed, Liranda interrupted him.

"It set itself on fire, and the girl survived?"

"Yes!" Dwin threw his hands in the air. "It was as if she simply touched a hot piece of steel!"

Liranda paid more attention to the story; her mind drifted when Dwin told of the baby imp that waved at the Yeveran woman named Mika Plum.

How was it possible that Mika's skin didn't melt off when the imp set himself ablaze? Why did an imp child not attack a human, but instead *wave to it*? That behavior was … oddly familiar. Liranda took a bite of a kraken tentacle and stood up. She adjusted the top of her shiny black dress and teleported to the Chambers of Aevum, a place where the deities could look through time.

The Chambers of Aevum were pitch black, except for a moving torch that approached Liranda. The light was carried by a two-legged creature with a hunchback and a long, giraffe-like neck that ended with a small head with one eyeball. This creature was called a Keeper.

"Liranda, deity of ignis, fire, and corruption. What year should I transport the most lustful being known to all?" The Keeper's words were slow with perfect enunciation despite its toothless mouth.

Liranda didn't dare look at such a vile and disturbing creature. Why would Baigh, the deity of aevum, create such a disgusting being? Liranda's voice was sharp and direct. "Life of Mika Plum, Yeveran, region of Celeste, continent of Irstia, world of Zonos."

The Keeper lowered his head and began to think. After a moment, he nodded and whispered, "Aevum." He extended a scroll to Liranda, who snatched it from his hands.

Liranda scoured through Mika's past. Fatherless child, daughter to the strongest healer in Celeste, low spell-to-age count, disinterest in magic, patriotic, hopeful, short-tempered, obsessive, territorial, bouts of anger, excessive anxiety.

She tossed the scroll at the Keeper's face. "Mika Plum's residence during the destruction of Yevera, region of Celeste, continent of Irstia, world of Zonos."

"Yes, Liranda." The Keeper passed his hand where the scroll scratched his face before raising his torch.

The darkness around her pulled away, and she was transported to a body of water. The blue sky was clear, and the sun beat brightly on the deity and the Keeper. The land around them changed at immense speeds. Smog covered the sky, water changed to ice, ice melted, mountains began to form, hills, grass, trees, animals, humans moving, roads, tents, a temple, buildings, a town, walls, black blanket covering the sky, the town on fire.

Liranda stood in front of Mika's home. She walked through the open door to see a woman named Cynthia throwing a pan at a female, whose name registered in Liranda's mind as Kathrine. No sign of Mika.

"Forward to Cynthia's death."

Cynthia and Kathrine moved through the fight, and Liranda followed them into the room. Mika was sent crashing into the closet just before her mother was butchered. Liranda smiled.

"Keep it moving until the child escapes the enclosure."

Liranda watched Mika struggling in the closet, screaming for help and the flames around her responding to her yells.

"Let me out! Let me get out! Somebody help me!" Mika screamed, and then something remarkable occurred. The flames replied in voices Liranda could understand, the voices that sounded like human children.

~ Mommy's in trouble ...
~ Mom needs help ...
~ Is she trying to get out of the closet ...
~ Yes ... she's trying ...
~ What's holding her in ...
~ The bed ... the bed ... the bed ... the bed ...
~ We're not strong enough to break it ...
~ Up here ... up here ... we just need to be stronger ...
~ Mom needs to give us more power ...

Liranda chuckled when Mika screamed, forcing the flames to grow in power and eat away at the beam that incinerated the bed, allowing Mika to escape.

Liranda clasped her hands together.

"Oh, Mika Plum!" she squealed.

Ignis paid the keeper some life essence for his service before opening a portal that allowed her to look into Mika's room, her adventurer's stone granting Liranda the ability to watch the young woman.

Mika lay on her back, eyes wide open and staring at the ceiling. Addie snored on the floor and, noticing the slight disturbance in space caused by the portal, awoke and raised his head.

Addie's alertness sent anxiety through Mika's veins. Without moving any part of her body, Mika's eyes scanned her room. After a moment, Addie thought it was just a dream, so he sighed and fell back asleep … but Mika could sense eyes watching her. Was Mika being watched by a ghost she couldn't kill? By a man who wanted to rape her? By a woman who wanted to slice her throat and steal her dog and money? By the imp's family looking for vengeance? Mika's breaths, choppy and fast, prevented Addie from falling asleep, so he went to the bed to check on her.

Noticing Mika's anxieties, paranoia, stress, inability to sleep, the wideness in her unblinking eyes, and the how she scratched at her thumb to the point that the skin began to peel told Liranda all she needed to know.

The deity of ignis activated her symbol, the ember, on Mika's stone.

"I've finally found my daughter," Liranda hissed, biting her lip. Then she smiled. "I've found Irstia's sorceress."

9. MARKET

The cool morning breeze swept under Sandra's olive-colored dress. The zephyr made the hairs on her arms rise, but she forced herself not to shiver. Arms crossed and leaning against the city's northern stone walls, she watched adventurers, traders, travelers, and soldiers converse and check their gear, waiting for the gates to open and release them into freedom. She scanned the crowd for Mika, though she figured she should look for a dog instead. Not finding Mika or her pup, she fixated on people's equipment, the interesting types of weapons, the magic denoted in their hair, and, most interesting to her, the rare armor some of them carried. The armor and gear brought back memories from years ago, when she was younger, faster, more energetic, more fun.

When she was an adventurer.

She remembered when she first started out, taking a risk in meeting with Oniusus, following him down the caves in Imbris to hunt for nagas—vile half-human, half-snake creatures of terra that plagued southern Imbris for decades. She remembered traveling to the eastern continent of Sytu and recruiting Rachel before climbing the summit of Mount Juliana and retrieving boots that allowed the wearer to not be injured when falling from great heights.

Sandra smiled at the memory of Rachel's astonished face when she saw a dragon guarding the treasure and how fast they ran down the mountain. Her smile faded when she remembered Rachel's screams at the bottom of the flooded caves in the Sea of Angels.

"Do not let go!" Sandra cried out, feet pressed against two boulders and clutching the Trident of Kymarinou with both hands.

Rachel's face was dripping with sweat that mixed with the tears on her cheeks. Her hold on the trident began to slip, and Rachel screamed in a way that Sandra didn't know was possible.

Sandra leaned over to see Rachel in waist-high water. The water's color was red from mermaids eating away at Rachel like piranhas, while others pulled her hair into the water. Rachel managed to free her opposite arm; the despair on her face was immediate the moment she saw muscle hanging from bones.

Sandra tried to pull Rachel up by pushing her feet against the boulders. She strained until the trident flew behind her, thudding against the sand. Springing to her feet, Sandra leaned over the edge. The blood thickened in the water, telling Sandra that Rachel's grip slipped from the trident.

Sandra's face betrayed no emotion when the memory rushed through her vision. She swept it away with several blinks and continued scanning the crowd. Still no Mika, still no dog. The gates cranked open, rising by thick black chains. People exiting went through one side, people entering came through the other, with guards checking stones, traveling documents, or trading memoranda upon entry. She saw a woman and man walk through the gates. They looked like twins, and their armor was as broken as their spirits. The woman, whose baby-blue hair was tied in a bun, leaned on the man and wept, triggering yet another memory for Sandra.

She was sitting alone at a campfire in the middle of a starry, moonless sky. The Trident of Kymarinou lay on the floor next to her, the adventurer's stone in her hands.

"I forfeit my adventure."

The smooth voice of a handsome and intelligent-sounding man filled her ears. "You wish to forfeit your adventure, which was to travel to the Sea of Angels, navigate through the caves, and launch Kymarinou's Trident into Aqua's Whirlpool, granting you access to the undiscovered treasures underneath."

"Correct."

"Forfeit of an adventure is considered dishonorable amongst the deities. As punishment, they will reject all further requests for adventure for the rest of your life. Furthermore, the Trident's location will be shown to any adventurer wishing to obtain it. Combat with you will be justified, should you refuse to surrender it. Is it still your wish to forfeit?"

Her voice trembled. Through the years, she had grown fond of adventuring.

"Yes."

She was instructed to travel to a city of her choice. She settled on Di'Abribel, where she was allowed entry. Then the symbols of the seven deities following her adventure faded from her stone and, due to her proposition, she became infertile. Sandra's lineage would die with her.

Sandra took a breath and continued watching the crowd. No Mika, no dog. She took another breath and felt the wind rush past her. She sensed eyes looking at her. Turning in the direction of the stare, she saw Mika waving at her with her free hand, the strap of her backpack clutched in the other. The biggest smile she had ever seen on Mika was present on that sunny day, and the flower on her head did not lie about her emotions.

Wearing a brown, long-sleeve shirt tucked into dark-green pants that were, in turn, tucked into calf-high black boots, Mika picked up her pace but was taken aback when Addie pulled at the leash wrapped around her waist.

Sandra controlled herself so she wouldn't smile. *Stupid child.*

"I couldn't fall asleep last night!" Mika was out of breath, not from exertion but from excitement. She looked at Sandra with her weird, wide eyes that seemed to analyze people's souls. *Crazy eyes* were what Sandra called them. The disturbing part for Sandra was that Mika didn't stare like that on purpose; it was her look all the time. Mika only seemed to blink when she snapped out of her *thinking* state that made her shake her head and rub her nose. Sandra had only seen this type of stare in people who were executed for committing mass murder.

Sandra moved herself away from the wall. "Sleep deprivation is not something to joke about."

Mika rolled her eyes. "I'll sleep at the market." She pulled at Addie's collar, releasing it from her waist and wrapping it around her wrist.

Sandra gave Mika a stare, then looked her up and down. "You brought coins?"

"Yes." Mika jiggled her hips so the coin purse would move.

"Tent, sleeping bag, flint and steel?"

Mika turned her body, closed her eyes, and gave a gentle smile when she made her backpack jiggle. "Yeah."

"Food, clothes, cooking equipment?"

Mika pulled at the straps of her backpack and nodded.

"Map and adventurer's stone?

Mika's eyes widened, her face lost color, and her flower began to hide in her hair from fear.

Sandra's voice remained calm. She used her chin to point at Mika's backpack. "Check your bag."

Mika slid her backpack off and dug through the front pocket. She took a breath and held her hand over her heart. "I have the stone."

"But no map."

"I don't need it." She swung her backpack around to her back. "I've memorized it … and it's a far walk back home!"

Sandra shook her head. "Are you set? I need to return to my shop."

Mika's face straightened. She looked at the gates, then back at Sandra. She shrugged. "I'm guessing there's no reason for me to stay any longer."

"Are you going to tie your hair in—"

"Why would I do that?" Mika snapped.

Sandra scoffed. "Do you not realize someone could grab it? It can get caught on something. It is much harder to clean. You need to make adventures easy, for anything can happen. Adventuring is not a joke. There are dangers lurking everywhere, and your hair is a prime target. Warriors stopped wearing capes decades ago for the same reason hair is cut or tied. Hair is a hazard."

"All right, all right, all right!" Mika threw her hands in the air. "I'll tie my hair when I exit the gates!"

Sandra scanned Mika's facial expression, hoping to catch the hint of a lie. When Mika began to hide her hands behind her back, Sandra knew.

"You are lying to me."

Mika's wide eyes widened, and so did her smile, until she hid her rebelliousness behind a giant grin.

"Mika," Sandra exhaled, "I sometimes feel like shaking your head until your brain rattles to where it is supposed to be."

Mika's face straightened. Her eyes became sad, and she moved her hands over her heart. "You just admitted your feelings to me ..."

Sandra rolled her eyes and touched her finger to her forehead. A black drop of tenebris appeared on her finger. "Come here."

"I'm not accepting another spell." Mika lowered her hands and shook her head. "You've lost enough spells to me already."

The wizard-turned-hairdresser approached her with the drop. "Stop being stubborn, Mika. I do not adventure anymore; most of the spells I know are useless to me. It is a waste to have learned these spells and to never use them."

Mika began to speak, but Sandra shushed her. She touched the black drop to Mika's forehead,

"This spell lessens the effects sunlight and lux have on you. You will not have to worry about sunburn if you use it."

Darkness dissipated from Mika's mind when she learned the spell. Tenebris required the caster to close their eyes, so she did so. She cast the spell and imagined the rays of lux being bounced from her skin. Once she opened her eyes, she realized the sun's heat didn't seep into her skin like before.

"Goodbye, Mika." Sandra walked off. "Do not follow me."

Mika took a step toward Sandra. "That's it?"

Sandra kept walking. She passed her fingers through her smooth and shiny hair, letting it hang behind her until it rested just above her butt.

Mika was dumbfounded. How could she and Sandra separate like that? After a minute of watching Sandra walk away without stopping, Mika shouted so Sandra could hear her. "I'll write you! And I'll send you a wedding invitation! I've paid my taxes in advance! I'll come visit! My home will still be here, so I have to, you know!"

Sandra smiled and shook her head. She straightened out her smile before she faced Mika. Sandra and Mika stared each other down, until Sandra gave a thumbs-up, forcing a smile out of the new adventurer. Mika kicked her feet toward the gates and began walking away with her companion.

Sandra was glad she was far from Mika. It'd be embarrassing to Sandra if Mika saw the tears forming in her eyes. Sandra cleared her throat and swallowed before continuing back to her shop.

Please be safe, Mika.

The Di'Abribeli walls rose higher than most roofs in the city and were thicker than most buildings. Mika was amazed at the size of the walls, marveling with her upward stare that caused her to be blinded by the climbing sun. Her eyes adjusted, allowing her to see the mages and archers atop the battlements, watching for threats. Noticing the massive spikes on the gates above her, she ducked her head into her shoulders and hopped over the holes in the ground. Once outside the walls, Mika looked at the beautiful open space around her with a gaping mouth.

The sun hovered toward the thick, fluffy clouds that seemed to be running away from Di'Abribel. The menacing rocky peaks of Adventurer's Pass to her northwest stood in the distance. They appeared to reach for the sky, trying to escape the grasp of the earth. To her east, short hills danced through the grassy landscape. Watchtowers spaced randomly through the hills would alert Di'Abribel of incoming enemies. Birds chased each other, and colored butterflies rested on flowers that swayed with the wind next to the cobblestone road. Some butterflies hovered in what felt like calm conversations.

Addie pulled at his collar, forcing Mika from her thoughts. She shook her head, blinked, and scratched her nose. She pulled back, preventing him from chasing a squirrel.

I'd better get going. Page isn't going to find himself.

Instead of going east toward Yevera, Mika took the long way north, following the cobblestone road toward the market. She knew to avoid Yevera; its lands were tainted by the necromancers, and they needed to be blessed before humans could pass through without falling ill from lingering mori.

Although her main goal was to get to Triumph, she hadn't been out of Di'Abribel since she arrived four years ago. She would sightsee on her way, taking little detours here and there. She hoped to reach the market near the Grand Waterfall before sunset. There, she would spend her first evening before traveling east through the Farmlands and resting at Mount Cabria, where she planned on camping for a day to relive the fond memories invested there as a child. Maybe she would hike to the top. Doing so would only add a day or so to her travel, but Addie had never been up a mountain—he might not do well.

After Mount Cabria, her plan was to bathe at Peak's Lake, where the sirens swam in the immaculate waters they called home. From the stories she'd heard, women were infatuated with the sirens. Men, on the other hand, either loved or were terrified of them. Mika didn't care about the stories; she just wanted to see one turn from a fish into a human, then back to a fish.

After camping at Peak's Lake, she would follow the road on the west side of the lake toward the north, passing the Lost Forest. Triumph—and Page—would be hours away from the bridge at the river between the Lost Forest and Peak's Lake. Although it was much safer to travel along the eastern coast, Mika did not have the patience or the resources to spend the extra days on the road just for safety.

I'll be fine, she thought. *Necromancers are not known to attack small groups.*

Mika walked and waved at passing adventurers, admiring the men's armor and studying the women's hairstyles; most hair was short or tied in small buns. To Mika, the most interesting things on the adventurers were the different weapons they carried. Broadswords, battle-axes, recurve bows, magical staffs, maces, swords.

"Is that a crossbow?" Mika asked a woman in leather armor.

"Yes," she said and kept walking.

"They are so interesting!" Walking behind the woman, Mika began reciting the mechanics of the weapon. "I've always wanted to shoot one!"

The woman stopped and gave Mika a *get away from me* stare. "Then go shoot one," she said and continued to walk away.

Mika stopped the moment the words left the woman's mouth. Mika glared at her, and anger began to boil. She clenched her jaw and ground her teeth but calmed herself when Addie whimpered, saliva pooled around his mouth, reminding Mika that she and her pup needed a drink of water.

Being friendly gets me nowhere.

*   *   *   *   *

The sun began to set, turning the misty clouds a magical pink that reminded Mika of the flowers on Professor Tovey's property. Mesmerized by a sky she had never seen before, Mika didn't notice the booms and claustrophobic noises coming from the market until she approached the first couple of stalls.

The market, dubbed Market 135 by travelers, adventurers, and traders of Irstia, was the size of a small town, but it was much, much louder than a city. Tents, stalls, kiosks, booths, and tables flanked both sides of the cobblestone road. Men and women of all ages buzzed back and forth, yelling, laughing, picking up items, admiring them, pulling out coins, and placing them on tables. Some bartered prices, others shook their heads in disagreement; all smiled when they agreed on an exchange.

Mika leaned on the shoulder-high sign that read MARKET 135. She exhaled and closed her eyes. After numerous uses of her sunblock and water spells, walking, and yelling at Addie to keep up for nine hours, she was physically and mentally exhausted. Addie pulled, and Mika yanked back in stress-induced anger. She scowled at Addie before walking deeper into the market, where she was stopped by a hired mercenary who acted as a guard.

He spoke with a rough, informal tone that told Mika he didn't care about her.

"Ye got papers?" He raised his chin and curled his lip upward to show his teeth. Many were missing from his numerous brawls.

Mika swung the backpack around and, without saying a word, showed the adventurer's stone. The tiredness showed in her open mouth and droopy eyes.

The mercenary took off his helmet and held it under his armpit. A tattoo went from his forehead, over a bald skull, to his cheek, and curved to the back of his neck. He signaled with his fingers to see the stone.

Too tired to care, Mika exhaled and placed the stone in the mercenary's hand, sliding her fingers away from the stone, causing the mercenary's hands to push up against the pressure. Addie watched his hands like a hawk and sneaked close to his legs, ready to trip him if he became a threat.

"Ye don't look like no 'venturer to me." He put his helmet on and held the stone to Mika. "Welcome ta one thirty-five."

He walked away when Mika took the stone. She could see the tattoo on his head continue down past his leather armor.

Not many people in Celeste had tattoos, and Mika associated them with strong warriors.

Continuing her walk, she sat in a chair next to a kiosk, tilted her head back, and dangled her fingers above her mouth.

"Aqua." But instead of water coming from her fingertips, her mind clouded and plunged her deeper into exhaustion, making her feel like she hadn't slept in days. Mika reached mental exhaustion from magic use.

Her head hung from the back of the chair, and she started sliding down, unable to feel Addie's tongue lick her hand. The chatter, laughter, and noise of the market drifted away into booming roars. Her mind tuned out the massive noises when she faded into a deep, twitching sleep.

A dream seeped into Mika's vision. She saw herself surrounded by fire. Left, right, behind, nothing but growing yellow flames danced around her. She wasn't afraid of the flames; she felt they were inviting her, asking her to join them. Reveling in the flames, Mika allowed them to approach, and they crawled toward her in unison.

"Hey ..." they whispered, growing in intensity with every word.

The flames surrounded her feet. "Hey."

They crawled up her legs. "Hey!" A volcanic inferno surrounded her.

Just when the flames began to crash into her from all directions, the next "Hey!" woke her.

A man's gentle touch clasped onto Mika's shoulder. He held a torch, hiding his facial features in the night sky.

"Is this your dog?" He let go of Mika's shoulder and offered Addie's leash.

Addie panted and wagged his tail. Mika could see dirt all over his fur.

Mika sat up on the chair, holding her head to ease away at the exploding headache.

"Yeah," she murmured, "where did you find him?"

The man's tone was arrogant. "By the south entrance." He looked back, then faced Mika again. "He was just sitting there under a bush." He offered the leash to Mika again. "I figured he was yours when he kept pulling toward you."

"Thank you." She accepted the leash and stood. "I've reached exhaustion, and my head is *killing* me."

The man laughed. "Yeah, I figured! I'm Lawrence, by the way." Lawrence moved the torch, and Mika could see he had a long chin.

"I am Mika Plum of Yevera." Mika curtsied, and the movement of her head intensified her splitting migraine.

"Oh wow … I thought most Yeverans left Celeste years ago. You didn't go with them?"

Obviously not.

"No," Mika took a breath. "I decided to stay."

Lawrence had shifted to the point that Mika could see his manly, defined jawline and his piercing brown eyes. "Well, I'm sure there's a reason for that. It's a shame Di'Abribel didn't cleanse the land and attempt to rebuild. Everyone in Celeste owes Yevera their freedom."

That's true, she thought.

"It's all political," he said. "I feel like Di'Abribel *chose* not to rebuild it. I mean, I guess it's pretty dangerous to do it."

Mika knew the land was tainted by necromancers and many, many healers, resources, security, and supplies were needed to cleanse her former home.

I would cleanse Yevera, no matter the cost.

"Would you like an escort to the inn? I notice you don't have a torch or anything."

She slapped her forehead and dismissed the thoughts of Yevera. "I forgot that too!"

Her eyes met Lawrence's.

Lawrence didn't need another word. With a smile that contained great teeth and a dimple, he waved for Mika to follow, and she mustered all her strength into keeping up with the man who Addie had no problem trusting.

They walked on the unlit cobblestone road. Mika thought she was dreaming when she remembered the buzzing market just a few hours prior. Now it looked and felt like a graveyard. With a plug and blow of her nose, her body told her she was not in a dream.

The nearest of the five inns, a tall building with candlelight shining through some of the windows, came into view.

Lawrence kept Mika entertained in conversation. He asked about her life, her interests, Addie, what she was doing adventuring, and when the conversation turned that way, about Page. One thing led to another, and Mika found him very disarming. He was also funny, making jokes about the things Mika disagreed with or didn't like.

They reached the front of the inn, its doors flanked by hovering orbs of lux. The two faced each other at the steps.

"Thank you so much, especially for helping Addie." Mika caressed her face, and Addie barked at the sound of his name, startling Lawrence. "I'd be frantic looking for him."

"I bet! Anyways, have a good night!" Lawrence turned and waved. "Good luck in finding your boyfriend!" The man turned to head back down the road.

"You travel at night?" Mika asked. "Aren't you worried about bandits and werewolves?"

Lawrence continued walking. "Shit. Good luck to them if they try to fuck with me!" Lawrence moved the torch so Mika could see him wink, and he cast a spell that surrounded Mika with several clones of himself.

Mika laughed and shook her head, and Lawrence's clones dispersed like clouds. Mika opened the door and stepped into the inn.

A cozy warmth from the fireplace hugged her like a blanket when she set foot past the threshold. One fireplace crackled at one corner, warming the few guests who sat on cushioned loveseats. All of them had weapons next to their chairs, and they all read books. A man with mean eyes looked over his book at Mika's hands, Addie, then at her face, studying her demeanor before he continued reading.

On the other side of the room, behind a counter, stood a young girl with greasy hair. She wrote in a book, looked up in thought, then continued writing. Mika walked to the counter, and the girl greeted Mika with a broad smile that revealed crooked teeth.

"For one?" she asked. Her cheerful attitude brought a smile to Mika's face. Mika tried to ignore the girl's flawed, stained teeth.

Mika nodded. "And a dog."

The girl leaned over the counter and cooed at Addie. "You are just too cute, aren't you?"

Addie wagged his tail.

The girl reached toward a stack of papers and grabbed a packet. "Dogs are no problem compared to other companions!" She began filling out paperwork, leaving Mika to her thoughts. She admired the paintings behind the counter. One painting was of a glorious knight holding a sword that gleamed with the rising sun. Another painting featured rolling hills with a red-and-brown house at the top. A single moon shone bright in the corner.

Mika's attention shifted to the counter, and she ran her finger across the smooth mahogany wood. She continued running her fingers until her pinky touched an open book, the book the receptionist was writing in. Trying not to seem nosy, Mika read the letters from the corner of her eye. The receptionist seemed to be writing a love poem.

The poem wasn't finished, and Mika looked at her.

She smiled at Mika with closed eyes. "What do you think? I'm writing a book of poems for the deities. That specific one is for Gral!"

Mika looked at the writing. "I wasn't able to read it, but you seem enthusiastic about it, so I'm sure it'll be good."

"Thank you!" The girl handed Mika a paper, and Mika filled it out.

Two gold coins for one night? Mika could feel the pressure in her jaw when her teeth clenched.

She was too tired to look for a spot to set up a tent, build a fire, and get enough sleep to cure her exhaustion. She had no light source to find a cheaper inn, and if she did have a light, she didn't know where to start looking for one. With reluctant hands, she reached into her coin bag and dug through the silver coins until she pulled out two of her four gold coins.

The receptionist accepted the coins and handed Mika a key with the number *115* engraved upon it. She pointed down the hall.

"I provided a room downstairs! You can leave the rear door open for the pupper to go potty while you sleep. To reach the toilets, just follow the torches!"

Mika curtsied, made her way down the hall, unlocked the door, opened the back door, stripped down naked, and scooted herself under the comfy sheets.

Before her typical anxious night whispers could set in, she fell into a long, dreamless sleep, knowing that Addie and the mercenaries would protect her from any danger.

*   *   *   *   *

Addie lay on the floor, looking out through the open door at the calm green hills that waved in the distance, reflecting the sun's bright rays onto his snout. His ears were pointed back, listening toward the front door, ready to confront any unwanted guest and protect his Mika. A bird swept from above, grabbed one of the strange creatures with the long, floppy ears, and took it toward the sky. The winged creature had found his own food, yet Addie still depended on Mika for his. Addie looked at Mika.

Still asleep, a string of saliva ran from the side of Mika's mouth, down her cheek, and created a puddle on the pillow. He'd never seen Mika sleep after the first few rays of light.

Addie sighed, remembering that Mika forgot to feed him last night. Now, at midafternoon, he was starving.

With one last look at Mika, Addie couldn't hold his hunger anymore. He decided to hunt for food, just like the winged creature had done. He would prove to himself that he could do the same thing his body and mind had been telling him he could since he was a puppy. Shaking off the stress, Addie sneaked through the back door and, hoping his mother would be safe, ran toward the smell of food.

The narrow and buzzing streets, people's equipment, armor, and weapons clanking with every step and movement, shouts and laughter, along with loud conversations … it all confused Addie. He tried his best to remain focused. First, he knew, he needed to find a source of water. A sharp pain on the paw sent a jolt that shocked his heart. Addie yelped. A man had stepped on Addie's paw.

"I'm sorry, little guy." The man knelt and offered his hand to Addie.

Addie sniffed his hand and determined he was trustworthy.

Holding Addie's paw in the palm of his hand, the man said "Vita," and a powerful golden glow flashed from his hand.

Using the tip of his tongue, Addie licked the man's face until his paw was released.

The human looked at Addie's mouth, noticing it was tacky with saliva. "Thirsty, aren't ya?"

Addie tilted his head at the word *thirsty*. He'd heard that word before but didn't know what it meant.

The man repositioned himself away from the road. "Aqua."

At the sound of the spell's name, Addie rushed under his fingers, delighted when water spewed like a river. The man's water, unlike Mika's, tasted so, so good, pure, clean! Addie drank until he quenched his thirst. The man ruffled Addie's ears and left.

Addie followed his nose, which led him in the direction of meat … cooking meat. He picked up his pace and sat behind a food stall, watching a skinny older man hurry back and forth from the grill to the counter—where he wrote on a paper—then back to the grill. He walked toward the pup and reached into a bag filled with charcoal.

"Go!" He stepped toward Addie. "Go away! Bad!"

Addie ran, and the old man gave chase, throwing a plate that shattered to pieces when it hit the ground.

"Shoo! Bad!" The man sprinted back to his stall and continued cooking and serving.

Addie lay on the ground and whined, but he continued to analyze the man's movements—how he looked at the food, the customers, the grill …

And how he turned his back to the uncooked meat on the counter every time he moved from the grill to a customer.

Addie kept watching the old man. His routine stayed the same after every customer. He placed a fresh slab of meat on the counter,

121

added spices and garlic, then turned around. This was the moment. Addie sneaked up, keeping his head low.

"What's your order?" The old man's mean voice startled Addie, forcing him to hide behind the counter. "What else?"

"Thirty silver!" Clanking of coins, shuffling of clothes, tapping on wood. "Any day now, sir!"

"I'm trying, man, hold on!"

Slap! The slab of meat was thrown on the counter. A thud was followed by the scrape of a knife, then a clank preceded sizzling. The mean old man should be facing the grill …

Addie stood. He inched his snout closer to the edge of the counter, closer, closer. The delicious smell of meat entered his nostrils and filled him with excitement. His mouth opened slowly, then his lips curled back, revealing his teeth until … the teeth sank into the delicious meat. With a smooth pull, the meat dangled from his mouth, and he made himself small behind the counter.

"What the!" The man scrambled under the counter, looked around and away until he groaned and pulled another piece of meat from a container. After the cutting, Addie sneaked away, and the meat flopped side to side in his mouth, its juices dripped onto the grass.

Addie's tail wagged with such force his hind end moved. He felt so proud of himself he ran circles around the slab of meat. When the burst of energy faded, Addie ate the meat, still hungry for more.

Addie decided to get more, this time, he was too excited to be careful. He scrambled close to the counter. His heart was pounding so, so hard, ready for another slab and another victory.

"Twenty silver for you, pretty lady …" The old man's voice was nice compared to before. "… or free if you meet me after." He snickered.

"Watch your filthy mouth and make the food, you disgusting pervert," the woman snapped back.

The old man laughed and slammed a slice of meat on the counter.

Addie tried hard to remember the steps and precautions he'd taken earlier, but excitement clouded his memory. He stood and snapped his head over the counter, opening his mouth and biting down on the meat. That's when his canine eyes met the old man's. The look of fiery rage reminded Addie of Mika, but unlike Mika, the old man held a bloodied cleaver. Addie's ears lowered. He shrank his head under the counter.

Failure. Trouble. Danger.

The man squealed and swung the cleaver, missing Addie's nose by less than a hand's breadth.

Addie tripped and fell. The old man circled around, swinging his cleaver at Addie's belly. Addie scrambled to his feet. Sparks flew when the cleaver struck a rock. An uncontrolled slash cut through Addie's leg.

Addie yelped.

Running with tail between his legs and a hind leg curled up to his body, Addie bit down on the meat. He looked back to see the old man had tripped on a rope.

Addie mustered all his strength to ignore the pain. If he didn't run, he would be hurting more.

"You son of a bitch!" The man rose from his belly and gave chase but was too far to catch up. A sting of curses followed Addie.

Addie limped back to the inn, eating the meat on his way there.

The pup peeked into the doorway and noticed Mika sleeping on her side, her face sunken into the pool of saliva on the pillow. Addie limped in, curled into a ball, and began to lick his wound clean. Instinct told him to keep the wound moist with his saliva, so he continued licking, hoping his mother wouldn't wake up from his licks and tell him to shut up. Worse, if she found out, he would be in big, big trouble.

*   *   *   *   *

The sun began disappearing, revealing a sky full of stars. The wind whistled into Mika's room through the open door, waking the young adventurer. Mika's eyes opened in a slow, hazy blur. She blinked once. Twice. She shut her eyes, but she sensed Addie staring her down.

Addie!

She jumped out of bed and relit the candles. She put on undergarments and ran outside. "Drink? Eat?"

Addie followed her, doing his best to walk normally despite the pain, and slid under her fingers when she cast her water spell. Addie

123

turned so his wounded leg was away from Mika's view. Although Mika was dehydrated, she waited for Addie to finish before she gulped down the liquid that came out of her own body. Her stomach growled, but the pain in her stomach couldn't take away from the pain she felt in her heart from having starved her baby.

"I'm sorry, I'm sorry!" she said. "You must be so hungry."

She dug through her backpack, stuck her hand into the refrigerated pockets, and grabbed a piece of meat and a handful of fruits that expanded when she pulled them out. She hovered the meat over Addie and waited a second before allowing him to eat. She slammed the handful of fruits into her mouth and munched away. Mika couldn't believe she'd slept for an entire day!

She shook her head before reaching for another handful of fruits. *Exhaustion is no joke.*

Grabbing another handful, she leaned against the wall and looked out at the night sky. The stars glimmered and shone in the heavens, the moons, Chey and Sumner, both in their new phases, were like hollow black sockets in the sky, reminding Mika of the symbol of tenebris. A howling breeze ran past and tickled her stomach, reminding her she wasn't wearing anything but underwear. The wind had blown away the torches leading to the toilets. With another howl and a powerful breeze, she picked up the scent of cooking food.

Soup with vegetables and ... She waited for another breeze. *Beef.*

With the whiff of food, she spun around and got dressed. She wore a green short-sleeved shirt, shorts that almost matched her skin tone, and brown sandals that matched her hair. She brushed her hair and teeth before shutting the back door and talking to Addie.

"So, I'm going to eat."

Addie tilted his head at the word *eat*, but he didn't move. He was lying on his side, on top of his injured leg.

Mika reached for the dagger on the nightstand. "I want no disasters when I come back!"

She strapped the sheath around her thigh, tightening it more now that she wasn't wearing long pants. She pointed at Addie.

Addie's heart sunk. Had she found out about the wound?

"Do you understand me?"

Addie began lowering his head in fear.

Mika stomped forward. "Addie!"

Addie opened his eyes wide, his ears hidden behind his head, and he lay on the floor.

Mika grabbed his snout and put her nose on his. "Be good." She kissed his nose.

Mika grabbed her coin purse and placed the flower behind her ear. Addie shook off his stress when Mika exited the room.

"Miss Plum!" the same receptionist from last night said. "How may I be of service?"

Mika knew to avoid looking at her teeth. Tonight, the girl's hair wasn't greasy, and Mika handed her a gold coin for an extra night. She knew traveling at night would be dangerous. "Where can I find food? I smell some delicious soup cooking."

The girl's eyes closed, and her smile widened. "Just outside. Turn left," she said, pointing through a window. "And you'll see a tavern a little walk away. They serve the best … the best minotaur urine in Irstia!"

Mika's mouth watered. Minotaur urine came from both the bulls and cows of those savage creatures, indigenous to the central parts of Imbris. Mika remembered the first time she heard of the drink, but she had tried it, knowing that other cultures in the world smoked cow secretion to achieve similar states of mind. Maybe, just maybe, she would also drink tonight. She thanked the receptionist and left the inn.

The door flew away from Mika's grasp the second a gust took hold of it. She forced the door shut and moved toward the loud building surrounded by undying torches. She hugged herself to stop the wind from hitting her skin.

A shadow from the corner of her eye got her attention, but when she turned to look, nothing was there. She wasn't scared; she knew markets were safe from criminals because everyone carried a weapon and help was always nearby. A considerable number of mercenaries also protected the markets and kept them safer than most smaller towns. Still, she hurried her step, wishing the deafening wind would subside. She might, in other circumstances, hear an attacker before she saw one, but not over the howling wind.

Making her way closer to the tavern, she was excited to be out of the city and into somewhere unknown. She could do whatever she wanted! She could say whatever she wanted, and no one would remember her!

No one knows who I am! This is a brand-new beginning!

A giggle escaped her mouth. How would she introduce herself? She could say she was a master assassin; a rich traveler who wanted adventure, a dog tamer who was looking for revenge for her lost tribe; or an empress from a foreign land traveling without an army! Excitement hurried her steps to the tavern. When she got there, she took a deep breath and opened the door.

The boisterous laughter and shouts ran into Mika's ears faster than the smell of alcohol, food, and sweat when she opened the door. Body heat radiating from the dancing and moving made her think the fireplace in the far corner was unnecessary.

An attractive, well-dressed man with long, black hair greeted her with a smile. He handed Mika a yellow stick, bowed, and extended his arm to the bar. Mika passed and scanned the loud tavern.

The bar was full; so were almost all the tables. She wanted to sit next to women—she knew they wouldn't try to seduce her—but it looked like every woman in the tavern was either flirting with or talking to another person. She set eyes on a table that sat three huge, middle-aged men built like bears and gorillas. One had brown hair running to gray, a goatee, and a war hammer standing by the head on the floor beside him. The man next to him had a messy hairstyle and a bushy beard. The last man had baby-blue hair and silver highlights. He slammed an empty mug on the table before chugging another one.

Mika circled her neck with her finger, doing her best to quell the insecurity and nervousness she felt upon laying eyes on the three men. Since there was nowhere else to sit, she took a breath and eased her way to the table. She had caught the attention of the men; two of them stared her in the eyes; the one with aqua-mastery hair kept his eyes on Mika's strong, defined thighs that pressed against her shorts.

"May I sit here?"

The man with the goatee and war hammer held his massive hand to his ear. "What?" His voice boomed louder than anyone's, almost quieting the tavern for a moment when he yelled. "Can you hear this child?"

"I astutely cannot!" the man with aqua hair shouted.

Astutely? Is he trying to sound smart?

The man with the messy hair was in front of Mika; he was eye level with her, even though he sat. He leaned close to her ear. "Care to be louder?" His whisper was sinister.

Mika balled her fists, but she relaxed them before they could notice. Unlike her fists, her growing anger didn't wane.

"Assholes! May I sit here?"

The men exchanged glances with gaping mouths and wide eyes. They looked back at Mika; their eyes shifted to her flower, then back at her. Her flower told all three of them, and anyone watching the exchange, that Mika was furious and not afraid. They shouldn't have called her a child.

The man with messy hair jumped to his feet and wrapped his arms around Mika's shoulder. "Of course, you may sit here!" He bent down and picked Mika up with one arm, sat her in the chair, and slid his drink in front of her.

Mika smirked and placed the yellow stick on a tall purple vase on the table, letting the waiter know she needed service. For some reason, Mika felt a rush of confidence from the chat. The confidence grew when all three men inched their faces closer, and each tried talking over the other to ask her questions.

"How old are you? You look so young!" The man with the aqua hair asked, spilling his drink on the table. He used aqua to magically direct it back into the mug.

Messy-hair man pushed him away. "You come here by yourself?"

"What do they call you?" War-hammer man's voice boomed louder than the others, but it wasn't the boom that caught Mika's attention, it was the question.

Mika deepened her voice, elevated her chin, and narrowed her eyes. She didn't shout; she forced them to get closer to her and looked at all of them with seductive eyes before continuing. "I am Mika Plum of Yevera."

The man with the aqua hair leaned in. "I'm Blake! I hail from—"

"Shut your mouth!" said the man with the war hammer. "No one wants to know your story. It sucks!" He turned to Mika and softened his face. "Miss, sorry for my stupid, want-to-be smart *ally*." He grabbed the purple vase and held it in the air. "Waiter! Hurry up!" He placed the vase as far toward the edge of the table as he could. "Tell me, not them, tell me about Yevera!"

Blake scoffed, turning red the moment Mika winked at him.

"Yevera is home of the *finest* and most *vicious* warriors of Irstia." Mika's voice hissed; she lowered it to make it more dramatic and bring the men's faces closer to hers. "Though the women are young, smart, and beautiful, they are just as brave, capable, and *bloodthirsty* as the men." Mika paused for dramatic effect, making herself hunch over before exploding up, slamming her hands on the table. "Legends say that a Yeveran never truly dies until his weapon—" and in a flash, Mika unsheathed her dagger and stabbed it into the table, "—has been *pried* from the corpse's hands." She bit her smiling lips and gauged their reactions.

Blake inhaled to speak, but Mika put her finger to his lips, flicking his bottom lip before she continued.

"A true Yeveran—" she dragged the dagger toward her, carving a line in the table, "—never fears anyone, because they know they'll emerge victorious from the battle." The dagger slid off, and she wiped off the wooden chips on the blade, flipped it in the air, grabbed it, and sheathed it. She sat straight with her chin held high.

The man with the war hammer locked eyes with Blake. The man with the messy hair nodded with an open, surprised mouth.

"Sorry for the delay! What can I do for you?" The waiter leaned close to the group.

Mika ordered the largest bowl of soup and a mug of minotaur urine.

The man with messy hair slid coins on the table for payment, but Mika flicked them back at him. "I'm a grown, nineteen-year-old woman." Her voice was stern and demanded respect. "I can pay for myself."

"She can pay for herself, Donald!" The man with the war hammer repeated and shook his head.

Mika leaned back. "Yes, Mr. War Hammer... I can. But ... I still don't know *your* name."

The man's face lost color. He scratched the back of his ear. "My name—"

"You better use your real name, old man!" Blake cried out in laughter.

Donald slammed the table and hid his face. Mika could tell he was laughing. When he raised his head, Mika could see tears in his eyes from the laughter. "The real name! No nickname and no surname!"

Mika opened her palms toward the man with the war hammer. "Give it to me!"

The man clenched his jaw and stared at his two friends. "Sta ..."

Mika couldn't hear.

"She can't discern you!" Blake laughed.

"Not so loud now, are ya?" Donald slammed his hand on the table, shaking the mugs. "Say it!"

Mika began to chuckle.

"Stacy!" the man with the war hammer cried out. "My name is Stacy!"

Blake laughed so hard he almost fell backward.

"He said it!" Donald looked at Mika with wide eyes and a smile that showed a missing canine.

Mika closed her eyes and covered her mouth. She didn't want to be rude and laugh at Stacy's name. Such a big, loud, and mean-looking man was named Stacy.

Stacy! she thought. *His name is Stacy!*

With the thought, Mika burst out in laughter; she rolled her head back and laughed with the others until her stomach hurt. Stacy sat with his hands on his lap. His red face told the others he was fuming with anger, embarrassment, or both.

Mika finished laughing and wiped the tears from her eyes, realizing the waiter had placed a steaming-hot bowl of soup in front of her. Staring at the food, she couldn't keep her seductive, narrow eyes. When Mika's eyes returned to their wide and analyzing state, she saw the carrots, beef, celery, lentils, spices, onion, bell peppers, and tomatoes in the soup that made her mouth water. She snagged the spoon and took a bite.

Delicious.

Halfway through the bowl, she took a break. Stacy, Blake, and Donald continued talking and trying to score Mika. She, in turn, kept playing her game.

She grabbed the mug of minotaur urine and held it to her mouth. Taking a whiff, she almost puked. She'd forgotten the best way to drink minotaur urine was not to smell it … or acknowledge that it was urine from a bull that stood like a human. Without taking another breath, she chugged and chugged and chugged and kept chugging.

The beverage splashed from the mug into her throat, forcing her tongue to dance in her mouth and savor every sweet, delicious, tangy drop of urine. Mika raised the mug until it was parallel to the walls. She placed the mug back on the table and wiped her lips with her wrist.

All three men stared in shock. Mika burped and blew it out as ladylike as possible. Although Mika wasn't an alcoholic, she was able to chug the drink because the only liquid she had consumed in the past twenty-four hours was the little bit she had at the inn.

"Who's joining me on the second one?"

Two drinks turned to three, four, then five, until Mika and the three men sat in a drunken haze, laughing and joking, poking fun at themselves and the other guests. Mika hadn't been drunk in a long, long time. She'd forgotten how giggly and happy she became.

Stacy was a blur, but Mika saw him drink a purple liquid from a small vial. He passed it to Donald, who drank and passed some to Blake.

She leaned on Blake's arm, one eye half-closed, the other wide open. She giggled, and Blake sat her up.

"Mika," he whispered, "how about we take you back to your room?"

Mika rolled her head to Donald and Stacy, who were eager for Mika's response.

Mika shook her head. "Oh, aqua-hair man, you, nor you …" She looked at Donald. "Nor you …" She looked at Stacy. "Will be lucky enough to even see me naked. Tonight. Or ever." She saw Blake's shoulders drop; his exhale carried the scent of alcohol.

Stacy leaned over the table. "Hey, we're not saying that, are we, boys?" He looked at his partners. "All we're saying is we'll keep you warm and safe tonight, you know. Cuddling and stroking your … hair."

Mika thought of a response. It took almost a minute.

"Okay, okay, okay."

The men looked at each other with excited eyes.

"But all you're doing is walking me to my room and leaving me there *by myself*!" she continued. "And if I wake up tomorrow, and I feel in any way, in *any* way, different than what I normally feel …" She hung her head and fell asleep, but the thought of all three men in bed with her woke her, and she continued.

"Then you, and you, and you … will find yourself shackled and naked. Your dicks will be tied together with a rope, and your balls will have a candle to them until they are cooked a crispy and delicious brown. Then!" She held a lazy finger in the air. "I will force you to eat your own dicks while I broil you to death. Understood?"

The men looked at each other. Blake inched away from Mika, and Mika closed her eyes and started falling back. She caught herself and swayed side to side.

"That's what I thought! No taking advantage of Mika Plum of Yevera!"

Mika opened her eyes, just in time to see a man with smoky-black hair, wearing a black cloak, slip something inside of a mug a few tables away. The action was weird, and it caught Mika's attention. She tried her best to fight the drunkenness and focus on the man. He walked away and sat at the end of the bar. His eyes never strayed from the drink.

Mika looked at the drink, now in the hands of a woman with bright-orange hair and pale skin. She drank sips of it at a time, never putting down the mug. Blake lurched in Mika's line of sight, but she pushed his face away and continued watching the woman. The woman began to cough.

The coughs became more vigorous until foam pooled from her mouth. Thick, white foam turned dark red when blood from her stomach mixed with saliva and mucus. She held her stomach and vomited blood before collapsing on her knees, vomiting again, and falling on her side. She convulsed until she lay still. The tavern fell silent.

The waiter knelt next to her. He used vita, but the vita rejected the woman's body, bouncing away from her, letting everyone know

131

the woman was dead. Mika's gaze snapped at the man with the cloak. The palm of his hand was pointed down, and a smoky-black mist danced within his palm. With a twitch, the mist slithered away, finding the most discreet path from the bar, down to the floor, between the stools, and seeping itself into the woman's nostrils.

Everyone talked and wondered what happened. Was she sick? Did she get poisoned? If so, by whom? Why? They began looking at their drinks, failing to notice the woman began to move.

The woman reached for the waiter's ears and pulled him down, sinking her teeth into his neck and ripping out his jugular. He pulled away, skin in her mouth ripped from skin on his body.

"Ghoul!" someone yelled, and the tavern erupted in panic.

Shouts of surprise covered his screams, as blood spurted from his neck onto a table and people. The ghoulish woman was on top of another woman and sank her fingers into her eyes before biting off her nose. A man cut off the ghoul's hands, while another grabbed and pulled her onto the floor. The ghoul squirmed away and pummeled him.

Blake, Stacy, and Donald were on their feet, stumbling over furniture to the action. The cloaked man released more mist that slithered into the dead waiter. The waiter stood and stabbed a man with a white shirt.

The cloaked man cast a mori spell. Taking aim at Donald, he launched a slow-moving ball that increased in speed as it moved.

"Donald!" Mika shrieked.

Donald dodged out of the way. Blake turned, and the ball collided into his arm. Pain filled Blake's face.

"I'm going to fuck you!" Blake stomped to the man, but his arm tripled in size until it exploded, sending a trail of blood into Donald's face.

"Blake!" Donald ran to his friend. "Blake!"

Blake leaned on the bar. Blood continued to spurt, and he fell to the floor.

"Stace, help me with Blake!"

Stacy and Donald picked Blake up, tied a makeshift tourniquet around his arm, and carried him toward Mika.

More ghouls were rising from the carnage.

Mika fell out of her chair and inhaled some of the mist. She coughed it out, worried she would turn into a … into a crazy! Into a ghoul! She stood, but her drunkenness caused her to tumble. She used the table as support to stand.

Blake created an invisible blade of pressurized ventus and decapitated Donald.

Donald fell, and Stacy delivered a devastating strike to Blake's face, knocking his undead friend to the ground. Stacy ran to Mika, poured purple liquid down her throat, and threw her over his shoulder.

Stacy placed Mika on the floor and punched a ghoul out of his way. They were now everywhere.

"Help me!" an undead human screamed.

Stacy smashed his hammer into the wooden wall of the tavern—once, twice. Wood flew into Mika's face. With a powerful roar, he swung the war hammer a third time, creating a hole that he pried open with his hands until it was big enough to fit Mika through. He grabbed Mika and launched her headfirst outside through the hole in the wall.

Through the hole, Mika saw Stacy fighting off a ghoul, each strike becoming slower and slower. He needed help. He needed help! Mika stood and caught her balance. She wobbled to the hole and tried to pick apart the wood, but she was too weak. Stacy screamed when a ghoul dug a knife into his forearm. He used the knife to stab another undead foe.

"I can't break this!" Mika shrieked.

After a punch that appeared to fracture the jaw of a ghoul, Stacy slid his war hammer through the hole. He continued fighting.

The hammer was heavy; Mika couldn't lift the head past her ankles, but she used it like a battering ram, beating the wood bit by bit. She felt like she was going to puke, but she kept hammering, ignoring the massive headache and her tired arms. Stacy's screams made her work harder until there was no wood left on the bottom portion of the hole.

"That's all I can do! Stacy! That's all I can do!"

Stacy's bloodied fingers wrapped around and tore away at some of the wood. She was sure he could fit now, but he didn't go through. The mist began seeping out of the hole, and she couldn't see her ally;

she could only hear his grunts and the cries for forgiveness by the undead within.

"Stacy!" she cried. "Stacy! If you don't come out, I'm going in!"

No answer.

"Stacy!" she shrieked.

Stacy dove through the hole and used his elbows to crawl out. Just before he stood, he let out a shout and faced the hole. A ghoul had Stacy's boot in its mouth; blood seeped between its teeth and onto the soil.

Mika recoiled when she saw the ghoul's scared, sad eyes. It thrashed its head from side to side and tried to pull itself and Stacy back through the hole. Stacy began to slide back through the hole when other undead pulled the one clinging to Stacy's boot.

In a desperate panic, Mika slid to her knees and sawed away at the ghoul's neck with her dagger, spitting away the blood that shot into her mouth.

Stacy helped by grabbing the ghoul's hair and pulling it, granting better access to its neck. Wet pops escaped the throat.

Mika reached the spine and chopped until she felt her dagger sink into flesh. The dagger slipped from her bloodied hands. She cleaned her hands and reached for her dagger. The pulling caused the undead's skin to peel from its neck.

Still biting onto Stacy's foot, the undead's sad eyes darted between Mika and Stacy.

"Kill me, please!" it mumbled from its lips.

Mika stabbed the undead's eyes, and when she withdrew the dagger, now covered in gore, Stacy punched the head. When Stacy retracted his fist, Mika stabbed. The cycle continued until the undead's jaw was broken, and it released Stacy's foot. The undead's still-living head rolled away.

Stacy and Mika sat next to each other; their panting filled the air but was soon smothered by screams and shouts around them. They locked eyes.

"That was a fucking necromancer." Mika's eyes were wide, and her voice returned to its regular pitch.

Stacy nodded. "Only a matter of time before they targeted this market. I knew they would."

"We need to stop them!"

"Us and what army? The paladins are barely keeping them in check." He stood, limped to his war hammer, and used it as a crutch for his wounded foot. "We need to leave. Now." He held his hand to the girl he was trying to bend over just moments earlier. Now, he felt like it was his duty to protect her.

"Fuck!" Mika shook her head, and she noticed her drunkenness was dissipating. "I need to get to Triumph! I can't go back!"

"I'll help you get there, but for now, we need to leave, or neither of us will get anywhere!"

Mika sighed and pressed the corners of her eyes. She cleaned her bloody dagger on her shirt, angry at herself for letting the weapon slip from her hands. Stacy limped away from the screams coming from deeper within the market. Mika followed. Stacy grabbed a vial from his pocket and drank half of it.

"It'll help with the drunkenness." He handed the rest to Mika. "Gave you some earlier."

Mika consumed the purple liquid. It had a putrid taste that made her mouth sizzle and smell bad.

The couple rested after a short walk. Stacy leaned on the large sign that read MARKET 135.

With a relieved sigh, Mika leaned on the sign and closed her eyes. Her head cleared from the alcohol, and she was able to think straight.

Stacy looked back at the market. The night sky reflected the reddening glow that came from fires at the opposite end. A blanket of blackness was beginning to form above them.

The large man spoke. "I can't believe they died like that."

Mika was silent. She figured he was referring to Blake and Donald.

"I can help you retrieve their belongings." Mika didn't know what else to say.

"Yeah …" Stacy's voice hinted that he wanted to cry. "But not today."

Mika looked back at the fiery and mesmerizing glow. "I will help. I owe you that much for saving us."

"Us?"

She held up the hand she used to hold on to Addie's collar. "Us."

She didn't feel a pull or see a leash. Her eyes widened, her heart sank, and she looked at her empty hand. Profuse sweating began the moment she felt the sides of her head press with stress. The drunkenness she felt earlier forced her to forget all about Addie.

She gasped. "By the gods, no!"

"What is it?"

"Addie," she screamed. "Addie, Addie. *Addie!*"

"Mika!"

Mika was at a dead sprint back toward the inn. The only image in her mind was Addie screaming in a corner, a blood-spattered ghoul gnawing away at his intestines.

"Mika, what are you doing?" Stacy took off after Mika, plummeting to his elbows the second he put pressure on his ravaged foot. He looked up to see Mika's hair flying behind her like a cape until she faded away from his view.

"Mika!"

10. STACY

She leaned forward. Her hands were open like blades to cut through the air easier, allowing her arms to swing with so much power the wind whistled in her ears. Stacy's shouts were drowned out by the sounds of her flapping sandals on the cobblestone road. Running against the powerful wind, tears began forming in her eyes, making it harder for her to see in the dark, moonless night.

Speeding toward a figure leaning on a stall made her slow her pace. She kept her eyes locked onto the dark figure and readied herself on her approach. A crunch of something beneath Mika's sandal caused the figure to jerk, and its head lolled around. With a choppy turn, it faced Mika. She slowed her pace to a quick walk.

Ghoul ...

"Run away ..." the undead woman said, its voice gargled and wet.

Mika slowed to a stop. She couldn't hear because of the crying wind.

The figure took a step. "Run ..." it repeated. "Please ... Run ..."

Mika tensed as the ghoul lunged at her. Mika blocked with her forearm, and its nails cut through skin.

Mika sprang away.

"Terra!" said the ghoul.

Green vines flew from its hands and wrapped around Mika's arm. The undead pulled the vines like a rope. Mika screamed and set her feet; the pull forced her to fall, knocking the air from her lungs.

The ghoul dragged Mika toward her; the vines tightened to the point Mika lost circulation. Ignoring the dizzying constriction, Mika hacked away at the vines until she was a foot away.

The ghoul scratched Mika's face. "I'm sorry!" It gargled a cry. "I'm sorry!"

Mika kicked, blocked a scratch, and swung her dagger, cutting open the cheek of her opponent.

"Help!" Mika squealed. "Help!" She pulled at her constricted arm.

Scratches to her face and body forced a distressed scream. With closed eyes, Mika swung her dagger, and the vines released. She opened her eyes.

A man wielding a sword and shield had cut the vines. He swung, cutting the undead woman's throat before hiding behind his shield to block the spurting blood and counterattacks. After a displacing kick, he pierced its undead heart.

The ghoul went limp, resting on the man's sword. Life essence escaped from the undead, entering both Mika and the man. The only memory Mika saw was the woman holding a baby. The woman's son.

The man placed his steel boots on the corpse's hips and pushed it off his sword.

He looked at Mika.

"Easy essence if you go after the weak ones." He walked away, striking the shield with his sword every time his left foot hit the ground.

Mika released a breath. Moving her gaze to the undead … No, not an undead, just a corpse now. The corpse of a woman. Mika looked into her sad, scared eyes, one of the few things the woman was able to control.

She was saying sorry …

The stinging of her wounds blunted her sadness. She could feel deep gashes from the nails on her face and cut clothing around her abdomen.

"Vita!" The beautiful golden glow radiated around her hand. She passed the healing magic through her face, exhaling when the burning faded. Passing it through her stomach, she gasped when the deep scratches closed, leaving no evidence of a wound. She stood and ran to the inn, applying vita to all her wounds, mindful not to reach the point of exhaustion. It would be horrible to pass out in this situation. Mika slowed her pace when she saw the bright lux orbs at the front of the inn.

There, she saw two ghouls. One twisted the knob, stopped, then pulled on the door. The other stared at the wall, swaying back and forth.

Mika stuck to the shadows around the side of the inn. She came across the wooden back doors. She scanned the first door, only seeing a brass knob.

No numbers.

Running down the side, she counted the doors.

One ... Three ... Five ... Seven ... Nine ...

A woman's shriek came from room eleven. The door rattled, followed by screams and cries. Mika quickened her pace.

Eleven! Thirteen! Fifteen!

She wrapped her fingers around the cold knob. She twisted her hand left and right. Locked. Was it stuck? She twisted her hands with more force, pushing and pulling at the door. An arrowhead pierced through the wood.

Mika gasped.

Had Mika's hand been a centimeter wider, the arrow would have cut her.

She composed herself and leaned into the door. "Hey ..." she whispered, "what room is this?"

No response elicited a quiet but rapid knock.

"Please, I need to find my room."

She heard someone touch the door through the other side.

A man whispered back. "One thirteen. We're barricaded inside. The inn is overrun!"

Mika stepped back. She looked at the door of her room and sneaked to it. She held her ear to the door.

"Addie ..." she whispered.

Still holding her ear to the door, she slid down, listening for any sign of life until she was on her knees, her forehead touching the ground.

Please, Angelis, please let him be okay.

She heard a sniffle, forcing out a sigh of relief.

"Thank Angelis and all her beauty! I'll be right there! I'll be right there!"

Her voice forced rapid breaths out of Addie. *He must be petrified,* she thought. Mika stood and reached for the doorknob. Grabbing it with her fingertips, she stopped, took a breath, and turned the knob.

Locked.

She looked for a keyhole but did not see one. She clenched her fists to the point her nails cut into her skin.

How could she have been so stupid to go out and leave Addie? Why did she have to get drunk? How in the world did she forget about her baby? Now she had no simple or safe way to get into her room. The anger she felt boiled inside her to the point she was walking in a circle. The circle then became a line that she walked back and forth. Tears of anger pooled in her eyes. Soon, she began hearing the tiny, distant whispers and voices that always came to her in times of undying rage.

Stop when you hear the voices, stop when you hear the voices ...

She closed her eyes, cocked her fist behind her head, and struck the soft ground, creating a hollow where her fist collided. The anger and voices dissipated the moment she released her anger onto something.

Think, Mika, think.

Mika looked up and noticed the second story of the inn had windows with exterior ledges wide enough for Mika to be able to stand on. The windows and their ledges were close enough to each other that Mika could shimmy from one to the other in case a room wasn't safe to enter.

Mika ran to the wall, jumped and kicked off the wood with her foot to give herself the extra inches she'd needed to grab a window ledge. She touched it with her fingertips but was unable to grab it. She crashed down and rolled out of the fall.

She stretched out. She hadn't practiced acrobatics since she got caught sneaking into the amphitheater two years ago.

Digging her feet to the ground, she leaned forward, exploded into a sprint, jumped, kicked up, clawed up the wall, and reached. Her palm slapped the top of the ledge, and she managed to catch herself.

A stressed breath escaped her throat.

She dangled on the ledge by just three fingers. She pulled her-self up, pushed on the window to open it, and shuffled to her feet along the ledge.

Her heart was pumping as if she'd just sprinted for a full minute. She forgot how much acrobatics zapped her energy. Before she continued, she deepened her breaths and calmed her heartbeat.

Looking through the window, she strained to see inside the pitch-black room. Mika poked her head in, closed one eye to adjust to the darkness faster, and hopped in, hoping the thud of her landing didn't alert anything inside.

Lack of eyesight amplified her hearing. Moans, running, and screams came from the distance. A muffled explosion from far away made her realize how hard she was breathing. She tried breathing through her nose, but her lungs needed more air. Her breaths were choppy and filled with fear. Walking blindly through the room, she held her hand out in front of her, moving in the direction of a light that came from underneath the front door.

A gentle collision with a mattress was followed by the caress of a dresser until her fingers met the wooden door. She slid her hand to the knob, unlocked, and turned it, opening the door to the hallway, lined with torches at every door. An undead figure stood facing a corner at the far end of the hall, where the stairs led downward.

Looking away from the ghoul, her eyes met with a torch. Her heart skipped a beat. *Fire!*

She reached for the torch, lifted it from its base, and slid back into a room that now glowed a dancing orange. Holding the torch like a sword, Mika swung it from side to side, its gentle, roaring *woosh* was like music to her ears. The dancing flames made her pupils dilate; the gentle crackles and pops seemed to match the beating of her heart. She scanned the room.

The room was identical to hers, except for a window instead of a back door. Since it was unoccupied, she turned and peeked her head out into the hall. The ghoul stood in the same spot, motionless, except for the gentle rolling of its shoulders. Straining to listen, Mika could hear sobs coming from the ghoul, sending chills down Mika's neck. She inched her way back into the room to think.

Remembering the fight at the tavern, she concluded the mist would resurrect people into the undead creatures, but only if they die, since she was still able to control herself. Images of beating the undead's head from Stacy's foot replayed in her mind, telling her that decapitating an undead won't kill it; neither will injuring its brain, which Mika did when she stabbed it through its temple.

How do I kill one?

Her mind raced through the events with the undead that used the vines. Cut jaw, severed vines, sliced throat, sword through the heart.

Sword through the heart. That was it. *Sword through the heart! Destroy its heart!*

She peeked into the hall. Sliding out against the wall, she inched to the ghoul. Transferring the torch to her opposite hand, she brandished her dagger and gripped it tight within her sweaty hands.

Sliding off her sandals, she extended her leg, placing her toes on the ground, pressing them against the cold wooden floor. Mika rolled her heel to the ground until all her weight was on one foot. Extending her other leg, she sneaked behind the undead man, avoiding its peripheral vision.

Just like the training ... She was a few feet away.

Toes ... Heel ... Weight on the foot ... Extend the leg ...

Pop! A joint in her foot popped. She froze, balanced on one foot. The ghoul snapped its head over its shoulder. Mika was inches from view.

Silence filled the room except for the tortured undead sobs, now turned to wails the moment it heard the pop.

Waiting ...

Her vision tunneled to the point she only saw the ghoul. Mika could feel the vein in her neck booming.

He's going to hear your heartbeat. Her leg began to shake.

The undead turned to the corner, and the wails faded to low sobs.

Mika swallowed and took a deep breath before dashing forward. She spun the ghoul around and plunged her dagger into its chest. The blade crunched off a bone and sank into its torso up to the hilt. The undead wretch's terrified eyes went wide; then came a horrible scream. She'd missed the heart.

Mika pulled out the dagger and sprinted up the hallway. The tapping of her feet was drowned out by the thuds of the undead man's heavy boots. Hair flopping behind her, Mika's heart sank when she saw the ghoul brandished a spiked mace.

Mika leaned forward, sheathed her dagger, and swung her arms harder, pivoting around a corner that led to a flight of stairs to the third floor.

She jumped, clearing four sets of stairs, stumbling but continuing up the flight. A hand wrapped around her ankle, and she fell forward. Elbows broke her fall.

She grunted and squirmed. The mace cracked against the stairs. Chips flew into Mika's face.

The undead raised the mace. Mika trapped it with her torch; she felt no pain from grabbing the fire. The undead pulled; she pulled harder. It wrapped its hand around the spiked head, and blood dripped into Mika's eye. Mika's fingers began to slip as her muscles cramped. She heard hurried voices in the distance.

"At the stairs!" she wailed. "I'm at the stairs!"

The undead stepped on her stomach, and she tensed before he could crush her intestines. The stairs dug into her back.

The voices became louder; they bounced around and concentrated in front of her where the fire burned.

Mika's fingers slipped. The ghoul cocked back the mace, and Mika held the torch in front of her. After a panicked shout, the torch exploded into a fireball. The voices dissipated.

It stumbled back, dropping the mace and tumbling down the stairs. Mika dropped the flameless torch, snatched up the mace, and swung it into the back of the creature's skull. Unable to pull it out again, she sprinted down the hall, reached for her keys, pivoted toward the stairs, and jumped down. Using the wall to break her fall, she alerted the numerous undead patrons that stood in the lobby.

They ran toward her.

She charged at them, dodging away from a ghoul that reached from a dark room. She dodged a jet of aqua, jumped out of the way of terra spikes, and crashed her elbow against the undead receptionist's cheek. Mika stopped, surrounded at both ends of the hall. She read the room number in front of her.

115.

Both groups of undead charged her.

She worked her shaking key into the hole, unlocked it, and stepped into her candlelit room. Mika closed the door and slammed the bolt locked. Thuds thundered from the other side of the door as she moved the dresser to the entrance.

"Addie! Addie! Addie!" Mika scrambled over the bed. Half of Addie's body was underneath the bed, and his tail wagged the moment he heard Mika. Stress and candlelight made her miss Addie's wound.

Addie wriggled and kicked his legs, but he couldn't free himself. Mika closed her eyes and breathed a sigh of relief. She slid off the bed and grabbed Addie's lower back and thighs. He peed on her hand the moment she touched him. With a pull, she slid Addie from under the bed. His face was buried inside her backpack.

"Oh, Addie." She rubbed Addie's stomach.

Her adrenaline was so high she didn't realize her nails were digging past fur and into skin. She pulled off the backpack, closed the open pockets, and looked around for her flower. Her heart skipped a beat when she couldn't find it. Her hand reached to her head, and she exhaled when she felt the flower hiding in fear.

Mika opened the back door, looked to make sure there was no danger, and stepped out with Addie's leash wrapped tight around her hand. Her feet were tickled by the grass, so she stopped to pull a pair of boots from her backpack. They expanded the moment she pulled them out. She slid them on and walked around the side of the building, shuddering at the fierce, persisting winds. Addie did his best to fight through the pain and not show his mother he was hurt.

Mika froze the moment she reached the road. The market had been overrun with an undead mob. What was buzzing with banter, laughter, running, and hopping earlier was now filled with cries and wails, shuffles and darkness.

A loud whisper came to her ear. "Mika!"

She turned to see Stacy crouched behind a stall. He waved Mika his way.

Stacy?

Mika sneaked to him and crouched in front of the man, wrapping her legs over Addie so he wouldn't move.

"What are you doing here?" she whispered.

144

"Trying to catch up to you." He looked at Addie, who did not look away from Stacy's eyes. "Is she yours?"

Mika became angry. Was he judging her?

"*Him*," she said. "And *yes*. Now, why are you following me?"

"You ..." Stacy stopped to think, trying to find the right words to say. He spoke and acted much differently than he did at the tavern. "Well, you told me you'd help me get their belongings."

Mika narrowed her eyes. "I don't believe you."

"You and I—" Stacy reached for Mika's shoulder, but Addie's growls stopped him. "—we need to leave. Now. We won't survive until the paladins and guards from Di'Abribel get here."

"Where are the mercenaries? Markets are supposed to be safe!"

A hint of a smirk appeared on Stacy's lips. "Mercenaries? They're useless. Would not surprise me if they fled when they realized what was happening. We need to get out of here. Now."

Mika peeked her head over the stall, looking at the silhouettes of the undead. They moved or stood in place, blocking the way east to the Farmlands. She looked behind her at the open fields that led to hills. She looked in front of her, behind Stacy, at the cobblestone road that led back to the largest city in Celeste, almost ten hours away.

Her eyes met Stacy's, and she leaned closer. "What do we do?"

He pointed to the hills behind her. "Necromancers surround the locations they raid while their creatures and casters do all the work. Anyone they see escaping is captured and sent to the forest, never to be seen again."

He peeked over the stall then looked at Mika. "The east exit toward the Farmlands? About seventy minutes of running, nonstop, dodging all the undead on the way there. There are more inns and people in the center of the market. More people, more undead." He slid his mangled foot between the two. "I can't make the run like this."

Mika looked at his foot. Half of his leather boot was missing, making the bones that had been scraped of skin and muscle visible to Mika.

"We might be able to heal this. Do you know vita?" he asked.

"Yes, yes, I do but only for myself. I learned the spell through a statue."

"Doesn't matter. You only need a baseline to start crafting your own spells. I'm no healer, but magic is magic, it's all the same... I would imagine myself healing someone else, visualizing my glow entering them. Try it. I think there's still time to heal it."

Mika pressed her fingers against her eyes. Stress squeezed her brain. She needed to start learning magic.

"Okay. Okay. Okay, okay, okay …" She held her open hand to Stacy's foot. "Vi-ta."

The golden glow radiated from Mika's palm, allowing her to see Stacy's bare foot. Flesh hung from Stacy's big toe. The next two toes were bones covered in dried blood. Repulsed, Mika looked away and placed the healing glow on Stacy's foot. Upon contact, the glow shattered. Mika's head throbbed, and she fell to the ground in a horrible daze, her mind's way of telling her she didn't know the spell she was trying to use.

She clenched her teeth and dug her nails into her hair. She wanted to lash out at Stacy for putting her through the pain she was feeling. The only thing stopping her were the undead foes just yards away.

"We'll have to go back to Di'Abribel and hope the paladins and guards meet us on the road."

Mika sat on her knees. "How the fuck do I do this?"

Stacy recoiled at her attitude.

"Well? How do I fix your fucking foot?"

He pulled his shirt collar. "Move your foot next to mine. Pretend to heal yourself, slowly inch your hands to my foot. It'll probably feel like you're trying to break through a wall. Push past it. Easy."

Mika locked eyes with Stacy. An angry exhale was followed by her sitting on her butt and moving her foot next to her partner's. She remembered Janice telling her something similar, something about a wall, years ago.

"Vita." The golden glow grew the moment it touched her boot, surrounding her foot in its beautiful light. With slow, steady movements, Mika began to move the glow toward Stacy's foot until she couldn't move her hand anymore. Her hand felt like it was hitting a wired fence.

"I feel a fence."

"Don't lose your focus. Imagine the vita glowing around you, wanting you to pass through. It's not fighting you; it wants you to push through with it. Focus."

146

Mika felt the life magic on the other side of the fence pushing her back, preventing her from learning more about its mysterious abilities. She closed her eyes, envisioning the wired fence with vita on the other side of it.

"It's on your side," Stacy reminded her.

Parts of the glow began to seep through the fence.

You're with me. We're together.

More of the glow joined Mika's side. She pushed at the fence with both hands.

"If you have essence, breathe it out."

"How?"

"Like … like you would a burp or the air already in your lungs."

She pushed against the wired fence, most of the glow on her side. She exhaled and saw the little amount of life essence she had in her soul leave her mouth. The life essence seeped to the other side and pulled at the glow. One of Mika's hands broke through. Stacy saw part of the vita surround his foot. The flesh on his big toe began to grow back.

Mika pushed harder on her opposite hand until it broke through. The glow surrounded half of Stacy's foot. Mika pushed her forehead against the fence. She put all her weight forward and walked. The barrier exploded, and she ran through. The glow that fought her rushed into her chest. She opened her eyes to see herself healing Stacy's foot.

"I did it." Her eyes wide, she looked at Stacy. "I did it, Stacy!" Losing focus, the vita dispersed.

"Vita." She hovered her hand over Stacy's foot. When muscle began to wrap around the bone, Mika's mouth dropped. Soon, the skin began to extend over the muscle, and nails grew and shone against the glow. Mika stopped when Stacy moved his foot away.

"Are you ready?" she asked.

Stacy stood. "More than before. Stay behind me, and stop for nothing and no one. We're not heroes. At all."

Mika nodded. Stacy took off in a powerful run, and Mika followed. The ghouls turned the moment they heard footsteps, setting off in a sprint after the man, woman, and dog. Shouts of anguish and despair filled the air.

Mika's heart exploded with fear. She ran through the grass, wanting to pass Stacy but knowing he was her best line of protection against the undead. He also knew the way out of the market and to the Farmlands. Stacy swung his war hammer, and a ghoul flew and rolled on the ground. They continued running, dodging, striking, and dashing away, trying their best not to be surrounded.

Stacy vaulted over a long stall.

"Jump, Addie!" Mika hurdled over. She heard a yelp and a crash, and her arm was pulled by the leash. "Addie!"

Mika jumped back over the stall, tossed Addie over, and vaulted across. A ghoul ran after her. She dodged. Pulling the leash made her notice Addie was limping; his hind leg was wounded.

"Stacy, wait!"

Stacy crushed the head of an undead with his war hammer. He ran back to her. "Mika, I know you love your—"

"I'm not leaving him!"

She carried Addie, slowing her pace to a jog and feeling the laceration on his leg.

Stacy swung his war hammer, sending another undead through the air. He picked up an undead child and snapped its spine on his knee before tossing it.

Mika placed Addie on the ground. "Come on, Addie!"

Mika set off in a run, pulling at Addie's leash.

Addie tried to keep up, but his leg wouldn't let him. Addie knew Mika would die if he couldn't keep up. Not only Mika but the nice man protecting them.

When she pulled, Addie pulled back, twisting his head side to side until his collar slipped off his neck. He sat and held his head low, refusing to look at Mika's panicked face when she felt no force coming from the opposite end of the leash. Mika planted her foot into the grass, twisting her body, her hair continuing in the way of her momentum.

Whether by extreme stress or aevum magic, the world around Mika slowed to a crawl. She moved as slow as everything around her, but her mind and her eyes moved at normal speeds.

She looked at Addie. His ears low in sadness, his head was crawling its way to the ground. He began falling to the side in defeat. Was he dead? Was he wounded? What was wrong with him? She could see no bleeding and no new wounds. An undead butcher held two meat cleavers. His movements were slow, but he sprinted toward Addie. Further behind Addie were multiple undead closing in, their legs in a run but moving slow, like everything else in the world at that very moment.

Mika's eyes shifted to Stacy. One leg swinging in the air, Stacy had lost his balance and was falling back. Stacy's eyebrows overshadowed his wide eyes, and his canines were visible. A ghoul had taken grasp of Stacy's war hammer. Another just finished cleaving a small axe into Stacy's forearm. Numerous undead foes approached from behind the one latched onto his war hammer.

A woman with puckered eyebrows and tears rolling down her face charged Mika with a spear. The spear was long, and it would crash into Mika's chest if she didn't move toward Addie or Stacy. If she didn't move toward one or the other, she would die with both.

Mika looked at Addie. He was curled into a ball, eyes closed, tail tucked between his legs. Addie was ready to die.

Mika looked at Stacy on the ground; he looked at Mika, hoping she would do something. Stacy wanted to live.

She looked at Addie.

She looked back at Stacy.

The pain in her lungs told her she wasn't breathing. They pressed hard, but for some reason, she knew the second she took a breath, time would return to normal. She looked at Stacy's eyes and waited until the woman with the spear was within reach.

Fighting through the pain in her lungs, Mika pushed the spear away. The undead woman's steps shifted toward the direction Mika sent the spear.

Mika's muscles felt like they weighed hundreds of pounds. Once the undead had her back to Mika, Mika released all the power she had and pushed her away. The undead stumbled forward. Mika's body turned the opposite way. She continued watching.

The undead caught her footing and shifted to her next target. She cocked back her spear and plunged it forward. Brain matter exited along with the tip of the spear as Stacy's legs shot up and stiffened before starting their descent back to the ground.

Tears filled Mika's eyes to the point she could barely see the ghoul butcher with the cleavers. A lump formed in her throat the moment she crashed her shoulders into him, forcing the old man to spin to the ground. The pain in her lungs too great, she took a breath, and the world returned to its normal speed.

"No!" Mika screamed.

Addie recoiled at Mika's touch.

Mika wailed.

She swung Addie over her shoulder and sprinted forward, mustering her strength to dodge an attack.

Stacy! Stacy! Stacy! Stacy, Stacy, Stacy, Stacy!

Mika looked back and saw him wielding his war hammer. An undead wretch, he lurched after her, too slow to ever hope to catch her.

Still able to see, feel, and think, Stacy's heart broke when he wondered why his life was less important than a dog's.

*   *   *   *   *

Rays of sunlight emerged over distant mountains at Peak's Lake. Rising in slow, methodical degrees, it seemed like the sun had no idea of the tragedy that had occurred in Market 135. The birds began to sing louder with each passing moment until they appeared to sing in competition with one another. With a final stretch, the sun cleared the mountains, continuing its journey to the top of the sky.

Her hair was a mess. Her legs shook from exhaustion, and her lungs begged for a break. Mika slowed to a stop, collapsing to her knees on the road that had now turned to dirt. She was miles from Market 135.

Mika hung her head and closed her stinging eyes. She didn't rub them; instead, she let them sting. She closed them harder to force them to sting more. When the stinging stopped, she felt the pain in her throat. Whether the pain came from the running or the crying, Mika didn't care. All she wanted to feel was pain.

You could have saved him. You could have saved Stacy. You killed Stacy. You killed Stacy. You killed Stacy, Mika.

Addie limped to her and sat next to Mika. Saliva had pooled in his mouth to the point he spat it out with every exhale. He locked eyes with his mother, but this time, he did not smile.

Addie.

Mika stared into Addie's yellow eyes. Her face showed no emotions, no expressions, just a blank, lifeless stare. She fell toward Addie. Too tired to move away from her, the pup let Mika latch on to both of his ears. Her forehead met his.

She was gentle with him, scratching his ears with her nails and giving him a kiss on the top of his snout. Tears began to form again. Mika pouted and closed her eyes.

Mika slid on top of Addie, her stomach on his chest; she could feel his pulsing heart. She cried, wishing she could be hugging Stacy, giving him a gentle kiss on the forehead or the cheek, telling him she was sorry, telling him they would recover Donald's and Blake's equipment together. Mika cried, burying her face into Addie's neck so as not to disturb the happy little birds above her.

*　*　*　*　*

There was no source of light on the top floor of the gloomy, quiet, and massive cathedral that Liam had called home for the past five years. Though it had no torches, no moonlight, no sunlight, and no lux orbs, everything on the top floor was visible thanks to tenebris.

He stood at the fourth floor of the cathedral. If he wanted to, he could jump and reach his hand to touch the ceiling. Still, he remained motionless, his eyes locked on to the spiral stairs on the opposite side of the building. Noticing someone moving on the floor below him, he shifted his gaze, seeing if he could recognize the person's walk. Before he could, the door he was standing next to opened.

"What's up, Liam? How was the raid?" Seth, a veteran lieutenant in a platoon of casters, walked toward him and leaned on the rail that would prevent someone from falling to their death. Seth's most prominent features were his long, curly hair; tailored clothes; and the fragrance he always wore, a musky wood.

Seth's relaxed posture and casual attitude helped Liam relax. Liam leaned back against the wall and rested an arm on his own head. "Not as many prisoners as we wanted. They either fought to the death or killed themselves."

"Any losses?"

"Take a guess." Liam moved his hands to his hips.

"One squad." Seth looked down below over the railing. "And half of another."

Liam chuckled. "Close, but no. Zero. None."

"No losses?" Seth hopped off the railing.

"None, Seth."

Seth clapped. "By Nessa!" He reached over and hugged his comrade. "Better to have no losses than no prisoners, man. Good job! You giving the report now?"

"Yeah," said Liam, his voice tight with anxiety.

Seth gave Liam a gentle smile. "Relax, man. I'm sure she forgot all about it or doesn't care anymore," he said. "That is if she ever cared in the first place. Just go in there and pretend nothing is wrong."

Liam was uneasy. "Just like that?"

"Trust me." Seth grabbed Liam's shoulder. "I've been doing this long enough. Just pretend nothing happened."

Liam nodded, faced the door, and knocked three times.

He waited with his hands behind his back, receiving no answer. He looked at the black door with the engraving of a human skull near the top. Still, no answer. Taking a deep breath, he knocked again.

"Enter." It was a female voice, and it resonated, loud and calm from within.

He opened the door and stepped into his leader's room.

Next to the door was a medium-sized bed with a blood-red comforter. Two nightstands flanked the bed, a human skull placed on each. A bookshelf decorated with several artifacts and stones stood next to a dresser that bore a large mirror with silver engravings. On top of the mirror was a belt made of leather and two human skulls. One skull belonged to a paladin commander, the other to the captain of a defeated enemy naval army.

On the other side of the room sat a desk before a round window that accepted every ray of moonlight from the sky. In front of the window, a woman with shoulder-length, mori hair and tenebris lowlights sat jotting something down in a thick brown book.

"Approach." The rhythm of her writing didn't change when she spoke.

Pretend nothing happened.

Liam stood in front of the desk and saluted by snapping his fist over his heart.

His leader continued writing, stopped, skimmed over her writing, crossed something out, set down her pen, and looked at her guest. She smiled and saluted back.

"Liam! How is your shoulder feeling?"

"Mistress Kathrine," he said, clearing his throat, "it's much better thanks to the potions Vicqua provided." Liam rotated his shoulder.

Kathrine had been recovering for the past few years herself, after a Yeveran healer had opened up her hip with a sword. Necromancers refused to use vita—the magic of their nemesis—to heal their wounds.

Kathrine's smile grew and she relaxed in her chair. "Marvelous. I'm assuming you're making an appearance regarding the raid on the market?"

Liam blushed at Kathrine's smile. His leader was one of the most stunning women he had ever seen. At seventy-three years old, Kathrine looked to be in her early twenties. Her mind was sharper than the blade she carried, and she was slender but with perfect proportions. Kathrine's eyes cut through anyone she looked at, making them wonder if she was about to slaughter them or pounce with sexual desire—something Liam could only dream of.

"Yes, Mistress." Liam pulled out a scroll. "I have the formal report."

"Perfect, take a seat!" She raised her hand to a chair.

Liam sat and scooted closer to the desk. He laid out the report for Kathrine to see. She leaned forward and read.

Liam watched her read. He passed his palms over his thighs, relieving the nervousness, and at the same time, wiping his sweaty palms. He bounced his leg up and down.

Her smile did not change. Her eyes scanned the report until she reached the end. Now, her eyes bounced from one portion of the page to the other, then back to the first, then to a random one. Her face began to straighten.

"Stop shaking your leg," she demanded.

"Yes, Mistress."

Kathrine continued reading. She stopped, reached for a notebook, and held it so that Liam couldn't see what was being written.

"Rendezvous with Lieutenant Amy."

Liam let her continue.

"Advise Amy she's in charge of executing an attack on Warrior's Edge." Kathrine locked onto Liam's eyes. "As she's raining down on Edge, you'll oversee the attack on Triumph and the paladin outpost there. Once both have fallen, both of you converge on Reach. Di'Abribel can't function after a loss that severe."

The corner of Kathrine's lips curved up in a smirk. "The war is almost over, Liam."

11. SYLISIA

In the dream, Mika woke up from the bed inside room 115. She looked around for Addie but couldn't find him. Something prevented her from speaking and calling his name. Forgetting the dog, she slid off the bed, noticing her backpack was strapped around her leg, where her dagger should be, and her dagger hung on her back, where her backpack should be.

Weird, she thought.

She walked to the door; her bare feet grazed wood floors that felt like carpet. Turning the doorknob, she stepped through the threshold and appeared at the market's tavern. There, she recognized the faces of all the people she saw die three nights ago. They did menial tasks—brushing the table, looking at a cup, talking. There were no voices, despite the moving lips. She moved without thinking, making her way to the table where she met Stacy, Donald, and Blake. This time, only Stacy sat at the table. His eyes followed her, and he took a chug from his mug.

Mika stared off into the distance. She looked at the fireplace, noticing the flames stood still and did not dance like natural fire.

"Isn't something weird around here, Mika?" Stacy asked in a gentle voice.

Mika continued staring into the distance. "I feel very relaxed. I've been here before."

"Yeah," he said. "Are you breathing?"

The scent of sweet firewood and sweat filled her nostrils. She looked at Stacy then around the tavern and then back at Stacy.

Stacy smiled. His eyes looked alive, and his movements were natural. He looked at his hands. Mika mimicked and looked at hers.

Her hands were massive, her fingers almost triple their normal size, and she had seven fingers instead of five. She looked at Stacy.

Stacy had his finger plugging his nose.

Mika brought her finger to her nose, plugged it, and breathed out. Her ears didn't fill with pressure. She inhaled and felt her lungs filled with air.

Am I dreaming?

She blew out again. When her ears didn't fill with pressure, Mika realized she was in a dream. The rush of a lucid dream waned the moment she realized she was sharing a dream with a dead person.

"I'm sorry, Stacy." Mika controlled her feelings. She knew that too much emotion would make the dream spiral out of control.

Stacy shook his head and smiled. "Don't be."

"I got you killed." Mika looked up at the ceiling and swallowed. She looked back at Stacy. "I killed you by not closing the door and letting Addie get hurt. I left you behind like you were nothing." Mika's dream began to fade.

She brought her hands in front of her face and clapped them once; the clap echoed through the walls and stabilized the dream. She ran her finger through the table, feeling the wood. The dream stabilized and became more vivid.

"I know our time here is short. I joined you to say that I have no grudges against you. No hard feelings. I'd forgive you, but nothing you did offended me. At all."

Mika hung her head. The amount of sadness she felt was greater in her dream than in waking life. The tavern around her began to crumble.

"This is my dream!" she shouted with tears in her eyes. She looked up at something, shouting at her unconscious mind that battled with her for control of the dream. "This is *my* fucking dream, and *I* control it!" The tavern stabilized. She took a breath and looked at Stacy.

He talked, looking into his mug. "Stand firm by your choices; they're the crumbs you leave behind as you move through life." He looked at Mika. "No one should judge you for a choice you've made, especially if they've never been in your situation or hold the values you do."

Mika gave the words some thought before speaking. "I don't know, Stacy. I don't know." Mika plugged her nose to remind herself she was still dreaming and to stabilize the dream. She lowered her head onto the table.

Stacy shook his head. "You've been inside your tent for three days. You are hours away from falling ill from lack of food. Mika. Mika…" Stacy waited until Mika looked at him. "You need to bounce back from this. Now."

"I know … I know … I know, I know, I know." The dream began falling apart. Mika clapped her hands and passed her finger through her opposite hand. The dream was shaky. "But how?"

Stacy raised his hand and pointed next to Mika.

Mika looked to her side. Sitting next to her was a figure of herself, the same way she looked that night at the market. The figure had a distant stare, and when Mika looked at it, it looked back at Mika with blank eyes.

"Your mind is what's holding you back," Stacy said, sliding Mika's dagger across the table.

Mika looked at the dagger, then at the figure of herself. "What do you represent?" Mika asked herself.

The figure turned to fog when it spoke, its eyes the only solid object. "I am the manifestation of everything inhibiting your progress." After speaking, the figure became solid once more.

The dagger appeared in Mika's hand. She raised it, placing the tip on the figure's neck.

"I don't want to perish," the figure said with a blank stare.

The dream trembled and crumbled, but Mika focused on the handle of the dagger to help stabilize herself. With a deep exhale that also caused her to exhale in her waking life, she pushed the dagger forward, feeling like it was pushing against a brick wall. She continued to push, pushing and pushing, until the dagger passed through the figure, and the figure shattered, falling into millions of swaying pieces of cloth that burned before they touched the ground.

"Live your life to the fullest, Mika. Don't worry about what happened. Honestly, the afterlife isn't that bad!" Stacy chuckled. "Donald, Blake, and I were joking about you just before we realized you were in a dream."

Mika watched the pieces of cloth get eaten by embers before she looked at Stacy. The dream settled. "How are they?"

"Better than ever." Stacy offered his hand to Mika. "Promise me you'll bounce back?"

Mika looked at Stacy's hand, at Stacy, his smile, then his hand again. She needed to compose herself. She was in a deep, deep state of depression and grief. Mika grabbed Stacy's hand.

"I promise. I promise I will." She moved through the table and to Stacy, sitting on his lap and placing her head on his chest. Stacy wrapped his arms around Mika and held her with big, strong, loving hands.

"Will I see you again?" Mika whispered.

"Of course, you will. After you've lived a wonderful life, filled with adventure and love!" He moved to look at Mika.

Mika looked up at Stacy.

"All three of us will welcome you with a mug of minotaur urine in each hand."

Mika chuckled and snuggled closer to Stacy. She felt her heart fill with warmth and her shoulders relax. She smiled. "My dream is fading."

Stacy kissed Mika's head. "Good morning, Mika."

Mika opened her eyes to see the inside of the yellow tent, the sun shining on the opposite side. She sat up to see Addie snuggling her foot and keeping his eyes toward the tent's opening. Mika had healed Addie the night after the tragedy.

Mika plugged her nose. Her ears filled with pressure.

Reaching into her backpack, she pulled out an apple and bit into it. She chewed, moved her foot away from Addie, and gathered her gear. When she finished the apple, she threw the core out into the wilderness and bit into another one. Pieces of her tent shrank in her backpack before she swung it over her back. She gripped Addie's leash, adjusted her dagger, brushed her hair, held her head high, puffed her chest, and walked east on the dirt road, following the sign that read CELESTE'S FARMLANDS.

From the dream, she only remembered sitting on Stacy's lap, but she knew something must have happened before that, because something deep inside felt different.

The dirt road, now barren of trees, gave her full view of the rising hills that led to the Grand Waterfall. From where she was, she saw the waterfall miles and miles to the northwest, its white waters rushing down from a mountain hidden by the clouds. Addie looked in the same direction. When Mika looked at him, he sensed it and turned to face her. Mika looked away on purpose, watching him through the corner of her eye. When he realized he wasn't being watched by her, he went on high alert. Something was watching him, but from where? He looked behind them, to the sides. He couldn't see any threats, so he growled to scare away any possible danger. Mika laughed.

She looked to the south, and in the distance, she could see glimmers of the stone walls that surrounded Di'Abribel.

Such massive monuments ... No wonder the necromancers hadn't tried to attack the city. To Mika, the necromancers were taking little tentative bites of Celeste at a time before they opened their jaws and lunged at Di'Abribel and Vicqua. Necromancers had time on their side, for mori magic slowed their aging.

Looking forward, to the east, she saw the colorful patchwork of farmlands spread across the hills. Mika wondered why the necromancers hadn't attacked Celeste's food source. Maybe they were eating from there too?

Mika began to think of the necromancers. She never gave them much thought after the attack on Yevera, despite them being a threat to Celeste—a *serious imminent* threat to Celeste. No cities wanted a united Celeste, which was the reason this single army of necromancers was so strong and so deadly. More deadly than the armies of Imbris or the clans of barbarians that come from Azilia. Where did they get their reinforcements? Mika didn't want to believe they came through Adventurer's Pass from Velonde. Rumors around the underprivileged sections of Di'Abribel were that the necromancers had a secret alliance with the County of Vicqua, and Vicqua allowed recruits to pass back and forth through Velonde, providing food and supplies to the Lost Forest.

Mika was lost in thought for hours. She didn't notice the adventurers, warriors, traders, and builders who passed her or said hello. She just thought of the necromancers. She could still remember the face of the one who killed her mother.

A blond guard slightly shorter than Mika stepped in front of her when she neared the red fence surrounding the Farmlands, interrupting her thoughts and bringing her back to reality.

Mika blinked, shook her head, and scratched her nose.

The guard adjusted his leather armor and stroked his facial hair before speaking in a direct voice. "Documents permitting travel."

Mika swung her backpack around and dug into the pocket holding the adventurer's stone.

The guard drew a double-sided, single-handed axe. "Stop!"

Addie braced for a fight. Mika's eyes locked onto the axe. Did he think she was reaching for a weapon? "You asked me for documents."

The guard took a step back. "Slowly pull your hand out."

Mika's eyes met those of the guard. She took the chance to grab the adventurer's stone. Pulling her hand out of her backpack at a smooth, careful tempo, she showed him the adventurer's stone.

"Drop it," the guard demanded.

"You're insane. It's literally—"

"Drop it!"

Addie curled his lips behind his teeth and stepped toward the guard. The guard backed away.

Mika slung a single strap over her shoulder and hung both her arms to her side. "You're being ridicu—"

"I said!" The guard struck the ground with his axe. "Drop what's in your …"

A drop of fire fell from Mika's fingertips, catching the guard's attention.

Mika closed her eyes. "Don't fucking yell at me!" She held her fists to her head the second she began hearing tiny, childish whispers crowd and bounce around inside her mind.

~ Just kill him ...
~ Dead guard ... dead guard ...

"Fuck!" Mika screamed. Her eyes snapped open. She scanned the guard from top to bottom before locking eyes with him.

~ He's single ... no one will miss him ...
~ Cut out his tongue and feed him his own shit ...

It was the first time Mika was able to distinguish what the whispers were saying. Mika was so surprised at the evil, putrid thoughts, that she dropped the stone.

The guard scoffed and relaxed his stance.

"Was that so hard? I allow you to enter."

Mika shook her head, blinked, and scratched her nose. She began to calm, and the voices waned. She shot a glare at the guard before bending over to pick up the stone.

She held it inches from his face.

"You didn't allow anything. I have a stone permitting travel." She lowered her hand. "Was that so hard?"

The guard spat at the ground. Mika kept walking.

She stopped just before she passed him, looked into the guard's eyes, down to his boots, then back into his eyes.

"Had to become a guard to be respected, huh?"

Mika smiled when she saw the guard's lips churn.

"I'll keep my eye on you, bitch."

Mika walked away. "Make sure to get a stepstool, midget."

"Won't need one to spot the flat-chested whore with the mangy mutt."

Undying rage rushed through Mika. The insult to Addie brought her blood to a boil.

Kids laughed in her head. Several voices now sang around her, spinning in circles at the edges of Mika's brain.

~ Skin him alive ... skin him and burn him alive ...
~ No witnesses ... no witnesses ... NO WITNESSES ...

The whispers sang their words, extending their syllables to make Mika's mind feel compressed, loud, cluttered.

~ *Addie senses your anger ... Addie will help you gut him ... feed him his guts ...*

She continued walking despite wanting to release a burst of anger, punch the floor, pull her hair, and torture and kill the guard. She didn't reply to his following comments. She wouldn't give the guard the pleasure of knowing he made her angry. What she didn't notice, though, was her fingertips.

~ *I can't believe you're letting him talk to your baby that way ...*

Her fingertips, with every sentence sung by the whispers, dripped small embers onto the ground. Had the embers touched the drying grass instead of the dirt, they would have started a wildfire, burning down the whole of the Farmlands and cutting off food to millions.

When her heartbeat slowed, the voices dissipated, her shoulders relaxed, and she took a breath, trying to match her steps with her breathing.

What are those voices?

The trek through the farmland was monotonous and uneventful. An entire day of rows upon rows of fruits and vegetables, farmers, guards, sun, sun, and more sun. She felt regret for not going through the section filled with livestock. She wanted to, but she feared Addie would lose his mind and do something stupid, like chase or kill the cattle. The boredom and fatigue, combined with the constant checks for documents, filled Mika's mind with annoyance. The only good thing about the farmland was the free food. She restocked her backpack and ate more than she had in a long, long time.

Mika passed through the eastern fence of the Farmlands, where she set up camp and rested for the night. The next morning, she woke up and packed her supplies.

"Have a good day, madam." A female guard with leather armor and a plate-mail helmet nodded at Mika.

"And you too." Mika curtsied.

A cool, light breeze swept through Mika's hair, making it sway behind her like a flag dancing in the wind. She remembered what Sandra said about tying it but pushed the memory away, knowing she would never, ever tie her hair in a bun. A sniff of the passing breeze hinted at rain.

She continued east, stopping in front of a wooden sign. Two arrows pointing west read The Farmlands, Di'Abribel. Two arrows pointed east read Mt. Cabria, ~~Yevera~~.

Her head dropped. She tried to push away the feelings and memories of Yevera. The memories of her mother, her classmates, her instructors. How would her life have turned out if something had gone differently that day? Would she have completed her assassin training? Would she have found a job as a scholar instead of a scout? What would her mother be doing at this very moment? Would Mika have married Page?

A tan paw moved next to her brown boot. Addie looked at the sign.

Caressing Addie between the ears brought a smile to her sad lips. "But I would've never met you, huh, Addie?"

Addie opened his mouth at the sound of his name and looked at Mika with his yellow eyes.

The duo continued east toward Mount Cabria and the destroyed town of Yevera. Mika let Addie free from his leash since he was beginning to learn not to chase after deer and rabbits. Addie protected Mika from the front, and Mika guided him from the rear.

Thick, gray clouds moved across the sun, promising a few days of rain, if not a storm. The clouds hid the peak of Mount Cabria, making the summit appear elusive and enchanted, as if it hid a chest filled with diamonds and rare, magical items guarded by a ferocious ignis dragon.

Thinking of dragons, Mika slid the flower from her hair. She looked through the lime-green pearl. With a little focus, the dragon's sight came into view.

The terra dragon flew above a yellow desert. The skies were clear, making the scorching sun seem like it was frying everything in its view. The dragon looked at the ground miles below, then behind himself. Its wings whipped at the air, and its body slithered in the sky. Behind him flew another dragon, the khaki color told Mika it was also a terra dragon.

Made a friend, didn't you?

Mika looked at the petals, neutral like her current state of mind. Sliding the flower into her hair, she felt the stem wrap around her ear. She continued walking, spraying Addie with water to tease him and keep him cool.

She continued her thoughts of the treasure.

Dragon? No, no ... Dragons seem nice ... A fiendish ignis demon with human skulls hanging from spiked horns is protecting the treasure.

The portrayal of the would-be beast surprised Mika; she'd never thought of a monster with human victims. Why were her thoughts so dark the past few days? Maybe it had something to do with the carnage at the market? Stacy's death? The whispers? She shook her head and continued walking, glancing up at the mountain.

What if, instead of a strong beast guarding the treasure, it was Mika standing watch? Mika, Page, and Addie. All three guarding the treasures hidden inside their castle.

Hours passed, and Mika stopped in front of a wooden road sign. An arrow to the east read REACH. To the north, through a narrowing trail, MT. CABRIA. To the west, THE FARMLANDS. Mika took a breath, reading the sign pointing south.

Scratched off, yet readable; Mika whispered, "Yevera."

This was the closest she'd been to her home since she left. She stared at the sign and frowned, her shoulders drooping. She refused to look back toward the ruins. She didn't want that sight in her memory. She went around the sign and walked north, following the trail to Mount Cabria, cursing the leaders of Di'Abribel for refusing to rebuild her town. Looking ahead at the massive mountain in front of her, distant memories came to life.

Once, Yeveran festivals took place where she stood. Mika would scream and shout at the top of her lungs during the wrestling competitions. Her champion, the smaller, skinnier man named Laouri, won all his fights on top of the wooden platform that now lay mossy and rotting in front of her.

She remembered teasing Page during their races up the mountain. His impromptu stories when they hiked one in front of the other. The story at the top of the mountain when they watched the stars. Only happy memories came from this mountain. Mika smiled at the memory of the fun she had when she was a child. Comparing her childhood to her life now, though, was painful. If only she could go back and continue the happy life she once had.

Shaking her head, she patted the fading Mt. Cabria Trail III sign. The looming storm, her mood, and the fact that Addie had never hiked a mountain, made her rethink her plan of reaching the summit. She set up camp, slept, then continued toward Page the next day, walking eastward on the grass toward Peak's Lake, home of the sirens.

*   *   *   *   *

Pink and fuchsia flowers surrounded the banks of Peak's Lake. Tall green mountains enclosed all but the south side of the natural wonder. The water ran off into a river that flowed south into the ocean. Trees of varying shapes and sizes were spread out in random clusters throughout the banks, providing shelter from the beaming sun that, for some reason, felt perfect. Not too hot, not too cold.

Just perfect.

Some sort of magic prevented the gray clouds from moving past the mountains. In the distance, Mika saw women bathing, while others talked at the edge of the water, and the more athletic ones swam, some from the shore to the small island in the middle of the lake, others to the other side of the water. Being inside the mountains of Peak's Lake made Mika feel relaxed, like she was in a different world, free from the dangers that lurked in Celeste and Irstia.

As she walked through a row of trees, sunlight rippled from the waters and into Mika's face. A fish jumped out of the water, forcing Addie to brace himself, ready to sprint after it. He'd never seen a body of water before.

"Go on!" Mika pointed. "Go! Go play!"

Addie looked at Mika, then the water, then Mika. He didn't want to leave her alone and unprotected if he couldn't get to her right away.

Mika held Addie's ears and put her forehead to his; she kissed his nose. "I'll be okay."

She slapped Addie on the leg and pushed him forward. Addie sprang with a tongue that flopped out of his mouth before he dove into the water.

She watched him play and swim, plugging her nose to make sure she wasn't in a beautiful dream. When her ears filled with pressure, she slid off her shirt and placed it next to a tree. She untied her boots, sitting on the floor to take them off. She wiggled out of her pants and rolled them next to her shirt. She took off her upper undergarment and covered her nipples with her arm, not wanting to seem indecent. Hopping on one foot, she took her underpants off with her free hand and tossed them next to her pants. She would wash her clothes after her bath.

Still covering her breasts, she walked to the edge of the lake. Addie swam in the distance. Mika reached her toes to test the pristine water. Ripples bounced from her toe. The water was at the perfect temperature.

Sliding her foot in, she touched the soft dirt underneath. She spun around, held her arms out to the side, and dropped herself into the water, blowing air out her nose when the water rushed onto her hair and face. Despite being submerged, she could see the sky as if she were out of the water.

With a sweep of her arms, she popped out of the water and swung her hair to her back, sending droplets that glistened in the sunlight and created a rainbow. Seeing how clean and nice the water was, she drank some, relishing the pure taste. It tasted better than water from the fountains in Di'Abribel. After a long bath using the sand as an exfoliant, she looked for Addie. He was returning from the island in the middle of the lake.

He swam far.

Mika fluttered her legs, extended her arms in front of her, and pushed herself through the water toward him.

"What are you doing?"

Addie swam toward her with a smile on his face. He faced forward, but his pupils followed Mika when he passed her. He turned and licked Mika before he latched onto her, scratching her chest and pushing her under water.

Water rushed up Mika's nose, and she exhaled to prevent it from going into her lungs. Any other day, anger would have pumped through her veins, and she would have smacked Addie, but the views and calmness she was feeling curbed her displeasure.

Mika slipped away and fluttered to the surface. "What are you doing, silly? Are you tired?"

Addie swam toward her with a smile and tired eyes. Mika treaded the water and reached for his paws. Floating on her back, she held on to Addie and fluttered her legs back to the shore.

She swam until her back touched the silken sands that felt like bedsheets. Mika closed her eyes, only to be ambushed by the slaps of Addie's tongue to her face.

Mika pushed Addie before she lay back down. A breeze that carried the scent of flowers made Mika close her eyes and inhale deeper.

A calming, mesmerizing female voice sang to Mika from the water. "Amazing smell, isn't it?"

Mika sat and saw a gorgeous woman with long, blonde hair and pink eyes swimming several feet away from her. Looking through the clear water, Mika could see a naked torso and below the waist, pink fish-like scales that ended with fins.

A siren! Mika's heart raced. *A siren!*

Mika tried her best to not show her excitement. "Yes…" She cleared her throat. "The sights are amazing." She forgot what the question was.

What do I say, what do I say? Mika swallowed. She could feel the vein on her neck pumping. "Do you tend to the flowers?"

"There's no need." The siren smiled with closed eyes, showing a mouth filled with white, razor-sharp teeth. "Our water keeps everything within the mountains alive and fed."

"Everything?" Mika said, looking around her. "The grass, the flowers, the people, the birds, the trees, the—"

"Do you mind helping me? This is the hardest part."

The creature was floating on her back, extending a hand to Mika.

The movement of the siren's fins caught Mika's attention. Every time her scales and fins touched the air, they turned into legs and feet, then back to scales and fins when they submerged.

Mika grabbed the siren's small, smooth, warm hand. Mika pulled up, and the siren did a quick flutter of her fins, propelling herself into the air with the help of Mika's pull.

Now standing out of the water, Mika saw the siren looked like a human except for her teeth. Standing shorter than Mika, the siren looked up and smiled with closed eyes. A dimple in both her cheeks kept Mika enthralled with the beautiful creature.

The siren exhaled. Her breath carried a distinct odor, one that Mika couldn't pinpoint, but she wanted more of the smell. Mika moved her head closer to get another whiff, but the siren moved away, caressing Mika's arm and breaking the physical barrier between the two. The siren moved around Mika and toward Addie. Mika's gaze followed, noticing two dimples that curved at the small of her back with every step the creature took.

"Look at you!" The siren slid to her knees and extended her arms to her sides. "Come here, you cute little baby!"

Addie rushed to the siren and brushed up on her chest, and the siren wrapped an arm around him before being licked in the face.

The siren looked at Mika with a smile so big it raised her cheeks and hid her eyes. "He is so adorable!" She giggled when Addie nibbled her ear. "What's his name?"

"His name is—"

"I can't hear you." The siren looked at Addie. "You're so cute, so cute!" She moved Addie away so he would stop nibbling her. Her pink eyes locked onto Mika's, and she smiled. "Do you mind coming closer?" She scooted to the side, and her voice became a deep, seductive hum. "I'd like to hear you better."

Without another word, Mika approached and knelt next to the siren.

The siren moved so that she knelt in front of Mika.

Using her arms, the siren accentuated her cleavage and placed her hands between her legs. She looked up at Mika with wide, interested eyes; she exhaled and smiled.

Mika widened her nostrils to accept more of the siren's breath. Mika's heart raced, her pupils dilated, and saliva began to form inside her mouth. Mika blushed.

"What were you saying?" The siren's smile widened.

"The, uh …" Mika wiped the forming sweat from her forehead. Did the sun get hotter? Something was causing Mika's temperature to rise. "The dog? The dog is named Addie. I saved him when he was young. I almost lost him several times, but he's very strong and brave, and he overcame his sickness …"

"I like him!" The siren nodded without stopping, she looked at Addie and leaned her face close to his, and when Addie's snout touched her nose, she kissed it. "He's super cute."

She is so sweet.

The siren looked at Mika and smiled with closed eyes. "What's your name?" The siren opened her eyes and straightened her face, eager for Mika's response.

Mika swallowed. She brushed her hair behind her ear in a smooth, controlled motion, twirling the ends with her finger. "I am Mika Plum of Yevera."

"I've never met a Yeveran before!" The siren leaned closer to Mika and exhaled. "Are they all as brave as you?"

Mika's face reddened; she rubbed her hands on her thighs and sat her butt on her feet. Mika *was* brave! She knew everyone considered her pretty, smart, or agile, but no one had ever called her brave. That, along with the siren's breath, was making Mika ... aroused. What she didn't know was that the siren's breath carried droplets of aphrodisiacs. Mika just sat there and smiled, continuing to rub her legs and wipe sweat from her forehead.

Noticing Mika's nervousness, the siren changed the subject. "What brings you to the lake?"

A deep breath helped Mika relax. "I've always wanted to visit, ever since I was a girl. I used to swim in the rivers of Yevera, pretending I was a siren." Mika laughed. "I didn't know it would be this beautiful." Mika slapped her forehead. "I meant the lake. The lake is beautiful. I mean, you are too. Not saying you're not beautiful, I think you're very pretty. Well, not just pretty ..." Mika shut her eyes and pressed her palm harder on her forehead.

Shut up! Shut up!

Mika noticed she had stopped breathing when the arousing smell of the siren's breath stopped hitting the receptors in her nose. She continued breathing, but her breaths were nervous and hard.

"Sorry." Mika had tired eyes and exhaled, trying her best not to bite her bottom lip and smile. "I'm just feeling very hot right now. What is your name?"

The siren smiled. "I am Sylisia." She had no last name, so she paused to introduce herself like Mika had. "... of Margarita Cove."

Mika broke her gaze with Sylisia to think. Margarita Cove, she realized, must be somewhere far to the east near the Valentina Islands. The first lands.

Sylisia moved her knees closer to Mika.

"Thank you for thinking I'm beautiful." She inched toward Mika some more, releasing more of her breath. Smelling the juices coming from between Mika's legs, she knew it was time to pounce on her victim.

"Mika," said the siren, moving closer and grabbing Mika's thighs. She leaned into Mika's face. "Do you know what we do here?"

Mika swallowed. Her voice when she responded came out as a breathy whisper. "What do you do here?"

"We sirens, we've been all over the world. We always travel together, but there's one thing incredible and unique about us."

Watching the movement of the siren's luscious lips made Mika want to throw her legs over the siren's shoulders and pull her down between her thighs.

"We don't reproduce like your species." She caressed Mika's legs, from her knees up to her waist, then down the inside of Mika's thighs when Mika inched them open. "We need gorgeous, smart, loving women like you to help us build the next generation."

Sylisia noticed Mika's bedroom eyes began to wane. Before she lost control of Mika, she exhaled and continued. "In return, we fulfill your deepest fantasies." The siren leaned back, smiled, and let her tongue out. Not only was her tongue long enough that it reached her collar bone, but Sylisia could also thicken it at will. A second, smaller tongue protruded from the first; it vibrated when Mika looked at it.

When Mika's jaw dropped, Sylisia raised her eyebrows. "I'll move all of it inside you, and no one will know about our little secret." She made her tongue move and thicken, waiting for Mika's consent.

Mika's heart raced with erotic adrenaline. The warmth between her legs had now turned into a dripping fountain. The thirsty saliva pooling in her mouth forced her to swallow. *What's the worst that could happen?*

"Okay."

The siren stood, latched onto Mika's cheeks, and raised her off the ground.

Mika released a moan, enjoying the gentle yet authoritative fingers of the siren. She opened her eyes and saw a different siren, one with coiled black hair, throwing a stick, then chasing after Addie.

Sylisia twisted Mika's chin toward her. "He'll be fine."

"Yes, ma'am." Mika's heart raced at the grip, the force.

She guided Mika to the water. "Go first, up to your waist."

Mika obeyed and walked until the water touched her waist. She turned around to see the siren dive into the water, her legs turning to pink fins and scales that matched her eyes. The siren swam underwater toward Mika, stopping in front of her. Then she rose from the water and looked into Mika's big, brown eyes.

"Ventus," Sylisia sang.

Wind encircled the two women in a bubble. "This will be your little room while under the water." The siren's voice was deeper, more seductive, more in control. *I know what I'm doing.*

Sylisia pressed her breasts against Mika's and stroked upward on her back until her small fingers wrapped around the back of Mika's neck, applying firm but gentle pressure to the sides. She pulled Mika to her lips, licked them, then kissed her. Mika relaxed and let the siren's lips suckle on hers.

The siren grabbed Mika's hand and placed it on the siren's belly, then up onto her breast. Mika squeezed.

After parting lips, Sylisia spoke. "Don't be scared. I'll keep you safe."

The siren picked Mika up, kissed her again, and both descended into the depths of the lake.

Out of instinct, Mika took a breath just before she submerged. Sylisia told her to breathe, so she did. Only air entered Mika's lungs. Lowering to the bottom of the lake, the dimming sunlight became darker and darker until Mika couldn't see. Then, teal-colored lights from the bottom of the lake appeared, revealing a stone temple at the lake's bottom.

The temple was lit with lights arranged around the perimeter and tops of the temple. Continuing the descent, Sylisia breathed on her, putting Mika into another erotic high.

A hot whisper came to Mika's ear. "You're a unique little princess, aren't you?"

Mika felt her ear being licked. Her earlobes danced around the siren's tongue before juicy lips exchanged saliva with hers. Soft hands squeezed Mika's breasts, and Sylisia's tongue licked down her neck, across her chest, over her breast, and circled her nipple.

"Ahh …" Mika pulled her head back. She opened her legs and could feel her own arousal as it ran down her thigh.

Kissing Mika's breasts, her stomach, her waist, and all the way down her thigh and to her ankle, the siren suckled her way up to position her face between Mika's thighs. Caressing the inside of Mika's legs, the siren took a whiff of Mika's scent then flattened her tongue and slowly, deliberately, licked at Mika, who made a moan she didn't know was possible to make.

The siren passed her tongue through again, again, again, then started kissing and suckling at Mika's sex. Unable to control herself, Mika's legs twitched at the attention. Mika's hands flew to massage her breasts in a desperate need for more pleasure. Sylisia smiled.

She wiped her face clean of Mika's juices, then licked them off her hand. "You taste good." She then extended her tongue, thickened it, and pressed it against her, and Mika gave a surprised, girlish yelp when the siren eased into her.

She's inside me! A siren is inside me!

The siren extended her tongue slowly, and drew it back, then extended it again, giving Mika pleasure beyond anything she had ever experienced or imagined—and all the time delving deeper and deeper.

Soon the avid viscous attention was almost frightening, almost painful, and were it not for the maddening waves of pleasure Mika might have pulled away. But she couldn't, for the manic all-encompassing orgasm building at the very core of her being threatened to unmake her entirely.

Mika twitched with each flutter and flick inside of her. Moving the tongue in circles to push against all of Mika's walls, the siren used the smaller tongue to lick Mika's clit, sending loving shocks throughout Mika's hips. Mika latched onto the blonde's hair and pushed her further in.

The orgasm began to build. A slow, rhythmic rise, she felt the tingle in the exact spot the siren kept hitting. The feeling continued to build, radiating through her until it exploded into an energy that burst inside her body, sending exciting shivers and pressure that made her thighs wrap around Sylisia's head. Her toes crinkled, and the siren released a hot, thick liquid inside of Mika.

Mika moaned "Oh … fuck …!"

Then she started to giggle. Her legs would not stop shaking, her nails dug into the creature's scalp. The siren continued moving inside of Mika until her muscles stopped shaking.

With a slow, gentle movement, Sylisia pulled her tongue out and held on to the end, carrying what seemed to be the most important thing in the world. A siren with brown hair and green fins swam to the blonde and grabbed an egg that glowed like fire. A quick exchange of words happened before the brown-haired siren swam to the temple.

Sylisia brushed Mika's sweaty hair behind her ears and kissed her cheek. Lowering Mika to the bottom of the lake, she wrapped her arms around the adventurer.

Mika laid her head on Sylisia's chest. "That was amazing."

Sylisia looked at Mika.

Mika looked at Sylisia.

Both smiled before she lay back on the siren's chest. Sylisia rubbed Mika's back with her nails.

Mika cleared her throat to speak. "What made you approach me?"

"Your fiery personality, mostly."

Mika looked off into the distance, thinking of the response. She relaxed her shoulders, nuzzled Sylisia's breast with her cheek, and began telling the siren about herself. Mika felt safe with her partner. She rubbed Mika's back without stopping. Minutes passed until Mika quieted down.

"I need to get back to my baby."

"I'm ready when you are," the creature fluttered her fins.

Mika leaned for a kiss, and Sylisia kissed her.

Sylisia wriggled out from under Mika and treaded water in front of her. She signaled for Mika to approach. "Ready?"

Mika wrapped her arms around Sylisia's neck and let Sylisia wrap her legs around her hips. The siren began swimming to the surface with Mika.

Mika looked down at the temple. It began shrinking until it faded away.

173

"What will happen with that egg?" Mika asked.

"Three days from now, your tribute will hatch from her egg in the form of a fish. As she grows into her teens, she will hibernate into another egg, eventually hatching into one of us. The human features will resemble you." The siren looked at Mika. "Brown hair, big eyes." She kissed Mika's nose. "Cute nose. The bottom portion will look pink, like mine, so will her eyes."

Mika's territorial nature kicked in. It would be her daughter, and she felt a longing love for her already. "Can I visit her?"

"Of course! You're part of our family now!" Sylisia stopped just before reaching the surface. "I know our child will be unique. I could sense it when I saw you."

"What do you mean?" Mika unwrapped her legs from Sylisia's waist, but still held on to her shoulders.

A smile appeared on Sylisia's lips.

"Come back in a few months and see for yourself." The siren winked. They both resurfaced, and Mika was told to tread water.

Mika did. Sylisia waved goodbye and swam away. Water rushed into Mika's air bubble until it filled and popped. Mika turned to see the same siren from earlier cuddling with Addie.

Upon seeing Mika, the siren skipped toward her.

"Have fun?" Her voice was deeper than Mika expected, but it sang with beauty. The siren didn't need a response; Mika's face and hair said it all. She dove into the water, her legs turning to white fins the minute they touched it.

Mika embraced Addie and reached for food inside her backpack with a smile on her face and soreness between her legs. Page crossed her mind, but she didn't feel guilty. In fact, she felt like jumping in for round two.

12. STORM

Thunder boomed, sending massive vibrations through the air and shaking the trees around them. Mika stood under a tree, watching the rain fall from the dark-gray clouds overhead. A thick mist extended from the top of the trees to the muddy road in front of her. Thunder rolled to her, then away, exploding nearby and making her flinch.

Addie heeled next to Mika, and he too watched the rainfall. Addie looked at Mika, noticing her lips twisted in a slight frown, her head shaking at the sight of rain and mud.

Mika held her palm toward the sky and used ventus. Wind shot up from her hand, and Mika adjusted her fingers until the wind curved itself, deflecting water away from her like an umbrella. With her other hand, she latched on to the straps of her backpack. Addie followed next to her on the quiet, muddy road westward away from Peak's Lake and north of Mount Cabria, where a small community of homes might provide shelter. Addie scanned for danger, his eyes sharp since his ears wouldn't be able to pick up a threat. Mika focused on the road, debating whether to set up camp or press on.

Hours into the trek, the wind picked up speed, driving the rain sideways into Mika's face. Every second, hundreds of drops made it feel like she was being cut by tiny razors. She hunched over, touched her cold, shaking palms together, and faced them forward.

"Ventus!" she shouted past the screeching gust.

A massive umbrella of ventus formed in front of her, blocking the aggressive rain that popped upon hitting her magical barrier. Condensation left her mouth with every exhale. Hair scratched her ears and whipped her back with every gust that made it past her blockade.

She looked back, making sure Addie was protected. He huddled close behind her, trying his best to stay within the barrier. She hurried toward the dancing flames in the distance, barely visible within the thickening mist.

Mika's feet caused the wooden steps to squeak when she mounted the raised veranda of the first home she saw. The nearest home was more than half a mile away, visible because of the lux orbs that guided toward the toilets. Rubbing her arms, she faced away from Addie when they went under the overhang of the house. He shook the water off his coat, splashing Mika's back and forcing her to stiffen. After a shiver, she knocked on the white wooden door. Seconds passed before she knocked again, this time louder.

No response.

She looked inside the home through a large, square window, seeing a shadow zoom into a room.

Someone is here.

She knocked again, this time hammering the door with her fist, hoping her knocks would be heard over the howling wind and pelting rain. She looked through the window, condensation gathered on the glass. She analyzed the barren living room lit by a raging fireplace. On the opposite wall, a steaming bowl of food sat on a small table; a lonely chair was pushed out from underneath.

Mika knocked on the window. "Hello?"

A male figure came into view from a room. Stopping, he faced Mika. The man lowered his arms and made a slow walk toward the door.

Mika positioned herself in front of the door. Ignoring the cold, she stood erect and held her arms down to her side. Uncontrollable shivers became cold trembles.

The door was opened by a tall, muscular man with messy black hair and burn marks on his forearms.

"Good day," she said with a curtsy—though cold forced her legs to shake. "I'm seeking shelter and have coins. Could you help us?" She waved her arm toward Addie.

Addie tried to be discreet by hiding his growls and tried to control himself by licking his nose. He stepped between the man and Mika, staring the man in the eyes.

Keeping her eyes on the man, Mika didn't notice Addie's reaction.

His eyes scanned Mika, from her eyes, down her side, to her feet. He glanced at Addie, then back at Mika. He smiled.

"Sure." He moved to the side, gesturing Mika to enter. "Please, come in."

Mika wrung out her hair and flipped it to the side. "Thank you so much!"

She had to nudge Addie forward with her legs. She and Addie went inside, though the latter only reluctantly. Mika made a beeline toward the fireplace. When she stood in front of it, the fire grew and curved toward her. She let out a final tremble, and her fingers began to hurt from the switch in temperature. She looked around the room when she heard the door close.

Although the smell of food filled her nostrils, the room was much more eerie than Mika perceived from outside. There were no ornaments on the walls, no plants hanging from the ceiling or near the windows, and no furniture except for the table, chair, and a tall bookshelf filled with books. A small, yellow, diamond-shaped shield lay beneath the window. The only sounds in the home were the pelting of the rain and the songs from the fire.

"Aren't you a bit tall for a shield that small?" Mika laughed, pointing at the shield.

Redness filled the man's face. He looked at Mika. "Isn't it rude to insult someone in their own home?"

A wave of heat flashed through Mika. How could she say such a thing, especially after being allowed in out of the rain?

"I'm so sorry!" Mika covered her eyes in embarrassment. "Please, please, please, I didn't mean it as an insult! I just, I'm just so nervous and cold ... I was trying to be funny." Her hands lowered to her mouth. She didn't look at the man.

"My name is Ron Stannard." He leaned back against the wall. "What should I call you?" He strained himself to keep his voice slow and calm.

"I am Mika Plum of Yevera." She curtsied, better now that she wasn't freezing.

Ron chuckled at her introduction. "A Yeveran?" He looked away, lost in thought. "When I was young, the first set of weapons my father taught me to make were for the Yeveran army during the Imbric invasion."

"Did you ever make a great sword with alexandrite set in the guard?" Mika's response was immediate. "It would've been for a Michael Plum."

Ron looked up in thought; after a few seconds, he shook his head. "No, a magic jewel would've been placed by, you know, an arcane magician long after we forged the weapon."

Mika's shoulders dropped.

"Must have been an important man, for his blade to have a jewel of aevum in it. Your brother?" Ron's eyebrows curved; his lips frowned.

"No …" Looking at the ground, she watched the glow of the fire dance on the wooden floor. "Michael Plum was my father."

Silence let Mika think of her father. She knew he would have protected Cynthia from the necromancer.

Ron took a breath to speak. "What is his name?" Ron asked, pointing to Addie with his chin, even though Mika wasn't looking,

"Addie Plum." Addie stood in front of Mika, creating a barrier between her and Ron. She noticed his mood, and Mika pushed his butt down for him to sit. Mika's eyes looked up to Ron's hands. His arms were crossed, hands hidden underneath his armpits.

Something's wrong.

She stopped for a moment, composed herself, and tried to maintain the same tone as before. "I saved him when he was young. He's very strong," she warned. "He killed an imp once."

Ron laughed. "He looks mean!"

Mika revealed her teeth in an attempted smile, but her lips didn't curve upward. She clenched Addie's ear. "He's not," she said. "Just loyal."

Something is really wrong here. Mika looked outside at the storm. She wanted to leave, but she couldn't be out there. She would die if she tried to set up her tent—that is if it was even *possible* to set it up in such horrible wind.

178

Mika continued petting Addie until Ron spoke.

"Well, Mika Plum of Yevera, would you like some food? I need to serve myself another bowl, since, you know, the one I have on the table is cold now. You're welcome to stay until the storm passes or until you feel like leaving."

The offer, along with Ron telling Mika she could leave whenever, helped her relax.

"Sure, I'll have some food. What did you make?"

Ron held up a finger and walked to the kitchen. A minute later, he returned with two bowls of food. Ron served Mika a bowl of rice with diced chicken and peas. Ron ate his food standing, and Mika ate hers at the table.

"This is delicious!" Mika said a little too loud after the second bite, startling Ron so much he almost dropped his bowl.

Ron took a bite, keeping his eyes on Mika. "Thanks. Cooking is a hobby of mine. I like making things, putting them together, you know, just creating something new and whole. I'm a blacksmith, so it just makes my work better."

"Makes sense," Mika said before filling her mouth with more food.

Once she finished, Ron approached. "Another serving?"

She looked at Ron. "Please, I'd love some more."

After the meal, Mika took off her flower and gazed into the pearl. Black. The dragon must be sleeping.

She set it on the table and untangled her hair. She gazed into the fire, and her pupils dilated. The fire danced in its mesmerizing rhythm, crackling and popping at random intervals. For odd reasons, the fire pulled toward Mika like a magnet. She dismissed the thought, thinking she was hallucinating from her tiredness.

Ron shifted, and her attention turned to the man who sat on the floor. One leg was sprawled out in front of him, and Ron rested his forearm on his raised knee. His eyes were deep in thought as he too stared at the fire.

The light from the fire shone on his sun-kissed skin, accentuating his narrow face riddled with acne scars on the cheeks and burn marks on the front of his face. Messy black hair ended just at the middle of his ears. Ron noticed her stare and looked back. His eyes narrowed for a moment before they returned to the fire.

After some conversation about Mika's adventure and Ron's skills as a blacksmith, Mika forced herself to get some sleep, telling herself that she and Addie would be able to win a fight against Ron if he tried anything with her.

Late in the night, she woke up to wipe the drool from her mouth. She noticed Addie had not lay down and was sitting in front of her, staring toward a brown door. Ron was nowhere in sight.

"You are awesome," she muttered.

We'll leave when the storm passes.

Nightmares filled Mika's dreams, and the childish voices spun around in her head.

~ There's something in the basement ... you need to check the basement ...

* * * * *

Mika moved the chair to the window the next day. The scene from the prior day had not changed at all; the few visible trees bent from the wind's onslaught, and the road had been taken over by the water. She rested her head on the cold glass, and her plane of view shifted. She looked at her reflection in the mirror, took a deep breath, held the air in her lungs ... and let out a long sigh. She'd had trouble sleeping the prior night. The uncomfortable position and bad dreams that she couldn't take control of ran through her mind.

I wonder what Page is doing.

"Ventus, Page." A moderate breeze swept from the northeast.

She remembered her map and wondered what the weather was like in Triumph. They weren't far from each other, and if the weather was anything like this, he was likely inside. She imagined him staring out of his window and looking at his own reflection, thinking of Mika. Her heart rushed with excitement, so much that she kicked her foot forward, striking the small yellow shield.

~ She heard that ...

~ She heard it ...

Childish voices whispered from below her.

~ Her ears perked up when it happened ... I saw them ...

Mika looked around her. She wasn't angry, so why could she hear the voices? Ever since she was a child, she knew the voices only appeared when she was in a state of extreme anger. She looked at her reflection and noticed the flower. The tips of the flower's petals were touching the pearl, telling her she was in a state of surprise, not anger.

A voice came from behind Mika.

~ Mommy is looking for you ... shut up ...

She spun out of the chair and looked behind her. Nothing but the fireplace and fireplace tools. Childish laughs came from below.

Addie whimpered, and Mika shook her head, thinking she must be feeling tired from the restless night and long journey. With a final look at the fireplace, she turned to Addie and rubbed his head. Mika looked at the shield.

The shield's face was on the ground. Worried it would get scratched, she picked it up. Above the shield's arm straps was a name carved and painted in red letters.

"Ashlynn Sorip," Mika whispered.

~ She knows someone is touching her shield ...

The voices came from a brown door next to Ron's bedroom.

~ She's crying ...

Voices came from the fireplace.

~ She's crying ...

"Mika Plum of Yevera," Ron's voice boomed.

Mika's heart raced, and her hands tightened on the shield. Her reaction caused Addie to spring to his feet and face Ron, who stood at the threshold of the kitchen.

"Ron!" She closed her eyes, held the shield over her chest, and exhaled. "You scared my heart out of rhythm!"

"How do you like your eggs?" Ron kept his eyes locked onto the shield.

Mika took a moment to let her heart settle. "Scrambled, please. No runny stuff." She relaxed her grip.

"Got it." Ron didn't move. "Do you mind, you know, returning my shield where it belongs?"

Ron didn't move until Mika placed it below the window.

"I kicked it by accident." Mika stared at the shield.

"If you're bored, you're welcome to the books on the bookshelf." Mika refused to look at Ron until she heard him walk away.

With a sigh, Mika returned her gaze to the window. Addie's claws clicked on the floor, and he approached her. Addie stopped and rested his head on Mika's lap. He too let out a sigh. Still staring out the window, Mika moved her hand to Addie's head and scratched the back of his ear. Feeling the flower relax into a neutral state, Mika reached for it and gazed into the pearl.

The dragon flew above the thick and fluffy clouds that hovered underneath a bright-blue sky then nosedived through the clouds. Passing through the mist, it dove at unbelievable speeds toward a pasture. It spread its wings, slowing its descent. With massive, black talons on both of its feet, the dragon latched on to the back of two cows, one in each foot.

"Food's ready," Ron said over the rain.

"Here too."

The dragon angled upward, soaring into the heavens, and passing the clouds before looking at its prey. The cows' wide, terrified eyes closed, and their cries fell silent as they passed out from the altitude.

Mika looked up. Ron stared at her with two plates in his hands.

"Food's ready, Mika Plum of Yevera," Ron repeated.

Mika smiled. "Any chance there's beef?"

A flash of lighting and a boom of thunder reminded her she was nowhere near her dragon, but the daylight told her it was somewhere in the continent of Irstia.

Ron slid a plate onto the table. Mika scooted in her chair.

Ron leaned on the wall and took a bite. "This is steak with eggs, mixed with rice and, you know, an assortment of vegetables."

"Thanks." Mika finished her bite and swallowed. "This is so good!" She looked at the plate; red liquid from the medium-rare steak seeped onto her scrambled eggs. "The steak is delicious! Where do you get all this from if you don't farm?"

Ron took his time chewing the food before he swallowed. His eyes never looked away from Mika. "A caravan of traders passes every week. They take food from the Farmlands to Triumph and, you know, turn around and bring items from there. Big trading business. Anyone can join."

Ron took a bite. Mika inhaled to speak, but Ron hushed her by raising a finger. He swallowed.

"I make weapons, repair equipment, sharpen tools in exchange for food, money, shit like that. My work is *so* good, they kill and cut the meat for me." He took a bite, swallowed. "My food box has the shrinking and freezing abilities your backpack does for, you know, storms and emergencies like these."

"I've yet to see your work. I'd like to. Is your shop in the house?"

"Just behind it." Ron's answer was immediate. "I built a shed, along with everything I need, myself. Took a lot of trips to Di'Abribel and Vicqua. I'm not letting any man say he took part in forging the weapons I make!"

Mika saw a proud glimmer in Ron's eyes.

"If your smithing is as good as your cooking," she said taking a bite, "then I have no doubt they give you the best of their crops." Mika scraped her plate clean. She moved her hands to her legs, signaling to Ron she was done eating.

"I'm stuffed." Ron said when he walked away from Mika and into the kitchen.

Mika rubbed her stomach, "Me too. Need any help?"

"I got it," Ron snapped.

Okay, then.

Mika returned to the window and fed Addie.

The rain continued to fall, so she gazed into her pearl. The dragon feasted on a cow, ripping out its intestines. Mika looked away right when a piece of flesh snapped from the cow's skin onto the dragon's mouth.

Gross. Hopefully the cow never woke up.

Mika stood and approached the bookshelf. The books were placed with the tallest ones in the middle, smaller and smaller books flanked toward the sides. The only time she'd ever seen a bookshelf so full of books was at the Di'Abribeli library. She pulled out the books and read the titles on the first page, *Small Unit Strategies.* Another one read, *Advanced Strategies of Human Warfare*. Another, *Beginner Strategies of Human Warfare*. Mika picked up a book encased in gold: *Ruling a Nation: Examples From all Kingdoms, Past and Present*.

Mika closed the book and saw her reflection in the gold. *This should be interesting.*

Mika began to read. *Ruling a Nation* began slow, the author explaining the reasoning for his book, but by the hour, the book's tempo had increased, giving detailed instructions and examples on various methods on how to govern and rule a nation. The book was balanced, advising of brutal ways to conquer, yet cautioning to ensure obedient citizens are not abused by their king. Addie began to whine for a bathroom break, but Mika ignored him, too focused on reading why being feared is more important than being loved. Addie whined, and Mika ignored. Addie whined again. Mika looked at him, then returned to the book. Addie began to circle at the door.

"Okay, okay!" Mika placed the book on the chair.

After a long break and a quick scolding of Addie for playing in the rain, Mika dried him off with ventus before opening the door and going back inside.

With a plate in his hand, Ron turned the knob to the brown door next to his room.

"Still hungry?" Mika joked.

Ron jumped. He faced away, then turned to Mika. His voice was deeper than usual, darker, his eyebrows furrowed down to his eyes. "I like to eat while I work."

Mika tilted her head to the side. *Didn't he say he was stuffed?* "I thought—"

"Mika Plum of Yevera," he barked, then lowered his voice when Mika took a step back. "I do not like being bothered while I work."

Mika opened her mouth, but Ron interrupted. "Nor do I like people seeing the inside of my workshop. Turn around until I close the door ... please."

Mika's eyes locked onto Ron's. She looked at the plate, Ron's eyes, the plate, then Ron's balled fist.

"Yes, Ron," she said, and with a slow turn, she faced the white front door.

"Thank you, Mika Plum of Yevera." He slammed the brown door shut.

Mika turned her head, noticed he wasn't in the room, and stared at the brown door. With so much going on in her mind, she didn't remember that Ron said his shop was outside. Mika grabbed the book, moved to the fire, and wondered why Ron's attitude had changed.

Maybe I said something rude again?

She sat in front of the fire and hugged her legs, staring into the mesmerizing dance of the flames before returning to the book and reading for hours and hours until nightfall.

That night, Ron brought out a game where Mika controlled sixteen black pieces, and Ron controlled the same pieces, just white in color. Ron called the game chess.

"My strategy is to think several moves ahead: working on getting there without my opponent finding out what I'm doing. Takes me a bit longer, but in the end, I have all my pieces lined up for a coordinated attack."

"Interesting..." Mika looked at the board. "This one moves like this?"

"Correct, that one moves diagonal as much as you want or until it collides with another piece," Ron instructed.

Mika pointed to the piece with a big crown. "And this one moves as much as I want in any direction, right?"

"Right, the queen."

"I'm going to call her the empress."

Ron sacrificed two of his best pieces so that a minor piece could take Mika's king. That made an impression on her, and Mika vowed to remember that move.

Mika lost every match, even when Ron played without the queen. Mika knew it was time to stop when frustration made her head heavy and anger showed in her face and eyebrows.

"I'm tired," she snapped.

Ron laughed. "Snack before bed?"

Mika looked at Ron. "What type of snack?" She began relaxing her narrowed eyes.

"Have you heard of bananas?"

Mika couldn't believe her ears.

"You have bananas?" Excitement made Mika jump from the chair.

"Just a few," Ron nodded. He waved Mika into the kitchen, and she followed. "Here." He threw Mika a banana.

Mika peeled it and took a big bite.

She spoke with a full mouth. "Bananas are magical."

Ron raised an eyebrow.

"So magical they help with dreams." She took another bite. "Makes them more vivid! More *real*!" Mika smiled, knowing she would have an amazing lucid dream that night because of the powers of the banana.

Trying to seem interested, Ron widened his eyes and nodded. "Amazing."

After the snack, Mika settled into her sleeping bag that she'd unrolled atop blankets on the living room floor. Addie cuddled between her arms, his snout resting on her shoulders, allowing him to keep an eye on Ron's bedroom door. She had finished reading *Ruling a Nation*, so she lay down with *Mental Warfare: Manipulation of the Human Animal* and read it in front of the fire. Hours and hours passed until she fell asleep.

Mika was dreaming ...

"Hey, hey," a whisper called out. "Hey!"

Mika opened her eyes. She was on a bed inside of Ron's living room.

A shadow in the corner waved at Mika. The feeling of a nightmare began creeping into Mika's heart. The shadow dashed past the kitchen door, looked into Ron's bedroom, then went through the brown door.

The brightest color in the room was the brown door, its brass knob shone like gold.

"Hurry!" the voice hissed.

Mika rolled out of bed and walked to the door. Her feet made no noise, but they felt so, so heavy. She looked down to see shackles around her ankles.

"I am free ..." The thought caused the shackles to become water that seeped into the floor. She heard drops fall into a puddle below her.

"Hurry!" the voice repeated.

Mika looked at the brown door and teleported in front of it. The door opened before she could touch the knob. In front of the door was a bright-red storm door with silver handles. It creaked open on its own, revealing stairs that led into a well-lit hallway below.

"Hurry!" The voice came from the basement.

Mika's heart rate increased. She knew it was beating faster, but she couldn't feel it. Instead, she heard it bounce from the walls around her.

THUD, THUD ... THUD, THUD ... THUD, THUD ...

"This is a dream." Mika was confident of it. "This is definitely a dream."

She plugged her nose and felt air run through her hands. An inhale filled her lungs.

"I'm dreaming!" she shouted. She leaned forward and braced herself to fly through the roof and into the heavens above, anxious to escape the creeping nightmare.

"Wait!" the voice cried. "Don't leave!"

Mika stopped.

"Please don't leave!" the voice repeated.

Mika looked at her hands. Tiny hands like a little baby, she counted three fingers. "This is a dream," she said. "What's the worst that can happen?" Mika hovered down the stairs into the bright room.

The stone hall was flanked by thick metal bars set into the ground ... cells. Prisoner cells, two on each side. Mika could smell the mildew in the walls; caused by the drops that had been her chain, they continued crashing into a puddle at the end of the hall.

"Over here ..." The voice was ahead of Mika, inside one of the cells.

Mika hovered forward. The feeling of a nightmare built with every second.

"Don't be afraid ..."

Mika reached the second set of cells. She looked inside the cell the voice had seemed to come from. The cell was lit through a window that let in the light of the moons. A metal cot was against the wall, but there was something behind it. Mika moved to get a better view.

Her heart skipped, and she felt the feeling of a full nightmare the moment she saw a pile of human bones and a skull. Next to the bones was the small yellow shield, and on it, the name Ashlynn Sorip was written in blood.

"Don't let her die."

Mika's dream began to crumble. It was hard for her to feed air inside her lungs. Several unrecognizable voices screamed at her.

"Your mental health is deteriorating!"

"She's going to die!"

"You're dying!"

Mika screamed. "Wake up! Wake up!"

"You need to save her!"

Human shadows crawled toward her.

"Don't let me die!"

"Wake me up!" Mika screamed.

A wet tongue slapped her face.

"Addie! Addie!"

Mika sat up, awake, in the living room. "Addie!"

She latched on to Addie. He'd taught himself to wake Mika during her inescapable nightmares. She took a breath and plugged her nose. Pressure filled her ears. She was awake. She was awake.

"Fuck," she whispered, sure she could hear her heart thumping against her chest.

She closed her eyes, took another breath, and reopened them. In front of her, the brown door next to Ron's bedroom stared at her.

She pushed Addie out of the way and looked at Ron's door, cracked with no light from the other side. Her gaze shifted to the dying fire, which seemed to come to life the second Mika looked at it. She looked at the brown door.

Sliding out of the sleeping bag, she sneaked to the door without making a sound. She grabbed the cold knob and opened the door toward her. Her heart sank when, just a few feet away, she saw a bright-red storm door with silver handles, the same color and shape as the one she saw in her dream. The brown door slammed shut.

Ron towered over Mika, his face distorted in a glower.

"Do not," he said, "go into" –he made a fist, knuckles popping– "the fucking basement."

"I'm sorry." She took a step back when Ron walked toward her. Addie barked. He was about to lunge.

"Go back to sleep," Ron demanded, pushing her out of the way and standing between her and the door.

She signaled for Addie to stop. Ron was, beyond a doubt, hiding something. Together with her dog, she could hurt him, immobilize him, kill him perhaps … but she had no right to attack him, not without knowing what was in the basement. But what if there were human bones?

"Go back to sleep," Ron repeated.

"Yes, Ron." Mika walked to her sleeping bag and slid into it. She stared at the growing fire with fearful tears rolling down her cheek.

I'm getting into the fucking basement, Ron.

13. ASHLYNN

Mika stood on the veranda, brushing her hair, and gazing at the shimmering sun off the puddles outside. The rain had stopped sometime in the night and left a cool, refreshing feeling in the air. It would be the perfect time for tea and a handful of angelwish berries. Her mind was brought back to reality when Addie zoomed past her.

"Addie! No!" Mika stopped Addie right before he jumped into a puddle.

Addie looked at Mika and lowered his head.

Mika flung her hair behind her and approached Addie. "Yeah, yeah. You're depressed. I get it! Life is so hard!" She stood him up. "Inside!"

Addie sprang to his feet and jumped over the stairs. He waited for Mika with a smile. Mika shook her head and rolled her eyes, enough for Addie to understand her mood. Instead of trying to cheer her up, Addie calmed down and waited for her.

Once inside, Mika sat in front of the fire, placed her chin on her palms, elbows on her knees, and looked at the flames. Thoughts raced through her head.

That storm door was red. It was fucking red! He's hiding something in there. I need to see what's in that basement. He's going to want me out soon, though.

"Mika Plum of Yevera," Ron called out to Mika in his normal voice. "Do you want your eggs like last time?" Ron acted like nothing had happened the prior night.

Mika turned. Ron was at the kitchen door with two eggs in his hand. "Yes, scrambled with no runny stuff." When Ron began walking away, Mika added, "Please!" The *please* was hard to say. She turned back to the fire when Ron disappeared into the kitchen.

Mika thought hard on how to get into the basement. Every scenario she played in her mind ended with Ron catching her at the brown door or before she opened the red storm door. His room was too close to the door, and so was the kitchen. If she managed to get inside, it would only be a quick peek. She only had a few hours, if that, to think of a plan to get inside that storm door and see what was inside the basement.

She looked at the door, then away, catching a glimpse of the chess table left out from the morning's play.

Ron's voice echoed in her mind. *"My strategy is to think several moves ahead: working on getting there without my opponent finding out what I'm doing. Takes me a bit longer, but in the end, I have all my pieces lined up for a coordinated attack."*

As she was thinking with her mouth open, Addie's pent-up energy caused him to jump up and lick her face. Part of his tongue slipped inside her mouth. Mika coughed and spit in the fire. She coughed again to get his saliva out of her mouth.

Ron's footsteps told her he was running. "Are you sick?"

"Huh?"

"Are you sick?" He placed the back of his hand on her forehead.

Her eyes widened. *This is my chance!*

"Yes ..." She faked a cough into her elbow and pretended to sniffle. "I've been shivering all morning. The storm must have bested me. Can I stay until I get better? I'll pay more ..."

"By all means," he said. "Just, you know, don't come close to me." Ron distanced himself. "I'll prepare some tea and add vegetables to your eggs."

Mika pretended that shivers ran through her body. "I'll try to sweat it out. May I have more blankets?" She was slow to move her sleeping bag closer to the fire and slide inside it.

Ron ran to his room and returned with armfuls of blankets. He placed them on Mika. She coughed when he was close to her, making him jump back.

"Watch where you cough, Mika Plum of Yevera!"

"I'm sorry." Mika hung her head to hide her smile. When she composed herself, she looked at him. "I don't want to keep you from work. I'm sure you have a lot of catching up to do after these few days."

Mika saw Ron's lips draw into a tight line, acknowledging he had missed work and couldn't miss any more. He composed himself.

"I'll make sure to make you breakfast, lunch, and dinner. Other than that, I'll be, you know, out in the, uh …" –he gathered his thoughts, and shook his head from side to side– "I mean down in the basement."

Mika faced the fire. "Thank you, Ron. You're the best." She moved a blanket over her mouth to cover her smile. *I'm winning this match, Ron.*

Ron hastened back to the kitchen, allowing Mika to think of her plan.

She figured he would go into the basement, either take food with him, or pretend he was working on something. If he hinted at something like that, Mika would pretend she was asleep but listen for his footsteps and listen to what he does, time how long he does each task.

If he didn't do that, he would go outside and into his workshop. He was so paranoid about the brown door that he might keep watch on Mika somehow. Mika decided she would get out of her sleeping bag, pretend to use the bathroom with half-closed eyes, and see if he watched her. On her return to the sleeping bag, she would leave the door open and listen for any footsteps or sounds giving away Ron's position.

Her excuse if questioned about the open door?

Easy, just tell him you're used to doing that in Di'Abribel for Addie.

She smiled, knowing that Ron and his books on strategy were the reason she was thinking this way. The book on manipulation seemed to have opened a door inside her mind that she was longing to unlock.

Several moves ahead of you, and you don't know what's coming, Ron.

Mika heard Ron's footsteps approach.

"Would you like to eat at the table?"

"No … I just got comfortable. I'll just eat on the floor." Mika faked a cough. "Fuck …"

Ron placed a plate and steaming mug within arm's reach of Mika. "I'll get more herbs from the traders. They should, you know, pass by today."

Mika ate her delicious food and drank her tea without saying a word. "Thank you, Ron. I wish I could taste it."

Ron took the plates and went into the kitchen. Mika pretended to sleep. She counted the seconds. Seconds turned to minutes. Eight minutes after Ron took the plates, she heard him whisper.

"Mika … Mika …"

Her heart began to race.

He gave a light knock on the wall. "Mika …"

She did not move. She refused to swallow the saliva pooling in her throat.

Footsteps came. The turning of a knob. A slight thud of a closing door. The creaking of the storm door. One second. Thirty seconds. One minute. Five minutes. Thirteen minutes. The creaking of a storm door. A turning of the knob. Silence. Heartbeat. Heartbeat. Heartbeat. Footsteps. The slight thud of a closing door. Footsteps. Kitchen. Footsteps across the living room.

He's in his bedroom.

Something metallic was picked up. Footsteps. The first deadbolt on the front door. The second deadbolt on the front door. The third deadbolt on the front door. Doorknob. Birds chirping, smell of fresh air. Door closing.

Mika began to count. One minute, three minutes, five minutes. Sliding out of her sleeping bag, she pretended to be half-asleep. She wrapped a blanket around herself and spun in a slow circle. Adrenaline burst through her veins when she saw Ron staring at her through the window.

Pretending not to notice, she went through the kitchen and out to the bathroom. She returned. Still pretending to be half-asleep, Mika noticed Ron peeking his head out from under the window, still watching her.

She opened the front door. "Potty?" she muttered.

Mika had never used the word before. For breaks, she always used the word *bathroom*. Addie knew what was going on.

Good baby.

She left the door open, slid back into her sleeping bag, and covered her head with a blanket.

193

One minute, seventeen seconds later, she heard Ron's footsteps walk past the front door. The stairs creaked from his weight when he made his way to the back of the house and toward his workshop.

Mika couldn't believe he was watching her, but it became the norm when Ron did the exact routine after lunch, and the next day after breakfast.

"Thank you, Ron." Mika slid her bowl of vegetable soup away during lunch the following day. Adjusting the blanket that covered her from head to toe, she crawled on the floor and into her sleeping bag. Lunch was gross today.

Ron picked up the bowl and stacked it into his. "Feeling any better?"

"My head feels like it's going to explode," she groaned, turning to face the fire. A sigh was followed by a fake cough. "Thank you so much, Ron."

"Anything for you, Mika Plum of Yevera." Ron walked to the kitchen and followed his routine of calling Mika's name, going to the basement, and returning before going outside and watching what she did.

Addie sat in front of Mika and stared out of the window, his gaze focused on Ron. After a few minutes, Addie's gaze followed Ron walking away. With some focus, Mika listened and listened until ...

Squeak.

The sound of Ron's footsteps on the stairs, along with Addie lying on the floor and letting out a sigh, told Mika it was time for the next step in her plan.

Mika burst out of her sleeping bag, forcing Addie to jump. She pushed the dog away, gathered all her blankets, and threw them inside her sleeping bag, forming them to make it look like she was still inside. Balling up a thinner blanket, she made the shape of her head and placed one final blanket on top of the bag. With a step back, she looked at the sleeping bag.

This should work.

She looked at the brown door. Addie's gaze followed.

"Stay," Mika commanded.

Addie sat, and Mika looked at the window before hurrying to the door. She grabbed the cold knob, turned it, and crossed the threshold, locking herself in the dark room with the bright-red storm door with silver handles.

Mika dashed to the storm door and flung it open. Her heartbeat quickened. Stone stairs led to a well-lit basement, the same as her dream.

She stepped onto the cold stairs, tiptoeing without making a sound. She descended enough to peek inside. Prisoner cells flanked a hallway. The smell of mildew rushed into her nostrils.

Mika reached the bottom of the stairs and stared down the hall.

She plugged her nose. *Not in a dream.*

Mika sneaked forward. She looked into the first cell. Nothing except a small window that accepted every ray of sunlight from outside. A thick stone wall separated it from the adjacent cell. This cell was mirrored by the cell in front of it.

Remembering her dream, she would find a cot and a pile of bones in the next cell.

But no shield. The shield is upstairs, right?

She walked to the next cell, holding her breath to prevent herself from screaming if something popped out at her. Stepping in front of the cell, Mika's eyes widened, and her jaw dropped. Her reaction mirrored that of a middle-aged woman in tattered leather drabs and shoulder-length black hair.

In a hurried whisper, the woman asked, "Who are you?"

Mika couldn't believe her eyes. She raised her hand to plug her nose.

Not ... dreaming ...

The woman dashed forward, clasped onto the thick bars of the cell, and tried to push her face through the gap between the bars. Her prominent cheekbones told Mika she was malnourished and weak. Bones pressed hard against her shrunken forearms.

The woman spoke fast, as though she would die at any second. "Who are you? Tell me who you are. I'm Ashlynn Sorip. Two Ns. Don't be scared. I'm human just like you." She smiled with wide eyes. "Hey, what are you doing here? Are you going to tell me your name? Hello?" She reached her hands between the bars and touched Mika's face.

Mika shivered at Ashlynn's cold hands. "I am Mika Plum ..."

Ashlynn smiled, revealing sharp canines.

"... of Yevera ..."

"Mika, you need to get out of here. You need to leave now. Call for help, Mika. Get an elder, a guard, a council member, or a paladin. Anyone. Get them here quickly. Please, Mika! You need to do it! Do it now! Go, go!"

"Okay … Okay … Okay, okay, okay." Mika walked away, still wide-eyed from her encounter. She ran through the hall and up the stairs.

"Please don't leave me here without sending help! I can't escape! Please! Mika, please!" Ashlynn cried out.

I won't … I won't … I won't, I won't, I won't. Mika tripped going up the stairs, hitting her shin on the edge. Adrenaline blocked the pain signals from touching her brain.

Mika closed the storm door. She peeked out the brown door, noticed it was clear, and tiptoed to her sleeping bag. Addie sniffed her, and she kicked him away. She threw a blanket over herself and crawled into the sleeping bag.

The fire in front of her had tripled in size, to the point that a normal person would try to tame it. Mika didn't care. The fire seemed to channel her ferocity, exploding into pops when Ron's face crossed her mind.

She closed her eyes, focused, then began planning a way to get out without calling suspicion on herself—or harm to Ashlynn.

Ron placed a plate with fried chicken, mashed potatoes, vegetables, and fruits in front of Mika.

"I'll usually eat fruits for breakfast, but these will go bad if I don't, you know, serve them today."

Mika leaned over the table with her hands between her legs. "I understand." Mika could not make herself look at Ron. She used the blanket over her head to hide her eyes.

Ashlynn Sorip. Mika's head drifted to the shield under the window. *Ashlynn. Sorip.*

"What's wrong?" Ron asked between bites, breaking Mika from her thoughts.

"Nausea." Mika looked at her plate. "I feel like I'm going to throw up. I just don't have an appetite."

Mika wasn't lying. Looking at her food disgusted her. The smell made her want to vomit, despite it being her favorite meal. There was a malnourished captive just below them, and she had been there since Mika entered the house. These thoughts made her flower's petals droop in disgust.

"I see," Ron said with long, drawn-out words. He approached Mika. "I'll take your plate. Maybe I'll eat it, you know, downstairs in my shop."

Mika couldn't control the shivers that ran through her body. Her shoulders lowered further.

Ron knew something was amiss. He towered over her. "Something wrong?"

Mika looked away and shut her eyes. *Fuck ... Fuck, fuck, fuck, fuck, fuck.* She could hear her heartbeat. The flames from the fire dulled.

"No ... nothing, Ron."

Ron took a step back. "Did you go into the basement?"

He saw her flower hide in fear, confirming his suspicions.

Mika froze, "No, well uh no. Of course not. Why would I do that? You told me not to, so I would never—"

Ron struck Mika with a plate, and she fell onto the floor.

Addie attacked.

"Ventus!" Ron roared. Blue electricity sparked, sending thundering booms throughout the house and electrifying Addie, stunning him.

Mika spun to her feet and charged Ron with her dagger. "Don't you hurt my—"

Mika tensed. Pulses of electricity attacked her muscles, and a horrendous cramp spread throughout her body.

Unable to move, she let out a broken scream louder than her pup. She fell, and the pulses continued, forcing her to scream louder.

A boot to the face.

"I told you to stay out of the fucking basement, Mika Plum!" A stomp to the stomach had no effect because of the convulsing muscles.

"Addie!" She shouted between the bursts of electricity. "Addie, *get him!*"

Ron opened the door, grabbed Addie by the scruff of the neck, and flung the crying dog out of the house. Then he slammed the door and locked himself in with Mika and Ashlynn.

Ron stumbled from exhaustion.

As quick as they came, the cramps were gone. Mika dashed to Ashlynn's shield and slipped her arm through the straps on the back.

Ron charged and swung a kick that crashed into the shield.

The shield hit her nose, and Mika stumbled. Her eyes watering, she missed the swing of her blade.

"Ron, stop!"

She dodged a punch.

Ron grabbed a fireplace poker and swung.

Mika blocked the attack, and Ron swept her feet from underneath. She landed on her tailbone.

She screamed.

"I told you…" Ron pummeled Mika's shield with his weapon. "…to stay…" He threw the pick and wrapped his fingers around the shield. "…out of …" He pulled, but Mika held on with all her might. "… the fucking…" Ron placed a foot on her sternum and pushed. "…basement!"

Mika lost the shield.

The shield swooshed through the air, the edge split open her skin, fractured her cheekbone, and cleaved her ear in half. Stars flickered, and her ears rung.

Ron stepped back.

She braced herself up with her elbow. Her hand traveled to the wound that prevented her teeth from clenching. She opened her bloodying eyes. Ron stood above her.

Arms shaking from pain and fear, Mika crawled back, never letting go of her face.

"You bastard," she whispered.

Ron slammed the shield into Mika's knee.

Agonizing screams rang out of her mouth. She hunched over and held on to her shattered joint. The shield slammed into the side of her temple, hurling her to the side.

Whimpers escaped her throat. Unable to move, she lay on the cold, quiet floor. Her vision, blurry and dark, saw Ron raise the shield above his head, rise to his toes, and squat down, sending the shield into Mika's face. She lay in front of the fireplace that faded to embers the moment she lost consciousness.

14. IGNIS

"Are you fucking serious?" Ashlynn's voice screeched along the basement walls. "Ron, what the fuck?"

Ron let go of Mika's hair and she rag-dolled down the stone stairs. Running to Ashlynn's cell, his voice roared like an enraged lion. "Shut your mouth, or I'll make sure you don't eat for the next week, you damned bitch!"

"Ha!" Ashlynn spat in Ron's face. "You think I care, Ronald? You think I give a fuck? Make me die, Ron, make me die and absorb my essence and be damned to the Abyss! Do it, motherfucker!"

Ron bit at the inside of his cheeks but didn't remove Ashlynn's spit from his face. Mika had tumbled to the bottom of the stairs. Ron stomped toward her. He picked Mika up by her long, beautiful hair and dragged her down the hall.

Mika's head felt like a pendulum, swinging and banging on an imaginary wall before curving to the opposing one. Every one of Ashlynn's screeching shouts intensified the headache.

Crash. The world shook. *Crash.*

Mika felt like vomiting, so she opened her eyes.

The hallway spun in spirals in front of her, further churning her stomach. A bump on the ground sent a sharp, stinging pain from her knee, down to her foot, and up her thigh. Her arms dangling at her sides, she realized her weapon hand was closed, but she wasn't wielding her dagger. She began to feel the pain in her scalp just before Ron let go of her hair. Her head bounced on the floor, sending booms into her ears.

Ashlynn's shouts continued.

Ron screamed at her to shut up.

"Make me, Ron!" Ashlynn sang. "Make me, make me, make me!"

Please ... Mika's brain burst with every shout. *Please, shut ... up ...*

The second Mika's thoughts ran through her mind, Ashlynn's voice began to settle until the only audible sound was Ron's heaving and the jingling of keys. Metal scraped against stone.

She was dragged into a cell by her hair before it was released. Her head bounced on the ground. Ron locked two thick padlocks on the metal bars.

"I'm going to slaughter you one day, Ron," Ashlynn whispered. "Then boil you in your own shit."

Ron locked eyes with Ashlynn. He was rubbing his hand with his fingers, balling them into knuckles, then relaxing them. He looked at his feet, took an angry breath, and stomped out of the basement. He slammed the storm door shut, sending painful vibrations into Mika's brain.

Mika stared at the stone ceiling, moving her head left and right to try to orient herself in the spinning cell. She brought her hand to her face. Electricity seemed to escape from her cheek into her skull the second she touched her wound, forcing her to wince and ball her hand into a fist. She would grate her teeth from the pain, but she could not close her mouth. Before moving her hand away, she felt a long, deep, bleeding cut on the side of her face.

Mika rolled her head to the side and closed her eyes, hoping for a peaceful sleep.

"Hey!" Ashlynn shouted, sending a shock through Mika's cranium. "Don't go to sleep! Don't go to sleep!"

Struggling to open her eyes, Mika looked at the cell in front of hers.

Ashlynn was squatting and pushing her face against the metal bars. "Get up, get up. You have to heal yourself. C'mon! Hurry!"

Why is she talking so fast? Mika looked at the ceiling.

"Heal your face before it's too late! Hurry! Do you know vita? Hello?"

Mika inched her hand to her face, again feeling pain on her cheek and nose. She was careful not to put pressure on her wound. Her neck felt tight.

"Heal, use magic! Say *vita* and quickly!"

"Ahh," Mika groaned. She couldn't speak right from the wound on her cheek. She tried again, only using her throat to speak.

"Aqua…"

A stream of freezing water sprayed her face, down her neck, and into her shirt. The coldness caused the headache to pierce into a single point at the top of her brain. She lay motionless and in pain, looking at the ceiling that looked so, so far away. Mika wanted to cry.

Angelis, please, help me. Please help me, this hurts so much …

"Vita!" Ashlynn shouted. "Vita, you idiot, use your vita spell!"

"Okay, right." Holding her hand to her face, Mika managed to groan, "Vita …"

The golden light blinded her and amplified the headache, but the moment her head touched the light, she felt amazing. Every time Mika stopped healing, Ashlynn urged her to keep healing herself in quick, rushed words.

"Keep healing, let's go, let's go. Keep healing. No way you're exhausted! Let's go. Let's go!"

After a few hours of healing her face, the tenderness disappeared, and the headache became manageable. In a slow, controlled motion, Mika sat up and looked at the woman in the cell opposite.

Ashlynn clasped her fingers high on one of the bars and leaned her head on her forearm.

"Well, your pupils are the same size now! I'm glad you know that vita spell. I couldn't have saved you from here. Goodness, I'm so glad you said you were from Yevera and not from Di'Abribel. The Di'Abribeli are assholes! You have to tell me everything that happened upstairs. We have to keep track of all the crimes he's committed! I already know what I'm telling the guards when I get out of this place. I heard the paladins are useful when it comes to this type of stuff, strangely enough. Do you know any paladins? Might expedite things. Oh, geez … am I talking too much? I don't think I am."

Ashlynn let out a nervous laugh and *continued* talking.

"You said you were Mika Plum? That's a cute last name. Never heard it before. Mika is pretty cute too. My name is Ashlynn Sorip, in case you forgot. Two Ns because my dad was an asshole and wanted to make my name *unique*." Ashlynn smirked. "How old are you? What are you even doing here? Have you passed through the Grand Waterfall? It's beautiful. I was there before I ended up here. Do you know Ron personally?"

Mika forced her eyes closed, unsure what question to answer first. Mika opened her mouth to speak, but Ashlynn cut her off.

"Ron is a fucking monster. I can't believe he did this shit." Ashlynn started pacing in her cell. Then she stopped. "Was it you that touched my shield?" She continued pacing. "Anyways, I'm able to hear what goes on upstairs, but I guess no one ever hears me scream from here. Were you able to hear me? He must have this basement protected from sound by magic, or he's just real fucking good at building shit. Did you see any sigils above the storm door? That's where they would be to mask the sounds. Although, I'm not sure if he is good enough to make a sigil!"

Ashlynn continued talking, her words quick, with little pauses in her sentences, forcing Mika to tune her out. Memories came back to Mika: lunch, the shield, the electricity, the fireplace pick, Addie.

"Addie …"

Ashlynn stopped pacing and talking. "What?"

Mika slid her knee behind her butt and, shifting her weight to her opposite leg, she cried out when she put pressure on her shattered knee. Crashing onto the floor, she held her wound, releasing dreadful screams when her knee sent shocks through her thigh, up her butt, and to her tailbone.

She rocked back and forth, ignoring Ashlynn's prolonged talking and explanation on the importance of healing her wounds the moment they happen. Mika's screams turned to cries when she wondered what happened to Addie.

"Who is Addie? I'm not from here, you know. I come from Sytu, so the names you people use are interesting. Oh—" Ashlynn covered her mouth. "I shouldn't say *you people*. I didn't mean it in a rude way! Just like, Celestials … Well, not Celestials, since you people aren't united … Wait, did I say *you people* again?"

Addie stuck his nose through the small, rectangular window that looked in on the cell. Hearing the sniffles above Ashlynn's rambling, Mika turned around to see a wet nose through the opening. He'd caught Mika's scent. Mika crawled to the wall with a smile of relief.

"My Addie," she whispered. Inching herself up the stone wall, she tried her best not to put pressure on her ruined knee.

Standing on her toes, she reached up to the window, sliding her finger over the stone, feeling the warm, wet tongue.

"I'm sorry. I'm sorry … Did it hurt?" Mika remembered the excruciating pain of the electricity. The inability to move just made it that much more traumatizing.

Addie scanned around before licking Mika's hand and smiling. He heard something, looked, then returned to Mika. Knowing Addie was safe made her flower come out from its fearful hiding, its pearls resting open from her state of trust with the dog.

Mika stayed at the window until her calf begged for her to come down.

"Give me a few," she whispered before sliding down the cold, rough wall. She sat her back against the wall and faced Ashlynn.

Ashlynn Sorip pressed her face against the bars of her own cell, staring back at Mika with a big smile on her face. "I've told you a lot about me." Ashlynn smirked.

No way! Really? Mika's patience with Ashlynn was thinning.

"Tell me about you? We're gonna be in here for a bit, but maybe now that there's two, we can plan an escape! That's a cool flower, but damn, you got a nasty scar there. I don't think you healed it in time for it to close properly. Your skin already started healing itself. Not to knock your spirits away or anything." Ashlynn smirked. "Maybe you can try to heal it? Might be a distance thing, I don't know; maybe it looks better up close … or not. You said you're Mika?"

Mika stared at Ashlynn, waiting for her to continue talking. When Ashlynn didn't continue, Mika responded. "Yes." She cleared her throat to make her introduction louder. "I am Mika Plum of Yevera."

"Sorry for the rushed introductions earlier. It's nice to meet you, Mika. Well, not under these conditions, of course." She released a stressed laugh. "I must be dreaming. I can't believe there's another person here with me. Obviously, not a good thing, but I haven't seen anyone

203

other than Ron in a long time. I think about a year! I got stuck in here in the season of growth, and I guess it's growth time again, right? All this rain hits pretty hard around here during growth, from what I've read. Can you believe it? I thought my troubles were gonna start in the New Lands, not in in Irstia ... especially not Celeste! Celeste, for crying out loud! Celeste!" Ashlynn shook and lowered her head. Her head sprang up when she had a thought. "Well, with the necromancers trying to take over, I guess people go on edge? Makes sense to me; I mean, necromancers are devious. They don't just destroy and take over, but they let the psychological part of war take its toll on the people! Their attacks are random and spaced out! You think they won't attack, then" –Ashlynn smacked her hands together– "*boom*, a necromancer attack!"

Mika looked at the cell around her little by little, having to stretch out her tight neck from the fight. She was surrounded by stone walls and a stone floor. The cells weren't dark, for there were plenty of torches on the hallway walls, and the sunlight made her cell brighter than Ashlynn's. Thick iron bars were set into the ground and rose to the ceiling. The gates to each cell were sturdy like a giant tree, immobile because of two thick padlocks.

"Where am I?" Mika looked at Ashlynn.

Ashlynn returned her gaze and shrugged her shoulders. "This is Ron's basement, obviously. You came down here yesterday morning, don't you remember?" Ashlynn stopped talking. She held her hand to her throat. "Damn, I'm so thirsty. Must be some poison he put in the food this morning."

It's because you talk so damn much.

Mika opened her mouth to reply, but she was cut off.

"You need to start healing your knee, Mika. Your vita is strong enough to heal you ... eventually. I would start soon, before it gets worse and the damage is permanent." Ashlynn smirked. Her pupils traveled to Mika's cheek.

Mika moved her hand to her cheek and felt the thick wound on her face. Starting perpendicular to her nose, just below her cheek bone, the cut traveled across the side of her face and to her ear. She cursed when she felt her ear had been split in half and hung like an earring.

"Ouch," Ashlynn said.

Mika let out a frustrated, angry sigh.

"Yes, ouch, Ashlynn. I don't need your remarks, thank you." Mika gave Ashlynn her back and began working on her ear. "Vita."

"Don't be mad at me. I didn't put you here! It was Ron! Geez! I'm just trying to be—"

"I am here," Mika shouted, her voice echoed through the walls, "because I was trying to help you get out of here safely! I could have left you, but I didn't! I stayed because I didn't want him to kill you when I left!" Mika's shouts raised to the point of a screech; the torches on the wall seemed brighter than ever. "So, let me heal myself like you're telling me to! Maybe learn how to realize when someone wants you to shut your mouth!"

The smile on Ashlynn was gone, and her eyes traveled down to her feet. She pushed away from the bars. "All right."

Mika saw Ashlynn's lips shake before she turned around and hid under the covers on her stone bed. Through the silence, Mika could hear the quiet, hushed cries that came from the cell across from hers.

Mika continued healing her face. She turned to the corner and rested her head on the wall. *Mika, you dumb* fucking *imbecile.* She shook her head and let out a sigh. *She hasn't talked to anyone but her captor in a year. Be kind to her.*

She looked at Ashlynn. Little movements of the blankets told Mika she was still sobbing. "I'm sorry for being mean."

Ashlynn's movements stopped.

"It's just," said Mika, "well, I'm quick to anger. Ever since I was child. I don't know why."

Ashlynn moved her blankets so that only her eyes showed. She didn't speak, but she looked at Mika, blinking every few seconds.

"Then I hear little whispers and voices. That's how I know I've reached a point that I need to calm myself. It's nothing against you … I'm just … I'm just dumb. I'm sorry."

Mika crawled on her good knee to the bars of her cell. She passed her arm through the gaps between the bars and into the hallway, reaching her hand to Ashlynn.

Ashlynn stood, covered everything but her eyes in the blanket, and knelt at the bars. She passed her arm through the gaps and reached for Mika's hand. Just the fingers touched.

Healing her wound, Mika slid to her back and extended her arm through the bars again and into the hallway, touching Ashlynn's fingers.

Ashlynn never let her fingers slip from Mika's fingers nor her gaze from Mika's face—it reminded Mika of Addie's stare.

Mika rested her head on the cold, hard ground and redirected her healing magic to her knee.

"Give me time. I'll figure out a way to get us out of here."

Ashlynn's fingers tightened around Mika's.

... and then we'll kill Ron together.

Magic exhaustion came upon her, so she drifted to sleep, waking up every now and then to thoughts of a yellow shield striking her face.

*　*　*　*　*

Ashlynn shuffled to her feet, startling Mika. Having been on the cold floor until sunset, Mika woke with uncontrollable shivers. She looked around the room that bloomed with orange colors from the torches and the sunset sky. The room looked a lot warmer than it felt.

"What's wrong?" Mika held her head.

Ashlynn rolled up a spare blanket. "Bastard is coming down." She tossed the blanket through the bars and into Mika's cell. "Warm up, it's dinnertime."

Ashlynn took a position with her back against the wall. She crossed her arms and waited. Mika heard the creaking of the storm door, followed by Ron's footsteps. The smell of food entered her nostrils.

Ashlynn locked eyes with Ron. He placed the bowl through the bars inside of Ashlynn's cell. Ron turned to Mika.

"Against the wall, Mika Plum of Yevera."

"Hey, stupid ..." Ashlynn made her voice rude and condescending. She had no problem being vulgar. "Can't you see she's freezing? She needs more blankets, fucking idiot!"

Ron forced his eyes shut. He ground his teeth in stress. "Against the wall, Mika Plum of Yevera!"

Mika began to stand but remembered her broken knee. She sat on her butt and slid herself with her hands until her back touched the wall. The window above her radiated orange onto the bowl that Ron placed in her cell.

Where's Addie?

"I saw him earlier. He checked up on you," Ashlynn's voice echoed in Mika's mind, startling her to the point she tried to stand. She locked eyes with Ashlynn.

Ron pushed the bowl further and walked away.

"Don't worry, I'll only be in your head when he's here. Pure privacy after." Ashlynn laughed in Mika's mind. Her voice was much prettier telepathically, for the natural gargles and imperfections in Ashlynn's throat were not present in Mika's brain. *"He'll leave soon since no one is upstairs."*

Ron went up the stairs and closed the storm door.

Mika slid to the steaming bowl and looked inside. Rice mixed with mashed potatoes, peas, and pieces of meat. Mika began to devour the food, healing her cheek to ease the pain when she chewed.

"You actually eat it? I rarely do. Like, what if he poisons it? What if he spits in it or takes a shit and mixes it with the food?" Ashlynn used a sigh as a break. "I do get hungry in here. I used to be so fit. I used to have muscles! Not manly but toned and firm! Anyways, is it good? Do you taste anything in it?" She looked inside her bowl. "Oh my goodness, it's white. What if he mixed it with his semen?"

"Ashlynn!"

"Sorry! I just think of this shit! Who feeds people they've kidnapped three times a day for no reason? It doesn't make sense to me. What if he dragged the ingredients through the dirt? Old ingredients?"

"I don't think he would do that," Mika said.

"Please don't tell me you're defending him! Please, *Mika Plum of Yevera,*" she mocked Ron, "please don't tell me you're defending him."

"Ashlynn …" Mika tried her best not to lash out at her fellow prisoner. "I'm not. I was with him when he would cook. He stayed in the kitchen the same amount I'd expect from anyone cooking a meal."

Ashlynn looked at her food. "But what if he put something in it?"

"I don't think he did." Mika looked at her bowl. "But it's clear he doesn't want to poison you. You mentioned corrupt essence and the Abyss—what did you mean by that?"

Ashlynn sniffed the bowl and approached the bars. "Yes! Yes! Corrupt essence! When you directly kill or cause the death of another *without* justification, mutual combat, or the use of a warrior's stone! Adds the years they were expected to live to your time in the Abyss, where hours feel like days, days feel like years, years feel like decades, decades feel like centuries!"

That's why he keeps her in here and hasn't killed her.

Ashlynn took a deep breath to continue her ramble, but Mika stopped her. "So, why would he add poop and piss and semen and nasty stuff that would poison you and cause you to die?"

Mika took a bite of her food and stared at Ashlynn to strengthen her point. The food tasted pretty damn good.

Ashlynn covered an eye and slid her hand down the side of her face. "You're right. I've just been so paranoid about everything since I got locked in here."

Ashlynn leaned back against the wall with the bowl in her hand. She wanted to say something, Mika knew, but she wasn't saying it.

"What's on your mind?"

Ashlynn stood silent for minutes until she slid down the wall. "It's been hard …"

Mika stopped eating and stared at Ashlynn, trying to figure out what to do or say. She hated dealing with crying people.

Curling into a ball, Ashlynn started to cry.

"I haven't seen my family, my friends, or my Zarl …" A cry of anguish escaped her throat at Zarl's name. Ashlynn continued crying. Not uncontrollable wailing, but soft, choked weeping that could not be contained. Mika knew Ashlynn didn't want to cry in front of her. A lump formed in Mika's throat.

"I want to go home. I just want to leave and never come back here." Ashlynn sniffled. "I don't care if he dies or gets arrested or gets rich or whatever … I … I just want to go home."

A few minutes passed until Ashlynn's cries wavered. "I want to see Zarl."

"Who is Zarl?" Mika slid closer.

"Zarl …" Ashlynn stayed curled into a ball. She looked up to the ceiling, lost in thought. She didn't speak for minutes.

"Zarl is my phoenix. My pet, I guess, but he's more of a companion." Ashlynn smirked, but her face straightened right after. "I don't say pet because pet sounds a little disrespectful. He's my friend, really." She took a breath. "I bought him from a trader the day I left Sytu. Zarl had died at a young age, so his resurrection power had already been used, which means that no one wanted him because, well, who wants a phoenix that won't resurrect, right? Anyways, I bought him, and we bonded on the ship to Azilia, that's just south of Sytu, can only reach it via water. Anyways ..." Ashlynn stopped talking.

Mika scooted to see if she was okay. Ashlynn's eyes were open, and she blinked, but she didn't talk.

"So, you were on the ship to Azilia?"

Ashlynn's eyes snapped to Mika, then returned to the faraway look at the ceiling. "Yeah, so we docked and explored all of Azilia. Horrible place, horrible, horrible, horrible. Good food ... incredibly good food. We took a ship west to Imbris. Beautiful place, not much adventure, though. Anyways, Celeste has always been one for natural wonders, right? So, we came to Celeste, visited Peak's Lake, knew to avoid the forest, hiked Mount Cabria, camped at the Grand Waterfall."

Ashlynn stopped talking again.

"What happened after?"

Ashlynn sat up. The sadness in her eyes along with her tone changed to rage.

"Ron. Ron fucking happened. That piece of shit and I started talking, normally like two decent human beings. Well, the fucking bastard makes a move on me, and I told him to stop. He doesn't stop, Mika. He forces himself until I use my shield to ... shit. So, my shield transforms into any weapon I choose and surrounds me in samurai armor, okay? I'm not a samurai, but the armor is in my culture, so I use it." Ashlynn smirked.

"Anyways, so me and him start fighting, and the little shit ends up knocking me out with his fucking halberd. Hit me right in the face until I passed out. He's not a good fighter, but his electricity spell is strong! Woke up the next day in a tent, bound and gagged, then brought here. He knew if he let me go, I would go to a council elder and have them see through my memory of what happened. He would've been castrated and forced into hard labor at Vicqua. That's why I've been in here! He's scared of the repercussions!"

"No one knows you're gone?"

"I'm sure my family in Sytu suspects something. I was sending letters every month! They're old and don't know where I am!"

"Tell me about Zarl."

Ashlynn sighed. "Phoenixes aren't big; they're the size of a large hawk or a small eagle. Did paladins bring eagles here? Anyways, he used to sleep on the trees, so I honestly don't know what happened to him or if Ron" –Ashlynn forced her eyes shut– "or if Ron killed him."

Ashlynn's mood swung back to sadness. Mika couldn't imagine going through what Ashlynn had, especially with Zarl. Not knowing if he was alive or dead ...

"Are you going to eat?" Mika asked, knowing to change the subject.

Ashlynn placed her bowl down, wrapped herself in a blanket, and lay on the bunk. "No need. I'd rather just die."

Anger boiled in Mika's blood. "Do not say that!" She hated the thought of surrender or giving up on life. It went against Yeveran tradition.

Ashlynn didn't reply.

"You need to eat! You look like a pile of walking bones!"

Ashlynn curled into a ball on her bed.

If only Mika could use ventus to force the bowl of food down her throat.

Ventus... Mika looked at the window in her cell. Addie's nose stuck through.

Mika imagined Addie's yellow eyes and mean face, the color of his fur and his silly smile. *Ventus, Addie.*

A strong gust of wind blew from Addie's direction, knocking Mika to the ground.

Ashlynn peeked out of her blankets. "What was that?"

"Ashlynn..." Mika locked eyes with the woman in the opposite cell. "If you eat, I'll tell you if Zarl is alive."

Ashlynn's eyes widened. "You can't do that!" She sat on her bed, and her blankets fell from her head. "Can you?"

"Eat first," Mika demanded. "Then we'll talk."

Ashlynn hurried to the bowl and scarfed down the food.

"Okay! Okay! That's enough ... No need to get sick."

"Your turn," Ashlynn spoke with a full mouth. She tried to fit her head through the bars.

"What does Zarl look like?" Mika passed her fingers through her new scar. She was happy her ear was able to recover with the help of her magic.

Ashlynn collected her memories. "Yellow flames on the body, blue flames on the beak, ummm, feet were flameless because he already resurrected." She looked up at Mika with worried eyes. "What else do you need?"

Mika closed her eyes, deep in thought. "Is Zarl a common name in Sytu?"

"I made it up because it was the sound he made when I bought him! Are you able to find him? What magic are you going to use? Is there even such magic?"

Mika held her finger up to hush her new friend. She imagined Zarl, an eagle surrounded by flames of different colors.

"Ventus, Zarl."

A moderate breeze swept Mika's hair from the west. Her eyes snapped open, meeting Ashlynn's smile.

"He's alive, isn't he?" Ashlynn was hopping up and down like a young girl excited to play with her friends.

Mika smiled and nodded. "Yes."

Ashlynn let out the stupidest scream Mika had ever heard before and started jumping up and down in her cell.

"He's alive! He's alive! Mika how did you know to do this? Are you sure he's alive? Who taught you that spell? It seems extremely useful, especially if you're like, a paranoid lord or a jealous wife!" Ashlynn laughed. "Oh goodness I can't believe he's alive!" She stopped, looked at Mika, and crashed her forehead into the bars. "Where is he?"

Mika thought for a moment. She used her spell to locate Page, a moderate breeze from the northeast hinted at Triumph. She used her spell to locate Sandra, a moderate breeze from the southwest suggested Di'Abribel. She used her spell to locate Zarl, a moderate breeze from the west. With Mika's recollection of the map of Celeste, along with the triangulation of Page and Sandra, Mika replied, "He's at the Grand Waterfall."

Ashlynn's eyes widened, but her reply was cut short when they heard the squeaking of the storm door. They locked eyes. Ashlynn nodded, placed her back against the wall, and crossed her arms. Mika slid on her butt and sat below the window.

"Go away! Go!" Mika whispered. Her sense of urgency made Addie scurry away.

Ron stomped down the stairs, muttering to himself and slamming something metallic on the stone walls. He placed a large metal bowl on the ground before going upstairs. He returned with another bowl and placed it in front of Mika's cell. He dragged his feet to the first bowl and placed it in front of Ashlynn's cell. He tossed a towel into Mika's and Ashlynn's cells and grabbed the bowls of food before returning upstairs.

"She still needs blankets, Ronald!" Ashlynn screamed, her voice taunted him, made him seem stupid. Ashlynn grabbed the towel and approached the metal bowl.

"Asshole didn't bring hot water since you got here. Don't feel bad, though, it's not your fault. Just been gross not being able to bathe. Over in Sytu, everyone... *everyone*, bathes every day. I was grossed out when I found other continents bathe weekly, some monthly... I heard people from the New Lands only bathe for special occasions! So gross. No offense to you, obviously." Ashlynn smirked. "You do smell nicer than most here."

Mika got on her stomach, crawled to the bars, pulled herself up, and grabbed a towel. Ron stepped at the base of the stairs and handed Mika several blankets.

"Thanks." Mika's response was out of respect. The moment she said it, she didn't realize why she did.

Ashlynn supported her thoughts. "Don't thank this piece of shit! Look what he did to you! Look what you did to her, Ron! You shattered her fucking knee! Her knee, Ron! She was already done fighting!"

Ashlynn locked eyes with Mika, then threw a small rock that hit Ron in the back of the head. Ron was still and silent. His eyes did not move from Mika's knee.

"Hey, bastard!" Ashlynn screeched. "You also fucked up her face! Look at her face! Look what you did to her cute little face!"

Ashlynn continued screaming obscenities, but Mika didn't listen to her. Mika's hands traveled to her scabbing wound. Mika didn't know what she looked like, but she imagined how horrible the scar looked. Although Ashlynn wasn't trying to insult her, Mika's mood plummeted. The moment it did so, Ashlynn's voice settled, and she quieted down.

"I'm sorry," Ashlynn said in Mika's mind. *"I didn't mean to say that. It's not that bad, honestly. It looks pretty neat. I mean, it makes you look strong. Like a man."*

Mika closed her eyes and moved her hair to cover the scar.

"Well, you don't look like a manly man, more like—"

Sadness overtook anger. *"Shut up,"* Mika thought, *"Just ... stop."*

Ashlynn let out a sigh. "Ron, get the fuck out of here so we can bathe. Thanks."

Ron faced Ashlynn; she spit at him, missing and striking the wall. Ron went upstairs, and the storm door creaked shut.

Mika tiptoed at the window. Petting her pup, she refused to speak to Ashlynn, but Ashlynn continued rambling about Zarl.

Mika attributed the rambling to Ashlynn being so lonely after being locked up in a cell for a year with no one to talk to. Mika bathed without saying a word. When Ashlynn went an hour without talking, Mika turned to see Ashlynn fluffing her blankets on the bed, trying her best to make the pillow more comfortable.

Ashlynn sensed eyes on her and looked at Mika. Despite the drop of Ashlynn's eyebrows and downcast eyes, Mika could see the tears that glimmered in the torchlight.

Ashlynn looked away, wrapped herself in a blanket, then got on her bed, curling up in a ball.

Mika turned back to Addie.

After staying alert and scanning for danger, Addie left and returned with a stick. Mika threw the stick far into the silver, moonlit grassland, letting Addie fetch it and bring it back. When Mika got bored, Addie lay on the grass with his snout through the open window. Mika rubbed his head and poked his snout before lowering herself to the floor. She grabbed her blankets and dragged herself to the bars of her cell.

213

"Would you like to hold fingers with me?" Mika asked, reaching into the hallway.

Ashlynn struggled to get out of her blankets. She poked her head out and saw Mika lying on a pile of blankets on the ground. Ashlynn sprang out of bed, lay on the floor, and met her fingers with Mika's.

"Thanks, Mom."

Mika chuckled. "Hey, you're older than I am." She looked at Ashlynn.

"Then what are you to me?" Ashlynn's voice was muffled from the blankets.

Mika looked at the ceiling in thought. "Sister," she said, gazing across the floor at Ashlynn. "I'm your sister."

"The strong sister that takes care of me?" Ashlynn's eyes widened.

Mika smiled; the idea was weird, strange, but a rush of happiness from Mika's territorial personality ran through her veins.

"Yes, of course. And I'll take care of you. It's what sisters do."

*   *   *   *   *

Mika and Ashlynn talked every day, nonstop. Mika confirmed that the long, quick, hurried sentences from Ashlynn were because of her loneliness and isolation. Soon, Ashlynn's speech became smooth and pretty. She was more controlled in her talking, in her manners, and in her movements. Still, Ashlynn talked a lot, but Mika learned to listen to her anyway. Ashlynn was intelligent, and she knew about weapons, tactics, strategy, information about all the continents and regions, magic, creatures, agriculture. Ashlynn knew something about everything.

"Favorite color and describe it using three words or phrases!" Ashlynn asked.

Mika thought of the color red. "It's powerful, a leader among all the colors, and ... it stands out. Everyone notices red."

"Now, same thing for your favorite creature!"

Mika didn't know why Ashlynn asked this, but she went along with the game. What else could she do in a literal prison cell? "Dog. Protective, loyal, attentive."

Ashlynn asked her to do the same for her favorite body or form of water.

"I've never seen one, but I'd say an oasis." Mika began to like this strange game, like she was learning a lot about herself, though she didn't know what she was learning. "They're like a unique treasure; not everyone can get to one. They provide safety, despite everything outside it being bad ... an escape from reality."

"You don't know your soul magic?" Ashlynn asked one day, sounding a little taken aback.

Mika stood on her good leg. She used vita on her wounded knee, allowing her to use it without hurting.

Ashlynn repeated her question in the same tone of voice. Mika glared at her sister. "No, I don't. I don't know a lot about magic, if you haven't realized from this past month."

"Oh, trust me, I have." Ashlynn moved her hand to cover her mouth. She stared at Mika in deep thought. "I'm going to figure out what your soul magic is, although I have a pretty damned good idea." Ashlynn moved her hand; Mika saw a smirk on her face.

The days went on, and Ashlynn, no longer as paranoid now that she had company, began eating more and more. She didn't look like a walking skeleton anymore.

"Exercise with me!" Ashlynn jumped in the air, placed her hands on the floor, kicked her feet out, did a pushup, and jumped back in the air.

Mika's form on the exercise was horrible, but Ashlynn corrected her.

Despite Ashlynn's malnutrition, Mika could not keep up with Ashlynn's workouts. After some conditioning, Ashlynn taught Mika basic and intermediate fighting skills.

"Okay, now, swing your arm," Ashlynn's voice was slow, and she stood the same way Mika did. "And pivot your foot like you're squishing a bug." Ashlynn demonstrated.

Mika followed Ashlynn's instruction; swinging her fist in an uppercut, she pivoted her foot.

"Good job!" Ashlynn screamed. "Now do it again, but use your hips to help you put more power into it. Good! Now move your foot back and send two thrusts into the neck with your dagger and twist it on the way out! Exhale with every strike, so it has more power!"

Mika used a stick Addie brought to simulate her dagger. "Why do I have to twist on the way out?"

"Bleeding." Ashlynn was quick to reply. "Makes them bleed more, it's harder to close the wound, even with magic."

"Have you tried escaping?" Mika asked, hiding away from the sweltering heat that came from the sunlight.

"None of my spells are strong enough to break through these bars. He put time into this place. Still, it's better than when he had me chained to the wall." Ashlynn smirked.

"I've been trying to think of a way out, but I just can't." Mika was practicing some dagger strikes, healing her knee with her opposite hand. "Maybe we can use Addie?"

"We *could* …" Ashlynn thought a moment. "I think I have a way to help with that."

Mika stopped to catch her breath. "Yeah?"

She walked toward the bars when Ashlynn waved for her to approach.

Ashlynn held her index finger to her forehead. A khaki drop of terra magic clung to Ashlynn's finger. "I used this spell to talk to Zarl."

"What do you mean?" Mika's eyes were wide. She didn't look away from the drop of magic.

Ashlynn extended the drop to Mika.

"Terra is an amazing magic, sis. It connects us to the planet and other creatures. It's how it connects you with your flower, and how the flower feeds itself when it's in your hair." Ashlynn shook her finger, coercing Mika to accept the spell.

Mika reached; the gooey magic stuck to her finger, and she touched it to her forehead. It felt like mountains shook and moved inside her brain until they revealed a long-forgotten and distant memory.

Mika saw different images of herself. Each image, she saw herself holding her forehead with one hand, the other hand touching a tree, another image showed touching a tiger, another touching a butterfly.

"Creatures, plants, insects, trees, animals … they all feel, they breathe, they think, they love, they strive for survival just like us.

We're all connected to earth, to terra. When we die, we decompose and become one with everything that has perished before us. The only thing separating humans from nature is the inability to communicate with each other." Ashlynn smiled. "Unless of course, you have this spell."

Mika ran to the window. "Addie! Addie come here!" Her eyes were wide as she scanned the area outside her small window. "Addie!"

Addie zoomed past the window. He tried to stop himself but fell onto his side and slid across the grass, forcing a yelp out of his lungs. He rushed back to Mika and licked her hand with a smile on his face.

"Terra..."

Mika held a hand to her forehead, then touched Addie's. She could feel what Addie felt: excitement, alertness ... hunger. Everything Addie could hear, Mika could hear also.

"Say something!" Ashlynn's voice burst through Mika's ears. "It has to be basic, very basic! You're still new to the spell; you can't just converse with them right away." Although Mika wasn't looking, she knew Ashlynn had smirked.

"I love you."

Mika's heart almost exploded. She felt a rush of happiness she had never felt before. The feelings had come from Addie the moment he understood what the words meant. He broke the physical chain and began running in circles with a smile on his face. He ran back and forth, his eyes wider than ever. He calmed himself, lay on his side, and tried to crawl through the hole.

"Damn, he actually loves you, doesn't he?" Ashlynn's words were direct, rude, and demeaning. "I thought he just wanted you for food and comfort."

"Huh?" Mika turned, confused, and looked at Ashlynn. "What do you mean?"

Ashlynn spit, placed her hands on her hips, and raised her chin. She mocked Mika. "*What do you mean? You're as stupid as that dog, aren't you?*"

Mika furrowed her eyebrows; her knuckles cracked when she made a fist. She closed distance to Ashlynn without healing her knee, anger masking the pain.

"Watch your mouth, Sorip."

Ashlynn mocked. *"Watch your mouth, Sorip."* She laughed, cocking her head back and holding her stomach. She looked at Mika with a smile on her face. "Or else what, Mika Plum of Yevera? You gonna come hurt me? You gonna come *kill* me?"

Mika's lips were compressed in rage, her blood infused with angry adrenaline.

"Please," Ashlynn continued. "You couldn't even save Stacy from a dead human. You think you're going to hurt *me?*"

"Don't bring Stacy into—"

"Oh, don't bring Stacy into it? How about your mother? You can't save your own fucking mother. You'd rather watch her get stabbed to death instead of helping her, and you think you can do something against me?"

~ *Kill her ... kill her ... kill her ...*

Mika's head trembled. She covered her eyes with her palm.

"Hearing the voices? Huh? Hearing the voices, crazy girl?"

I'm not crazy, I'm not crazy.

"Stop!" Mika dug her nails into her scalp. She pulled her hair to inflict more pain on something ... on someone. She faced the corner. If it weren't for the cells separating the two women, Mika would be ripping through Ashlynn's neck with her nails.

~ *She called you crazy ... she called you crazy ... she called you crazy ...*

The childish voices circled inside Mika's head.

"What's wrong, Crazy Mika? Don't have anyone to help you out of the mess you're in? Is that it? Can't depend on someone this time, can you? Maybe if you spent less time getting fucked by sirens, you'd be more useful right now! Oh, wait ... no, because even at home, you have to rely on the government to provide for you ..."

~ *We can kill her... we're here next to you ... let us kill her, Mommy ...*

~ *Mommy, let us kill her ... we can kill her ... she can't defend herself ...*

Ashlynn stopped her insults. Mika tapped her forehead on the stone wall, ground her teeth, and dug her nails into her palms.

"I knew it ..." Ashlynn was alarmed. "I knew it! Mika, look!"

Ashlynn's change of mood angered Mika further, she spun around and held her arms to the side. Ashlynn's cell was darker than usual.

Ashlynn's eyes widened and her jaw dropped. "No, no, no. Mika, lower your hands …"

Mika ignored Ashlynn. She heaved, her chest rose and lowered, and the shaking of her head was uncontrollable.

"Mika …" Ashlynn stepped back. She created a boulder from terra and used it as a shield. "Sis … look at your hands …"

Mika moved her eyes, bouncing them from Ashlynn's face to the shield, to Ashlynn's feet. Mika looked at the hallway; the torches were extinguished.

"Your hands …" Ashlynn cowered in the corner.

Mika looked at her hands. Her eyes widened the second she saw a massive ball of fire hovering above her palms. Its roaring flames popped and swirled around her fingers.

Mika jumped back in fear. She shook her hands, trying to get the fire off her.

It burns! It burns! It burns! It burns! It burns! It burns!

~ Mom … stop … Mom, it's us … stop, Mom … Mom …

Mika realized the burning was her brain trying to rationalize the fire. She lifted her hands to her face and looked at the base of the flames. When the fire became too bright for her, the flames dimmed themselves.

~ Hi, Mommy … you finally acknowledge us …

The voices came from the flames.

The amount of stress overtook Mika. She lost focus, and her control over the fire waned.

With a pop, the flames slithered away, laughing and saying goodbye to Mika. The flames returned to the torches in the hallway.

Mika's mouth was wide open. She looked at Ashlynn hiding behind her terra shield.

"I *knew* it …" Ashlynn undid her defenses and jumped to her feet. "I knew it!"

"What the fuck was that?" Mika couldn't control her breathing.

"Mika!" Ashlynn latched on to the bars of her cell. "Haven't you realized the patterns?"

"What just happened, Ashlynn?" For some reason, she felt like crying.

"Mika! Listen, listen, listen ... You anger quickly. I did that on purpose!"

Mika locked eyes with Ashlynn. "Don't start."

"No, no, no, no. Listen, listen, listen, Mika ... when your mother died, you were inside the house, and the fire was everywhere. It was affecting the necromancer; she couldn't breathe. It was destroying your house ... it was baking your mother. But, Mika, you managed to get out. No burns, no heat exhaustion, no dehydration, not a single singe on your body."

The memory of the burning house replayed in Mika's mind.

"Then you tell me about the imp. Mika, did you know an imp's fire is so potent that it can burn through metal in seconds? For some reason, you, little Mika Plum, are attacked by a blazing imp and come out with blisters! Blisters!"

Mika remembered the nauseating pain caused from the imp's fire.

"Then you go back, and a baby imp, who only knows the difference between family and foe, perceives you as family! Unheard of! That does not happen! Ever!"

Ashlynn calmed her voice. "Then you tell me that Liranda, the deity of ignis and corruption, who only follows matters of war and depravity of humans, decides to follow your boring little walk through the roads of Celeste?"

Mika gave the statement some thought. "So then, I can control ignis ..." She looked at her hands; they had not been affected by the fire. "So what?"

Ashlynn slapped her forehead. "So what? *So what?* Mika! Okay, history lesson! A master of ignis is referred to as a sorcerer, right? By laws of the deities, all sorcerers were culled centuries ago because they were too powerful and unpredictable. Liranda and her ally, Mooredoth, deity of terra, fought a holy war against all other deities because of this. In their victory, and to prevent a second holy war, they decided the world will have only one sorcerer, born at a time only Baigh, the deity of aevum, knows. This sorcerer, though, could harness almost all of Liranda's power. A human with the powers of a deity!"

Ashlynn took a deep inhale. "Anyways, when that sorcerer dies, a random countdown is started for a new one, and a continent can produce only one sorcerer, ever."

Everything started to make sense to Mika. Just before she confirmed, Ashlynn told her what she suspected. "Mika, when you felt Addie's love for you, the torches in the hallway turned blue from the strong rush of emotions. When I made you angry, they hovered to you until they concentrated themselves in your hands."

Mika looked at the torches on the walls. That was why fire always fluctuated when she was around it. That's why it inched closer to her when she was within its reach. That explained the siren's comment of the *fiery personality*, why the egg glowed like a flame. That was why the pops and roars of fire sounded like beautiful music to her ears. Had she paid more attention to her mother and been more interested in magic, maybe, just maybe, she would have realized this sooner. Mika's soul magic was ignis.

Ashlynn broke her thoughts. "You have the ability to be the most powerful spellcaster in the continent ... in the *world*! You've been gifted with the ability to command imps, demons, incubi, ignis dragons ... *any* of Liranda's ignis creatures! You can harness the power of the sun!"

Ashlynn rushed to the bars of her cell.

"Mika Plum of Yevera, you are the only ignis user in the *world*. You are the sorceress of Irstia."

*   *   *   *   *

Mika was quieter than usual following the days of her revelation, appearing to be in deep, deep thought. She would stare at the torches for hours ... hours upon hours. Her lips would move, as if she were responding to something the fire said. Ashlynn understood, so she didn't talk much, but she was scared. She just hoped her sister wouldn't hurt her. She hoped and hoped because, throughout history, sorcerers had been known to be insane, unpredictable, depraved, cold-blooded murderers.

Perhaps Mika would be different.

Ron brought bacon, eggs, and potatoes for breakfast. Since Mika wasn't talking, Ashlynn did a quick workout and decided to take a nap after her meal. A desert filled Ashlynn's dreams.

Zarl stood above a metal shield and dug his enflamed wings onto it, burning the metal, creating a horrifying screech and filling her dream with the toxic smell of burning metal. Zarl moved, and the shield scraped stone under his feet. Zarl began burning into the shield again, only this time, the smell was much stronger, the sound so close it caused her to wake up.

Her eyes fluttered open, and she looked at the window.

Still morning.

A shadow behind her caused her to jump to her feet. She froze when she saw her cell was open; smoke was rising from a melted lock on the floor. With an open mouth, Ashlynn looked at a figure just taller than her. Fire protected the figure's rear. The fire masked the figure's expressions but shone against the ugly scar on its cheek. Ashlynn cleaned her eyes, and she saw Mika's flower; its petals were opened in happiness.

With gentle fingers, Mika shut Ashlynn's jaw and moved Ashlynn's hair behind her ear. The young woman smiled, revealing the most perfect set of teeth Ashlynn had ever seen. Mika grabbed Ashlynn's hand, guided her through the cell, and into the narrow hallway.

Ashlynn stepped over the spot where their fingers spent clasped together night after night. Then she came to her senses and stopped. Mika tugged at her, but Ashlynn wouldn't move. She shook her head and covered her face, releasing small sobs into her cold, sweaty palms. She extended her shaking arms to her sides and looked at Mika with red, crying eyes.

Mika tilted her head and, with soft eyes, walked forward, closing her arms around her sister. Ashlynn let out a single, loud cry that sent violent quivers throughout her legs. Mika returned the embrace, and Ashlynn fell to her knees.

"Oh no you don't." Shuffling forward, Mika pulled Ashlynn to her feet. "We need to go. Zarl is waiting for you."

15. SISTERS

The storm door creaked open, and Mika tiptoed to see through the small gap between the floor and the door. Except for a small ray of light coming from under the brown door, they were in darkness.

With a hand still on the storm door and a hand applying vita to her knee, she stepped up the stairs, careful not to make noise but quick at the same time. Although Ashlynn was frozen behind her, Mika could feel the impatience resonating from her sister. She sensed every feeling except fear emanating from Ashlynn.

"We need to find my gear," Mika whispered, setting the storm door against the wall.

She slid over the floor, placed her ear on the brown door, and listened for noise. There was none, and she waved at Ashlynn to approach.

"We need to find my gear and grab your shield, or we won't survive the walk to Reach."

Ashlynn placed her ear at the door, listened, then put her face inches from Mika's. "Reach?" she whispered, "Why not Triumph? Isn't Triumph closer? What about Page?"

"No." Mika shook her head. "The Lost Forest is on the way. Can't risk you falling out next to that place. You haven't walked in a long, long time. Travel south, rest at Peak's Lake, ask the sirens to swim us across, then hike through the valley into Reach."

"That doesn't make sense! I've been working out! You can't keep up with me!"

"Ashlynn," Mika placed her hand on Ashlynn's shoulder. "Push-ups and crunches use different muscles than sprinting, running, and walking. I assure you, you will *not* make it if we have to run."

When Ashlynn looked at Mika, she noticed Mika's eyebrows had risen into a worried curve. "I'll trust you, sis."

Mika wrapped her fingers around the cold doorknob and turned it in a slow, controlled movement. A slight pull of the door prevented the latch from scraping against the doorframe. The door opened outward, and blinding sunlight flashed onto her eyes, as fresh air scratched the inside of her nose. A smile crossed her face, despite having to wait until her eyes adjusted.

Where would my gear be?

Ashlynn was quick to reply, her voice echoing in Mika's mind. *"Check his room! I heard him go in there after he knocked you out."*

Mika sneaked to Ron's room. She turned to look at her sister. Ashlynn had taken her final tiptoeing step to her shield.

Ashlynn grabbed the edges of the shield with both hands and held it in front of her. A huge smile that revealed her sharp canines appeared. Ashlynn snapped the shield around and slid her arms through the straps. She stood motionless for a few seconds, inhaling until she exhaled in a slow, proud fashion. She turned to look at Mika.

Mika stepped into a messy room that had a thick scent to it. An unmade bed sat in the middle, pushed up against a wall that led to a closet. Across from the bed was a dresser with several items atop it. A pile of clothes lay squished next to the dresser.

Mika surveyed the room. She sighed and turned to Ashlynn. Her sister walked with a smile on her, and eyes on the shield.

"Ashlynn, look on that side of the room." Mika pointed her finger. "Brown backpack, silver dagger."

Ashlynn nodded, peeked out the gleaming window, and began opening and closing the drawers of the dresser.

Mika knelt on her good knee and looked under the bed. Nothing. She stood up and swung her hair behind her head and lifted the mattress.

Ashlynn went into the closet.

Nothing under the bed.

"I found it!" Ashlynn ran out the closet with a smile on her face. She waved at Mika. *"Hurry!"*

Mika ran to the dark closet. There, she saw an open wooden chest. Mika's silver dagger was on top of her brown backpack. She lunged for her dagger, gripping the cold grip with her trembling hands. She unsheathed it, making sure it wasn't damaged, then strapped it on her thigh. Adjusting the straps, she was surprised to notice she had gained some weight under Ron's care. She maneuvered her arms inside the straps of her backpack, looked inside the chest for anything else of hers, and stepped out of Ashlynn's way.

Ashlynn dug through the chest, throwing aside items, coins, equipment, and books until she reached a folded white-and-blue dress with wide sleeves.

"Gotcha!" Ashlynn held the dress close to her chest and smelled it. Her chest lowered with an exhale.

Mika slid her backpack off and opened the biggest pouch. "Put everything in here. It'll all fit because it will shrink."

"No," said Ashlynn, closing the backpack. "This is all I need. I wore this to Dad's funeral. Everything else can be replaced."

Mika looked at Ashlynn, the open chest, then back at Ashlynn. "Let's go."

They stepped out of the closet, and the front door slammed open. Ashlynn raised her shield in front of her. Mika froze. What seemed to be an eternity passed until Mika whispered to Ashlynn. "The bed ..." Mika guided Ashlynn forward. "Under the bed, go, go, go."

Ashlynn crawled under the bed. Ron's footsteps stomped to the kitchen.

"Hurry, Ashlynn, hurry."

"I'm trying, Mika!"

Mika slid to her stomach when Ashlynn gave the all-clear. Ashlynn grabbed on to a leg of the bed, held her arm out to Mika, and pulled Mika under.

Ron's booming steps made it into the bedroom.

Ashlynn faced Mika. Her warm breaths slapped Mika's face. Mika's warm, choppy breaths misted Ashlynn's cheeks.

Ron passed the window; his long shadow hid Ashlynn's expressions. Ron let out a frustrated exhale.

"Why is he here? It's not lunchtime. Does he know we're gone? We're vulnerable from this spot."

Mika remained quiet. When Ron moved to the dresser, she replied, *"I don't think he knows we're gone."*

Ron opened a drawer and slammed it shut before opening another. *"I think he's looking for something he forgot. He's not looking for us."*

"You're right. Shit. You're right." Ashlynn tilted her head toward Ron. *"I'm so fucking scared right now. I'm so fucking scared, Mika. Burn him with your ignis!"*

Mika could imagine the tremble in Ashlynn's voice if she were able to use her throat to speak. *"I don't know how to summon fire. I need to pull it from something like the torches. He'll be gone soon."*

"Fuck!"

Mika ducked her head into her shoulders. Ashlynn stayed still, but her eyes widened.

Heartbeats.

Ashlynn placed her hand over Mika's mouth. *"You're breathing too loud. He's going to hear you!"*

Mika blinked before nodding.

Ron sat on the bed; it sank and almost hit both the girls on the face. "Where is it?" he asked himself. He went into the living room, then the kitchen.

"Did we close the chest?"

"Shit! We didn't! I need to go close it!" Ashlynn began crawling out.

Mika grabbed her by the ear and pulled her back. *"Are you stupid? Stay where you are!"*

Ashlynn was hurt by the comment, but she exhaled and closed her eyes, opening them when Ron stomped into the living room.

Mika saw Ron's feet at the threshold of the door. They pivoted away, and he opened the brown door leading to the basement. Stomps hurried down the stairs. Mika had left the storm door open.

"Move. Now." Mika dug her elbows into the wood floor and crawled from under the bed. *"Move, move, move!"*

Her heart thudded, and she knew Ashlynn's was in the same rhythm as hers. *"What happened? What happened?"* An accidental bang of Ashlynn's shield on the bed forced Mika to crawl faster.

"The basement!" Mika was halfway out from under the bed.

Ron shouted something from the basement.

"He's coming from the basement!"

Mika pushed herself to her knees. The searing pain forced her onto her stomach.

Ron blew through the brown door and stood at the threshold of his bedroom. Mika looked at his balled fists, his torso, then rested her eyes on his red, rage-filled pupils.

"You fucking bitch!" Ron dashed to Mika.

Her flower hid.

He grabbed her hair and slammed her onto the living room floor. "Where's Ash?" He spat. "Where's the Sytui?" He slammed her head on the floor.

Ashlynn shouted a terra spell that surrounded her in a misty brown.

Ron turned, released Mika, and ran into the kitchen.

Ashlynn sprinted out of the room in full samurai armor. The armor's helmet hid her face behind a grinning demon with large, pointed canines that protruded past the chin. She grasped a two-handed katana. She faced the kitchen, then ran to Mika.

"Are you okay?" Ashlynn's voice was deeper and much more serious. "Vita." A flash of vita cured Mika's dizziness. "Use ignis!"

Healing her knee, Mika stood and called to ignis. Flames from the fireplace rushed to her hands, but they were weak. She was an amateur ignis user and didn't know how to control it.

Ron stepped out of the kitchen with plate armor on his forearms. Under the plate forearm guards were brown gloves that held on to a massive, black halberd with silver engravings. Ron's face was hidden under a black executioner's mask.

Ashlynn slid her feet apart with wide legs and held her katana in front of her.

Mika unsheathed her dagger and held a weak flame on her opposite hand. Like Ashlynn taught her in the basement, Mika placed her weight on the balls of her feet and held her dagger close to her breasts. She slid forward and stood next to her sister. Emotions masked the pain in her knee.

Ashlynn broke the silence. "Ever dance with two women, Ronald?"

Mika could see Ron's anger when he tightened his grip on the weapon.

"I'll distract him, you get the door!"

Ron took a step, and the halberd cut through the air.

Mika dove to the door. Ashlynn dashed, sliced his thigh, opened a gash in his arm. Ron grunted. Ashlynn readied for a counterattack.

Mika unlocked the top deadbolt. She slid her hand down to the middle one. "Watch out!"

Ron's weapon crashed into Mika, and she lost focus on the ignis. Ron held her to the ground with his boot.

Mika screamed, and her back cracked.

Ashlynn cut, and Mika scrambled to her feet.

"Ventus!" Ron snapped his hand to both girls.

Blue electricity thundered its way into Mika's body; she tensed and cried when cramps ran through her muscles. Her face smacked the floor. Ashlynn hid behind a wooden shield, insulation from Ron's electric attack.

The halberd swept Ashlynn off her feet and swung toward her pelvis.

"Shit!" Ashlynn used her hands to slide back.

The halberd sliced through her armor, carved through her femur, and stuck itself onto the wooden floor.

Ashlynn's focus withered. Her armor dissipated. She howled, and her blood painted the walls. "Vita!" she managed. The healing magic stopped the bleeding. She used her working foot to back away.

Ron grabbed Ashlynn's severed leg and cracked her in the face with her own limb. He threw her leg and choked the warrior. "Talk shit now, Ash!"

Electricity coursing through Mika faded. She ran to the door, unlocked it, and swung it open. It crashed into the wall, catching Ron's attention.

Ron looked at Mika in time to see her boot curve into his chin.

A tooth flew out of Ron's mouth before he fell to his back.

Mika picked up her sister, who continued applying vita.

Mika wobbled to the door. "We need a torniquet!" she gasped. "We can't fix a severed limb!"

They hobbled past the threshold. The sun burned her open sweat glands. Ashlynn screamed Mika's name on the way down the front steps.

"Almost there, come on." Mika didn't know what to do. They were both hurt, both on the verge of being immobile. Ron would catch them in seconds. Her boots met the grass. She wiped blood from her nose. Her eye caught a glimpse of Ashlynn's thigh.

A creak from the wood behind her forced her to look back. Ron leaned against the railing.

Mika continued wobbling. "Ven …" Ron inhaled.

Mika pushed Ashlynn away. Ashlynn fell forward and rolled. Mika faced Ron, exhaled, and protected her sister.

"… Tus!" Ron shouted, and electricity thundered from his hand, crackled on the wood, then reached Mika. She fell to the horrible, excruciating pain of the electricity. This time she didn't scream; she fell on the grass and convulsed on the ground.

"Get help! Get help, get help, get help!"

Ashlynn stood with crying screams. She hopped a few feet. "Terra!" Her shield turned into a cane, and she used it to gain some distance from Ron.

Ron picked up the novice sorcerer, looked around, restrained her weapon hand, then ran inside with Mika under his arm.

The man sat Mika down and cracked the back of her head onto the wall to further stop the woman from fighting back.

"Drop your weapon, Plum." Ron pushed the halberd against Mika's throat. He pushed Mika's arm further up her back, causing a stinging pain in her shoulder. "I'll break your fucking arm!"

No point in fighting; he won. There's always another move. Help is on the way. Drop the weapon. Drop the weapon. Don't fight …

Mika released the death grip on her dagger. It fell with such perfection, its tip stuck to the wood floor. Although her face looked away, her gaze was stuck on Ron's.

"Who broke the padlocks?"

Mika didn't reply.

Mika closed her eyes and opened her mouth in a painful frown when Ron forced her arm further up her back. "Who broke the padlocks?" he repeated.

"Ashlynn."

"How did she do it?" He stopped pushing up on her arm.

"I was asleep," Mika replied in disgust. "I don't know."

Ron pummeled Mika's face. "Tell me how she broke the fucking locks!"

Mika swirled the blood in her mouth before she swallowed it. She looked at Ron and didn't reply until she was punched again.

"Do you want me to guess? I told you I don't know!"

"Where is Ashlynn going?" Ron's grip cut circulation to her hand.

"She planned on going to Triumph. Has connections there with a guy named Page."

Ron closed his eyes and applied pressure to his eyeballs. He held Mika by the hair and removed her backpack. He pulled out her Dragon Flower when he saw the petals were pointing straight at him in anger. He removed her sheath, turned her around, grabbed her arms, and restrained her hands behind her back, holding both wrists with one hand.

Ron guided Mika through the brown door and into the basement. He stopped in front of the first cell, slid it open, and pushed Mika inside. Mika refused to walk in. Ron shoved her in, but she refused to move.

"Damn it, woman!" He let go of her hands, picked her up by the pants and hair, and threw her into the cell with so much force that Mika flew into the opposing wall, crashing into it and rolling on the ground.

Although her body was contorted and uncomfortable, she had no energy, no will to get up and fix herself. Mika refused to move. She was inches from defeat.

Ron locked the first padlock, left the basement, and returned with a wooden box of tools and supplies. He placed another lock at the top of the bars, so high he needed a stool to reach it. He attached a chain and two more padlocks at the top. He then reinforced the padlocks, bars, and chains with black terra magic.

Once he was done, Mika could sense eyes on her.

"If I find Ash, I'm going to kill her." Seconds passed until Ron moved, picked up the box, went up the stairs, and slammed the storm door closed. A clink told Mika the storm door had been locked from the opposite side.

This time, unlike before, escape would be impossible.

* * * * *

"Mika," a whisper entered her ears. "Mika!"

Mika looked out the window of her cell. Ashlynn's eyes darted back and forth; she squinted because of the blinding sunlight.

"What are you doing here?" Mika was stern. "You're supposed to be getting help. Ron is looking for you!"

"I know, sis. I've been evading him these past few hours. I had to use my dress to make a tourniquet, and all the sticks I found kept snapping. Can you believe this?" A noise Mika didn't hear startled Ashlynn, and she looked up.

She looked back at Mika after a moment. "Rabbit. The grass and trees tell me where Ron is, and they're covering my tracks. Anyways, that fucking bastard. My leg! Can you believe it? My fucking leg!"

Ashlynn slid her leg around and showed Mika the bottom of it.

Mika looked away at the sight of her bones, tissue, and muscles. "Ashlynn! I don't need to see that!"

Ashlynn began to move it away. Mika stopped her. "Wait. Let me see the tourniquet."

Ashlynn showed Mika the makeshift tourniquet she made with her dress and a rusted metal pole. The tourniquet was just above the cut at the middle of her thigh.

Mika churned her lips. "I'm not going to give you healing lessons, but you need to place another one to the highest part of your leg."

Ashlynn moved her leg and looked at it. "Okay, I'll look for another metal pole because they're so easy to find." Ashlynn let out a nervous laugh but straightened her face when she saw Mika's eyebrows furrow.

Ashlynn slid an apple into Mika's cell. "I saw your pup. He's okay. He was sniffing me. I think he knows you held me. Are you able to break free?"

Mika shook her head and lowered it. "He reinforced everything with some sort of black terra. I held my fire to it, and the voices told me they can't burn it. Even if I could," Mika pointed behind her, over her shoulder, "there are locks at the top that I can't reach."

"Ouch …"

Ashlynn's stupid side comments, as always, boiled Mika's blood. "Look, before I head to Peak's Lake—"

"No. Go south, take the road east around Mount Cabria. Follow it south, then east. Once you come to the bridge, Reach will be only a day away."

Ashlynn was quiet for a moment. "I thought you said to go through—"

"No!" Mika held her head in frustration. "No ... I said *we* would go through Peak's Lake. *We* don't know how the sirens will respond to *you*. Just ..." Mika rubbed the sides of her head with her fingers. "Play it safe and follow the road."

Following Ashlynn's request for Addie to catch Mika's scent, she took off her shirt and gave it to Ashlynn. Mika slid herself down the cold wall until she met the warm spot where she was sitting earlier.

"Mika ..."

Mika sighed. "Listening."

"I'm sorry we couldn't get out."

"Me too." Mika knew Ashlynn couldn't see her, so she hung her head in defeat.

"But I'm going to get help. And when I do, the guards will come with an army to kill this bastard. Just stay strong for me, please."

"Right."

Seconds passed until Ashlynn spoke. "You know, when I was young, before my father passed ..."

Mika rolled her eyes; she was not ready for another rambling story.

"... well, he lay on his deathbed with just me in the room. Mom had gone to cook food. I had been crying for days and days. I couldn't stop. I felt like ... I felt like I wanted to die too. Like the world couldn't go on without my dad. He had promised me so much. Adventure, wealth, exploration, stories ... I wanted to adventure with him ... I knew I wouldn't be able to do it alone. I loved him so much. He taught me everything and shaped me into the person I am today."

Mika remembered losing her mother. She had the same thoughts Ashlynn did years ago.

"I'll never forget the last thing he said. Do you know what he said?"

Ashlynn waited for Mika to respond.

Mika cleared her throat to speak. "What did he say, Ashlynn?"

Ashlynn's reply was immediate. "He said, *'Don't give up hope. Once hope fades, the soul follows. When hope runs through a person, she can achieve whatever she wants.'"* Ashlynn cleared the lump in her throat and inhaled. "His last words were, *'Nothing is more resilient than a person who has sprouted the wings of hope.'"*

Mika pressed her lips together and closed her eyes.

Wings of hope ... like Angelis's wings.

"Mika, please fly on the wings of hope. Fly on them until I bring help. Please. Please, promise me you'll fly."

Mika opened her eyes. She looked up, shifted her weight, and stood. Ashlynn clasped Mika's face and pulled at her. Mika looked at Ashlynn. She studied her bruised, heart-shaped face and brown eyes.

"I'll fly as high as you want me to ... so long as you are with me when I reach the top." Mika tilted her face onto Ashlynn's hand and grabbed her wrist.

Ashlynn smiled, a smile not of happiness but sad relief. "I love you, Mika."

Mika closed her eyes. She didn't want Ashlynn to see the tears that formed at the sound of the word. No one except Cynthia had told her that before.

Mika's lips trembled. She released a pout that caused spittle to crash onto Ashlynn's face. "I love you too ..."

Mika cried in Ashlynn's hands, loud, uncontrollable cries that forced her shoulders to shudder and shake. Cries that forced her throat to tighten and her eyes to sting from the tears. Cries that made her scream and curse that stupid imbecile who promised he would find her.

Control yourself. Please, she needs to go. She needs to get help. She's hurt.

Mika composed herself enough to open her swollen, red eyes. She looked at Ashlynn. "Okay. Okay. My wings are open." Mika touched her sister's face. "Promise me you'll come back."

Ashlynn kissed her hand. "I promise, Mika." Ashlynn looked into the cell; her eyes bounced to analyze the inside until she met Mika's eyes again. "It's what sisters do." She stood and used her shield, now a cane, to walk south toward Mount Cabria.

When she was out of view of Ron's house, she picked up her pace, tilting her wobble toward the valley leading into Peak's Lake, contrary to Mika's orders.

16. HEROINE

Ashlynn dug the cane into the ground and leaned on it, both of her hands gripping it with a force that caused her knuckles to pop. Her cane wobbled, wobbled, wobbled, until she lost her balance and fell. The deep, compressing pain from the two tourniquets on her leg shot to her hips. She lifted her face from the ground and opened her dry mouth. Heat exhaustion had set in, to the point that she was not sweating, all her muscles hurt, and confusion had taken over. Her once-pale skin had sunburned, leaving it red and hot. Despite her searing skin, she managed to graze the pink and fuchsia-colored flowers that waved in the wind. Her cracked lips smiled when she saw the pristine waters of Peak's Lake.

Ashlynn took a breath and fought her way to her knee. She leaned on her cane and hopped to her feet. She needed to keep going. Not only was she in danger—and minutes from dehydration—but Mika expected her to be back with help. Mika would never forgive Ashlynn if she gave up and died. Being so close to the water made Ashlynn's wings of hope flutter. If she used magic to drink water, she would collapse.

She hopped forward, her eyes set on the perfect waters. The winds shifted and pushed from behind, helping her toward her goal.

She exhaled. Her mouth was pasty and parched. Ashlynn was moments from death, but she didn't know it. Her primal instincts told her to get water into her mouth.

Splashes of water and running alerted her to danger, but she didn't think to fight. Nothing was more important to her than water. She kept hopping forward. Lean, hop, stand, move cane, lean, hop, stand, move cane. Lean. Hop ... stand ... Ashlynn collapsed.

"She needs water! She needs water!" A woman with a deep, mesmerizing, intelligent voice knelt over Ashlynn. The woman rolled Ashlynn onto her back and touched Ashlynn's face.

"We're here to help. Just stay awake."

Although Ashlynn's eyes were closing, she saw the woman tying her hair into a ponytail with green cordage.

The woman pointed at the water. "Lukewarm! Not cold!" She retracted her lips when she analyzed Ashlynn's maggot-infested leg, revealing a mouth full of razor-sharp teeth. "You! Come here!"

Multiple footsteps ran to and surrounded Ashlynn. Gasps escaped their mouths when they saw Ashlynn's leg.

"Cover her face from the sun," the siren continued. "You grab her legs. Take her to the tree."

Ashlynn felt small arms under her armpits and around her legs. The cane rolled out of her hand and turned into a shield before it hit the ground. The sirens ran with Ashlynn in their arms; another sprinted to the women and began sprinkling water into Ashlynn's mouth.

Ashlynn's tongue danced around her gaping mouth, savoring every sprinkle of the delicious water. The siren increased the amount when she noticed Ashlynn leaning in for more. Ashlynn opened her eyes to see a blonde siren with pink eyes smiling at her. A dimple appeared on each of the siren's cheeks. She squeezed a vegetable, allowing green liquid to drip into Ashlynn's mouth.

Shade covered Ashlynn, and her back was placed on the trunk of the tree.

"What is your name?" the siren with black hair and a deep voice asked to keep Ashlynn's mind active.

Ashlynn took moments to reply, "Ashlynn Sorip ... Two Ns ..."

"Nice to meet you, Ashlynn Sorip." The siren cleaned Ashlynn's saliva from her chin. "Can you tell me what happened?"

Ashlynn's head rolled to the siren. She licked her cracked lips to make speaking easier. "I didn't get your name, it's rude." Ashlynn adjusted herself. "It's rude of me not to ask for your name. What is your name?"

The siren swirled her tongue in her mouth to gather saliva. She held it out and lathered spit on her hand. "I'm a siren, and my name is Delarah." She passed some saliva on the corner of Ashlynn's mouth, her bottom lip, then her top lip.

When Ashlynn moved her lips to speak, she noticed they were not chapped or dry like before. Siren saliva contained healing properties. "Nice to meet you."

"Help me understand you better." Delarah nodded at a siren that whispered a question in her ear before turning to Ashlynn. "What happened?"

Ashlynn looked at Delarah's eyes; her pupils were a scary orange color but had a pretty shape.

"I was attacked ... I was attacked by Ronald Stannard. He ... he almost killed me; he hacked my leg off with his halberd." Ashlynn coughed. "Sorry, can I get more water? I'm very thirsty. I've been trying to get here for the last couple of days. There were no traders on the way. Literally none. It felt like the world ended. I couldn't buy supplies. I need to get to Reach. Can you swim me across the waters?" Ashlynn looked at the siren with blonde hair and pink eyes, the one giving her sips of water.

Delarah lathered saliva on Ashlynn's face. "We can't do that. We don't provide escorts ... but once you feel better, you're welcome to cross on your own."

Ashlynn pulled away. "Are you serious? Why can't you help? Mika is in trouble! She's being held captive!" Ashlynn shifted to stand. "I need to get Mika some help!"

Ashlynn noticed the blonde siren's eyes. "Wait! You're Mika's little friend!" Ashlynn pointed her finger right at the blonde siren's nose. "You're Sylisia!"

The sirens looked at each other. Delarah nodded, allowing Sylisia to speak.

"Where is she? What's happened to her?"

"She's still with Ron. She sent me to get help. We were held captive in his house. The house with the raised veranda and white door.

There's a closet with a brown door, then a red storm door that leads to the basement. She's in there." Ashlynn looked at Delarah. "You need to help her. Mika's been here before. She said you were her family, that she produced a queen or something? I don't know." Ashlynn began to stand. "I need you to help me. We need to kill Ron and free Mika!"

Delarah held a gentle hand to Ashlynn's shoulder.

"You need to rest." Delarah glanced at Sylisia then back. "Sirens aren't fighters. We can't defend ourselves, which is a reason we move from place to place so often. We can't do anything to help Mika."

Ashlynn covered her face. The siren was right … their only defense is their seductive power, their ability to swim away, and their magical capabilities to create havens that block the emotion of anger and conquest. With no fighting skills, no offensive magic, no protection from the magic surrounding the lake, the sirens were nothing more than pretty rabbits that couldn't run fast.

"Mika gave you a child!" Ashlynn was fuming, despite the lake's magic. "She is part of your family! The least you can do is swim me across to the valley! I need to get to Reach!"

The two sirens looked at each other. Delarah signaled for Sylisia to follow her. The two distanced themselves so Ashlynn couldn't hear them and began to talk in low voices.

"Terra." Ashlynn used a spell that allowed her to hear the vibrations in the air through the flowers and the grass.

Sylisia spoke. "… across will help Mika. She's the heroine's mother."

"If it were Mika, we would help. But this woman is *not* Mika, and she has done nothing to benefit us. Her mind won't consent for a tribute either." Delarah's voice was stern.

Sylisia looked at Ashlynn. Delarah followed her gaze.

"I've obeyed your commands since I was born." Sylisia looked at her leader, and the leader looked at her. "Silence me for my disobedience, but today I will defy you."

Sylisia walked to Ashlynn. "We can swim you across! A favor to Mika." Sylisia began applying saliva to Ashlynn's sunburnt skin. "Help me, please!" She signaled to Delarah. "The sooner she gets to Reach, the sooner the heroine's mother can come visit her baby."

237

Delarah's mood didn't change. She helped apply saliva until Ashlynn's sunburn faded.

A young siren with auburn hair and purple eyes gave Ashlynn her shield. Sylisia guided Ashlynn to the water, encased her in a ventus bubble, and carried Ashlynn underneath the waters of the lake. Ashlynn held on to Sylisia and rested her face on her neck. She smelled like flowers. Ashlynn held her breath, worried Sylisia's scent would drug her.

"You don't need to hold your breath, silly!" Sylisia laughed. "I know why you're doing it. Our breath only affects those women who really, really want to do something with us. If one doesn't want to, our breath and scent does nothing."

Ashlynn looked at Sylisia's eyes, then her mouth. She inched her nose to Sylisia's mouth and inhaled. Sylisia wasn't lying. Her breath didn't smell like anything but salt. Ashlynn relaxed, looked at Sylisia's eyes, and spoke. "Mika really liked you. Like, a lot. Not just because of … what happened, but I think she has a crush on you. I think every time she talked about you, she had a smile on her face. Did you make her fall in love? Anyways, what's with this heroine? Sounds intense. From Mika? Is it because she's a sorceress? Can you help me understand?"

Sylisia looked at Ashlynn with an eager smile. "Would you like to meet the heroine?"

"Well, yes!" The excitement curbed the pain in Ashlynn's leg.

Sylisia let out several squeals and whistles from her throat. Ashlynn had heard similar sounds from dolphins when she sailed to Azilia. Sylisia continued the sounds until they were returned. Ashlynn looked ahead, to the side, behind, around. When she looked below, a siren zoomed toward and around them, circling and circling, causing Sylisia to laugh. She stopped, and the other siren stuck her head out from behind the blonde's shoulder.

"Hi, Mom!" This voice sounded like a young version of Mika.

Ashlynn saw a child siren with big, pink eyes and chestnut-brown hair staring back at her. The siren had Mika's button nose and looked almost like her, just more feminine. Ashlynn looked down to see Mika's siren fluttering pink fins.

Sylisia replied, her voice playful, "Hey, hey, hey! This is one of your human's friends! Her name is Ashlynn. Two Ns. What do we say when we meet someone new?"

"Hi, Ashlynn!" Mika's siren swam down, then up, ending closer to Ashlynn than before. "You're really intelligent! I can sense it!" She swam circles around the two. She stopped and waited for Ashlynn's response with wide, interested eyes and a smile.

Ashlynn wasn't going to miss the opportunity. "Why do they call you the heroine?"

The young siren's smile broadened even while her eyes narrowed. It looked like she was going to give chase to prey.

She swam back and held both of her arms in front of her, palms to the surface. Blue fire exploded from her hands and caused bubbles and smoke to rise.

"Because I, Vivinia of Peak's Lake, am the siren who will lead our species into the waters of the deep ocean and colonize an island, where we'll destroy all predators and take up permanent residence!" She extinguished her flames. "Our forever home is waiting!"

Sylisia laughed. "Okay, darling, okay." She shook her head and looked at Ashlynn with a smile on her face. "Children are wild!"

Vivinia laughed. "Can I go back to playing?"

"Yes, you may! It's your turn to hunt food tonight! Let's try to find something on land!"

"Okay! I'll get us a bunny! Bye, Mom!" And with that, Vivinia swam away.

Sylisia giggled. "She's happy all the time like me and has Mika's energy. Wild combination!"

"What about her age? Isn't she just a couple of months old? I mean, from what Mika told me she was here just a few days before I met her. Do siren age like fish?"

"Sixty-six days, to be exact! Our species does age like fish. Early stages are fast, but when we reach adulthood, we stop aging for a long time."

A school of young sirens swam toward Ashlynn and her escort, forcing Sylisia to spiral and dive deeper. She turned around and used her squeaks and whistles. They were deep and fast. Ashlynn knew Sylisia was upset.

Sylisia continued swimming. "Mika's offspring will reach adulthood on day one hundred. Twenty days before that, we teach her the ways of a siren." She looked at Ashlynn and smiled, "The training of her voice, her movements on land, her singing, all the things humans admire about us."

Rising to the surface, they emerged. The bubble of ventus surrounding Ashlynn prevented her from ever being wet, and she was taken to the shore.

Ashlynn saw a siren with long black hair and red fins approach from the water.

Sylisia submerged, collected a raw fish filet brought by the other siren, and dove out of the water, turning into a complete human in midair. The sunlight gleamed around the water that flew off her.

"Here. The others grabbed some food for you." Sylisia handed Ashlynn the filet. "Sorry it's not cooked!"

Ashlynn scooted back. "No worries! I'm from Sytu; we eat raw fish all the time!" Ashlynn accepted the fish. "We wrap it in seaweed and rice. It's so, so good. I can't wait to eat some more. Have you eaten rice before?" Ashlynn dug her teeth into the raw meat. She pulled it from her mouth and chewed her food.

"Can't eat rice!" The siren smiled with closed eyes and pointed her fingers at her razor-sharp teeth. She held her pose for a moment before she dove backward into the water without creating a splash. "Reach is a few hours through that valley." She pointed behind Ashlynn, "Completely safe until you reach the last mountain! You'll see the signs!"

"Thanks for the help! I owe you!" Ashlynn finished her meal.

Sylisia paddled away. "Don't be silly! Just make sure you come back with Mika! I trust you'll save her!" With a wink, the siren submerged herself and swam deeper and deeper until Ashlynn couldn't see her anymore.

* * * * *

"Documents permitting travel?"

The guard at the gates of Reach wore full plate armor painted purple and gold. Ashlynn couldn't tell his expression, but she could see his eyes were locked on her severed leg.

Ashlynn leaned on her cane. She took a breath to speak, allowing the beautiful, salty scent of the ocean to enter her nostrils. Despite the calming scent, her frustration did not wane.

"Documents? Documents? I don't have any documents, sir. I don't even have a pack of supplies!" She shook her head. "I don't have a *fucking* leg! I barely avoided being raped, and then I was held hostage for a year! You guards are ridiculous with this *documents* bullshit!"

Unlike Mika, Ashlynn despised guardsmen.

The guard scratched the back of his neck through a small opening between his helmet and breastplate.

"Look," said Ashlynn, "I need to speak to an elder or someone in charge, because there's someone else in danger! I'm here to get help! I'll give you all the documents I have once you raid Ronald Stannard's house in the subdivision north of Mount Cabria!"

"Stand by." The guard removed his helmet. "Your name?"

Ashlynn hadn't expected him to be overweight, and his small eyes didn't help his double chin. "Ashlynn Sorip. Two Ns."

The guard pulled out a whistle and blew into it five times. "You do know that subdivision isn't in our jurisdiction, correct?"

Ashlynn rolled her eyes. She continued leaning on her cane, refusing to sit down in case the guard attempted to apprehend her for a stupid rule or violation he made up. Ashlynn felt an extreme urge to speak, but she would not speak to this person.

A guard with no helmet, and thick, curly, silver hair and engravings on his armor approached. A sword on his hip and one on his back told Ashlynn this guard was agile and fought with two weapons at once.

He looked Ashlynn up and down, then at the overweight guard. "What's wrong, Coastal Guard Daniel?"

Daniel explained the situation and referred to his supervisor as Coastal Captain Rashawn.

Coastal Captain Rashawn held his head close to Coastal Guard Daniel's ear. He whispered something that made Daniel crinkle his lips.

"Yes, Coastal Captain."

"Miss Sorip," said Rashawn. "I apologize for the delay in allowing entrance into the town. Would you mind if I help you walk to our healer's location?" He held his arm out to Ashlynn.

Ashlynn held her arm out, and Captain Rashawn swung it over his neck. He assisted walking Ashlynn through the gates. The coastal town of Reach was busier than Ashlynn had expected. Trading stands at every corner sold mostly seafood. Octopus, swordfish, dolphin, whale meat, and a thick, long, snake-looking thing that wrapped around several stands. The other stands sold housewares, decorations, small tools, and other supplies citizens on the coast would need.

Most of the homes were single story, while the important-looking buildings were two stories high. Further in the distance, Ashlynn saw massive ships spread throughout the harbor and further past the coast. Reach had conquered several uninhabited islands with their navy.

"If your navy is so powerful, why don't you combine forces with Di'Abribel, Vicqua, and Warrior's Edge?" Ashlynn asked.

"Ego, politics, money." Captain Rashawn's voice hinted at disgust and disappointment. "None of those leaders want the other to have more control. Stupid if you ask me. Necromancers would be dead if they all quit their squabbling."

Rashawn stopped talking when people walked past him. When they were out of earshot, he continued. "I'm just waiting for someone to kill them all and take over the towns and cities in Celeste. Don't give a damn who it is."

Coastal Captain Rashawn took a turn, then another, then went down a long alleyway until he made a final turn outside of a small home. He knocked on the door. An old gentleman with long, golden-blond hair with baby-blue highlights answered the door.

"Another one?" He sighed. He looked at Ashlynn with his tired, brown pupils. The purple, almost black bags under his eyes told Ashlynn sleep was rare on his schedule.

Coastal Captain Rashawn let go of Ashlynn. "Necromancers didn't get this one. Guy named Ronald Stannard did. Heard of him?"

The healer passed an uninterested look at Ashlynn's leg. "Never. All right come in, miss. I'm not carrying you." The man turned around, revealing a slight hunchback, and walked further into his home.

"He'll take care of ya. Get with me in the barracks after you feel better, and we'll discuss this Ronald guy then." Coastal Captain Rashawn began to walk away.

"No!" Ashlynn hopped toward Rashawn. "You can't just wait for me to get better! Ron still has Mika! She's literally in there by herself!"

"Understandable, but she is not in danger."

"You don't know that! He cleaved off my *fucking* leg!"

"When you tried to escape," said Rashawn. "Get with me after you've recovered. My mind will not change." Coastal Captain Rashawn turned, and Ashlynn watched him walk away.

"Damn it," she whispered. With a sigh, she used her cane to help herself into the healer's home.

Ashlynn stood at the doorway. She looked around at the disaster of a house. Table upon table scattered with items everywhere; jars of weird liquids were rolled on the floor. Pots of herbs and plants were squished together on the windows to get as much light as possible. Bookshelves had been hung from the ceiling to create room, and candles in random locations told Ashlynn the place was a fire hazard.

The healer tapped his foot on the ground and stood with his arms crossed. Ashlynn met his gaze, and he pointed to a room. Ashlynn hopped through the house, careful not to knock anything over. She felt that if something were moved, it would create a falling domino effect and wreck the whole house. She passed the healer and caught a whiff of his musk. Old, dried sweat combined with fragrance to hide the odor caused a barfing reflex in her. She hid the reflex with a cough.

"Sorry, I'm just thirsty. I haven't had any water since Peak's Lake. Did I tell you I met a siren?" Ashlynn tried to be cordial.

The healer was uninterested. "Mm-hmm, keep it moving now."

Ashlynn stepped into the room. Bookshelves with jars, books, and dried herbs lined the walls of the room. A lit candle on every shelf reminded Ashlynn of the fire hazard. A long table in the middle of the room had a pillow on it, along with guards to prevent someone from rolling off it.

"On the table." The healer walked to a bookshelf and picked up a bottle with yellow liquid. He popped off the cork.

"I really don't feel—"

"If you don't feel safe—" the healer shouted and locked eyes with Ashlynn. His eyebrows were furrowed and his eyes wide. "—you can get on out! I'm not wasting time on you!"

Ashlynn kept her gaze on the healer. She scoffed. She continued her stare, noticing the healer's only movement came from his inhales and exhales. She lowered her eyes, hopped to the table, and lay down. She turned her cane into a long shield and placed it on her chest, covering her torso and pelvis, worried the healer would fondle her.

The healer walked to Ashlynn, raised her head, and put the bottle to her mouth. Ashlynn drank the tasteless solution.

Looking up at the ceiling, her head began to feel bubbly, fuzzy. She wasn't in control anymore. "I'm feeling very strange ..." She began to sit up.

"Good!" the healer spat. "Maybe you'll shut up!" He pushed her down and splashed a burning liquid that sizzled when it seeped into her leg.

Whatever Ashlynn drank made her too weak to fight or sit up. Her eyes began to close. The last thing she saw was the healer holding a hacksaw to her leg. Ashlynn's consciousness faded the moment an exhale escaped her parted lips.

*　*　*　*　*

"Where in the Abyss did this snow come from, man?" The chattering of the necromancer's teeth was audible from within his closed mouth. He hunched closer to the small fire that melted the snow from around them. Everything was white despite the night sky.

Captain Liam let out his breath to admire the condensation. "I don't know. Means we gotta finish this raid quick. Scouts should be back soon."

The moment he finished his sentence, four scouts were seen running back into the tree line. The pitch-black, moonless sky hid their movements from the paladins and guards in Triumph. Aqua magic covered their tracks in the snow.

"Cap," Ty said between breaths.

"Spill it."

"One paladin at every tower with hundreds of archers on post. Damage to the walls hasn't been fixed. Oil at the top of the gates. Noticed the roofs of the houses behind the walls have been flattened and used as garrisons for archers. Paladin outpost to the north shows usual movements."

Liam took a minute to think. "How are they handling the snow?"

A scout named Allan spoke. "Prisoners and workers clearing it up within the city. Road between the paladin outpost and Triumph is covered in it."

"Do they know about the raid on Warrior's Edge?"

"They do. Doesn't look like they're sending reinforcements."

Liam looked past the trees to Triumph; the fires inside the watchtowers flickered like stars in the night sky.

"Allan, go with Ty. Tell Group Two to set up an ambush between the paladin outpost and Triumph." He looked at the other two scouts. "You two, tell Group Three to cancel their ambush between Triumph and Warrior's Edge. Have them flank Triumph from the south." His heart began to race, and he bounced on the balls of his feet.

"Raid on Triumph begins in two hours."

*   *   *   *   *

"The cold came early this year." Page placed a mug of warm milk in front of Amirra. He scooted a chair close to his wife and took a sip from his own mug of milk. He added cocoa to his, and it had the perfect amount of cocoa, sugar, and milk.

Amirra looked at the child she carried. The child looked at Amirra with wide blue eyes. His chubby cheeks twisted when he turned his lips into a smile. The baby released a happy giggle, and Amirra looked at Page with the biggest smile he had ever seen on her.

"I am delighted his eyes are as monumental as yours."

Page smiled at Amirra. He loved her beautiful voice and her thick accent, happy that after all these years, it was still there. He took a sip of his milk.

"Have you pondered on his name?" Amirra stroked the child's cheek.

Page leaned his elbow on the table. He looked past Amirra and to the dwindling fire in the fireplace. He passed his hand over his shoulder and felt the knob where his arm used to be.

"I think we should name him Carr."

Pity flashed on Amirra's face. She didn't hide her expression from Page because she kept no secrets from her husband—and why *should* she hide her feelings?

"What do you think?" Page looked at his wife.

Amirra moved her chair closer to Page. "The remorse in you flies higher than a dragon, does it not?" She wrapped her arm around him.

Page leaned his head on his wife's breast and embraced her with his only arm.

"We shall honor Sergeant Carr's sacrifice by bestowing his name upon our child."

Page passed his finger across his baby's forehead, then held the baby's face in his hand. He lifted his head, grabbed Amirra's mug, and handed it to her. "Drink some."

He was grateful for Amirra's help; she'd been there for him since he crawled out of the Lost Forest and into her arms the day of the retreat. She was the only person who risked her life by waiting for him.

Amirra blew into the mug and was about to take a sip when the sound of horns boomed into her ears. Her heart raced. She looked at Page—his eyes were wide, and the couple stared at each other. The horns sounded again.

"I must depart!" Amirra stood and placed her mug on the table with so much haste it tipped, and its contents spilled. She ran to the bedroom, and Page followed. Another hum of the horns vibrated through the walls.

"Three means necromancers," Page whispered.

Amirra placed Carr on the bed and wrapped him with blankets. She sprinted to the closet and donned her full paladin armor; its pure white colors and golden engravings denoting the rank of commander. She grabbed the helmet, looked out the window, then dropped the helmet on the floor. She turned to Page, gave him a long kiss, then dashed out of the house, grabbing a glass-steel shield on her way out.

Amirra ran toward the center of the town, trudging through the calf-high snow. Her eyes were trained on the sky. She cursed the moment a mori ball curved into a house in the distance. It exploded, sending screams from the direction of the explosion. A blanket of tenebris was almost done covering the last star.

"Indoors!" she shouted at those who peeked out of their homes. "Indoors at this very moment!" They complied upon seeing her armor.

She continued to the center of the town. The town's king, his general, and his two colonels ran into a house. Amirra followed, bursting through the door. The men greeted her and made a spot for her to stand at a round table. The table showed the town of Triumph on a board. Every building, every road, and every wall was represented in shallow relief; buildings stood as small blocks. Amirra reached down and removed the house hit by the ball of mori.

King Lillian crossed his arms and passed his hand over his chin. His voice was calm and soft. "Talk to me," he said.

General Tim leaned over the table and used chalk to make a circle at the west gates.

"Necromancer pavisers blocking our arrows from striking the approaching necromancer warriors. Spotted at least one platoon" – he passed the chalk in a straight line further west– "of necromancer knights easing in from here."

Necromancer knights were seasoned fighters. They meant trouble.

General Tim scratched his scruffy beard. "South gates are under siege by shadow horse archers." He stopped to think. "I think they said magicians are behind them. We were able to kill two scouts that tried assassinating our archers. Several platoons of necromancer swordsmen and spearmen on both sides." Shadow horse archers were archers on horses that dissipated to shadows before being struck, making them almost impossible to kill, but useless in melee combat.

A short woman in a dressing gown ran from the kitchen with a jug of water and several mugs. She sprinted back to the kitchen. Her husband, who only wore underpants, ran with a bowl of soup and placed it on an opposite table.

The colonel with brown hair and massive muscles looked at Amirra. "Will your forces join us from the north?"

"My paladins are commanded to protect Triumph with their existence. Reinforcement time, three minutes following third trumpet."

The second colonel, a lanky man with a crossbow slung over his back, leaned on the table. "Six minutes have passed since the third trumpet." He tried his best to keep himself from sounding demeaning.

A man in a thick bear jacket ran into the house. His pointed hat told Amirra he was an officer in the Triumphi army.

"Sir—" He stopped in front of the lanky colonel.

The colonel pointed his thumb to the table. "Speak to the table, Lieutenant."

"Gentlemen, lady, necromancers have executed an ambush *here*." He pointed north, between the paladin outpost and Triumph, then looked at Amirra. "Paladins are in combat with walkers; no reinforcements available." The lieutenant looked for questions, noticed there were none, and continued. "Triumphi spearmen are holding all the holes in the walls. Our healers eradicated the mist."

He waited for orders. His colonel told him to stay.

Amirra refused to show emotion. She leaned over the table and analyzed the map. "We are at loss during this siege."

The room fell quiet except for the homeowners serving water and soup. It could be hours or days before the siege ended. Amirra continued looking at the tabletop.

"Is there possibility of raising gates, making it appear as if accident?" Amirra knew the sole reason the officers in the room didn't start an outburst is because they knew her reputation as a strategist.

General Tim replied after a deep exhale. "It's possible. What are you thinking, Commander?"

She pointed to the west walls. "Our archers incapable of striking necromancer warriors because pavisers." She pointed further west near the platoon of necromancer knights. "Behind of knights will be magicians to impede Triumph spellcaster magic. Necromancer knights are capable killers."

The explosion of the house next to theirs shook the ground and paused the planning. When the ground settled, the lanky colonel removed the house that appeared to have been struck.

Amirra continued after a brief check of her surroundings, and she pointed to the south gates.

"Archers unable to strike shadow steeds with mounted archers." She pointed at the north walls. "Paladins engaged in life-or-death fight with walkers. If walkers losing, knights reinforce and defeat paladins."

She looked at General Tim. "We open gates by *accident*, drop oil before time, archers continue firing on necromancers. Necromancers think mistake made, necromancers enter through west gate, think they easy win." She pointed at King Lillian. "You shall be on steed and seen fleeing to town center, to here."

King Lillian bit at the inside of his lips.

"Once we are encircled, I summon lux sun under tenebris clouds. Lux sun invalidates tenebris magic. Lux sun weaken walkers. Walkers die, paladins enter behind necromancers from west gates, flank necromancers. We leave south gate open, allow necromancers flee to south gate, Warrior Edge flank from south, if able to, then … victory."

King Lillian had sat on a chair by the time Amirra finished her plan. He shook his leg with such force his chair rattled. "Anyone have any better ideas?"

The room was quiet. The colonel with the big muscles slurped on his spoonful of soup.

"Lieutenant, bring me my horse. The rest of you, relay the plan and execute it immediately." He watched his officers leave, then stuck his gaze on Amirra. "This plan of yours will cause many citizens to die."

Amirra pressed her lips together. She knew citizens would die, but there was no way to prevent it. Not only that, she knew she would collapse from magic exhaustion the moment she summoned the lux sun. This was the best plan, given the circumstances, and she was willing to sacrifice herself for her town and family to live. She inhaled and let all the air out through her nose.

"If necromancer win, everyone captured, everyone tortured, everyone dies."

17. ROSA

Mika looked out the window of her cell. The sun's powerful rays reflected from the snow and into her eyes. Mika didn't need to squint; in fact, she could barely see past the small, dark blur of her vision.

Every month she spent in the basement took a toll on her eyesight. Not from anything she did or anything in the cell, but from the offer she made to the deities five months ago during the season of growth. What first started as shrinking vision was now a full blur; her peripheral vision was gone, and it was like looking through a keyhole twenty-four hours a day. She could see shapes but not details. Mika knew that in a few more days, she would be blind. The deities now owned her eyesight, a payment for failing her adventure.

Knowing this, she continued looking out the window, taking in the last season of endurance she would ever see. Even though the snow was melting and dying under the sun's heat, the scene was peaceful and quiet. The tree branches further ahead were bending under the weight of the snow, and no birds chirped on this quiet morning. Mika shivered in her blanket and sighed, hoping Addie wasn't uncomfortable from the cold.

The storm door unlocked, opened, and Ron's footsteps made their way down the cold stone stairs. Today, he was dressed in tough boots, thick trousers, and a heavy furry coat made from bear hide. He carried a steaming bowl in his hand.

Mika couldn't see any of this. All she saw was Ron wearing thick clothes and carrying something round.

Mika limped to the wall. Ron placed the bowl on the floor.

"Hey, Ron." Her voice was sweet and manipulative; all the books she'd read revealed her sociopathic tendencies. "It's getting cold. Can I get more blankets? If you could, I'd also like another book. War strategy or leadership, please! The manipulation ones are scary ..."

Ron didn't reply. He walked up the stairs and locked the storm door.

Weird ... he usually replies. Mika wondered what was wrong with him. She could feel a different energy emanating from Ron.

She picked up the bowl and held it inches from her eyes. Thick oatmeal sprinkled with cinnamon and brown sugar. Mika scarfed down her meal and scraped the bowl with her spoon. With a burp, she tossed the bowl out of her cell. The bowl bounced back when it hit the bars of the cell across from hers.

She waited and waited.

Today, Ron didn't return to pick up the bowl or bring items she requested, further telling Mika that something was not right.

Still, Mika went on with her usual routine. She prayed to Angelis the first hour after breakfast. Then she brushed her hair with her fingers until the sun shone on a particular crack on the wall. After, she applied vita to her injured knee; she was now able to walk without having to heal herself. Through so many months of constant vita manipulation, she understood how to think of the magic, how to twist her fingers, and what to concentrate on to use more powerful, complicated vita spells. When the healing glow and thinking of bones, muscles, tissues, and all other body parts bored her, she would read, but she finished her most recent book, titled *Seductress: The Power of the Female*. She had read so many books on psychology, war strategy, leadership, unit tactics, and military tradition, she felt like founding an army of mercenaries and taking over a town.

Since Ron didn't bring a new book, she skipped reading and began to focus on the torches on the wall.

Mika held her hand to the torches, and the fire replied by pulling toward her. Once she heard their voices, she knew they were listening.

~ *Hi, Mommy ... Mommy's calling ...*
~ *Hey, give that back ...*

~ Shut up, stupid ...
~ DON'T CALL ME STUPID ...

"Come here," Mika said, laughing at the little voices. They sounded so cute, so childish, free, playful. The flames from the five torches flung themselves off and slithered to Mika. They stood in a line in front of the sorcerer.

~ What's the white stuff ...
~ Did it come from the sky ...
~ I think that can kill us ...
~ Don't say that ...

Mika learned that the more she argued, the more she yelled, the more explosive, unpredictable, uncontrollable the voices, and the fire, became, but being the owner of an obedient dog prepared her for this moment.

"Shut up and come here."

Mika held her palm to the ceiling, and the flames slithered together until they formed a ball of fire in her hand. The fire twisted, pulled, pushed.

~ It's my turn today ...
~ No, it's mine ...
~ Hey, you had it the day before the other day ...
~ THAT MADE NO SENSE ... IT'S MY TURN ...

"Pick." Mika's voice was calm but stern, as though she talked to an upset child. "Pick before I send you back home."

The flame stopped pulling and hovered above Mika's palm. Its warmth comforted her, and the growing roars were a beautiful song to her ears. The voice was much clearer now.

~ Aww, Mom ... he's so mean ... a bully ... no one else likes him ...

She threw the ball of fire, recalled it, stretched it between both her hands, and held it with both palms and pushed it forward like a flamethrower. The flame escaped with so much force, Mika had to push forward to prevent her hands from parting. If only she'd known all this when she tried escaping with Ashlynn.

Mika tossed the flame forward, sending it through the bars of her cell, into the opposite cell, and out the window before she pulled her arm back. She watched the flame fly too fast on the return; she pan-icked, twisted her hand up, and the flame disappeared over the window.

"No!" Mika slapped her hands on the ground. Now she had to go all day without fire in the basement. Ron would wonder why the flames went out, but he would relight them at dinner.

Mika hung her head. *Dammit.*

A gentle hum approached from the cell. Mika looked up and saw the flame slithering through the window until it hovered in the middle of the cell.

~ See ... we can learn too ...

Mika smiled. "Never said you couldn't." She held her hand to the flame, and it approached. Mika smiled at her new power, wishing she could see what they looked like underneath those childlike voices.

Addie panted, telling Mika he had visited her for the day.

~ Wait ... WAIT ... before you go ...

Mika looked at the fire that began to slither away and separate onto the five torches.

~ Say our name ...
~ Yes ... YES ... say our names ...
~ Call to us ...

Mika held her palm to the ceiling. "Ignis!"

The flames on the torches disappeared, and a ball of fire explod-ed out of Mika's palm, hovering above her skin.

~ You can only use us when we're around ... for now ...
~ Yes, but ... close your palm and open it ... then call our names ...

Mika closed her palm. In a slow, controlled motion, she reopened it, and the flame was gone. She looked at the torches. No flames. She listened for voices ... nothing.

"Ignis." The same ball of fire popped onto her hand.

~ See ... SEE ... you can save us for later ...

Mika held her palm to the torches, and the flames slithered away in childish laughter. Mika watched them dance in their natural rhythm until they noticed she was watching. They pulled toward her, but she looked away and gave her attention to her pup.

Today, Addie brought her gifts. He first dropped a small acorn that rolled through the window and into the cell. He ran away and brought a smooth, black rock. Lastly, Addie brought a long, wooden stick. When Mika grabbed the stick, Addie spread his legs and smiled.

Mika laughed. She threw the stick far through the small hole, trying to her best to watch Addie run after it. She knew his tongue was flapping up and down from the side of his mouth. Using her spell to communicate a thanks, Mika ordered him to hunt for food.

After Addie left, Mika sat with her back to the wall and looked at Ashlynn's cell. She twirled the acorn and rock in her hand.

"Ventus," she said, imagining Ashlynn's face, "Ashlynn Sorip."

A moderate breeze blew from Di'Abribel. Ashlynn had moved from Reach to Di'Abribel overnight.

Mika's eyebrows furrowed. She pressed her lips together. Her nails scraped against the stone floor.

Four months had passed since Ashlynn escaped. She was still alive. So, why wasn't she bringing help? Why hadn't she sent a group of guards or a group of paladins or a mercenary? Why had she not sent anyone? Ashlynn would've had to pass just a few miles from Mika's location when she went from Reach to Di'Abribel, yet no help. What was keeping Ashlynn from sending help? What if the guards were friends with Ron? What if—here the flames grew in potency— what if they were protecting him because he made them weapons?

The anger in Mika forced her to her feet. She used Addie's stick to practice her fighting moves. She practiced the moves and did the workouts her former prison mate taught her.

"Why do you want me to do these five moves over and over and over?" *Mika had asked once, rolling her eyes and dropping her hands to her sides.*

Like always, Ashlynn's reply was instantaneous. "Because it's better to know these five to perfection than to know hundreds of them and mess them up when your adrenaline is through the roof! When I was training with my dad, he told me that under stress we resort to our last level of training. You want your last level of training to be a move you only practiced once or a move you practiced hundreds of times?"

Mika did push-ups, remembering another conversation.

"Are fights fast?" Mika had asked. "I feel like they end within seconds."

When her arms shook and she wasn't able to do another push-up, Mika kicked her legs through her arms, lay on her back, and did sit-ups.

"Super-fast! Mika, they're not like the fights you see at plays or read in books. Fights can be over in a few seconds. Didn't you see how fast you tired after fighting that imp? No one can last over five minutes in a full fight, exerting maximum energy and force. End the fight quick. Fight dirty. Fuck honor!"

Mika practiced her favorite move. She practiced it slowly, increasing her speed until she did it so fast, it became sloppy. All of Mika's moves were simple, explosive moves that used her natural agility and stamina to duck and dash around her opponent. No fancy kicks, no spinning strikes, just fast shuffles of her feet from side to side, back and forth, combined with quick slashes, thrusts, and strikes.

The sweat dripped from her forehead and onto her face, despite the cold. She was on the twenty-seventh repetition of the fourth move when she heard the brown door open. Mika stopped, slowed her breathing, wiped her sweat, and sat at the wall.

Ron's descent was slow and heavy. He carried a large knife in his hand, turned to Mika, and leaned his back against the bars of the opposite cell.

Mika couldn't see his facial expressions, but after looking him up and down several times, she realized he was brandishing a weapon and not a new book.

"Mika Plum of Yevera." He refused to look at her. "Do you know what happened last night?"

Mika did her best to hide the heavy breathing from her workout. "What happened last night, Ron?"

Ron closed his eyes. He exhaled and leaned his head back against the bars. "Necromancers attacked Triumph and Warrior's Edge."

Mika's eyes widened, and her heart pumped.

Page ...

She wanted to stand and look out the window, to see if she could get a hint of what happened, but she kept her composure to let Ron continue.

"Warrior's Edge was destroyed. Razed and tainted. No known survivors."

No one spoke, and the only movement was the rising of their chests with each breath.

"And Triumph?"

Ron lifted his head and looked into Mika's cell. "Necromancers were defeated at Triumph." He refused to look at her. "Only a few guards, soldiers, and citizens lost their lives. Heroic victory."

Relief passed through Mika. If she weren't controlling her emotions and reactions, she would have exhaled and smiled. Ron had made no attempts to hide the knife.

"Ron ..." Mika squinted to get a better look at the large weapon. Ron's fingers gripped and ungripped the tool. "What's with the knife?"

Ron clenched the knife.

"Ron?"

"Things've been hard, you know. Necromancers raiding towns and settlements brings a lot of unrest to the traders. There's been less and less traders the past few years. Every month, less than the one before." Ron passed his hand across his face.

Mika spoke. "Necromancers don't attack small groups of travelers or—"

"They are now, Mika Plum of Yevera!" Ron stepped to Mika's cell and wrapped his hand around a bar. "They've been killing off traders to hurt Di'Abribel and every other town's economy and supply lines! Justified killings of civilians because they're furthering war efforts!"

Mika closed her mouth. It made sense to her. No trading between towns means less revenue, less supplies, less luxuries for people to enjoy, and more unrest, making traders justified targets.

Ron began opening the top padlock, the one that, if Mika could burn through the black terra, was too far from her reach.

"Ron ..." Mika scooted to her feet. "What's with the knife?"

"In a week or so, people I trade with are coming to help me move everything." He wrapped the chain around his hand, another weapon. "We're getting out of this region, you know?" He unlocked the second padlock. "These cities, towns, and paladins don't do shit to stop these ..." Ron shook his head. "All worthless. All of them."

Mika's voice was desperate. "What's with the knife?"

Ron stopped. He hung his head. He struggled to get the words out. "Can't let my reputation falter, you know, when they see this place ... when they see you." He slid open the bars and stopped at the threshold. "You'd live another year or two, if that. Sorry, Mika Plum of Yevera. A few years in the Abyss is better than decades of hard labor in prison, you know?"

The chain dangled from his hand.

"Ron…" Mika backed into the corner. "Ron, please, just let me go," she whispered. "Please, Ron, like Ashlynn, I won't say anything. Please, Ron, I have Addie. I have my flower … I can't even see. I'm blind now, Ron." She tried to sway him. "You're not a bad person. I know there's kindness in your heart. I knew it from the moment you helped me. This doesn't need to happen, Ron. You're like my father now." Mika knew Ron had lost a wife and son. "You're supposed to protect me …"

Ron closed his eyes and shook his head with such vigor, Mika didn't know how he didn't get dizzy. He closed the distance and swung the chain.

Mika ducked, and sparks flew from the wall.

"Ron, stop!" she squealed, dove over her bed, and crawled to the exit.

Ron pulled her by the ankle. She blocked a slash with her forearms. Her flesh split open, but adrenaline blocked the pain.

Ron mounted Mika.

She bucked; he sank his weight on her hips. The knife sunk into her palm, just over her heart. Blood dripped to her chest.

Addie's animalistic barks bounced from every rock in the wall.

Mika's elbow prevented Ron from pushing further in. "Ron!"

Ron bore down on the knife. "Why … won't you …" Ron smacked, keeping his hand on her face; he pushed it down, forcing her to face the hallway.

Painful crackles escaped her mouth. The sharp pressure on her palm was forcing involuntary twitches on her fingers. Her neck felt like it was going to snap.

~ *Mommy is going to die … Mom is going to die …*

Keep fighting! Keep fighting, Mika!

~ *We need to help her … need to help her …*

Mika dug her nails into Ron's face. Ron pushed her head, and she twisted her body so her neck wouldn't snap.

257

Flames slithered from the torches into a ball of fire.
The knife poked her chest.

~ CALL OUR NAMES ... YOU NEED TO SCREAM ...
~ YOUR HAND ... USE YOUR HAND ...

Mika let go of Ron's face and opened her palm. "Ignis!"

~ We're with you ...

"What the—"

Mika slapped Ron with the ball of fire. The flames exploded into hundreds of smaller flames on impact. Ron held his face and screamed.

Mika clenched the knife, anticipating the pain. "Vita!"

The golden glow appeared on her stabbed hand; she yanked the knife and dashed toward Ron. Her poor eyesight contributed to the missing strike. She jabbed it into Ron's stomach, backhanded him, and ran out of the cell.

Not seeing the first step, she tripped. Her shin crashed onto the corner, and the sweat on her forehead dripped into her eyes, furthering her blindness. She crawled up the stairs, slid herself over, and slammed the storm door shut.

The lock, the lock ... She struggled to see in the dark room, and she couldn't find the lock to the storm door.

She kicked open the brown door, and the daylight helped her see better. She ran into Ron's room, stumbled around the bed, into the closet, and reached around in pitch darkness for the chest.

Her hands felt the corners. She unlatched the chest and flung it open. She felt inside. Pointed glass, smooth pearl.

Flower.

With shaking hands, she passed the stem through her hair. The flower retracted inside from fear.

Smooth leather, small straps. Backpack. She swung it over her head.

The storm door slammed open. "Mika!" Ron shouted. "I'm going to fucking kill you!"

Thick handle. She grabbed the sheath, and, with trembling hands, attached it to her thigh.

Mika jumped over the bed.

Ron exploded through the brown door.

She hid behind the open bedroom door and did her best to quiet and slow her breathing.

Silence.

Ron heaved. He stomped into the room, standing motionless and listening for any noise.

"Ventus!" Electricity sparked around his hand.

The thought of the spell made Mika's legs weaken. Not only was it painful, but Mika couldn't fight through it if it touched her.

Ron flipped the bed and shot electricity. "Where are you, Mika?"

He swung his fist onto his wooden dresser; the loud thud shook the walls. He ran into the closet. Electricity exploded the moment he went inside.

"Mika Plum of Yevera!"

He ran out of the room, passing so close to Mika that she could see his angry eyes underneath a burned face that oozed blood and white pus. He entered the kitchen.

Mika sneaked out of her hiding spot and to the dresser, pulled out a large drawer, and dumped the clothes on the ground.

Please work. Please, please, please work.

Thundering from the kitchen forced her to duck.

She did her best to run in silence through the living room and to the door. She reached it, unlocked the top deadbolt, unlocked the second, and stopped when she heard a thundering behind her. She spun and used the wooden drawer as a shield.

The electricity exploded and seeped into the drawer. The wood acted as an insulator, preventing Mika from being paralyzed and electrocuted. As she blocked the magic, she felt around the door.

Clunk! The third padlock unlocked.

Addie leaned on the window and barked through the glass. Spittle flew with every bark. Thick, sharp teeth were visible past retracted lips.

Mika turned to open the door. Ron crashed into her.

Addie barked louder. He ran to the door and scratched it. Ron picked Mika up, swung her over his head, and slammed her on the ground.

Mika took seconds to recover. Ron grasped her hair and dragged her toward the basement, where her blood wouldn't spray the walls when he killed her.

Mika thrashed left, right, spun in circles with her hair being pulled and twisting into a knot. Ron stepped through the threshold of the brown door. Mika held on to the doorframe with both hands.

Mika pulled. Ron pulled back.

Mika's scalp felt like it was going to tear. She saw Addie barking at her. His angry eyes almost hid the fear that showed on his ears. Her hands began slipping. Part of her hair flopped over her eye; the sweat made it stick to her eyelashes.

Fucking hair! Fucking hair! Fucking hair!

She unsheathed her dagger, held it behind her head, and curved it to the ceiling. The stinging on her scalp faded, and her head bounced on the ground. Ron crashed into the wall with several feet of Mika's hair in his hand.

Mika pushed to her feet and dashed to the door. She twisted the doorknob, looked at Ron, and flung open the door. Sunlight beamed from outside.

"Get it, Addie!" Mika pointed at Ron. "Get it!"

Addie dug his nails into the wood. They clattered on the floor until he leaped onto Ron. Ron blocked Addie's teeth from digging into his neck by sacrificing his forearm.

Ron ran to his room, brandished the knife, and stabbed Addie in the stomach, forcing the dog to let go of his forearm before he locked himself in the bedroom.

"Addie!" Mika squealed. Worry curbed her anger; Addie's life was more important than Ron's death.

Addie yelped and bit at his side.

Mika ran to Addie and dragged him outside, healing his wound and ignoring the hole in her own hand.

"Hang on, Addie!"

Mika dragged Addie down the stairs and set him on the snow. The blood dripping from Addie's wound turned the snow pink, then a deep red.

Mika knelt next to Addie, applying the healing magic, and focusing on the dog's organs and muscles. With concentration, thought, and focus, Addie's wounds began to close.

Addie stood and thanked Mika by licking her face. Mika continued kneeling. She placed her hand on the cold, melting snow. Her eyes were wide, her breaths deep and slow.

I'm out. I'm out.

Mika looked around. The snow covered the trees and porch, reflecting the sunlight into her eyes. The delicate cold kissed her cheeks and ears. Like a human using his fingers to cover his mouth in surprise, the tips of her flower touched the pearl.

She raised a hand to her nose and squeezed it. She looked at the house's red roof, the raised veranda, the white door, then she blew out. The moment her ears filled with pressure, she realized she wasn't in a dream, making her collapse into fits of crying. She closed her eyes and screamed, rocking back and forth and hugging her arms.

"I'm out," she managed to say. Addie approached her, and she wrapped her arms around him, crying into his neck. Her shoulders bounced with each inhale; her throat felt tight and closed.

"I'm out."

She covered her face, noticing the cut on her hand. The feeling appeared; it felt like her hand was struck with a blunt object instead of a knife. She'd be all right, she thought, for she could heal her wounds, and the pain was just for a moment.

"Vita," she said with a shaking, crying voice. Tears rolled down her cheeks and fell into the snow. She applied the magic to herself, and the wound disappeared in seconds.

She looked up. Ron's house was but a blur.

"Ventus Page," a moderate breeze brushed from the northeast.

Mika knew she wouldn't make it to Triumph in her condition. No cold-weather clothes, food was probably rotten, no eyesight. She was so unsure, so doubtful of herself the past month that she never thought she'd be out of Ron's basement, and now that she was out, the situation was much, much worse than she had ever imagined. She looked at the open door to the home.

He's still alive ...

Thoughts passed through her mind on how to kill her former captor.

Burn him alive. Boil him in his own shit. Boil him, heal him, then boil him again. Over and over and over …

She stood, feeling the crunching of the snow beneath her boots. She closed the distance to the house, went up the steps, and stood in front of the door, standing in the exact spot she stood on the first day of the storm five months ago. She looked through the window, catching a glimpse of her reflection; her mind was distracted by the length of her hair.

She noticed the horrible, long scar that looked wider than she thought it was. The wound hadn't healed properly; new, scarred skin had formed within the cut that ran all the way to her ear.

Her hair was a mess, long strands here, short strands there; most of her hair ended just below her ear. If she didn't look like a boy before, she did now.

To Mika, her eyes looked normal, just big, brown eyes staring back at her. In reality, though, her eyes were wide. Wide and piercing, much, much more than before. Mika did not blink.

Mika looked past her reflection. Her eyes focused on the blurred door leading to Ron's room. She moved to the front door and stopped. Addie heeled next to her.

She ran every possible scenario through her head. Ron opening the door with the halberd, Ron using electricity, Ron hurting Addie again, Ron killing Addie, Ron recapturing Mika, Mika dying, Ron and Mika dying. Ron, Mika, and Addie …. She looked at the flames in the fireplace, reminding her that she could use the fire to her advantage, burn down the house.

Ron is still inside. What if that makes him come out? He'd want revenge … and it would be mutual combat if she did that. If he burned in the house, she'd consume his corrupt essence and be damned to the Abyss. She shook her head.

I've won. I shouldn't let greed turn this into a loss.

With a balled fist, she absorbed the flames before turning around and stepping down the raised veranda, healing her knee only when it hurt. Deciding not to kill Ron made her mood plummet. She wanted to collapse, curl into a ball and cry, hug her dog until nighttime, but she refused—that would just show defeat. It would show that she'd been tortured inside the cell and that the thoughts of being in there still haunted her.

Her boots sank into the snow. *I'll rest when I finish my adventure.* She pulled out her dagger and cut the longer strands to match the shorter portions of her new hairstyle

She rubbed Addie's ear and continued walking, widening her eyes to help her see past the blurry, keyhole vision.

Mika reached the road. It had been cleared of snow, but the work was done quickly, and the results were a mess. She felt eyes on her, so she looked around. Her eyes rested on the window of a wooden house with a raised veranda and red roof. As if a taunt by the deities, her eyes returned to normal for just a moment, the moment long enough to make Mika's eyes meet Ron's.

He stood motionless behind the window of his room, watching her, unable to go after Mika because he knew a neighbor would witness the fighting.

Mika looked away first.

She held her head high and walked north toward Triumph, and her eyesight diminished again to its new blurry, dark normal.

Walking through the cold, Mika cursed at herself for not packing cold-weather gear. She held her arms across her chest. Both hands held small flames that warmed her skin and dried her boots. The fire warmed her and didn't burn, but if she held it close to her clothes for long enough, they would melt or ignite.

Addie loved the snow. He leaped into the air and crashed down, sinking into the white, powdery phenomenon. He tried to force Mika into a chase with a smile on his face, but when she didn't return the smile, his ears lowered in sadness.

"Aww, are you sad? Did you spend five months trapped in a hole?" Mika knelt next to him and grabbed his face. "Terra." Mika communicated with Addie.

Addie's feelings were happy and filled with relief that Mika was back in her life, but worry was rooted under the relief. He was terrified of losing Mika again, and he was trying to cheer her up by being happy.

Mika kissed Addie's nose. Addie licked Mika's face. "Don't worry, it won't happen again."

Addie wriggled away from Mika's grasp, spread out his legs, and ran circles around her. He took off away from the road, then sprinted toward her. Thinking he would stop, Mika fell on the snow when Addie crashed into her. Addie stood above her and licked her face with a smile and wide eyes.

Mika fought to push Addie away, but he fought back.

"Okay! Okay!" She laughed and kicked her feet. She grabbed his paw, but he nibbled her arm.

Addie played with Mika, and she played back, grabbing his head and bringing it close to hers only to nibble on his ears. "Rawr, rawr, rawr!" she teased.

The snow began to seep into her clothes, and the thought of being cold ran through her mind. A warm lick to the face told her that being cold and wet didn't matter. She needed to enjoy the moment she was in. Her smile widened, and she rested her head on the snow, letting Addie continue his onslaught.

She heard a man yell. Addie stopped and looked in the direction of the shout, releasing a light bark. A woman's shout made Mika sit up. Mika saw a female figure running toward them with a whip. The man brandished a shovel.

Mika stood, pushed Addie away, and stood in front of him with her arms spread out. "Stop! Stop!"

The man and woman slowed to a stop.

Mika widened her eyes to help see the couple better.

The woman said something to the man in a foreign language, language from the New Lands.

The man raised his hands, telegraphing *I don't know,* they exchanged words until the woman looked at Mika.

The woman's accent fluctuated in pitch, her voice small and pretty. "Thought you were trouble!" The woman laughed, showing Addie her perfect, pearly white teeth. "Where you go?"

Where you go ... Maybe she's asking where I'm going and she thought I was in trouble?

"Triumph." Mika looked back at the man, making sure he hadn't approached or changed his stance. "I'm going to Triumph."

"Ah!" The woman lit up. "Me—"

"Rosa!" The man's voice cut her off, causing Mika to widen her stance and wrap her fingers around her dagger. After Ron, she lost trust in men.

The man told the woman a few things, and Rosa nodded. She faced Mika.

"Goodbye! Please road off one minute!"

Walking away, the couple said something to each other. The woman nodded in agreement and stepped into a large wooden carriage pulled by two brown horses. Rosa began to climb onto the driver's seat, but the man stopped her. He said something and grabbed the whip.

Kissing his cheek, Rosa went inside the carriage. The man sat at the driver's seat, adjusted himself, and urged the horses forward.

Thudding from the horses' hooves on the soft dirt and rattling of the wooden wheels filled the air. One horse grunted, and the other shook its head. The man didn't look at Mika when he passed. Through the window of the carriage, Mika saw a shadow looking back at her.

The door to the carriage swung open, and a child jumped onto the snow, sinking for a second before running to Mika with open arms.

Mika took a step back, unsure of what to do. Addie barked.

Rosa jumped out of the carriage. "Lila!"

Lila ignored Rosa and crashed into Mika, wrapping her arms around Mika's waist, and resting her head on Mika's stomach.

Mika stood with arms spread and wide eyes that first looked at Rosa, then at Lila. Does she hug back? Does she push her away? Who was this girl with short, wild, curly hair? Why was she so excited to see her?

Rosa came toward them, and Lila looked up at Mika with big, round, light-brown eyes.

"Miss, do you have more angelwish?"

Angelwish? Angelwish! That's right!

The memory rushed into Mika's mind. This was the girl she returned the gold coin to in the Di'Abribeli market!

Mika relaxed her shoulders and placed her hand on Lila's back.

"No, no," Mika's voice was soft and higher pitched. "I'm out of angelwish right now."

"Pardon!" Rosa caught up. She rubbed her rosy cheeks. "Mine sister crazy!" Rosa grabbed Lila's wrist, yanked her back, held her finger to Lila's face, and scolded her.

Lila had no problem showing her pouty face and angry eyes during the scolding. Lila didn't look away until her older sister did. Rosa began to walk away, but Lila stayed still, pulling back when her arm was yanked toward the carriage. Rosa knelt in front of her and asked her something.

Lila looked at Mika, then at Rosa, and replied. Both seemed to be having an argument that ended when Lila pulled out a handful of silver coins.

Rosa sighed, looked at Mika, and stood. "What are you called?"

"I am Mika Plum—"

"Of Yevera!" Rosa pointed a finger at her as if remembering her.

"Of Yevera." Mika felt the urge to complete her sentence. She felt a slight insult from not being allowed to finish her introduction.

"Remember of you!" She interlocked fingers with Lila and walked to Mika. "I called Rosa!" She used her hands to talk.

"How are you?" Rosa grabbed Mika's shoulders, kissed one cheek, then kissed the other before taking a step back.

Mika looked around to hide the shivers that ran down her back. She needed to keep moving, find food, and get warm. She had no time for conversation.

"Good, thank you."

Mika's feet pointed away from Rosa, subconsciously telegraphing that she was ready to keep moving and that she wasn't interested in speaking.

"Grandiose, grandiose!" Rosa smiled. She looked down at Mika's feet, and her face straightened. She understood Mika's body language. "Have good travel Triumph!"

Mika nodded, thanked Rosa, and whistled to Addie. The dog heeled next to Mika, and Mika walked forward, her steps small so she wouldn't trip on something. She heard Rosa's and Lila's warm clothing move back to the carriage, followed by Lila's small, childish voice.

Rosa asked something.

Lila replied.

Rosa shot a response back; she sounded upset.

Lila screamed and ran toward Mika. Mika turned around.

Lila held Mika's hand. "You are cold?" she asked in a voice losing its accent.

Mika pressed her lips together. She couldn't lie to a child, but she didn't want to show weakness. She opened her mouth but then closed it and exhaled out her nose.

Lila snapped at Rosa, shouted something, and pointed at Mika's clothes.

Rosa scratched the back of her neck. After a moment, Rosa held her index finger out, telegraphing for the two to wait.

She ran back to the carriage and met with her husband, Antorio. Based on the body movements, he was asking what was going on and was impatient about the situation. His alertness was through the roof, as he looked around every few seconds.

Rosa seemed to plead with him until he shouted a single word. He repeated it under his breath, faced forward, and placed his head on his hand, resting his elbow on the armrest.

Rosa ran back to Mika and Lila. "Sorry! Yeveran, you want ride Triumph? Carriage safe and warm. Dog welcome."

Mika looked at Addie, who was sniffing the air with a smile that made his tongue flop out of his mouth. It would be smart to accept the offer. Not only would it cut her travel time by a few days, but she'd have food and warmth and wouldn't die from being blind. Mika looked at the carriage.

Food and warmth, but she'd be dependent on someone else, again, for something. What would she say of her first, and likely last, adventure? That she received help the whole way? That she was unable to fend for herself? A shiver ran down her back from the cold.

They'd probably do the same, and they're not in my situation.

"Okay," she said. "I'll go with you."

Lila hugged her, and Mika placed her hand on Lila's head.

"C'mon, Addie," she said, walking to the carriage. Lila entered first, then Rosa. Mika stood at the stairs.

"I need to dry my pup."

Rosa reached for something and held out several towels. Lila jumped out and asked for a towel before wrapping it around Addie and drying his front side. Addie licked Lila's face. Mika dried Addie's rear before he jumped into the carriage.

"Thank you!" Mika held her palm to Lila.

Lila returned the high-five. "Yes!" She grabbed the towels and jumped into the carriage.

Mika grabbed onto a handhold, pulled herself up, and stepped inside.

A long bench rested on the front of the carriage. Rosa sat near the window. Opposite the bench were two chests, and all four walls each had a small white candle with a smaller flame dancing on top. Lila sat between Mika and Rosa. Lila scooted next to Mika until both of their arms touched.

Mika closed the door. Rosa slapped the wall twice. The carriage began to move.

What would've happened had I never returned that gold coin?

"Arrive day and half," Rosa said. She asked Lila something.

Lila translated. "Dinner."

"Dinner at night, but keep moving." Rosa exhaled, smiled, and rested her head on the wall before closing her eyes.

Mika hadn't talked to anyone but Ron since Ashlynn left. Mika understood Rosa was tired, but she needed human interaction. "How were the New Lands?"

Rosa didn't respond. Rosa's eyes gazed past the roof; she seemed lost in thought. Her lips wrenched, puckered, pressed together, and they parted before she exhaled.

"Bad dream."

Lila butted in. "Nightmare."

Rosa corrected herself. "Nightmare."

"Tell me more." Mika could sense Rosa didn't want to talk about it, but she was curious. She would never venture to the New Lands, and stories from there would take years to reach Celeste.

Rosa rubbed the front of her neck with her fingers. "No order, no laws." She looked at Mika, "Corrupt essence? None. Every person kill any innocent person, justify. Everyone kill everyone for new magic, new rulers, new kingdoms. No corrupt essence like here make New Lands …" She used her hand to help her think.

"Uncivilized?" Mika helped.

Rosa pointed at Mika. "Uncivilized! Crazy go everyone!"

No corrupt essence meant that people could kill each other without justification or mutual combat. Just people killing people to learn new spells, which in turn could be used to kill more people. Not until someone came out as ruler would the New Lands obtain their name and corrupt essence be possible. Mika dreaded the idea.

"Monsters everywhere," said Rosa.

"Pirates," Lila butted in. She scooted closer to Mika and rested her head on Mika's arm.

"Pirates." Rosa's voice began to shake. "If monsters not attack village ... pirates attack ... much prefer monster raiding ..."

Rosa looked out the window; her gaze followed a passing tree, then another, then another until she shook her head.

"Monster not do rape."

The sentence caused Mika's heart to skip a beat. She heard sniffles coming from Lila.

Look what you caused, stupid.

"Me and Antorio do bad thing there." Rosa looked at Mika. "But thing need for survive." She closed her eyes and shook her head. She blinked several times to dry the tears. She swallowed. "But we safe now." She nodded, attempting to convince herself. "We safe. Yes. We reach Triumph, eight day after, boat go Sytu. Sytu safe. We arrive Sytu, and rest forever. Happy family. War, pirates, monsters no more ... Forever rest."

A shaky exhale was followed by Rosa's smile. Mika was close enough to see her pretty teeth.

"Please, now, no more speak New Lands."

"Thank you for sharing your story with me." Mika looked to Addie. He was battling sleep, but he kept his eyes on Rosa, somehow knowing the reason she was sad.

After a quick talk about what Rosa and Lila would cook for dinner, the carriage fell silent. Rosa fell asleep with her mouth curved into a natural smile. Lila played with the straps to Mika's dagger until she fell asleep on Mika's arm.

Mika moved herself so her back was in the corner, and she moved Lila's head to her chest. Lila fell asleep to the rhythm of Mika's heartbeat.

Bored, Mika pulled the flower from her hair. The flower's petals were erect and upright, the bottom petals curved around the pearl. For some reason, she was in a deep state of anticipation. She gazed into the pearl.

Through the dragon's eyes, she saw the inside of a cave. Blue lights illuminated the dark area, and a smaller, baby dragon smiled back at her. The dragon acted just like a puppy, squaring off in a playful stance with a smile on its face. Mika's dragon swung a paw at the baby dragon, and the baby dragon rolled onto its back. Its snakelike tongue hung from the side of its mouth like Addie's tongue did. Another dragon approached and nuzzled Mika's dragon. After a loving nuzzle back, Mika's dragon walked away, spun in a circle, and curled into a ball, facing his partner and child before falling asleep.

They made a baby! A rush of excitement ran through Mika, and her flower responded to her feeling of joy by arching its petals toward the stem.

She placed the flower back in her hair, the stem curved around her ear. *I can't wait to meet all three of you!*

With that, Mika looked out the window. The Lost Forest eased its way into view, but she wasn't scared. The only feeling she experienced was excitement—for in less than a day, she would be reunited with Page. She wanted to get up and shoot fireballs into the sky.

"Are you okay?" Lila whispered.

Mika's elevated heartbeat must've woken her. "Yes, yes, sorry. Let's go to sleep."

"Nighty-night." Lila adjusted herself, snuggling closer to Mika.

Mika smiled and closed her eyes.

I'm so close .... This bad, bad dream is almost over. He'd better have a good excuse for not looking for me.

Mika brushed Lila's hair until both of their heartbeats pumped at the same rhythm, their inhales and exhales matched, and they both fell asleep inside the moving carriage.

18. FOREST

Thickening spirals of fire rising to the heavens filled the black room. Tiny embers drifted down like falling leaves, only to spin and whirl on the flames that erupted from the lava of the floor. The only spot not consumed by fire was the circle surrounding Mika.

Mika saw a double of herself with two pointy black horns protruding from her forehead and curving to the top of her head. Her long, burgundy hair and golden-blonde highlights draped to the small of her back. She hid her hands behind her back. Mika's fiery doppelganger smiled as flames seeped out of her body.

Focusing on the horns, Mika began feeling fear, causing the dream she was in to begin its descent into a nightmare.

"Horns are for followers of Liranda, deity of fire and corruption, the deity of evil and ignis." Mika recited the passage she was taught years ago in school.

The double's smile grew. "Let us in, Mika ..."

~ Let us in, Mika ...

The fire surrounding Mika grew with every syllable the ignis children spoke.

Mika looked around her. "No, no, I can't ..."

The fire encircled her where she stood.

She looked at her double. "My loyalty is to Angelis! I'll fly on her angel wings!"

The dream trembled.

271

All the flames shot up to the sky and converged into a mighty meteor, making a path straight to Mika.

"We're not going to hurt you, Mika." Her double walked to her.

The meteor closed in.

Mika's eyes shot open, and she looked around the candlelit carriage. Her breathing was heavy, and she began to move, only to be stopped when she noticed Lila's weight on her lap. The hand she placed on Lila's hair after dinner hadn't moved, and Mika didn't want to wake her. She looked at the other corner of the bench. There, Antorio slept.

It was just a dream.

Taking a deep breath, she looked at the blurry silhouette of Addie curled up on some blankets. Mika held her breath, counted to five, then let it out through her nose. When her heart slowed, she began to close her eyes. She would have fallen asleep had it not been for the small flicker of the shadows.

What was that?

She focused on a spot at the opposite corner of the carriage, the only spot where the candlelight was not hitting. Focusing and squinting, she figured it was a passing spirit, the type people only see from the corner of their eyes late at night.

She bowed her head and whispered, "May you find the light that guides you out of this realm."

After showing respect for the dead, she raised her head, looked at the shadow, and noticed it had taken the form of a slim human.

A gentle, older voice, as might come from a loving grandmother, bounced in her mind. *"Don't be scared, young one. It's me, Nessa."*

Mika looked at Lila; she was about to toss the child off her lap and bow in front of the deity of darkness and emotions, the deity of tenebris.

"Please, do not move and wake the child. I feel your need to bow to me. I ask you stay where you are."

Nessa's shadow began to take shape. She was sitting on a chest with one leg over her knee and her hands resting in her lap. Her posture was erect and firm.

Although Mika eased her hands, she began to straighten herself in her seat. What now? What to do? She'd never been visited by a deity. She didn't know anyone who had. Only thing she'd been told is to bow, bow and wait to be spoken to. Nessa's shadow cleared more. Her features were visible to Mika despite her failing sight and Nessa being surrounded by nothing but darkness. Mika could see Nessa with perfection.

Nessa's jet-black hair was tapered on the sides, and she had long bangs that hung low to her eyes. Haunting gray pupils were surrounded by black irises, her physical trait. A smile with black lips rested on a pale and skinny face. Nessa's bony arms showed numerous circular tattoos. The rest of her body was covered by a black cloak.

"Oh dear! I am smitten by your new hair!" Nessa moved her head so that Mika could see her haircut better. *"I'm a supporter of short hair on women."* Nessa smiled and turned back to Mika.

Mika wanted to say that she hated her new hair, but she refrained from doing so. *"Thank you, Nessa."* Mika tried to make her thoughts speak in a happy tone. *"I had to cut it yesterday."*

Nessa chuckled, but her body didn't move, in fact, her body didn't seem to inhale or exhale. *"I heard what happened. I'm delighted in your escape! It would've been such a shame for Irstia to lose such an important and powerful person."*

The compliment sent excitement and happiness through Mika. She didn't try to hide her emotions because she knew Nessa could read them regardless of how hard she tried.

"I've come to you tonight with a proposition. Would you like to hear it?"

A proposition? From a deity? Mika's response was almost faster than Ashlynn's responses when the two spoke.

"Yes, of course."

When Mika shifted in her seat, Lila moved. Mika brushed her hair to lull her back to sleep.

"Look outside." Nessa turned to face the window. *"What do you see?"*

Mika looked out the window; the view was perfect despite having been blind moments before falling asleep. Nessa asked her such a broad question. Where to start? The black skies, a couple of clouds, two full moons, stars upon stars, the trees of the Lost Forest, tall grass, the window …

"I see everything."

Nessa chuckled; this time the chuckle was genuine. *"Oh dear, not what I meant, but good. You see the effects of the night vision spell I've bestowed upon you, along with the restoration of your eyesight."*

The statement made Mika realize that she could see every minor detail from outside. Nessa continued speaking. *"I was referring to the Lost Forest."*

"The Lost Forest." Mika looked at Nessa. *"Main base for the necromancers waging war on Celeste. The necromancers are your children."*

Mika felt a rush of anger. She remembered Nessa could read her emotions, so the anger dissipated into fear. The fear turned into disgust and, combining with anger, Mika felt contempt and hatred toward Nessa. Mika sat back on the bench. Clenching and unclenching her jaw, Mika glared at the deity of tenebris.

Nessa looked at the candle near the door.

Mika looked to see what she was looking at, then continued scowling at the deity.

Nessa formed herself into a shadow and reached for the flame. She reached and reached and reached and reached, but her shadow was never able to touch the dancing ember. She sat back and returned to her physical form.

"Enough darkness can drown lux's light, but no amount of darkness can quell a fire's glow. Fire will always destroy darkness." Nessa rested her elbow on her leg and placed her chin on her fingers. *"Would you like to be the fire that destroys the darkness within the forest?"*

Mika's eyes softened. *"Elaborate."*

"Oh, dear ..." Nessa let her hand hang over her leg. *"The necromancers in Celeste ... their secondary magic is tenebris, making them my children, of course. I love them."* She waited to feel Mika's anger before continuing. *"But they're not loyal like the necromancers in other continents. Their leader, Kathrine, only cares about conquering the region, Irstia, and rising through the ranks and becoming a lich."* Nessa sat back, intertwined her fingers, and rested them on her lap before looking out the window. *"There's a child of mine in the Lost Forest, a captive, prisoner."*

"You want me to get her out." Mika was direct; she had no more time for banter.

Nessa smiled. *"Him. I want you to get him out. The life of this witch is worth more than this whole army of necromancers. He has sacrificed a lot for me, and he will sacrifice much, much more if he is able to live."* Nessa looked at Mika. *"In return, I'll bestow upon you a spell and ensure you are compensated monetarily."*

Monetarily. Mika had heard stories of deities giving coins to people who served them, a reward to loyal followers. The coins given as offerings from humans to the deities was used as to not ruin economies. Mika didn't need money. She didn't need spells. The only thing she cared about was finishing her adventure and seeing Page again. If she were going to accept a proposition from a deity, it would be on her terms.

Mika raised her chin. *"No."*

Nessa blinked. An unintentional reaction.

Mika crossed her ankles and placed her hands on her lap. If it weren't for Lila, Mika would have mocked Nessa's posture.

"I want several spells, all spells bestowed immediately. I want enough life essence to teach myself whatever vita spell I want." Mika leaned forward. *"I want your allegiance in any request I make on any deity stone, forever. I also want this family to be protected from all necromancer attacks until they arrive in Sytu. Lastly, you* will *vouchsafe my eyesight. Immediately. Forever."*

Silence filled Mika's mind. Nessa was staring back at her with a blank expression. Irstia's sorceress looked at Lila and her brother-in-law, at Nessa, then at the candle Nessa used to demonstrate her weakness. Mika called upon the flames.

They detached from the candles, slithered to the center of the room, and combined into one small ball of fire. Mika pushed the flame, hovering it inches above Nessa's head.

"I know your weakness; therefore, I do not fear you. Accept my counteroffer or find someone else to do your bidding. I couldn't care less about you or your pathetic witch, Nessa."

Nessa read Mika's emotions: pride, confidence ... dominance. The petals on Mika's flower were spread wide, its tips pointed forward in anger, telling Nessa that her power to read emotions was not being influenced by another deity, magic, or strange phenomenon.

"So be it." Nessa noticed she had slumped, so she straightened herself. *"I accept your counteroffer, and the spell I have bestowed upon you is the spell of night vision. In the forest, night vision will reveal a blood-red trail, providing guidance to the necromancer cathedral. Only once my pris-*

oner is freed will the trail guide you out of the forest's unnatural ability to shift like a labyrinth."

Mika moved the fire away from Nessa when she felt a darkness in her mind fade away, revealing two new spells.

"Now then," said the deity, "the second is an arcane spell that will work on the minds, hearts, spirits, and emotions of others. Say whatever you please, and whatever emotion you call upon, they will feel. Life essence absorbed will be multiplied in the Lost Forest, and I shall follow all your adventures, conquests, and builds until you perish. Kathrine, leader of this army of necromancers, possesses an active warrior's stone, any necromancer in the Lost Forest will kill you with justification, and you can do the same to them."

Nessa began to fade away.

"You're forgetting something." Mika placed her hands on Lila's arm and head.

Nessa continued fading. "This family is protected against tenebris and mori until they reach Sytu." Nessa disappeared. "Make haste, dear. All captives will be executed at the next moonrise."

Mika hovered a flame where Nessa was sitting. When she didn't see the deity of tenebris, she leaned back and relaxed. Mika felt a strong hate toward Nessa, as if the hatred were rooted in her lineage. When sorcerers and sorceresses were plenty in the early years of the planet, they marched alongside paladins against necromancers and witches—masters of tenebris—before Liranda and Mooredoth declared war on the other deities.

Mika shooed the flame away, and they slithered back to their respective candles.

Fuck that whore and fuck her necromancers.

Mika leaned her head against the wall.

And fuck that prisoner too.

Dreaming, Mika flew on her dragon, carving away at the darkness with fire that shot from her hands.

* * * * *

Clunk!

Antorio closed the chest after he grabbed two apples and a leather flask filled with water. He jumped off the still-moving carriage and sprinted to the driver's seat. Rosa hopped off the driver's seat, almost falling on her face when her feet touched the ground. The entrance to the carriage passed her, and she ran to grab the handle before skipping a step on the way inside. She opened the chest and pulled out three filets of fish coated in salt.

"Goodness!" Rosa's small voice made Mika happy; her beautiful smile made her happier. Rosa opened the window, brushed the salt off the fish, and gave a piece to Mika and Lila. "Fish good not cooked." She took a bite to demonstrate.

The filet was a large piece, pink and slimy. It reminded Mika of Ashlynn and her talk about eating fish wrapped in rice. Mika opened her mouth and lifted the food to her face. She stopped when she caught a glimpse of Addie sitting down, his eyes pointed at the filet.

She lowered her food and tore it in half, giving one to Addie before eating the rest. The fish was salty because of the preservation method, but it wasn't bad. She danced her tongue inside her mouth to get all the tiny bits from her teeth and into her stomach. When the feeling of being watched set in, she faced Lila.

"For you and your doggy." Lila had torn her filet in two pieces and offered them to Mika.

Addie drooled, Mika slapped him on the top of the snout and pointed a finger at him. Addie licked the drool from his mouth and sat back. Rosa told Lila something in their language. Lila turned and said something back. Rosa stared at Lila and replied after a few seconds.

Lila turned to Mika. "For you and your doggy."

Looking at the food, Mika had a difficult time saying no … and a harder time saying yes. Eating a child's food? Giving a child's food to pets? That didn't seem right. She looked at Addie, then looked out the window to the trees surrounding the Lost Forest.

What type of food is in there? How long will I be in there for? What if—

A bump that shook the carriage broke Mika from her thoughts. Two knocks from Antorio told them everything was fine.

Extending her hands, Mika accepted the fish. "Thank you, Lila. Why don't *you* feed Addie?"

"Yes! Here, here!" Lila smiled. "Eat food!" She retracted her small hand when Addie eased the piece into his mouth.

Mika ate her slice and hugged Lila. Lila gave her a long, strong hug in return. Mika kissed the top of Lila's head and eased her away.

"I have to go." Mika looked at Lila, then Rosa.

Lila's eyes widened, but Rosa answered first. "Why? To?"

Mika took a breath and told the two about Nessa appearing in the middle of the night, Nessa's proposition, Mika's counteroffer, and the fact that she was blind but not anymore. The carriage fell silent after the story was told. A bump followed by two slaps broke the silence.

"You going to?" Rosa spoke. She passed her hand through her black, wavy hair; her eyes were tired from piloting the carriage all night.

Mika nodded and shrugged her shoulders. "I'll be okay. No deity would intervene in the world for something unimportant." Leaning forward, Mika stood and walked to the door. Addie jumped to his feet, ready to follow.

"Mika!" Lila hopped off the bench. "Please do not leave." She wrapped her arms around Mika and rested her head on Mika's stomach.

Mika moved Lila away and lowered herself to her level. She pushed Addie before he was able to lick Mika's face.

"Have food ready for me in Triumph in a couple of days, okay?"

Lila nodded and sniffled. Her eyes had watered, but she did her best not to cry. Mika stood, and Lila hugged her.

"Thank you for helping me, Rosa. I'll invite your beautiful family to visit me and Page before you leave."

"Thank you, Mika." Rosa stood, hugged Mika, and kissed both her cheeks. "Heavens protect you." She reached into the chest, pulled out a brown coat with white fur, and put it on Mika.

Mika opened the door.

"Terra." She communicated to Addie to jump from the moving carriage. Addie jumped and shuffled his feet, preventing him from rolling on the ground. Mika stepped on the stairs and jumped out, taking a few steps but still falling to her knees.

Releasing a breath, Mika stood and looked back. The carriage door closed, and Lila waved her little hands from the open window. Mika crinkled her mouth and fixed her posture.

The massive trees of the Lost Forest stared at her. Although it was the season of endurance, and none of the trees behind her had leaves, the trees of the Lost Forest were lush and full of life. The snow had melted, leaving wet patches and puddles of mud everywhere except, for some reason, the ground below the trees of the Lost Forest. The grass was dry, almost as though the snow never touched its plants.

She looked at Addie. "Ready?"

Addie took a breath, licked his nose, and panted.

"Let's go." Mika took off in a jog, smiling when she realized her knee did not hurt anymore. Jumping over a puddle, she picked up her pace upon landing, slapping a sign as she passed by.

Lost Forest. Keep out!

Her hand stung, and she brought it up to her face.

"Ignis."

A ball of fire appeared. Mika closed her hand and stored the flame. Her breathing heavy, she remembered she hadn't run in months. She took a breath, controlled her breathing, and slowed to a walk. She touched the first tree of the Lost Forest. Its rough bark scratched her hand when she rubbed the tree up and down; the scent of fresh wood entered her nostrils. She closed her eyes to let her brain take in more of the scent. When she opened her eyes, she was surrounded by looming trees. A thick, gray mist seemed to attach itself to her skin and feed into her pores. The moisture inside the forest was starting to make Mika's armpits sweat.

Ears low and tail between his legs, Addie huddled close to Mika. He looked left and right, wondering where the sunlight went. Mika looked up to see the sky was screened by a knotted canopy of boughs. No sunlight seeped through the leaves yet, unsurprising to Mika, everything was visible inside the warm and humid forest.

She chuckled and shook her head. She looked behind her, no road, no dead trees, no sky, just more of the forest and more of the mist. Mika yawned and stretched. Her eyes were watery, and she realized it was hard to breathe in the mist, to the point she had to strain herself to inhale more air.

Panting, Mika used the tenebris spell Nessa taught her, the one that would guide her into the forest and let her see in the darkness. A blood-red mist came into view, floating back and forth, making a path in front of Mika. Turning around, Mika noticed the mist did not point to the exit.

No turning back now.

She took her first step forward and began following the red mist deeper into the Lost Forest.

Minutes turned to hours as she walked. With no sun to help her tell time, she gauged her trek by the number of cramps she had in her butt, hamstrings, and feet. She leaned on a tree and massaged the side of her glute; she pressed on a knot in hopes that the cramp would go away. She stopped for another water break. She felt the onset of exhaustion as soon as water began to stream from her fingertips.

She remembered a conversation with Ashlynn, who had told her she needed to eat greens to help her combat exhaustion or let her mind recover on its own. Deciding not to cast any more water, she kept her mind active by analyzing her surroundings. She could only see gray mist and trees upon trees. No sounds other than Addie's panting told her there was nothing alive around her. There were, though, yellow orbs everywhere except in front of her where the red mist guided. The orbs seemed immobile.

Addie whined.

Mika ran to him and grabbed his snout. "Quiet."

Addie blinked and pulled his head back.

Mika reiterated that they needed to be quiet, using her communication spell to do so. After stretching out her leg, Mika looked around her again. Nothing had changed in the forest.

Mika focused on a set of yellow orbs—her first guess was fireflies or fairies.

Maybe if I throw a fireball at them ...

She opened her hand. "Ignis." The exhaustion returned, but she focused on the closest set of yellow orbs. She cocked her arm back and, just before she launched the roaring ball of fire, the orbs disappeared and reappeared.

It blinked.

A couple of the yellow orbs turned to face each other. Whenever they moved, they revealed their strange figures: four long skinny legs, a tail that curved up and over their gray muscular bodies, and a mouth that opened side to side. She noticed the tails all pointed at her with something that oozed a green liquid.

Addie guarded the rear.

The figures moved closer.

Mika summoned another flame. She widened her stance, puffed her chest, and spoke with a loud, firm voice. "Another step, and all of you die."

Keeping the flame active made Mika's exhaustion soar. She wouldn't be able to last another minute holding the flames. As she struggled to keep her eyes open, her blinks became longer, until her eyes began to droop and close on their own. Just before she extinguished the flames, the monster closest to her took a step back, looked at its pack, and they all ran away, making no sounds when they did so.

Mika extinguished the flames. She reached down to rub Addie's ear and quickened her pace, thankful her bluff worked.

After a couple more hours of walking and making sure the monsters with yellow eyes weren't following, she came upon a large crate in the path of the mist. Mika crouched, listened for movement, and looked for threats. She concluded the area was clear, so she jogged to the large crate and looked inside. There, she found spinach, zucchini, lettuce, green apples, pears, broccoli, and brussels sprouts, all green fruits and vegetables. A brown leather book was placed on the corner. She opened the book and read the only page inside:

> For those traveling to and from the cathedral who have reached mental exhaustion.
>
> Remember:
> The food needs to digest before you start feeling better, so take only what is necessary.
> Stay safe,
>
> Major Lieutenant Seth

Mika tossed the book back into the crate. She took off her backpack and stuffed it with food, shrinking them into the refrigerated section of her bag. She grabbed broccoli and threw it onto the ground for Addie before she devoured some apples. The rest of the food in the crate, she grabbed and threw far into the mist, hoping to sabotage the necromancers' movements. She knew that any amount of damage to them would be beneficial.

Unable to throw the spinach leaves, she ate what she could and left the rest in the crate. She stopped and realized she shouldn't have thrown out all the food, so she hoped that keeping the spinach in the crate would make the next passing necromancer think the food had run out instead of being sabotaged. Satisfied with her work, she continued following the red mist; her high metabolism began digesting the food quicker than most, curing her exhaustion within minutes.

The crate and booklet reminded her the forest was not deserted but sheltered enemies, so she kept her steps fast, but not so fast as to come upon necromancers ahead of her all of a sudden.

Her caution paid off.

19. TENEBRIS

Necromancers were up ahead.

Pivoting her foot, Mika dove headfirst into the mist and shrubs. Sensing the urgency, Addie followed, and he crawled on his belly with eyes trained on Mika.

"Stay!" Mika whispered.

She faced forward, moved a patch of grass, and stared at a large open field where a massive cathedral made of black stone stood like a mountain. In the open field surrounding the cathedral were tents, tables, chairs, firepits, training dummies, stables, and necromancers going about their day. The necromancers didn't seem to know she was there. They cooked, ate, trained, exercised, cleaned, talked, laughed—everything a normal army would do.

Mika wondered if she had begun to daydream before she noticed the cathedral; its appearance was so sudden. One moment there was mist in front of her, the next the cathedral and necromancers snapped into view.

She raised her head and looked for the blood-red mist. Her gaze followed it to her side, deeper into the forest and not into the cathedral. Looking back at the camp, she noticed a huge black circle over a vertical rectangle on the face of the cathedral—the symbols of tenebris and mori. Looking further up, she noticed the sky was covered by a black cloud, the same black cloud that she'd seen years ago when Yevera was destroyed. To necromancers, the cloud provided all the benefits the sun provides.

Someone running behind her forced her to freeze and her heart to race. A tall man in tight necromancer leather armor sprinted past her, out of the tree line, to the field, and into a silver tent.

She slowed her heartbeat and waited. She took the time to study the area outside the cathedral, in case she needed to sneak to the front entrance. While she watched, a necromancer in black plate armor and no helmet exited the tent. He held a flap of the tent open, revealing a great sword with parrying hooks on his back. The running necromancer, despite having sprinted about five hundred yards seconds earlier, did not seem tired when he exited the tent. They both walked in silence toward the edge of the tree line, toward Mika.

In slow, inching movements, Mika sank herself closer into the ground and covered her face with mud for camouflage. Addie sank himself also.

As the men got closer, Mika could make out the voice of the armored necromancer; deep, rough, it hissed every word that came from his throat.

"Talk to me, Ty."

Ty held his fists to his hips. "We thought the gates opened by accident or that someone from the south team had sneaked in and opened them." He looked down at the ground. He rubbed the inside of his nose with his thumb, looked at it, and flicked whatever he had picked away.

"Went in, saw the king on his horse galloping to the town center. We followed, surrounded him. A ray of light manifested below the blanket into a lux orb brighter than the sun. Ain't ever seen nothing like it. All our spells useless, we were surrounded. Captain Liam died first."

"Did you get a look at the paladin who summoned the lux sun?" The armored necromancer stopped and looked past the trees. He was yards away from Mika.

"Yes, General Nicholas."

General Nicholas waited. Ty understood to keep talking.

"Woman, lux hair, light-blue eyes, bit darker skin, not from around here judging by the accent. Tall." Ty hovered his hand at eye level to General Nicholas, showing the approximate height of the female paladin.

284

General Nicholas stroked his thick beard that accentuated his muscular jaw.

"Amirra." He clicked his tongue and balled his fist. "The paladins have Amirra in Triumph."

"Amirra." Ty passed his hand through his hair. "She's in Triumph? Why not Di'Abribel? Reach?"

"Change out, head to Vicqua, tell them we need reinforcements." General Nicholas turned back to the open field. "On your way out, tell Liam's army to double-time back. I don't give a damn if they're injured or tired."

Ty began to move. "Yes, sire. We need to restock the exhaustion crate; it's empty. Stalkers must've taken the food."

"Are you serious?" The general's voice was angry, but controlled.

Ty nodded.

"Find someone to take care of it. Priority."

"Yes, sire." Ty ran off toward the cathedral.

General Nicholas took a breath and stood still, watching the movements inside the camp.

Mika studied the necromancer knight: jet-black hair cut into a military fade and a thick, black beard. His strong, muscular physique and black armor made her cower. Heavy and thick plate mail with no fancy adornments or useless add-ons, it encased the massive man from neck to toe. A shiver ran down Mika's spine when she looked past his waist.

The armor around his thighs was surrounded by small, pointed spikes, all the way down to his boots. The boots themselves had three spikes at the shins. When the necromancer knight unclenched his fist, Mika noticed his gauntlets had razor-sharp blades protruding over the knuckles. That armor was meant to kill more than it was meant to protect.

She felt a deep feeling of regret for anyone who had faced General Nicholas—and anyone who would face him in the future. General Nicholas walked back to the silver tent. Mika tried to control her breathing and heart, but after looking at Nicholas, she could not control her anxiety. No one had ever made her feel the way Nicholas did.

Several necromancers younger than her carried boxes of food from the field and began running toward Mika's path until they passed her. Ty followed, galloping away on a champagne-colored horse, reminding her of his journey to Vicqua.

They're allied with Vicqua! That explains everything! They get supplies from the necromancers in Velonde, through Adventurer's Pass, to Vicqua, and Vicqua gives them food from the Farmlands!

How could she prove this to the paladins or the Di'Abribeli elders?

After making sure the area was clear, Mika crouched and lay low, following the red mist that led her around the open field and behind the cathedral.

Still within the trees, the mist took a sudden curve *into the ground.*

"What the heck?" she whispered, gazing at shrubs and grass in front of her feet. She took a few steps back and stopped when the red mist continued entering the ground.

Crawling forward, she moved away some grass, threw a stick, and swept away some dirt. A hatch of rotting wood with a rusted iron handle lay in front of her.

Mika lifted the rough handle. She stopped when the wood creaked, looked around, noticed no one watching, and opened the hatch. Mika could see several stairs leading underground. Poking her head through the opening, her night-vision spell waned.

"Tenebris," she whispered and imagined darkness dissipating.

Gray night vision came back, allowing her to see the continued descent of the stairs. Audible dripping spoke of standing water below.

She got up, grabbed the hatch, and began to close it.

"Go on," she told Addie.

Addie shuffled to his feet and sped down the stairs. The stick Mika threw earlier hung from his mouth.

Gripping the hatch, she slowed her descent until the hatch closed. Stepping on each stair, she passed her hand along the stone walls to help her in case she lost her footing. Her heart was throbbing from the descent. Her mind told her to turn around and run away. It told her that this wouldn't end well. Deep down, she knew it wasn't fear of the necromancers or the cathedral, but from the memories of going down the stairs of Ron's basement. The stairs that took away months of her life and plunged her into the state of hatred she now felt.

Her boots filled with ice-cold water, and the sloshing inside her socks forced a grunt of disgust out of her mouth.

She lifted her boot and looked down, tracking slow, concentric ripples expanding into the darkness. But something was wrong. She bent over and passed her fingers through the invisible water, watching more ripples flutter away and bounce back when they hit the walls. At the opposite end of the hallway, she could see a set of stairs. Was the water invisible because of magic? Or was it that her night-vision spell didn't allow her to see the water?

She communicated to Addie to take the lead. Still carrying the stick, Addie jumped in.

Mika took a step into the chilly water. She took a step down, then another, and a few more until she reached the bottom and the water rested just above her waist. She sloshed forward, as fast as she could, to get out of the cold water making her body temperature plummet and her hands shake in front of her.

Addie ran up the stairs and shook himself dry. Mika's toes crashed against a stair, but she was quick on her feet and didn't lose her footing. She made her way up, leaning against the wall. Once she was out of the water, she threw off her boots, slipped out of her socks, and jumped out of her pants.

"Ignis." Her teeth chattered.

A flame appeared on both of her palms. She passed the flames up and down her legs, and Addie huddled close to the fire. When she was warm, she reached into her bag, looked for dry clothes, and changed. The rest of her clothes were laid out on the stairs to dry.

At the top of the stairs was a steel door with two flanking torches. She rushed up, absorbed the flames, opened the door, and peeked into the other side. She absorbed the flames flanking the opposite side of the door before taking in what was in front of her.

Although a pillar blocked half of her view, she could see a colossal metal brazier hanging from the ceiling by four chains. Inside was a massive fire that helped illuminate the long wooden tables below it. Standing in rows, the tables had benches where necromancers—both male and female and of different ethnic backgrounds and a few with magic masteries—sat eating their meals from metal bowls. Mika estimated about fifty necromancers sat at the tables. They laughed, debated, talked, read, even wrote, just like normal humans would.

I guess that's all they really are, humans, after all.

She expected the inside of the cathedral to have a disgusting smell, but it smelled clean, like a room that had been cleaned with lemons.

"I'll be right there! Let me go drain the water!"

Mika's eyes snapped to a necromancer walking toward her. He faced the tables and held his index finger in the air. Mika scooted herself back and began closing the door, hoping the darkness would hide her. The necromancer faced forward, revealing his chunky face, big stomach, and bald head. He had a genuine smile that showed his teeth and made the corner of his eyes crinkle. Mika slid back into the tunnel and inched the door shut.

"Go …" Mika whispered, pointing to the bottom of the stairs. "Go down, go down!"

Addie noticed the urgency and ran down the stairs, stopping just before his paws hit the water.

"Stay!" She pressed her back against the wall, as her heart boomed against her chest. She held her breath when the door opened. Her shaking hand clutched her dagger.

They killed your mother. They destroyed your village. They killed Stacy. Show no mercy. They're all rats.

The necromancer stepped inside and closed the door.

"Why …"

Although he faced Mika, he was looking up at the flameless torch above her, sensing that something was wrong.

"Tenebr—"

Mika plunged her dagger up the underside of his chin; it shone through his gaping mouth.

He fell back, and both tumbled down the stairs. The freezing water zapped her breath when they sank to the floor.

She twisted the dagger, holding it with both hands when he tried to pull it out.

Die, you fucking rat!

With a hand to his throat, she pushed her thumb against his trachea. He shut his eyes. She squeezed harder, her twists more vigorous.

She released the dagger and squeezed his trachea with both of her thumbs. Bubbles escaped her mouth when she yelled. The cracking sounds underneath her fingertips were amplified by the water.

The necromancer coughed up bubbles and took a breath that filled his lungs with liquid. His bloodshot eyes rolled to the back of his head, and he went limp.

She looked at him from his eyes, down to his neck, then emerged from the water. She took a breath, washed off the blood on her hands, and wrung out her short hair.

I killed one ...

Mika reached into chilly water, pulled out her dagger, and dried it before putting it back in her sheath.

I really killed one ... A thrilled breath escaped her mouth. Her hands were shaking from excitement.

I killed a necromancer! She bit her bottom lip. *I killed* someone!

Bending over one more time, she stuck the fingers of both her hands into his mouth and braced herself, exhaling when she pulled him out of the water and up the stairs.

She let the necromancer's head crash onto the steps. His face pointed at her, his mouth curved into a painful gape that revealed his top teeth, all stained with blood. Her crinkled eyes and eager smile straightened when she saw his life essence exit his nose and enter her chest.

She closed her eyes, accepting the visions.

She saw her victim being given a token by an important-looking man in necromancer attire. Then, she saw a campsite full of necromancers laughing and joking, drinking from brown mugs; they couldn't stop laughing. The last vision made Mika clench her dagger, for a black cloud spread under the afternoon skies, drowning out the sun and surrounding Yevera in darkness.

He was part of the raid. Her mood swung from ecstatic to depressed. She was trying her best not to cry.

~ *He was one of them ... He was one of them ... HE WAS ONE OF THEM ...*

Her sadness turned to anger, the uncontrollable anger that made the voices, the fire, talk to her.

~ *He's the one who made the cloud ...*
~ *He's the one who made them start the fires ...*

They told her the truth; he was the reason the Yeverans had to set their homes on fire.

~ He needs to pay ... he needs to pay for killing our mother ... he killed our mother ...

Yeverans couldn't see because of the black cloud that blocked the sun, the cloud that allowed the walkers to carve through her friends and allowed the necromancers' magic to be more powerful.

~ THIS FAT BASTARD WAS TOO SCARED TO GO IN AND FIGHT ...
~ HE WAS TOO SCARED TO BE A REAL WARRIOR ...

What can I do?

She pressed her hands to her face and applied pressure, rubbing them on her temple and through her hair.

~ Make them remember ...

This voice belonged to a beautiful woman.

Make them remember? How do I make them remember?

~ Carve her name into his skull ...

Mika noticed her dagger was enflamed with a fire that caused the blade to glow a hot red. She looked at the necromancer's bald head; his bloodshot eyes and open mouth disgusted her.

She knelt next to him, spat in his face, and held her dagger inches from his forehead.

"For those you were too scared to face," she said.

She held his head with her free hand and carved into his skin with her dagger. The action made Addie's ears cower. The smell of burning flesh ran into Mika's nostrils.

Addie used his snout to move the dagger away from the necromancer, telling Mika what she was doing was wrong.

Mika latched on to his snout.

"Stop it," she hissed, her wild, piercing, wide eyes cutting through Addie.

He took a breath and stayed next to her side. Whether she was doing good or evil, he would protect and never leave her.

Mika continued carving with her enflamed knife until she was satisfied with her work. She straightened herself and read bloodying letters on the necromancer's skull.

Y E V E R A

She stood, but before she took the first step, the voices rang in her ears. One voice in particular sounded almost motherly, so loving and caring...

~ *There's more we can do ...*

What can we do?

One of the torches by the door ignited with a yellow flame.

A row of small yellow flames appeared across the necromancer's neck. Understanding, Mika knelt next to the necromancer, placed her dagger on his neck, and pushed down with all her weight. She moved her blade back and forth, sawing through the necromancer's skin, forcing Addie to look away.

~ *Ah ... hahahaha ... oh, Mika ...*

Her movements became more and more aggressive, more brutal as she was egged on.

~ *Mika ... you are doing so well ...*

Mika reached the crushed trachea, carved through it, and reached the spine. She moved his head back and hacked away at the necromancer's bone with her dagger until it split.

~ *That's it ... make him pay for what he did to your mother ...*

Mika finished carving through the rest of his neck. She stood, holding the necromancer's head by the hole under his chin. Her own head lolling forward, she gritted her teeth together.

~ *Go now ... finish it, sweetie ...*

With a slow walk, she made her way up the stairs. She reached the torch with the yellow flame, opened the necromancer's mouth, and fed the torch in between his teeth. After a bit of twisting and turning, she faced the top of his head to her and read the carvings on his skull.

Y E V E R A

She cleaned off her dagger on her pants, sheathed it, and leaned back against the wall, letting out a long breath. Then she smiled. When she opened her eyes, her smile grew. The fact that she just killed a human, someone with family, friends, pets, a life, hobbies, goals, ambitions, desires, and feelings, didn't matter to her. Mika could finally say she took the life of a human, and she was proud. And what she did after? A psychotic smile that showed her teeth appeared on her face when she realized his friends would soon find her work.

Addie approached, and she knelt in front of him. She communicated to him that the necromancer was a mean and evil person. There was no reason to be afraid. She hugged and kissed him, took a breath, and eased the smile from her face. She still needed to complete her side of the deal, and she didn't know when *the next moonrise* would be.

Mika stood, got naked, ran down to the necromancer, stripped him of his clothes, and put them on herself. Though loose in the midsection, the length fit her well. She dried the clothes with a flame and put her backpack on Addie, hiding the flower in one of the pockets.

"I love you," she said, hugging him.

"Stay," she communicated. "Danger."

When Addie understood, she communicated that she loved him, stood, and walked through the door and into the dining room. She faced the door and closed it, taking a deep breath. A man flashed a torch in her face.

"Done draining the water?" He asked.

Mika jumped. She turned with scared, wide eyes and faced a necromancer with long, curly hair. High tailored clothes accentuated his defined pecs and muscular arms that flexed when he moved the torch in his hand to his face.

The flame revealed a pointy nose and a strong jawline.

"Sorry," he said. "Didn't mean to scare you, sister." He smiled, but the smile went away, and his face straightened.

Mika swallowed.

"Hey, you have …" He inched the torch closer to Mika's body. "You have blood on your robes."

Her face dropped to her chest. He was right.

She looked at the necromancer, her voice deepened, and she moved her hands to show more expression.

"I get bloody noses. I'm just stressed is all." All conscious acts, she passed her hand through her hair and rubbed her neck.

"I understand. It's been stressful for all of us." He moved and relit the torches.

Mika caught a whiff of his woody fragrance, making her shoulders relax and her lungs inhale more of the scent.

When he finished lighting the second torch, he turned to Mika. "I've never seen you before. Did you come in with the last batch of recruits? Cool scar you have there."

"Thank you." Mika felt the scar with her fingers. "And yes, I did. Still trying to figure everything out." She looked toward the dining necromancers, the enormous brazier, then back at the necromancer in front of her before she gave a curtsy. "I am Mika Plum." It felt awkward not finishing her usual introduction.

He bowed. "I'm Major Lieutenant Seth. We don't use last names around here. We are all brothers and sisters wearing the same uniform." He began walking away. "Make sure you eat."

He passed Mika, giving her another whiff of his fragrance.

With one last look at Seth, she walked to where the other necromancers were eating. If her ad hoc disguise worked for a lieutenant, then it was sure to work for the other necromancers. She made her way to the food line.

The food was inside of covered cooking pots that rested on a counter. Mika grabbed a bowl and utensils before serving herself fried chicken tenders and mashed potatoes mixed with sprouts and broccoli. Holding her bowl with both hands, she faced the tables. The image reminded her of morning and afternoon school meals in Yevera, the best part of the day after the grueling workouts. A table full of young women and an empty seat caught her eye, and she approached.

"May I sit here?" Mika asked.

A blonde with a small nose looked up. "Of course! You don't need to ask!"

Mika sat and took a bite of the chicken. Delicious juices squirted into her mouth.

"… but it's pretty easy to learn how to draw," said a teenager with brown hair and downturned eyes. "You just have to practice. It took me years to get where I am today."

A busty necromancer with chunky cheeks and black hair smiled. "They're very pretty, Sarah!" She handed Sarah a blue notebook.

Sarah smiled and looked at Mika. "Would you like to see some of my drawings?" She slid the notebook across the table.

Mika accepted it. With food still in her mouth, she flipped to the first page.

The drawing was dark: a girl sitting on the ground crying. Around her, black lines represented shadows, or darkness ... something evil. The words *I DO NOT BELONG HERE* were shaky. Dried portions on the page told Mika that Sarah's tears were falling onto the sheet when she made the drawing. Mika continued to analyze the image before skipping a few pages forward.

In the same drawing style, the girl stood in front of a tall man. The man was covered in smokey clouds; he was Gral, the deity of mori. He held a bloodied dagger in one hand and touched the girl's shoulder with the other. The words *You are my child. It's not your time* were written above him.

A journal, Mika concluded, *a journal with drawings instead of words.*

Mika savored another bite of the chicken. She looked at Sarah. "Which drawing is your favorite?"

Sarah reached over and flipped the pages. "This one," she whispered and handed Mika the notebook.

Mika's pupils dilated at the drawing's beauty. The skies were colored a beautiful blue that blended into white streaks of clouds. Despite the daylight, two moons shone brightly over a green field with an assortment of flowers. Sarah looked up to a man in necromancer armor; he handed her a pendant. The words *The family I always wanted* were written in pink. A love heart was drawn in red underneath the two humans.

Mika continued looking at the drawing, but she was lost in thought. She always thought the necromancers would be evil, inhumane people who hated everything, including each other. It was hard for her to accept that they all cared for their own. Calling each other brothers and sisters, they were nothing compared to the people in Di'Abribel or in Celeste. Not even in Yevera did Mika see such camaraderie.

"What do you think?" Sarah's voice crept into Mika's ears.

Mika continued looking at the pages, still half lost in thought. "I'm ..." She looked at Sarah. "I'm glad you feel welcome here."

Sarah took the notebook. "This place has been a blessing. I can't imagine myself anywhere else in the world." She smiled and closed her eyes, exhaling a breath that lowered her shoulders, "What'll you girls do when this war is over? I'm thinking of staying … forever."

The blonde girl spoke. "I'm getting out! No more necromancy for me. I'm going back to the Andtun Islands and raising a family. I want two babies."

Sarah and the blonde looked at the busty necromancer with bangs. She shook her head.

"I'm using the payment they give me to sail. I want to watch the stars from the middle of the ocean."

All the girls looked at Mika, and Mika looked at them. "I'm going to go find …" She reached for her dragon flower but remembered she had left it with Addie. She lowered her hand, followed by her head. For some reason, her mood was plummeting. "I'm going to adventure and find a dragon."

"You girls are leaving me?" Sarah sat back; her downturned eyes lowered more.

"Not yet we're not! Not yet at least!" the blonde said. "Are you girls ready for the meeting?" She rolled her eyes, trying to bring the happy mood back to the table.

"I have a feeling something went wrong on this one." The busty necromancer adjusted herself in the seat.

Sarah placed the book in a leather bag. "Your intuition is always right, Linda."

"Yeah," Linda shrugged. "I won't be there. I have prison duty tonight, unfortunately. I think they're having me execute them with Josh. We're both low on essence …"

"Nope, nope." The blonde shook her head. "I'd rather miss out on essence than work the prison." She stood, grabbed her bowl, and walked away. "See you girls there. I have to drop my bag off."

"I'd rather miss out also." Linda's gaze dropped.

Sarah stood, grabbed her bowl, and kissed Linda's head before slinging her bag and walking away.

Linda began to stand, but Mika stopped her when an idea rushed through her mind.

"Would you like to switch?" Mika grabbed Linda's bowl and placed it in hers. "I'm extremely low on essence, and I don't mind working the prison."

Linda's smile widened more than her eyes. "Really?"

"Yeah!" Mika matched her smile and wide eyes. "Just take me there, so John knows it'll be me instead of you!"

"Do you mean Josh?"

Mika's face reddened. She shook her head, closed her eyes, and smiled. "Yes, yes, I meant Josh."

"Okay." Linda jumped off her seat. "I'm up for it!"

Mika matched her enthusiasm and mocked her facial expressions. "Right! Let me put these away, and I'll follow you!"

Mika and Linda walked side by side. "Do you ever feel bad executing prisoners?" Linda asked, her voice low.

Mika sensed the dissatisfaction in Linda, so she replied in a way that would please her. "They're humans, just like us."

Linda stopped and looked at Mika. "They are! They really, really are!" She sighed and shook her head. "I just wish we could finish this war. All the senseless killing and bloodshed will stop then."

"Why do you think it's taking so long?" Mika probed.

Linda continued walking. "My intuition tells me it's because of the paladins. They're being defensive ... I think all their recent losses have them like that. Or they're trying to buy time until they figure out how to navigate the forest. Honestly, I don't think they know about the spell that will show them the way through the maze."

Mika nodded. *They will soon.*

They walked in silence through the halls and to the back wall of the cathedral. A long, winding staircase led them to the second floor. At the opposite end of the second floor was a heavy metal door with a small window protected by metal bars. Linda knocked four times, and a young man with uncombed hair opened the door. He looked at Linda, then at Mika, then back at Linda when she spoke.

"She's taking my spot."

"Sounds good." Josh stepped aside, allowing Mika through.

Linda hugged Mika. "I never got your name."

"I am Mika," she said. *Plum of Yevera ...*

"I'll let you know what was said at the meeting. Thanks again. Please be safe. My intuition tells me something bad will happen soon." Linda held her breasts with her arm to prevent them from bouncing when she ran toward the stairs.

Mika stepped through the doorway. She was met with the scent of old sweat and feces when she entered the prison. She held her hand over her nose and mouth. "Ugh, this is disgusting!"

"Yeah," said Josh. "Faster we kill them, faster we get out of here. Already got the first one out there." He pointed to the middle of the room. A naked man was bent over with his arms tied behind his back.

Mika took in her surroundings. In front of her was a large, horse-shoe-shaped desk with books, papers, and candles. In front of the desk was a long, wide hallway flanked by cells on both sides. The second floor of the room also had cells on both sides. A spiral staircase led up to the second floor and to the ceiling, where a blood-red sigil, a crossed-out S inside a circle, rotated in the air. Unknown to Mika, the sigil prevented anyone without necromancer attire from casting magic.

Josh handed Mika a double-sided axe with a crimson emblem between the black-and-silver blades. "You first?"

Mika's eyes widened when she accepted the axe. She looked at the opposite side. "This is …" she brought the emblem close to her face: a crimson square behind a black battle axe. "This is of Yeveran descent!" She looked at Josh. "This is Yeveran workmanship!"

"Is it? Where is that at?" Josh's lips were pouty, but he seemed interested in Mika's statement.

Mika held the piece of her history. The only relics and weapons from Yevera left, to her knowledge, were the ones carried by the survivors on their trip to Di'Abribel. Mika knew the axe she held specialized in decapitations and was carried by Yeveran executioners. Josh must not know or remember about Yevera.

Her lips grew into a smile.

You'll remember Yevera how I want you to, Josh.

"It's long gone now, an ancient civilization of powerful, fearless, beautiful warriors." She spun the axe in the air.

"There's a lot of weapons in the back," said Josh. "I'm sure you can keep it if you ask Liam. Are you ready?"

"Following you, Josh." She grasped the axe with both hands, admiring its workmanship with an eager smile on her face.

Josh marched forward; his posture was erect, and he walked with class.

They stopped in front of the naked man. Immobile, his arms were bound, legs attached to a tie-down on the floor, and his head stretched out, placed on a bloodied beheading headrest that protruded from the ground.

"Release me and fight me like a real man," the bald prisoner hissed. "Don't be a fucking coward, *Joshua.*"

Josh slapped the prisoner's back, leaving a handprint that welted the moment he lifted his hand. "Shut up, old man. Mika, would you?"

Mika positioned herself beside the prisoner. She tightened her grip on the axe. Her hands were sweaty, but she didn't want to show weakness by rubbing them on her clothes.

"Yeah, come on Mika, you little whore. Maybe if you do it fast, little Joshua here will look at you differently. Maybe he'll look past that scar and ignore your measly tits."

Mika's hands had gripped the axe with such force she felt it was going to break.

"You're letting him talk. Just kill him." Josh held his chin high and had his arms across his chest.

The prisoner tried to move when Mika widened her stance. There was an angry desperation in his voice now. "Come on, you useless bitch. Prove that you're good for something, even if it's not fucking."

Mika rested the axe on her shoulder and rotated her hips.

The prisoner's words were a torrent of panic now. "You're nothing, and you will always be nothing. The paladins will come and skull-fuck you before they kill you! No one will let you take Celeste, and all your dead friends will have been for nothing!"

The axe swung through the air. The room fell silent after gasps and shouts bounced from the walls. A head thudded and bounced on the ground. A body wearing necromancer robes collapsed.

"What the fuck?" The bound prisoner tried to move; his eyes were wide, looking at Josh's head, which continued rolling on the ground. "What the fuck? What the fuck! What the fuck!"

Mika backhanded the prisoner across the mouth. "Shut up or you're next."

She remained still and waited for Josh's life essence. It exited his decapitated head and entered Mika. She coughed, coughed again, and vomited.

"It's corrupt! It's corrupt essence!" an older lady yelled from inside her cell.

Corrupt essence? How? I just killed a necromancer ...

She looked at the body, then the head. She vomited again; blood was mixed with fried chicken and mashed potatoes. She ignored the visions from Josh, instead focusing on why she just absorbed corrupt essence. She wiped the stressful sweat from her forehead.

Shit, shit, shit. I'm bound to the Abyss ... I'm bound to the Abyss. How? This must be a mistake. This must be a fucking mistake!

The room turned into an uproar. Mika's mind was screaming the same questions they had. Prisoners screamed, yelled, asked questions, shouted for help. They thought they were next.

"Shut up!" Mika stood. "Shut up!" The room fell silent.

She looked at the body and thought of every reason why his death produced corrupted essence. *Noncombatant? No, he's a necromancer. Innocent? No, his leader has a warrior's stone. Surrendered? Can't be, he had more of a chance to fight than the one in the tunnel.* She couldn't waste more time thinking.

She addressed the prisoners after using ventus and aqua to clean the vomit. "I'm here to help. How do I get you out?"

All prisoners talked at once.

"One at a time! If there is another uproar, I will leave all of you in here!"

The bound prisoner began to talk. "You have to—"

"Not you," Mika interrupted. She towered over him and looked at him from the bottom of her eyes. "You're not allowed to speak to me."

The bound prisoner closed his eyes.

A man with a crackle in his voice spoke from the second floor. "The sigil on the ceiling. It's stopping us from casting magic! If you hit it with something, it will break. I can get us out with a few spells I know!"

Mika swung the axe to cut the rope holding the bound prisoner's head. She ran to the stairs and used the railing to propel herself up. Passing the second floor, she continued and reached the top of the stairs. The blood-red sigil rotated just inches above her. She touched it; its glassy texture reminded her of her dragon flower. She plunged her axe into it, and it shattered into millions of pieces that disappeared before they touched the ground.

Mika looked over the stairs, and a few cells opened. Clothed but bald prisoners emerged and began opening the closed cells. Mika hurried down the stairs, and by the time she reached the bottom, all the prisoners were free. When her boots touched the ground, the whispers quieted, and they faced their rescuer.

A man wearing a jet-black coat walked up to her. "Tell me," he said, inching his face closer to analyze her scar, "are you the sorceress?"

Mika felt uncomfortable with him being so close. She placed a hand on his chest and moved him away from her. He complied.

To answer his question, Mika opened her palm and summoned a ball of fire. Gasps filled the room.

The man in the jet-black coat turned around. "Ladies, gentlemen, this is the one! This is the one who has been shown to me in dreams by Tenebris herself! You've heard me talk about her, and now ..." He looked at Mika, then back at the crowd. "Now she is here in front of me! In front of us! In front of you." He started pointing. "And you, and you, and you!"

He faced Mika. "Sorceress, what is your name? And what will you have us do?"

She looked at the crowd, and they stared back at her. What now? What does she say? What does she have them do? Kill the necromancers! Take over the cathedral and Celeste! But how does she convince so many people to risk their lives to do so? She remembered the spell Nessa taught her, the one that would let her manipulate people's emotions. Maybe it was time to test it out, along with all the knowledge she learned during captivity.

She turned around, went up a few steps so everyone could see her, and whispered, "Tenebris," imagining people's hearts and minds being filled with ...

Hope.

"I am Mika Plum of Yevera."

She analyzed the crowd. "I know you're afraid." Her voice was loud and deep. "I know you're scared, and I know you were just minutes from death, but our fight is not over. None of you are defeated, and none of you will be defeated by the rats that have plagued our lands."

Anger.

300

"These vile excuses for humans must pay for what they've done to you, to your family, to our children. Only together, only under my hand will we be able to stop them. I did not come here with an army; I did not come here with a team. I came here on my own! If a lone person can do this much ..." She held her hand toward Josh's body. "How much can we do when we are united?"

A man raised his fist and shouted.

Excitement.

"All that is left is for us to escape and return to our families and form an army that will put the paladins and their useless tactics to shame. An army that will surpass any that has risen before in Celeste and Irstia. An army that will purge this curse that has been haunting us."

Cheers erupted in the crowd.

"More necromancers will die tonight, by my hand, and by yours!" She tasted the vomit in her mouth. "The Abyss will not stop us from killing them! Necromancers of the Lost Forest, in the name of Celeste, I, Mika Plum of Yevera, herby declare war on you!" She held her axe to the sky. "For Celeste!"

"For Celeste!" the crowd boomed.

She watched the crowd's eager eyes. Their smiles hinted that victory was within reach. She wanted to join them. She wanted to go with her new followers and fight out of the Lost Forest with them ... but she couldn't. Something held her back, and that something was the most important thing in her life.

Mika looked at the man in the jet-black coat, handing him the piece of Yeveran history. "Night vision will get them out of here. You're in charge. Kill as many as you can on the way out."

I need to return to Addie.

20. EXTINGUISHED

Standing in the corner of the canteen, Mika held her palms toward the massive brazier that hung from the ceiling. Concentrating on the flame, she guided it upward and brought it crashing down on the wooden tables. The fire exploded in a roar, sending embers and burning oil throughout the dining room. Mika stood in awe at the destruction she caused, not once blinking from the bright flames in front of her. Shouted commands and the sounds of panicked boot-falls were all around her. A massive horn sounded from above.

Seth ran toward Mika, his eyes showing nothing but fierce determination. He raised his arm to block his face from the burning flame.

"What happened?" Seth looked at Mika, scanning her up, down, front, and back. "Are you hurt?"

"I …" Mika widened her eyes and shook her head, feigning the appearance of being shocked. She forced fear out of her voice, making it tremble. "I don't know!"

She pretended the fire bothered her.

Seth wrapped his arm around Mika and guided her away from the growing inferno and to the center of the cathedral. Looking back, Mika ordered the flame up the stone pillar and further toward the kitchen.

"Someone cast aqua!" Seth shouted. He used his body to block the heat from reaching Mika until he walked her to safety. The fire made the inside of the cathedral a golden orange color.

An older female raced to the inferno, brought her arms back, and shot them forward, placing her palms together toward the fire. "Aqua!"

Gallons of water shot from her palms with enough force to make the necromancer stumble back. She doused the flames. Mika curved them upward. The fire seemed to understand and formed from flames into lava before crashing down onto the woman like a wave from the ocean.

Don't kill them! Just wound them! I can't afford any more corrupt essence!

The fire slithered away.

The burning necromancer ran from the lava, wailing, her arms spinning like pinwheels. She ran past a group of fellow necromancers who gave chase. The men took off their clothing to help pat away the flames.

"The flame is alive, I know it." Seth watched the lava climb up the walls and pillars, spewing out a lava rock that missed an armored necromancer by an inch.

Mika hid her hand under her cloak, clenched it, watched the lava compress; when she opened her hand, the lava exploded rocks and doubled in size. She shifted her fingers, and the lava began crawling toward her and the necromancers.

"Move!" A short necromancer pushed his way through. "Terra!"

His hands shook; it looked like he was straining to push up. His hands rose, and rocks broke through the cathedral floor and blocked the lava from spreading.

Mika shifted her hand, and the lava spewed forward, splashing onto the necromancer's face. He stumbled and screamed, breaking the concentration on his magic. The lava continued.

Necromancers used ventus to blow the lava back, aqua to douse it, terra to reroute it, and magical barriers to protect each other from the heat and fire.

Mika crouched when the lava exploded a rock. Making sure no one was watching her, she raised her hand and twisted it, causing a section to spiral past the second floor. Closing her hand, the rising lava closed into a ball. Mika opened her hand, and the lava spread across the air, creating a slow-falling blanket above the shocked necromancers.

She forced her hand down, causing the fire to plummet and bloom into a blazing calamity, engulfing everything underneath and incinerating the necromancers who tried to fight the inferno.

Don't kill them! Just make them suffer!

The lava pooled away from the necromancers it engulfed, leaving them in a circle filled with sizzling gore and charred flesh. Their screams bounced and echoed through the once-quiet cathedral.

A woman with shoulder-length ash-black hair with jet-black lowlights approached, offering her hand to Seth. She pulled him up once he accepted the help. The female wore a belt with two human skulls hanging from it. More necromancers approached, and having learned the necromancers were the enemy, the inferno erupted toward them, trying to grab them and suck them into the lava. The female with the belt of skulls shot her arms to the side. Shouting a mori spell, each necromancer was surrounded by an ashy barrier that protected them. With a sweep of her arm, a powerful wind pushed the lava away from all her troops. The lava crashed onto the adjacent wall and slithered up it.

The necromancer undid the barriers.

"You, you, and you four—" She pointed at a few necromancers that included Sarah and Linda. "—check the prisoners."

The group sprinted to the spiral staircase.

"You two," she said in a voice calm but direct, "recall all scouts. Everyone outside in a defensive perimeter around the cathedral."

"Yes, Mistress Kathrine." The two men sprinted toward the door.

Kathrine noticed Mika and signaled for her to approach.

Mika couldn't move. She studied the woman's facial features. Angry eyes rested on an oval face, a turned-up nose flared when she breathed, and her lips parted, revealing grinding, straight, white teeth. Mika recognized Kathrine, the necromancer that butchered her mother more than six years ago. As if the murder occurred the night before, Kathrine had not aged a single day.

Mika hadn't noticed her eyebrows began to hide her eyes and that she too was grinding her teeth.

"Hurry up!" Kathrine screamed. Anger was clear in her powerful, authoritative, intelligent voice.

Mika approached her. *Kathrine. Her name is Kathrine.*

Kathrine closed her eyes and took a breath, then stood straight and looked into Mika's eyes. They were the same height. Mika returned the stare, her face straight, hiding the hatred, anger, and lack of fear she felt. She was glad she was not wearing her flower.

Kathrine lifted her chin. "Someone is controlling the fire. Set up a sigil on the roof."

Mika nodded.

"Mistress Kathrine," Seth said as he approached, "I'll go with her."

Kathrine snapped a glare at Seth. "I want results, *not* conversation, Lieutenant."

Seth nodded, waved toward Mika, and set off in a sprint to the staircase.

Looking away from Kathrine, Mika increased her speed until she trailed behind Seth, whose curly hair danced behind him when he ran—hair like Mika's before she had cut it.

Kathrine. Kathrine killed my mother.

Seth cleared the first five steps with a single leap and used the railing to help him move up the stairs faster. Mika followed, but Seth had such technique that he left Mika far behind. She was heaving by the time she reached the second floor. Seth was far ahead; it seemed like he'd done this millions of times.

Mika stopped to catch her breath. She leaned over the railing and looked below: the inferno fought back the necromancers pushing against it, but it was no match for their magic. In a few minutes, it would be gone. Mika guided it away from spells and had it snake around the necromancers. They ran away, but one woman was caught in the middle. The lava reached up to her face and another rushed between her feet, causing her to fall. The lava slithered over in slow inches, pulling her in when she tried to pull away until she was covered in a blanket of lava.

Since Mika was still in combat, the necromancer's essence was invisible when it entered Mika's chest. Still, Mika could taste the corrupt essence's dry, sandy texture. She tried to cough it out but vomited over the railing.

Why is this happening?

A second vomit caught Seth's attention.

"Mika!" he shouted from above.

She jumped. *Shit, he knows.*

"Mika, are you okay?"

Mika was quick. "Yes!" She pretended to vomit again. "I'm just" –and she almost said *exhausted*– "dizzy! I'm dizzy!"

"We'll get rest when this is over. Push through, you can do it!"

Mika spit out the rest of the vomit. Before she continued, she caught a glimpse of the tunnel door next to the cafeteria, beyond which hid Addie. The fire understood—the lava concentrated there, making it the hottest portion, but keeping the door itself untouched by the fire.

I hope he's not scared.

With a final look at the growing catastrophe and the necromancers' attempts to stop it, she made her way up the stairs and caught up to Seth at the top. The stairs swayed when Mika moved.

"This is going to fall!" She clasped onto the railings and stood motionless.

Seth laughed. "You think this is scary?" Seth pointed at a ledge, ignoring the swaying staircase. "We have to shimmy through *this* now."

The ledge extended just a foot from the wall. Below the ledge was four stories of nothing but air. At the bottom, a floor covered in glowing lava.

Mika grimaced; the floor seemed to stretch away from her when she looked down. "Couldn't have built it easier?"

Seth stepped on the ledge, putting his back to the wall. "We could have," he said, "but that would've made it easier for enemies to destroy sigils." He began to shimmy away from Mika.

Mika watched him shimmy. Pebbles fell from the ledge.

"You coming?" Seth asked, still shimmying away.

Mika didn't reply, but she moved onto the ledge.

Why am I here? Why am I even doing this?

Placing her heel on the ledge, her tiny feet made her feel more balanced than Seth seemed to be. She moved heel to heel toward him, scraping the back of her boot against the wall.

"Don't—" Seth's robe latched onto something on the wall, and he yanked it away. "Don't look down." He kicked a pebble off the ledge. The moving object caught Mika's eyes, and her gaze followed the pebble diving into the lava.

The distance from her to the ground made her dizzy. She stiffened, her foot slipped, her opposite leg tensed, and her heart exploded with a fearful, surviving rush. A shout escaped her mouth.

"Don't move! Don't move!" Seth's voice was quick.

She tried to dig her nails into the wall behind her and shut her eyes, but a wave of dizziness started to well up in her, so she opened them again and looked at the ceiling, only a few feet away from her reach. She shuffled toward Seth, only concentrating on what she felt on her feet.

"I'm okay," she lied. "I'm okay."

Explosions came from below, followed by distant shouts.

"The prisoners escaped!" Seth cried out.

Mika opened her eyes.

Colors of magic exploded from the second floor. Mika saw the prisoners and necromancers casting magic at each other in an array of loud, mesmerizing, colorful spells of every affinity. Mika forced the lava to reach toward the necromancers, shifting their focus and interrupting their spells.

"We need to hurry!" Seth quickened his pace.

Mika looked for Sarah and Linda on the second floor. The fact that prisoners burst out unwounded told them the two girls she talked to just moments earlier had been killed, sending an awkward sting into her heart.

I hope they didn't suffer, she thought. Deep down, though, she knew both girls and the other four necromancers were tortured.

They reached a narrow platform that extended past the ledge. Seth leaned over and looked at the battle below. Mika stood by his side, focused on the growing lava, proud of the destruction and chaos she was causing. She walked behind Seth.

Two prisoners, a man and a woman, ran across the catwalk of the second floor. The woman pointed at Mika and Seth, pulled her arm back, and sent terra spikes toward Mika.

"Watch out!" Seth cried out.

He pulled Mika by the arm and spun her behind him, holding her in a protective hug. A thud followed, and Mika looked down to see a large terra spike protruding from Seth's abdomen. Seth struggled to breathe. He pushed Mika back and spun around.

"Mori!"

A mysterious black ball formed between Seth's hands. He launched the ball through the air, and it struck the woman in the stomach. Mika watched in horror as the woman's stomach bloated until it burst, sending bits of her intestines and skin flying in front of her. She stood lifeless, her spine began bending back, and her head touched her ankles before she fell to the side.

Oh, no ... Mika ground her teeth.

Seth launched another ball of mori that collided with the man's legs, which expanded and burst. His torso seeped blood, leaving a trail that followed him as he crawled away.

Seth lowered himself to his butt and extended his legs in front of him, leaning back on his palms. Mika, still dumbstruck, realized he risked himself for her.

"Remember," he said, sighing every few words, "when you rise up in ranks, the most important thing must remain those you are commanding."

Seth looked at Mika. His face was dripping with sweat, one of his eyes was closed, and the corner of his mouth was open, revealing a string of saliva that moved with each of his breaths. He looked away and began to stand.

"How are you going to get down?" She pointed both her hands to the spike and looked Seth in the eyes. "There's a spike through your stomach! You won't be able to shimmy!"

"We have deadlier things to worry about." The necromancer lieutenant turned around and stood at the edge of the platform, drawing a blood-red circle above him.

Mika looked down at the fighting. She watched the prisoners retreat to the back of the cathedral, below the large, winding stairs. The inferno now engulfed the second floor. She looked up at the sigil—Seth had finished the large S inside the massive ring. One more line, and all the prisoners would die.

Mika had to do something. She couldn't let him complete the sigil, but doubt began to creep in. The necromancers weren't bad—not intrinsically—they were just like her, just like her friends, like Sandra, Stacy, Rosa, Lila. They were human beings with feelings. The belt of skulls appeared in her mind.

Kathrine.

Mika knew she wouldn't be there if it weren't for Kathrine. She'd be at home, with her mother, with Page, in Yevera. The sigil was seconds from being active.

Kathrine needs to die; so does anyone that stands in the way of that happening.

"Seth?" Mika stepped toward him.

"Yes, sister?"

She braced a leg behind her. "I'm sorry."

With a heavy heart, she took a step, summoned a ball of fire, and released it on Seth. She raised her foot and kicked him off the platform. Mika refused to watch Seth fall in a ball of fire, down into the lava below.

Using her dagger, she destroyed the unfinished sigil and waited for Seth's essence. She tasted the dry and sandy mist and leaned forward before vomiting twice. After a moment of thinking, she made her way onto the ledge and shimmied back to the staircase. On her way down, she tried her best to ignore Seth's visions, showing her images of a beautiful baby and a young woman; the scene of a mystical, green island with dragons flying in the distance; and his young son and daughter laughing with him when they fed a set of hungry, motherless kittens.

He was a good person.

A slow walk down the stairs let her think, but she composed herself when she reached the bottom floor, now entirely engulfed in lava. The inferno parted, making a path for Mika to walk on the charred floor, showing every necromancer in the cathedral that she—the girl with short brown hair, a scar across her cheek, and wearing their uniform—was the one responsible for the destruction.

Mika walked through the opening the flames made for her, encasing her in a tunnel of ignis that hid her from the necromancers casting magic toward her. She held her arms out, touching the thick, smooth lava.

~ *Mommy ... why can't we kill more ... why don't you want them to die ...*

~ *We killed one of them ...*

~ *And the one you sent down from above ...*

"My children, lead me to Addie."

309

They obeyed, opening a burnt path for her to follow. She picked up her pace toward the door, pulled it open, and stepped through. Addie, frightened, stood at the sight of his mother.

Mika zoomed down the stairs and into the freezing water that had risen to her chest, forcing Mika to swim instead of wade. She changed into dry clothes upon reaching the opposite side and placed the dragon flower in her hair, its petals bent upward in anticipation. She ran up the stairs and opened the hatch, peeked her head through, noticing hundreds of necromancers sprinting toward her from the cathedral.

"Go!" she screamed, pushing Addie outside. "Run!"

She pulled herself up and set off at a dead sprint. She used her night-vision spell to guide her out of the forest, following the blood-red mist in a different direction than before.

"That way!" Mika pointed.

Addie saw where Mika pointed and followed her finger.

A ball of mori zoomed past Mika and caused a tree in front of her to explode. Wood flew everywhere. Mika covered her face. She tripped but caught herself before pushing through the foliage that scratched her face and arms. Her eardrums rang from the explosions. The red mist curved to the side, setting her up for a spell.

"Ignis!" She flung a ball of fire at the chasing necromancers. One moved out of the way; the other used his shield to block the fireball.

They slowed. "A sorceress?"

"Keep going!" a deep voice hissed.

Mika's breaths were hard and fast, and her heart was exploding. Her feet sank into the moist dirt as she fled. She hopped and vaulted over fallen trees, stepping on some to propel herself into the air. The wind whiffed by her ears.

"Don't let her escape!" she heard a man cry out.

Kathrine's voice zoomed into her ears. "I want her head!"

Aevum essence of many colors glowed ahead. A necromancer teleported out of the essence, swinging a sword. Mika ducked, raising her shoulders for protection. Seeing her life flash forced a curse out of her mouth.

Addie turned around to attack, but Mika ordered him to keep running.

She sped up and held her palms together. "Ignis!"

Separating her hands, a flame stretched in the middle. She sent the stretched flame toward the necromancers, and it grew into a massive wall of fire that charred everything in its path, roaring like a lion on its way toward the casters that chased her.

Screams and orders followed. Within seconds, they were further and further away, to the point she couldn't hear them. She slowed her pace to catch her breath. Jogging, she followed the mist and ordered Addie to curve around when the mist did. A mysterious black wall appeared in front of her, separating her from her pup. She slid to a stop.

"Addie!"

Two more walls appeared to her sides, these farther apart. Mika turned around. Her heart dropped when she saw General Nicholas in full necromancer armor slow to a walk. He summoned a black wall behind him, enclosing himself and Mika and a few trees inside a square the size of a small house.

"Sorceress." His voice, muffled by the helmet, still had the sinister hiss. "How did I catch up to you when I'm wearing triple the gear you are?"

Mika looked at the general's armor. The spikes on his legs and boots stared back. She didn't reply.

Nicholas drew his great sword. "You killed and wounded my troops, all while wearing our uniform." He assumed a wide stance. "I'd say you're crazy, but you're a sorceress; you already know you are."

Crazy. Crazy. Crazy, crazy, crazy, crazy, crazy.

Mika drew her dagger. She clenched it and set it on fire until it burned a bright red.

"This is your last day alive, General Nicholas." Mika too assumed a low stance. She narrowed her eyes.

Nicholas raised his arm. "Ventus!"

Wind pushed Mika toward him. Nicholas dashed, connecting his heel to her stomach.

Mika stumbled and launched a fireball before she hit the ground. Nicholas dodged. Mika scrambled to her feet. She ducked under the parrying hooks and stuck her dagger into Nicholas's plate armor.

She stopped, and so did he. Only the first few inches of the dagger penetrated through the armor. Mika heard chainmail underneath.

311

Nicholas laughed, wrapped his fingers around her head, lifted her, and slammed her onto a nearby tree.

Mika crawled. Nicholas stepped on her and struck her head with the sword's pommel. Blood trickled down her skull.

He kicked her. The spikes fractured her ribs and opened a hole in her lung.

"Vita," she mustered, closing her wounds and crawling to her feet. She held on to a tree for support.

"Holding a sword since age two." Nicholas followed behind her. "First swordfight at age three." He carved into her back with the talons on his gauntlet.

Mika grunted and sprinted away, gaining distance to continue healing her ribcage.

"First kill at seven, six kills by ten ..." Nicholas ran to Mika, grabbed her head, and slammed her face on his knee.

The bones on her face shattered. Tears filled her eyes.

She lay on her back for a few seconds before getting up. She continued healing her ribs and assumed her fighting stance.

"... joined the necromancers at thirteen and killed my first paladin at sixteen." He shook his head. "Yet you think *you* can kill me? You think you can *wound* me? You think you can tire an *elite* necromancer knight?"

He feigned an attack, and Mika flinched.

Nicholas laughed and grabbed her head. "This is for Seth."

He kicked upward; the spikes on his shins pushed into Mika's pelvis.

"Vita!" she howled, healing her pelvis; she curled into a ball on her knees. The healing magic cured the pain. With a healing hand on her pelvis, blood trickling into her mouth, and shaking legs, she inched herself up until she stood in her fighting stance, ready to kill her enemy.

His hand snapped to her neck, and he lifted her. "Why do you continue to deny your death?"

Mika looked through the visor and into his eyes. "Because I still hold my weapon," she cried, sending her dagger's blade at Nicholas's helmet.

The dagger dinged off without causing a scratch.

"Well," Nicholas chuckled, "time to let it go."

He slammed Mika on the ground, dug the spikes into her stomach, and used the blades on his gauntlet to saw away the wrist Mika used to hold on to her dagger.

~ *HE'S KILLING US ...*

Mika screamed and squirmed. She saw blood spurting onto his helmet; her hand wanted to open, but she kept it shut. Addie's yelping barks were muffled.

Addie! Addie!

~ *She's going to die ... Mom is going to die ...*

Mika tried to move.

A ball of fire formed over her chest.

~ *Shout our name ... Shout our name ... SHOUT OUR NAME ...*

Nicholas finished carving through the first bone on her wrist.

"Ignis!"

The ball of fire sparked, disappeared, and then reappeared in a massive explosion that sent Nicholas onto his back. His magical walls faded.

Mika mustered her strength to get up, but the pain throughout her body was intolerable; the squirts of blood from her wrist caused a rapid decline in her temperature.

"Vita ..." The healing magic flickered and waned, for the explosion exhausted her.

She sprinted forward, but only a few feet before she slowed. She sprinted forward again, but it was slow, and she only took one step. She walked, fell to her knees, and used her empty hand to support her weight. Still holding on to her dagger with a half-severed hand, blood from her wrist formed a pool under her chest that mixed with thick saliva from her mouth. Unable to hold herself up, she fell to the side.

A high-pitched squeal entered her ears, and tears filled her eyes when she realized it was Addie crying. Her baby was watching her die.

She opened her mouth. She closed her eyes, then reopened them; her vision was blurred. With her last living breath, she mustered enough strength to whisper, "Addie ..."

Her mind shut down, and she began the slow, deep, terminal gasping that made her breaths sound like a breathing tunnel.

21. AEVUM

A clear blue sky stretched for miles and miles of uninterrupted heaven until it curved over the green mountains in the distance. The trees made the mountains seem like they had thick, bushy hair flowing from the peak, down to the lake whose waters mirrored the color of the sky. The wind pushed at the calm water, its ripples forming a gentle reach onto the cut grass that sparkled in the sunlight. The grass continued closer and closer until tiny toes on little feet appeared. The toes crinkled when looked at, and Mika felt the tickling of the grass on the webs of her feet.

She stood closer to the ground. Her legs were thinner, and when she brought her hands in front of her face, they were small, uncalloused, younger, smoother. A brush of her hair told her it wasn't short, but it wasn't the longest it had ever been. Mika passed her soft fingers across her cheek. She didn't feel a scar running across the side of her face.

What's going on?

She moved her head around, noticing the streaks of white clouds that seemed to have been painted by a passing brush. She looked for the sun, but she couldn't find it. She plugged her nose.

I must be dreaming.

When pressure built up in her ears, she realized she was awake just like before … but … what was before? She closed her eyes, trying to remember what she was doing just before this moment. She re-

314

membered Ron in the cell, a knife in his hand. A drawer she used as a shield. Addie being stabbed. Rosa's carriage. Falling asleep. Talking to Nessa. Going to sleep, dreaming of her dragon, and …

Her closed eyes tightened; the force she used made crow's feet next to her eyelids. What happened after? She delved deep into her mind. What happened after the dream?

What happened after the dream?

Mika couldn't remember. She shook her head and turned around. Just feet away, a man with blond hair and highlights that changed colors was standing with a smile on his face. Her heart raced, but it slowed when the man knelt to her height.

Taking a step forward, Mika studied the man's big, light-brown eyes. She took another step, analyzing his small ears. Another step led to another, then Mika stopped when she studied his button nose. The nose told her everything she needed to know.

"You're my father." She was alarmed by her high-pitched voice.

The man's smile widened, revealing his teeth. "You're my daughter."

Mika stepped forward. She felt no overpowering emotions, no need to run to her father, Michael Plum, no crazy thoughts, no questions, no butterflies in her stomach. The only feeling running through her body was an immense sense of respect, a sense of belonging, a sense of friendship toward the man killed in war when she was just a child. Her legs stopped moving when she was feet away from him.

She held her arms out just a few inches from her waist and closed her eyes. Her foot moved behind the other, and a slow, little crouch gave her father the most perfect curtsy he had ever seen.

"Nice to meet you," she said, smiling with closed eyes, her face pointing toward his feet. "I am Mika Plum of Yevera."

After she recovered from her curtsy, he extended his palm to his daughter, allowing Mika to place her hand on his.

"And I am Michael Plum," he said, kissing Mika's hand, "of the same."

Mika's smile grew so much, so fast, that her cheeks began hurting the second she revealed all her teeth. Her father held his arms out, forcing tears into Mika's eyes. She nodded with a smile, letting the tears run down her cheeks and onto the grass. With a leap forward, she threw her arms around him.

Michael gave his daughter the tightest hug she'd ever received. Mika had never received a hug so close or so true. She could feel their heartbeats pump in the same rhythm, at the same speed, and at the same moments.

She closed her eyes, pushing more tears out before she released a cry that made her words shake. "Daddy ..."

The hands on her shoulders tightened, pulled her closer, and held her in the safest place in the universe. If all armies of the world were marching against her at that moment, she knew she would not be harmed.

She stopped breathing when she sensed another presence. She opened her wet eyes, blinking to wipe away the tears. She didn't want to let go of her father. In front of her stood her mother, Cynthia, in a pure white dress. Being a devoted follower of Angelis in her life, massive, golden, angel wings had grown on Cynthia's back. Cynthia smiled and shook her head, her hair swaying with each shake.

Still hugging her dad, Mika reached a hand to her mom; her hand shook when she couldn't stretch it any further.

Cynthia's smile churned, and her eyes watered, but she gathered enough strength to make her way to her family. She grabbed Mika's hand, knelt, and hugged her daughter. Michael held both of them in his arms. Cynthia grabbed Mika's face and squished her cheeks, making her lips pout into a kiss.

Emotions too high caused Cynthia's words to be broken. "You've grown so, so much."

Mika curbed her emotions. She had to be strong to help her mother feel better.

"Booot ..." she said in a silly voice because Cynthia still held on to her cheeks, and because she wanted to sound funny for Cynthia, "... I 'till look like ah baybee."

Cynthia laughed and shook her head. She moved Mika's hair behind her ear and took a breath to speak, but nothing was said.

Mika reassured her. "It's okay." She didn't like her high-pitched voice; she did her best to make it deeper. "You can tell me."

Cynthia smiled but then straightened her face. "Do you know why you look like this?"

Pulling away from her father, Mika looked at herself. Small, but not undeveloped, she had the body of a teenager. She wore an over-sized red shirt that hid her blue shorts. She looked at her mother with a tilted head and an arched eyebrow. Michael knelt next to Mika.

"This is what you looked like on the happiest day of your life," Cynthia said, playing with the top of Mika's hair. "Do you know what day that was?"

Mika was lost in her mother's gaze, trying to think of what the happiest day in her life was. Several random moments came to Mika's mind, but she couldn't pinpoint which was the happiest. Mika shook her head, just enough for Cynthia to see, but not enough to make Cynthia's hand leave her hair.

"It was the day you woke up in Di'Abribel." She stopped playing with Mika's hair and tilted her daughter's chin so that Mika looked her in the eyes. "There was a wooden box with blankets just at the foot of your bed. You leaned over, inched your face closer and closer to the box, and then …"

The memory ran through Mika's mind, making her muscles relax and her face settle into a mask of serenity. "Addie reached up and licked my nose," she said.

"Yes," said Cynthia, "Addie reached up and licked your nose. He hopped onto the bed and jumped on you until he ran out of energy." Cynthia moved to meet her eyes with Mika's distant stare. "It was the day he recovered from his sickness, three months after you found him under the tree. He was what you turned to when you had no one, and you succeeded in saving him."

Mika's eyes widened. "He's been a nightmare!"

Her parents burst out laughing.

"No, it's true," she said. "He's nuts!"

"We have noticed!" Michael pulled Mika close to him. "We laugh every time!"

Mika's face straightened when she realized her family could see her actions. Her thoughts ran through every private moment she'd ever had, the one with Sylisia the most prominent. Her face reddened. Her eyes widened, and she looked down in embarrassment.

Michael reassured her. "Don't worry, Princess, we knew when to give you privacy."

"Those are things you don't think about in the moment!" Mika cringed and covered her face. "Goodness I'm so embarrassed."

Cynthia and Michael smiled at each other.

They sat together, looking at the lake underneath the mountains. Mika learned about her father, a Yeveran champion who specialized in swords and aevum. He told Mika stories about his life, how he met Cynthia. The most interesting story was the one where Yeverans annexed Mount Cabria, wrenching it from the hands of the Vicquic, her father taking a key role in the battle. He continued, telling Mika how they planned to move from Yevera to Azilia, only to be stopped when the war with Imbris started.

Her mother talked to Mika about the afterlife, how it was a realm of unimaginable power, technology, feelings, and visuals.

"Imagine the greatest feeling you have ever felt, the greatest sights you have ever seen; multiply those by hundreds. That is what the afterlife is like. It's beyond comparison to the living realm."

Mika stared into the distance. "I think the most wonderful feeling I've ever experienced was hugging Dad and opening my eyes to see you standing in front of me," she said. "Your wings are spectacular."

Cynthia extended a wing and hugged Mika with it. "That's what happens when you're devoted to your deity," she said. "They repay you in the afterlife."

Mika accepted the soft hug of the wings. She inhaled, held her breath, then exhaled.

No point in waiting any longer.

"How did I die?" Mika felt Cynthia's wing twitch at the word.

Her father took a breath. "You're not dead, Princess."

He looked at Mika, and Mika looked back.

"Though in the living realm," he said, "you're just one breath away from expelling your essence."

Mika's question wasn't answered. "But, then … I am confused."

Michael looked at the peaks of the mountain. He bit the inside of his lip before telling the story, every detail, every one of Mika's choices, from the moment she woke up in the carriage, to running into the forest, assassinating the necromancer at the stairs, freeing the prisoners, killing Seth, and fighting Nicholas. With every description, memories popped into her head, and she remembered it like it was acted out in front of her.

"You're a hero, Princess. Those prisoners you saved are minutes from exiting the Lost Forest. They'll make it to Di'Abribel and spread stories about you. Stories about the lone woman who saved them from torment and death, the one who was unafraid to don her enemy's uniform ... the sorceress who decapitated a standing necromancer with a single sweep of an axe he himself handed to her."

Mika's gaze fell to the lake. She watched the gentle ripples continue to crawl onto the shore. How does saving the prisoners make her a hero? Is it that hard to decapitate someone? Mika remembered feeling angry before she did, so maybe that helped?

Mika knew there was more, and she was ready for answers. "Why am I here?"

Resurrection was a rare occurrence, only happening in the legends of strong warriors.

"When you killed the necromancers—" he said, stretching his arms in front of him. His elbows popped, and he returned his arm around Mika. "—you absorbed corrupt essence because you wore their uniform and killed them while wearing it, an act considered dishonorable in war."

That explains it. Mika sighed and closed her eyes. She passed her fingers across her forehead. *They posed no threat.*

"Josh, Seth, and the others you killed had enough years in them to leave you in the Abyss for centuries; hundreds and hundreds of years of suffering and nothingness."

Mika felt a distraught energy coming from her mother, but she didn't want to worry her, so she ignored the feeling by not trying to comfort Cynthia.

Mika swallowed. "So, now what?"

Her parents looked at each other.

"There's a way you can redeem yourself," her father said, looking at her. "You have to serve Liranda. Redeem yourself by being devoted to your soul's mother. You are the only child of Ignis, and she and Mooredoth are the only ones who don't want you to die in your adventure."

"The only ones?" Mika's head snapped to Cynthia. "Mom?"

319

She refused to look at Mika. Her gaze was stuck on the distant skies, her lips pressed together.

"Mom?" Mika shook her mom until Cynthia mustered the courage to look at her daughter. "Mom, is this true? Angelis doesn't want me to succeed?"

Cynthia forced her eyes closed. Answer enough. The acknowledgment cut through Mika's heart.

Mika reeled on her feet, then ran away and covered her face. How could Angelis not be on her side? How could the deity she had prayed to, served throughout her life, worshiped, and given offers to, want her to fail on her adventure? What had she done wrong for Angelis to want her to fail … to lose her eyesight … to die? She remembered being in Sandra's room, watching the Angel Wing glow its beautiful golden color, thinking that the deity of vita was on her side.

My deity … my deity betrays me, abandons me like I'm trash … like I'm nothing.

Thinking of her time in Di'Abribel, how she was treated by her fellow citizens, how the wife of the builders left her without asking her to go, how Page never came back for her, how Ashlynn didn't send help.

I really am nothing …

She turned to her parents, who were running to catch up to her. "No."

"No?" Michael repeated, slowing his pace until he reached his daughter. "No what, Princess?"

Holding her head high, she didn't care if her tears showed, if her voice shook. "I stand by the mistakes I made, and I will pay for the lives I have taken unjustly."

She puffed her chest but made no effort to hide the sadness on her lips.

"Return me to the forest," she said, "where I shall die in the same way and by the same enemy the Yeveran men did five years ago."

Obeying her wish, the afterlife opened a portal with crystal colors next to the dying adventurer. Beyond the portal, Mika could see the thick, disgusting silver fog that danced around the trees of the Lost Forest. She looked at Michael and Cynthia. Her parents looked back in shock.

She chuckled, shook her head, and raised her shoulders. "I'll see both of you in a few hundred years."

Michael took in a breath to speak and stepped forward, but Mika raised a finger. She pointed the finger toward him, ordering Michael to back off. He complied.

"I like when you call me Princess." Mika looked at the portal. "Build me a kingdom for when I come back? That way I can be a real princess. You'll have enough time to do so." She gave Michael an involuntary sad look that shattered his heart.

Mika the sorceress gazed at the healer.

"I'm sorry I couldn't save you, Mother." Mika looked down when the memories of Kathrine killing Cynthia ran through her head. "I love you. I love you so, so much …"

With pursed lips, Mika gave Cynthia one last look. Cynthia's features, however, had grown stern. *Wouldn't surprise me. Everyone else I've loved has hurt me.*

Mika looked at the portal, took a deep, deep breath, and exhaled. She leaned forward to walk, but Cynthia's voice fractured her thoughts.

"You're forgetting your promise."

Mika would have kept moving, but the word *promise* rang in her ears. She would never break a promise, so what was her mother talking about?

She turned her head toward her mother. Cynthia used a wing to point at something behind Mika. Curious, Mika turned her head; seeing nothing, she turned her whole body around. She shut her eyes and curved her lips in disgust.

The scene around her had turned from the beautiful mountain to the gloom of the Lost Forest. Just feet away from her, she saw her adult self in the fetal position over a pool of thick, dark-red blood. What disturbed her was not her body, her blood, the holes on her side, nor the half sawed-off wrist that still clung to her dagger by two fingers, but Addie.

Addie was frozen in time.

In a protective stance between Mika and something he perceived was dangerous, Addie's face showed nothing but sheer, brutal anger. His ears betrayed his feelings, though, for they were pointed back in fear. Addie was ready to die for Mika.

"You made him a promise," Cynthia said, her voice sharp.

Mika had never heard her mom speak to her in anger. *I'll take care of you,* is what you told him. Now you leave him to die because you're scared of going back."

Mika stepped toward Addie and moved to pet him, but her fingers passed through him like he was air. Mika wasn't *scared.* Mika wasn't scared of anything anymore. She was disappointed.

Angry.

Furious.

Furious at Angelis and all the worthless deities that followed her adventure. Disappointed that they would abandon her ... but wasn't that what she's doing to Addie now? Now, she was abandoning him.

She spun around. "Send me back. Send me back right now."

She ran to her parents, a desperate look in her wide, unblinking eyes. "He needs me. He needs me right now! Send me back. Send me back!"

"Mika!" Michael held his daughter's head. "It's okay! It's okay!"

She stayed still, but she was still desperate, bouncing on the balls of her feet.

"Nothing is happening in the living realm. Time is frozen until I release my hold on it." He took a deep breath, coercing Mika to follow suit. "It's okay."

It's okay.

She nodded. "What do I need to do?"

"I've dedicated my life to serving Baigh," he said, "and he's blessed me with the ability to manipulate time in the living realm as I please. Didn't seem like an extraordinary power, until the moment you ran through the market and made a choice between saving Stacy or saving Addie."

Mika frowned. "Stacy ..."

"It's okay," Michael knelt to her height. "He knows everything we plan on doing right now. He too loves you very, very much."

"I felt so bad," she whispered and yanked her head away from Michael's clasp before lowering it.

Michael raised her chin with his fingers. "Don't let his sacrifice be in vain. Mother can heal you." Michael touched his forehead, and a crystal drop with changing colors bounced on his fingertip. "And I can give you the power to kill your opponent."

When the crystal droplet touched Mika's forehead, her mind rushed through time. She saw herself standing in a circle, sharp arrows zooming to her in all directions. When Mika shouted *aevum*, they slowed to a crawl, allowing Mika to perceive time a lot quicker than everyone else. It was the same spell used when she ran through the market.

Mika shook her head. "I can't kill him … even if I dig my dagger into his armor, I can't reach his skin."

"Princess—" Michael lifted her chin higher and brushed snot off her nose. "He was quick to don his helmet and has no chainmail protecting his neck." He made a motion of stabbing Mika's neck with his finger. "We all know how much you love necks."

He blinked and smiled. Mika smiled back, her eyes widening.

Cynthia knelt beside her husband. "I've served Angelis and Gral throughout my life and devoted all my worship to them. I can bring you back from the brink of death and heal all your wounds."

"Can you heal my scar?" Mika was quick to answer, her hand passed through her cheek.

Cynthia narrowed her eyes and smiled. "I can, baby."

Mika seemed to come to life.

"But I'm not going to. That will be the staple people will look to when you lead them to victory."

Mika tilted her head. "What do you mean?"

Her father stood and grabbed Cynthia's hand. "You'll see in time. It's the only glimpse Baigh bestowed upon us."

He then guided Mika to her body and began pushing her down. Mika felt eerie lying inside of her own almost-dead body.

"Aevum the second you go back." He kissed Mika's forehead. "Make it quick. Kill the necromancer knight. The second you inhale or exhale, the spell will lose its magic. I love you, Princess."

"I love you too, Dad."

Cynthia whispered, "Vita."

A powerful golden orb appeared on her hand, and she passed it through Mika's ruined wrist. "A true Yeveran never drops their weapon."

Mika and Michael spoke at the same time. "It must be pried from their dead fingers by their brothers or sisters."

Cynthia passed the healing orb through Mika's chest, over her heart, her lungs. "I'm restoring your energy. You'll feel as if you got the best rest of your life after this." Cynthia finished by passing the orb through Mika's ribs and all her muscles.

Knowing she was going back to face death, that a single mistake could cost her life, made Mika afraid.

"I'm scared," Mika whispered, hoping her father wouldn't hear. His hand on her hair told her he did.

Cynthia kissed Mika's forehead. "It's okay to be scared. Those who are truly brave are the ones who act in defiance of fear."

Mika looked at Cynthia, took a breath, and held her mouth open. Cynthia smiled and copied her daughter.

At the same time, they both said, "I love you," something they used to do when Mika was a child.

"Get yourself and Addie to Triumph." Michael's voice was stern. "Complete your adventure, then return to Di'Abribel and unite Celeste under your name for Liranda."

The idea dumbfounded Mika. *Me, unite Celeste? He must be crazy. I'm on my way to see Page and leave this place forever!*

Her thoughts were cut short when the mist around her began to thicken, seeping into her open pores. The calmness of the heavenly realm left her. Her body began pumping all the neurotransmitters that culled her happy mood and made anger, hatred, and stress sail through her body. Her heartbeat quickened, her eyes widened, and her teeth clenched. She heard Addie's barks slow into her ears as time resumed its normal passage.

"Now ..." her father whispered.

Mika took a breath. "Aevum."

The world crawled.

Mika began pushing herself up. Her arm made a slow move as it pushed away from the ground. Her muscles flexed and bent; the muscles on her neck contracted when she looked to the side, locking her eyes on the skin visible under the back of Nicholas's helmet. Her knees sank into the ground, and the toes of her boot curved when she shoved them into the dirt, readying her body to propel forward. Her fingers scratched into the moist floor, driving her nails down and filling them with the black mud that covered her clothes. Her thigh contracted, and her muscles shifted until they pushed her forward.

Addie's head turned slowly, recoiling, and flinching a methodic flinch when he saw his mother sprinting toward him.

Mika took a step; focused on Nicholas, she didn't see the branch she stepped on but felt the languid exaggeration of the snap it made beneath her foot.

Nicholas began to turn.

Her toes pushed against dirt. Her thighs flexed with every move.

Nicholas saw the sorceress healed of every wound except her scar, running toward him at full speed, a red-hot dagger steaming in her hand.

Mika clenched her teeth when she saw Nicholas's eyes widen. A slow stumble over his own feet telegraphed his surprise. His arm rose to grab the sword on his back, but his feet were crossed. He was off balance. His opposite hand swung at Mika's face.

The duck from the girl under his fist seemed unnatural, almost an immediate reaction. The unmissable strike was met with nothing but air. Extending from her duck, Mika leapt, soaring higher than she'd ever jumped. Her feet landed on Nicholas's torso. Her hand gripped the cold, smooth steel of his helmet. Her thumb wrapped around the visor. She pushed his head back, further revealing his unprotected neck. Standing on Nicholas's chest, Mika raised the burning dagger in the air and squatted down.

She watched the pupils of his wide eyes move to the dagger. He began letting go of his sword just as the blade sank through his unprotected throat.

Nicholas closed his eyes; the dagger stuck through the opposite side of his neck.

Mika let go of his helmet. Her hand inched toward the blade until she grabbed it. Her lungs began to scream. With a powerful push of her thighs, Mika kicked herself off Nicholas, her dagger cutting through his trachea and opening his neck. Blood began to squirt from the necromancer's fatal, unhealable wound, onto Mika, and she made her slow descent to the ground. Seeing blood rush toward her face in a dark gout, she closed her eye just before it hit her, smiling when she felt the warm squirt slap her cheek.

Her open hand felt grass, telling her she was about to hit the ground. With a final look at Nicholas, whose leg was kicked up as he fell onto his back, she felt more and more of the ground touch her hand, her forearm, her triceps and shoulder. Her back crashed onto the ground.

And the spell was released, and time exploded to normal. Mika leapt to her feet.

"Go, Addie!" she screamed.

The blood-red mist guided her, and Addie ran ahead. Shouts behind her, balls of mori flying past her, explosions and debris. She propelled herself through the shrubbery. Countless necromancers sprinted behind her. Kathrine slid to her knees next to Nicholas.

Mika vaulted over a tree and jumped over another. A ball of mori exploded inches from her, sending her flying to the side. Addie was looking at her.

"Keep fucking moving!"

A necromancer teleported in front of her. Mika swung her flaming dagger, missing, but making the necromancer fall. Her feet were leaving a massive trail of fire in her path.

"Ignis!"

Two fireballs appeared. Spinning them in circles, she sent both to her sides, creating a similar trail to hers in hopes the necromancers didn't know which way Mika went.

"Split up!" she heard someone yell, telling her the distraction had worked.

She ran faster, kicking Addie in the butt and forcing him to keep moving. A crystal teleportation portal opened, and a female necromancer emerged with a blade.

Addie, looking back at Mika, didn't notice the threat.

"Addie!" Mika cried.

Addie looked in front of him. He flinched.

Both her hands on the weapon, the necromancer cut Addie in two.

"*Addie!*"

Her eyes tunneled into the necromancer.

The necromancer summoned a mori missile but turned to see Mika swinging her dagger. The necromancer slid forward, wrapped her arms around Mika's legs, and lifted the sorceress off the ground.

Mika's head knocked a rock, and she squirmed out of the necromancer's grasp. She tried to mount the woman, but the necromancer wrapped her legs around Mika's waist and pulled her hair. Mika jabbed her blade into the necromancer's stomach, stabbing her again, again, again. The necromancer moved her hands to stop the onslaught, but Mika stabbed the flaming dagger into her face, sternum, stomach, temple. The necromancer's legs relaxed.

Then a mace connected with Mika's face.

She rolled off and stood. A vortex of raging fire surrounded her in hellish flames that controlled themselves. Two necromancers threw every mori spell they knew at Mika. The ignis created a wall that blocked mori. The vortex sprang forward, encasing their heads in a flaming orb of fire until they fell to the ground. The skin on their skulls was melting off.

Mika heaved; she bit at air with her eyes wide, but her face relaxed the moment she heard Addie's yelps.

Like a mother hearing her screaming child, she ran toward the yelps. When she jumped over a boulder, she saw the bottom half of Addie lying lifeless on the ground. Just feet away, Addie used his front legs to crawl away from the pain.

"No … No … No, no, no, no—" Mika picked him up, but he screamed when she touched him.

"Vita!" She cried, holding a healing light over Addie's bleeding wound, stuffing his guts back into him.

The healing magic quieted his screams.

"Addie!" she cried, "Addie, no!" The tears in her eyes made her vision blurry. She struggled to breathe past the cries of anguish.

She looked up to see blue skies. Blue skies that told her the trees were not as dense, blue skies that told her she was almost out of the damnable forest.

She ignored the pain in her arms and adjusted Addie so he would stop sliding off her. Tears rolled down her face. She sprinted through the snow and toward the bridge just yards away. She looked at Addie. Addie looked back at her and licked her hand.

"Don't, Addie, please don't." She closed her eyes.

Her boots met the stone on the bridge. She remembered Addie giving her the same look the day she rescued him, giving her the same slow lick on her hands.

Mika crossed the river and slid to her knees. Addie's blood continued to drip, coloring the snow a bright red, drowned by the powerful glow of vita.

"Addie ..." Her voice was near unrecognizable from the snot and tears in her throat. "Addie ... please ..."

Mika continued healing, continued applying the golden glow that kept him alive. How could she fix this? How could she make him stop losing blood? How could she keep half of him alive? It was impossible.

She pushed her face on his neck and screamed his name.

Her mind began to tremble, and as her thoughts became hazy and blurry, the golden glow began to flicker. She forced her eyes closed. The tears felt like burning ashes in her eyes. Her lips wrenched.

The golden light flickered away. Using the last bit of magic in her, she communicated to Addie all her sorrow. Regret came from Addie's heart, for he thought it was his fault. He thought if he had just been a little faster, just a little smarter, just a little stronger, he would've lived, and his mother wouldn't be sad.

"Addie!" She shook him. "Addie, it's not your fault! Addie!" She fought through the exhaustion to heal him.

Addie closed his eyes and licked her flickering hand. She felt Addie's final breath kiss her cheek before her eyes shut from exhaustion.

*   *   *   *   *

Liranda looked at herself in the mirror. Her burgundy hair was combed straight, and her bangs draped down, ending above her black, pointed horns just above her eyebrows. Black eyeliner wings gave her seductive hazel eyes more pop than any other woman in the universe. She turned her face left, turned her face right, then faced straight. She smiled, grabbed a dragon flower with white petals and a red pearl, and placed it in her hair, the same side her soul daughter, Mika Plum, placed hers.

She turned to the closet and slipped into a sheer red dress that showed her breasts, hips, and ass to full effect. She looked at herself in the mirror once more, satisfied with what she saw.

She considered heels, but kicked them away, deciding that she would attend the weekly gathering barefoot. Her fingers filled with embers, and she opened a portal that would lead her out of her realm and into the realm of vita.

"Liranda!" Kymarinou, Liranda's nemesis, greeted her with a smile. "You're late!"

His physical trait of scales and fins was invisible everywhere except when underwater.

Liranda looked around, disgusted at the white sky and flocks of angelic beings above her.

The deities turned to greet her, surprised she had teleported, not to her usual chair on the round table, but just behind Nessa's chair. Nessa, unlike the other deities, did not turn to greet her. She sat motionless in her seat.

"I'm not late." Liranda's voice was smooth. "I just know when the party will start."

Liranda snatched Nessa by the hair and dragged her out of the chair. Gral, Baigh, and Kymarinou, the only ones not following Mika's adventure, stood from their chairs in surprise. The rest sat and waited.

"What in the Abyss is happening?" Baigh's voice was high pitched, contrary to his old and wise appearance.

Liranda twirled Nessa around and raked her nails across her face. The three deities erupted and ran toward them.

"Nah, ah, ah!" Liranda stepped back and shook her finger. "You don't know what's happening."

Nessa held her scratched face, refusing to look at any of the deities. Liranda circled behind and yanked her hair and kicked the back of her knees in until Nessa knelt like a slave in front of the deity of ignis.

Liranda sank her nails into Nessa's scalp, pulling her hair at the same time. "Little Miss Nessa, here, has intervened in the human realm and caused Mika Plum, Irstia's sorceress, my one and only child ... to die. Isn't that right, Nessa?"

Liranda pulled her hair so that Nessa looked up at her.

"Correct," Nessa muttered.

Liranda's movements were dramatic. She swung her arms up and to the side when she spoke.

"And as we all know, an intervention that results in the killing of 25 percent or more of one's children is considered an act of war! An act of war in which the aggressor ..."

And here Liranda whispered into Nessa's ear. "You."

"An act of war in which the aggressor is not allowed to call upon her allies!"

Liranda threw Nessa on the floor, placed her foot on her head, and twisted. When Nessa closed her silver eyes in pain, Liranda released her, slid over the round table, and sat at her chair. She placed her elbows on the table and touched her fingers together.

"Deities, please sit."

Baigh sat.

Gral and Kymarinou helped Nessa to her feet before they sat. Nessa sat at her chair. She didn't look up from her unserved plate.

"You knew that would happen, didn't you?" Liranda stared at Nessa.

Nessa didn't answer. Like a child being scolded, her head lowered and kept lowering with every word.

"You diverted the necromancers away from the prisoners, or should I say, *your* prisoner, and led them straight toward my child." The anger in Liranda showed in her dragon flower and the embers dripping from her fingertips. The golden table absorbed the flames.

Liranda looked at Angelis, who held her head high. She spread her wings, telling Liranda that she was not afraid of her.

"Your daughter brought Mika back to life with the help of *your* son," Liranda said turning to Baigh.

"And then," she said, "*then*, the thing Mika cares about more than life itself, more than some stupid, married boy, all her belongings, all her friends, her own fucking life ... is stripped away from her at the snap of a finger."

Liranda looked at Rend. "For lux's sake, after everything going on with my baby, what'll happen when Mika finds out Amirra is married to her long-lost lover?"

"Who knows?" said Rend with a shrug. "She's a crazy, deranged sociopath. Who can tell?"

Liranda chuckled, taking in her fellow deities. "Who can tell? When I have a good *fucking* idea."

Liranda locked eyes with Nessa, who mustered the courage to hold her gaze.

"Instead of declaring war and having all my creatures destroy you and your realm forever," she said, "I'll have an intervention of my own. All the deaths that come from my intervention will be blamed on you."

Liranda made sure Nessa and all the deities understood. Deaths blamed on deities zapped their powers and life essence, making them weaker until they restored their losses.

"Your realm lost forever." Liranda leaned forward, her fingers intertwined, but her thumbs continued to touch. "Or the souls of a few thousand people on your hands?"

Nessa refused to answer.

"Answer me!" Liranda slammed her hands on the table, ready to pounce on Nessa.

Nessa closed her eyes. "The latter."

"Perfect!" Liranda smiled and threw her hands in the air. "Let's get this party going! I've been dying to talk to you all about my Mika!"

22. AWAKEN

The sun began its slow descent behind the mountains at Adventurer's Pass. The golden glow of the ball of fire mixed with the dark-blue sky to give the hazy clouds a purple tint that radiated onto the fluffy snow. No birds sang, no insects chirped, and no footsteps crunched on this quiet night. The only sounds in the air were Mika's sniffles and the chattering of her perfect teeth. Still holding on to Addie, Mika sat herself to her knees and curled into a ball.

All that kept Mika alive were the boons of Liranda and her unsolicited intervention in the living realm.

A tongue of flame appeared in Mika's hand, and she passed it over her skin, warming herself until her trembling slowed. She looked at Addie's corpse, his eyes closed, mouth open with a tongue hanging out like it always had. He lay in Mika's arms, lifeless and stiff.

Still holding on to his body, she knelt over and began moving away a portion of snow, ignoring the shattering cold in her wet hands that made her fingers feel like solid stones. She reached the moist dirt and began digging away with her nails. She got the idea to use her only tool, her dagger, to help dig the hole deeper and wider. She raised her dagger above her head and pierced it into the ground, moving away only small portions of dirt every time. She worked and worked, not once stopping for a break or to see her progress.

The crunching of snow and whispers told her a couple was approaching.

She continued digging.

Maybe they'll help me. She sniffled and wiped her snot on her shirt. *Maybe they'll tell me it'll be okay.*

Mika didn't want to ask for help, but she would accept it if it was offered. Not wanting to seem rude by asking, she continued digging her dagger into the soil, pulling only inches of dirt at a time.

The footsteps came closer and closer. "Dude, she's bleeding," a man whispered.

"Nah, man." Shuffling of clothes. "It's the wolf she's holding." Footsteps walked away. "Just leave her, she's a crazy."

Mika continued digging. Tears filled her eyes; she let out a pout and forced her eyes shut. The image of Addie crawling away from his other half was seared into her eyelids. Opening her eyes, she caught a glimpse of the two men walking away, one looked back at her in disgust.

Mika continued digging.

Leave her. She's a crazy. Leave her; she's a crazy. Leave her, she's a crazy. Leavehershe'scrazy. The sentence repeated in her mind until she was brought back to reality when she swung into the hole and met nothing but air.

Mika set Addie into the cavity, careful not to hurt him when she placed him on the ground. She stood, crossed her hands over her pelvis, and looked into the hole, at the corner of Addie's mouth.

All the people she loved had been killed, yet she'd never witnessed a funeral. Her father died somewhere on the border of Celeste and Imbris. Cynthia's grave was a burnt home reduced to a pile of ashes carried away by the winds. Her grandparents perished somewhere in Adventurer's Pass trying to escape the Imbric War. Stacy, she was sure, received a funeral, but she wasn't there to see it. All the men she went to school and trained with as a teenager were consumed by the evil, dark forest that was home to the army that killed poor Addie.

She knew some cultures burned their dead and preserved the ashes, but she had no means to collect Addie's. Some buried their dead; their bodies would decompose in the ground, and depending on how good of a person they were, a tree would sprout. The better the person, the bigger and more powerful the tree. Others took their dead to sea, an offer to Kymarinou; they hoped he would turn the dead into legendary sea creatures before sending them to the afterlife.

Instructor Tolin, Mika's magic instructor in Yevera, had once said, *"Where I'm from, the perished are burned. Their souls intertwine with the smoke as it rises into the air. Wherever the smoke goes, so does their soul."* It was the only time Instructor Tolin was serious and not being an arrogant asshole—and the only time Mika paid attention in magic class. *"To see the world with the wind is the greatest gift we give them."*

"You always liked exploring, didn't you?"

Mika placed branches inside the hole and summoned a flame. The childish voices weren't playful this time. Instead, they were serious.

~ He is called Addie ...
~ Get on the small twigs first ...
~ Don't talk so loud ... Mom is about to cry ...

Whispering to each other, they combined until they were large enough to ignite Addie.

~ I liked Addie ...

Mika stared at the fire. She remembered Addie's face, always happy and smiling at Mika. How his tongue was always flapping from the side of his mouth. He was always doing something he thought was fun. His protective nature when she was in danger kept her worry-free through the rough streets of Di'Abribel.

Liranda spoke to her with a sweet voice. "Say something, Mika."

Taking a second, she spoke without thinking.

"Addie was a good person ..." She didn't dare call him a pet. "He always liked to have fun, and his spirit was never, ever broken. Never sad ... His personality kept me positive ... Kept me ... alive."

She shook her head and looked up, hoping a tear didn't roll down her cheek. She remembered Addie fighting for his life the first time she saw him.

She struggled to speak past the lump in her throat. "If I could go back ..." Her voice was deep; she flexed it to prevent her voice from shaking. "If I could go back, I would let you chase all the rabbits you wanted to chase, eat all the yellow hats you wanted to eat, and jump on all the people you wanted to jump on, and run as far as you could and bark as loud as you wanted."

She let out a small gasp. "And I would give you the biggest hugs, and the biggest kisses, and the biggest boops on the nose." Her hands covered her face. "And I would feed you the biggest pieces of meat and yell at the people you barked at." She forced her eyes shut and pressed her teeth together. "I'm sorry …" Her voice trembled. "I'm sorry I couldn't keep my promise. I'm sorry I didn't love you more than I could have."

She cried into her hands, refusing to fall to her knees. She bit her hand, trying her best to make her shoulders not bounce from her cries.

"I'm sorry, Addie." Her lips trembled. "I'm sorry I was always working. I'm sorry I was always going to Sandra." She screamed to be able to say the words. "I'm sorry I thought my garden was more important than you." She covered her face, her legs shook, and she fell to her knees. "I'm sorry I was a bad mother."

Mika shoulders bounced, as did the cries that escaped her throat. She hugged herself because there was no one else to do it for her—no Cynthia, no Michael, no Sandra, no Janice, no Ashlynn, no Stacy, no Sylisia, no Page, no Addie … just Mika. The thing that helped her push through the hardest time in her life would no longer smile with her, eat with her, cry with her, or hold her. Mika's wings were shattered.

The smoke rose in the air; the crackling of the flames kept the moment tender after the tears subsided. The night sky allowed the orange flames to flicker and take a slow, melodic dance on the snow. Mika watched the flames through the night, keeping her warm and providing years and years of happy memories, memories that would be seen in Mika's life essence, memories that Mika would someday write about and tell her human children and siren offspring.

The flames flickered away, and only ashes remained inside the hole, visible under the now-rising sun.

Goodbye, Addie. She held her head low and walked toward the sunrise, toward the town of Triumph. *I will love you … forever.*

*   *   *   *   *

The wind from Mika's spell pushed her back, causing her to place her foot behind her for balance. She reached the middle of Triumph's housing district. The roof of every house had Rend's flag, the five-pointed star, creating a patriotic feeling that reminded Mika of her home in Yevera. The flags flew in the wind, and Mika thought it strange that the wind inside the town was warmer than the wind outside of the damaged walls.

I could build a life here with Page.

People went about their day, all with smiles on their faces. Some pushed wheelbarrows, hawking their wares; others performed acrobatics or played instruments in the snowless streets, bowls in front of them allowed passing pedestrians to leave coins as tips. Paladins marched throughout the town; the fighting paladins wore plate armor, the scouts wore leather armor, and the magicians wore robes. Some magicians carried staffs, expensive magical weapons that amplified the power of spells and slowed magical exhaustion. She continued walking against the direction of her find spell that led her to Page's home.

After a few minutes, Mika set her eyes on a white house with a slanted roof at the end of the town. The yard had gravel rocks leveled around a large oak tree. A wooden ramp led up to a dark-gray door adorned with stained glass that sparkled at Mika. Rend's Star was engraved in the middle of the door, magic keeping the star lit a bright yellow. Mika walked to the edge of the ramp.

"Ventus," she said and imagined his face. "Page."

Almost blowing her onto the ground, Mika caught herself by grabbing the rail. Her heart skipped a beat, and her lips curved into a smile. She took a step up the ramp, making sure not to make any noise. She stopped, then backed away.

I need to bathe.

She jogged away, back into the center of the town, toward a pristine, white fountain.

"Where can I find somewhere to bathe?"

An older lady selling topaz jewels crinkled her nose and eyes and smiled. "Over there, dear." She pointed a crooked finger. "The public showers are before the inn."

Mika curtsied and sprinted to the showers. On her way there, she saw Rosa's carriage in the distance.

Rosa and Lila are probably at the inn!

She was glad they made it to Triumph safely, and she was looking forward to Rosa's and Lila's cooking.

She jumped out of her clothes and showered in the steaming aqua; powerful lux from the paladins was used to heat the waters. The young woman grabbed a towel from a stack and dried herself, then dressed in her only remaining clothes: a brown collared shirt with short sleeves and pink pants. She skipped out on wearing Rosa's coat. She adjusted her hair the best she could and jogged toward Page's home. Her heart burst with excitement; she couldn't hide her smile. She tiptoed up the ramp, trying her best to not make noise until she reached the door. Mika saw her reflection on the door's glass. Looking into the glass, she studied herself.

Her eyes were swollen from crying for the past couple of days. Dark circles under her eyes told everyone she had gone days, weeks, without proper sleep. A scar on her cheek brought memories of Ron striking her with the shield. Her once-beautiful hair was now disheveled and thin. The only perfect thing on her was her beautiful smile and her dragon flower, its petals erected upward in anticipation.

He loves me and won't care what I look like.

Her heart racing, she raised her shaky hand and curled her fingers into a fist. She held it inches from the door, looking at the glass one last time. She looked herself straight in the eyes before knocking in a gentle, happy rhythm.

Mika heard footsteps from inside.

They grew louder until she could hear the turning of bolts and locks. Mika stepped back and clasped her hands together in front of her pelvis. She stood straight and lifted her chin. The door opened, and Mika's smile broadened until her cheeks hurt. Page stood at the other side of the door.

Mika did nothing but smile.

Page looked back with wide eyes, an open mouth, and a missing arm.

Mika lowered her arms to her side, shook her head, and chuckled. She smiled at Page and spread her arms out, closing her eyes before dashing forward. Mika collided into Page, but something felt strange. Something about this hug wasn't normal.

She opened her eyes to see Page's arm extended, his palm resting on her sternum. A grim look on Page's face was followed by a light push that put Mika outside of the door's threshold.

Page took a breath. "What are you doing here?"

Mika stood with a gaping mouth and her shoulders lowered. She didn't know what to do. She just shook her head and swallowed.

"Page, it's me—" She held her hand over her heart. "Mika Plum of—"

"Yes, I know who you are. Just answer my question."

Mika recoiled. A lump began to form in her throat, and tears appeared in her eyes. "Why are you being like this?"

"Mika, what are you doing here? I haven't seen you in *years*!"

Mika scoffed. Maybe he was playing a trick on her, one of his stupid jokes that would always send her into a spiraling rage. "I thought you died!"

Page shut his eyes and shook his head. "I don't know why you're here. Go back home."

Page shut the door, reflecting Mika's pitiful look back at her. What just happened? What was that? Was he being serious? He wasn't playing … his jokes only last for a few seconds, and he always smiled at the end. He wasn't joking. He wasn't joking. He was being serious.

He's being serious.

Her lips began to shake, followed by her hands, then her whole body. She hugged her arms and began to rub them, trying to warm herself; it suddenly felt so cold. She heaved, she looked around her, rocks, ramp, rail, tree, sky. She shook her head and shut her eyes.

It's a dream. It's a dream. It's a dream. Wake up, wake up, wake up! Addie! Addie, wake me up!

She pinched her nose and blew air out of it. When her ears filled with pressure, she had to hold herself up using the rail. She couldn't believe what was happening. Why was he being mean? Why was he so rude? What happened to his arm? She looked back, noticing the door was still closed.

Her legs shook with every step. She looked at the bottom of the ramp; her mind showed an image of Addie looking up at her, lowering his head upon seeing the exchange, seeing Mika's failure.

She closed her eyes. She saw Addie being chopped in half. She saw her wrist being sawed off, Ron almost killing her in the cell, Ashlynn's leg being cleaved in the living room, a shield gliding through the air and onto her face, Stacy dying because of Mika, Mika being burned by the imp in the forest. None of that trauma, none of that hurt, none of those things would've happened if she didn't know Page was alive. She opened her eyes. The image of Addie was still there. Addie was still sad.

Turning around, Mika ran up the ramp and hammered the door with her fists, yelling at the top of her lungs. "Page!" The glass rattled with every strike. "Page! Open the fucking door!" She shrieked, and her voice cracked. "Open the fucking door, Page!"

She delivered an onslaught of fists and kicks. She twisted her hips, cocked her arm, and slammed the door with her forearms, not noticing her blood splatter onto the glass and ramp. After her fit of anger ended, Mika stepped back and noticed her bleeding arm and dazed vision. Her face relaxed, her eyes perked when she heard the door unlocking.

A woman with platinum-blonde hair opened the door. Much taller than Mika, the woman's light-blue eyes were overshadowed by eyebrows that curved downward. Page stood behind her with his hand on his head.

Mika sneered. "Who the fuck are you?"

The woman glared down at Mika, and when she spoke, her tone was authoritative, with a strong and elegant accent. "I'm Amirra, head general of the paladins in—"

"And I am Mika Plum of Yevera. Move out of my way."

Mika locked eyes with Page. Her eyes softened, and a smile began to form. She ignored whatever Amirra was telling her.

"Page—" She held her arms toward him, inviting him in for a hug.

Amirra slapped Mika's hands down. "I command you off this property!"

"I'm not afraid of you, Amirra."

Amirra saw Mika's flower, its petals confirming she was in a heavy state of anger, then joy when Mika's gaze turned to Page, back to anger when Mika's eyes met Amirra's. Amirra knew normal people do not shift from one mood to the other so quickly. Something was wrong with this woman's mind.

Mika moved toward Page, pushing Amirra to the side.

In a heartbeat, Amirra sent volleys of punches to Mika's face, causing the young adventurer to stumble to the side. Amirra followed through and delivered a powerful punch to Mika's liver, then her chin, and completing the combo with a kick to the ribs.

Mika fell to her knees, dazed and almost knocked unconscious. She grunted, tightened her fingers on her stomach, and pressed vita to her face.

"Be grateful I do not kill you!" Amirra pointed.

Mika's pupils dilated. She could feel the vein on her neck pulsating. Hiding an ember in her hand, Mika began to stand, only to stop when she saw a bright glimmer on the ground. Her arms went numb and almost buckled.

On the ramp lay her dragon flower, shattered into hundreds of pieces. It had been knocked out of her hair when she was attacked. Amirra raised her foot to reveal more fragments of the flower under her boot, causing the flower's pearl to roll down the ramp. Mika dove and grabbed the pearl.

She held the fading pearl in her hands.

"No ... No ... No ..." She looked into the jewel, through the dragon's eyes; she saw it spiraling from the sky. "No, no, no, no, no, no!"

The dragon crashed on the desert sand, creating a cloud of dust that spread all around it.

Its partner and child ran up to the dragon. It released a howl and looked at its tail. The dragon's tail began to melt into a gooey liquid the color of the pearl.

Tears filled Mika's eyes. "Please ..."

The dragon clawed at its melting tail. Its child, frantic, looked at its parents. The dragon's mate clawed at the tail also, trying to make the melting stop, but the melting continued, increasing its speed until it consumed the lower legs. The dragon tried to crawl away. The dragon looked back, its torso melted, the wings followed, the neck. The pearl melted in Mika's hand, seeping through her fingers, it dripped onto the wooden ramp. Mika looked at Amirra.

Amirra looked back with a hand over her mouth.

"That," she whispered, "was not my intention …"

Mika looked at Page. Page had his eyes closed and his fingers pressed to the side of his head.

"I've never been mean to anyone …" Mika's vision blurred from her tears. "My dragon … Addie and my dragon …" Mika curled into a ball and held the melted pearl to her heart.

That poor family. That poor dragon. They'd be alive if … Amirra …

Amirra and Page went inside without saying a word. Although Mika didn't see it, Page looked down at the girl he once loved, wondering what had gotten into her. Wondered why she changed so much. He shook his head and closed the door.

"My beautiful dragon …" Mika talked to herself. She closed her eyes and hugged herself.

Liranda spoke. "My poor, poor baby."

Even with her eyes still closed, Mika could see a small flame in the distance of the darkness.

"What did they do to you?" The voice came from the flame, and it made a slow walk toward Mika.

Mika sniffled. "I don't deserve this …" She breathed out. "None of them deserved this."

The flame was closer. Mika could see a woman with an hourglass figure and horns on her forehead walking toward her. "Of course, you didn't, Princess."

Mika recognized Liranda by her horns and her burgundy hair.

"… and they didn't either." Liranda knelt in front of Mika. She combed Mika's hair behind her ear and cleaned the tears from her eyes with her thumb.

Flames appeared from all around them; their violent roars, unpredictable pops, and the smooth crackles surrounded Mika. Whenever Liranda spoke, the flames quieted.

"I know a way you can make this right."

Mika didn't reply, but Liranda knew she was listening.

Liranda summoned a flame. The flame expired and was replaced by a crimson-red warrior's stone.

"Let us in… Let us in to help you exact your revenge on everyone, everyone that has threatened this beautiful place you call home, everyone that has ruined the beautiful life you once had … Everyone that has caused your dragon and your precious Addie to perish."

The warrior's stone shone with the colors of all the deities, telling Mika every single one of them would follow her conquest.

"Poor Page." The flames grew bigger; Liranda lied. "It's not like him to be like that. Would he do that to you? What if he's being held hostage by that woman?"

Mika's breathing quickened, and the flames exploded with every one of her heartbeats.

"Let us in." The flames crept toward the two. "Free Page." The flames consumed Liranda and were centimeters from Mika. "And unite Irstia under our name."

Mika's decision would make her allegiance to Liranda. Anything Liranda wanted, Mika had to do. All Liranda's traits of corruption, evil, destruction, and conquest, would enter Mika's heart.

"I'm the only one who ever really loved you, sweetie."

The words sliced Mika. She was defeated; she had nothing to live for anymore. Addie was dead, Ashlynn was missing, and her dragon was gone. What would it matter if she succumbed to the fire? What would it matter if countless others suffered because of her? No one ever helped her, so why should she care about anyone else?

Mika reached for the stone. "Okay."

The flames rushed into Mika. She felt a flurry of heat. Every organ in her body felt hot, a heat that made her want to die. She opened her eyes and stood, grasping the rail with both hands, immediately and profusely sweating. The heat dissipated, and her mind was like a fire that burned away every element known to man, filling her with knowledge of tens of hundreds of spells. The flames concentrated in her heart, and her mind filled with the corrupted thoughts of every sorcerer that came before her: evil, destruction, anguish, conquest.

"For today, I bestow upon you just a fraction of a sorcerer's true power! Kill the woman that destroyed your dragon!" Liranda's psychotic laugh bounced. "Your hands are untainted by those you kill today, and the stone will protect you until the continent is united! Set off the spark that will awaken your greatness!"

"Ignis." Two balls of blue fire flickered in Mika's hands and grew to the size of a watermelon. The heat radiated onto Mika. The power of the flames caused her hands to shake. She approached the door, looked at herself in the mirror, ground her teeth, inhaled, and cried at the top of her lungs. "Ignis!" She sprang her arms forward, releasing a flame that blew open the door to Amirra's home.

Mika dashed inside, ignoring the voices and roars of fire.

~ KILL THEM ...

She set fire to the ground, furniture, walls, and roof. The roars and pops became almost unbearable; the house began filling with black smoke and fire.

~ Mom is strong ... Mom is SO STRONG ...
~ We found a baby ...

Amirra gathered lux into her chest. The ray of light ran to Mika.

Mika plummeted to the floor. The beam exploded from Amirra and tore through the walls and into another home. Amirra raised the beam up toward the heavens, destroying her roof and requesting the assistance of the paladins in and around Triumph.

"Ignis!" A flame crashed into Amirra's stomach, interrupting her spell.

Amirra healed and sprinted toward Mika, a lux sword in both of her hands.

Amirra swung her swords with speed and technique. Mika used a barrier of fire that cracked until it shattered into millions of pieces. The sorcerer dodged a hack. She flattened herself on the floor to duck under a kick.

Amirra swung down. Mika rolled to the side, propelling fire toward Amirra's forearm, charring it and making the lux sword flicker away. Amirra raised her fists, wiped her sweat, and closed distance.

Mika swung her enflamed dagger.

The paladin blocked the attack and delivered a fist. Mika stumbled.

"She's charging at you!" Liranda screamed.

Mika uncovered her face to see Amirra dashing forward. Mika thrust the dagger.

Amirra sidestepped, locked Mika's elbow under her armpit, and arched her back.

Snap.

Mika let out a crying scream, and both fell to the floor.

Amirra wrapped her arm around Mika's neck.

Mika's vision blurred.

She latched on to Amirra's face and didn't let go as she called to ignis and released smoldering lava onto the squirming woman.

Amirra released Mika's neck. Mika's fire increased in potency. Mika scrambled away and kicked the paladin before healing her dangling arm.

The paladin rose to her knees and held vita to her face. Her agonizing cries would have saddened Mika long ago, but now, they just made her smile. The fire continued its violent pops and roars. Amirra began to stand, only to be shot to her knees by a fireball to the chest.

The sweet smell of burning human flesh, along with her children laughing, screaming, having fun, excited Mika. She stepped toward her next kill.

"How disgraceful," Mika said, sliding her dagger into its sheath, "for a paladin to have such pitiful cries."

Mika grabbed both of Amirra's wrists and pulled them away from her face, revealing scorched flesh and the white goo of Amirra's melted pupils seeping from her eye sockets.

"Oops!" Mika giggled. "That was not my intention!"

Casting a wall of fire under Amirra's knees, Mika began to laugh when Amirra screamed.

"Make it slow, children. Make her melt the way our dragon melted."

The flames obeyed, all crashing down on Amirra; the pops and swooshing roars covered her screams. Victorious, Mika looked for Page through the black smoke and red flames.

Page sat with his back against the wall, his legs spread in front of him. He was forcing his eyes shut and coughing. The black smoke was making it hard for him to breathe. He rolled out of the way of a collapsing beam from the roof.

Mika ran up and cast a protective barrier around him. She smiled when he began to breathe normally.

"Oh, Page," she shouted over the roars of the fire. "Oh, Page." She straddled Page's legs and caressed his face.

"I'm sorry it took me so long to save you." Mika looked down at his lips, then at his beautiful blue eyes.

She rubbed away hair from his face, wiped his sweat, and hugged him. "I missed you so much, Page. I'm never letting you leave me again." The hug tightened. She pushed herself away. "Why do you look so mad?" She giggled. "Aren't you happy to see me?"

"Where's Amirra?" Page's nostrils flared. Based on his lips and eyes, Mika couldn't tell if he was enraged, depressed, or worried.

"You're safe, baby. You're safe. She won't hurt you anymore. Ever. I'll keep you safe. I'll keep you safe forever!" She chuckled, trying to hide the pain in her eyes. "I'm a sorceress!" She held her hands to the side and summoned a flame on each.

"Mika, where is Amirra? Where is Carr?"

Mika didn't reply, just shook her head. He must be so scared, in so much shock to be asking about Sergeant Carr. She would be scared too if the house she was in was on fire, her lover a sorceress, her captor dead. It was a lot to take in. She needed to get him to fresh air.

She smiled at Page, a genuine, true smile … until her face began to relax when Amirra's life essence entered her body.

"Hold on …" She closed her eyes. "Let me enjoy this moment."

Through Amirra's eyes, Mika saw the once-powerful paladin piercing a thick, golden rod into the ground at the top of a large, rocky hill. Amirra unfolded a flag, Rend's five-pointed star. Amirra looked back to see an army of tired paladins behind her. Their broken, dirty armor and tired spirits proved they were victorious over a massive, deadly battle.

Mika saw Amirra walking down the aisle of a church until she reached the groom. At the altar, Page leaned over and kissed Amirra in their matrimony. Hordes of happy shouts from the seated crowd filled her ears.

Then, Amirra held a baby with dark-blue eyes the same shape and color as Page's eyes. The baby looked back at Amirra with a deep, curious look before its lips curved up until they parted, revealing a smile with no teeth. They continued curving up until the baby's eyes were squished between its cheeks and eyebrows.

The visions faded. Page sat inches from Mika.

"Is this why you didn't look for me?" Mika locked eyes with Page. The flames in the home began to seep into her body.

"Mika, what did you see?"

"Is this why you didn't look for me?" Horns of fire swirled above her eyebrows.

"Mika, I'm sorry—"

"Answer me, Page!" She grabbed his shoulders and pressed them against the wall. "Is this why you didn't look for me?"

Page tried to crawl away, wincing at the pain on his shoulders.

"It's been years, Mika! What did you expect? We were kids! You set my house on fire and murdered my wife, Mika! You're fucking crazy! I didn't—"

He squirmed when her dagger sank into his cranium.

"Do you know what I've done to get here, Page? Do you know how much I've lost for you? Just for you! Just for you! Just for you, Page!" Mika twisted the dagger inside his skull.

His arm reached up to grab her forearm; he gargled a shout.

Mika's face was inches from his. "For you to tell me I'm *crazy*?"

The flames rushed inside her. "I died with—"

A moan escaped her mouth. "I died with *my* baby! I died with *my* baby for you, Page!"

"You could've written me! I waited for your promise! That doesn't make me *crazy*!"

She closed her eyes; she saw Addie's innocent smile.

She yanked Page onto his back and dug her thumbs into his eyes.

"*I'm not fucking crazy*!" she shouted.

The concentrated ventus that escaped her hands combined with blue fire that rushed into Page's face until it blew a hole in his skull, sending his fried brain onto the opposite wall. The flames around the house gone, now absorbed in her body, allowed the paladin reinforcements to barge in with weapons drawn.

Mika faced the paladins and, in a final cry of rage, released the absorbed fire in an explosion, creating a mushroom cloud that announced the pulverization of Triumph to every person in Celeste.

23. EXPANSION

Kathrine stood motionless in front of two columns of black caskets, twelve caskets in each column, and one casket in the middle at the end. The ceremony honoring the dead was over, and everyone had left to resume the rebuilding of the cathedral. Kathrine passed her hand over each of the caskets, walking to the next, then the next, until she stood at the casket at the end—the casket belonging to General Nicholas.

Kathrine closed her eyes, breathed deep, and did her best not to collapse onto the general's casket. All their memories together, from joining the necromancer ranks, to their last dinner in the canteen, crawled through her head. The most prominent memory of him repeated itself.

She remembered not being able to look away from him when they were teenagers; both were bound and kneeling in front of each other on the deck of a ship below the star-filled sky.

"If you can't free her," a necromancer instructor had told them, his steps heavy on the wooden floors of the ship, "she will die. No instructor assists during this exercise." The instructors wrapped a piece of cloth around Kathrine's mouth and strapped a large boulder to her knees.

Nicholas didn't look away from Kathrine. He smiled.

"I'll save you." He would need to free himself while being beaten, disarm one of the instructors, then jump into the water and save her.

The instructors lifted Kathrine into the air and threw her overboard. The night sky was the last thing she saw before she sank into the arduous, freezing waters that made her brain feel fuzzy. Bubbles escaped her nose, and she sank thanks to the boulder tied to her knees. The pressure in her ears made it feel like they were going to explode. The boulder touched the ground, releasing a cloud of sand around her, and she was like an erect board, floating but immobile at the same time. It felt like minutes had passed, but it was just a few seconds. The minutes seemed like hours, but she had only been underwater for a minute. She waited; her lungs began to compress and decompress, but she forced herself not to breathe.

I'll save you, *she thought.* I'll save you.

A hand wrapped around her wrist. A blade cut through the rope, then through the skin on her knee by accident. She extended her legs and swam up, moving her body like a fish. She opened her eyes. The two moons shone bright beyond the surface.

Just a few more ... just a few more ...

She opened her mouth wide and took a giant breath through her mouth and nose at the same time. Still bound by her hands, she floated on her back.

The instructors leaned over the ship with eager grins on their faces. Nicholas and Kathrine were that much closer to becoming commanders in the necromancer army.

Nicholas cut the rope around her wrists.

She let her arms float to the surface.

"I told you I would save you." Nicholas placed his arms around her and helped her swim to the island two miles away from the shore, where their next phase would begin.

She coughed. "I never doubted it."

"Mistress Kathrine!" A scout burst in through the door, breaking the necromancer leader from her thoughts.

She gave Nicholas's casket two taps and turned to the scout. "Approach."

"Triumph!" He was drenched in sweat, his uniform cut. It was hard for him to speak. "Triumph was obliterated!"

"You're not making sense." The thought dumbfounded Kathrine.

The scout stood at attention, and Kathrine waved at him to relax.

The scout rested his hands on his head, allowing more oxygen into his lungs. "Triumph was just destroyed. An explosion came from within." The scout was unable to control his coughs. "I got here as fast as I could."

"What about the paladin outpost?"

"Also gone."

Kathrine jogged out the door and into Lieutenant Amy's quarters on the third floor.

Lieutenant Amy was studying a map of Celeste on the wall. Next to it was a map of Di'Abribel. Not expecting to see Kathrine enter her quarters, Lieutenant Amy didn't move.

"Lieutenant Amy." Kathrine's voice broke Amy's concentration.

Amy snapped around and saluted. "Mistress Kathrine!"

Kathrine returned the salute. "Prepare your army for a full assault on Di'Abribel."

Lieutenant Amy began jotting Kathrine's instructions in a red notebook.

"Pillage the Farmlands on the way; rest at the Grand Waterfall before your siege."

Amy's heart pumped with excitement. *This is it*, she thought. "Yes, Mistress Kathrine!"

"Who is your worthiest, bravest, and smartest soldier?"

Amy looked away in thought. "An archer by the name of Zain. He's young but has proven his bravery and leadership in battle countless times."

"Perfect. Tell him he's promoted to master sergeant in charge of Seth's army. Half of his army will travel east, then move south onto the northern walls of Reach."

Lieutenant Amy wrote down Kathrine's instructions.

"The other half of his army will march south from here, rest at Peak's Lake, then wait until the first half is in position at Reach before acting as reinforcements. The plan is to make Reach underestimate our forces. Questions?"

"What if the sirens refuse to provide shelter while they wait?" Lieutenant Amy walked to the map and focused on the vast area of Peak's Lake. "The lake is under their control."

"Reach gathers purified water from the lake," Kathrine scoffed. "They're part of Celeste, making them our enemies. Furthermore, they're nothing but creatures; killing them will grant us essence. Have them purge the siren presence, no matter if they help us or not. Have his army use tenebris before entering the lake so they're not influenced by the calming magic. Any other questions?"

Amy scanned through her notes, flipping the pages back and forth. She shook her head.

"Then get on with it, Major Lieutenant Amy. Congratulations on your promotion."

* * * * *

Rosa and Antorio sat side by side at a dinner table and smiled at each other before they kissed. Little hands reached for silverware and ate the tomato and basil noodles wrapped within the tines of the fork. Lila looked out of the window and past the town of Triumph and toward the ocean. A large ship was docked and being prepared to set sail. This was the last memory Mika saw; the memory came from Lila.

Mika was on her knees, alone in a crater she created. Around her was dust that, because of the sun, was colored a light gray like the top of a wild mushroom. The only trace of buildings was their skeletons—beams and foundations which, along with nine statues further ahead, were the only things standing in the town once known as Triumph.

Mika looked at her hands and then her body. She felt her hair, her clothes, and her backpack. Being the one who cast the explosion, she was uninjured. Her hands fell to her knees, and her eyes met the portion where Page lay before the catastrophe. So many thoughts ran through Mika's mind, the memories of everyone she killed, the thing she just did, the fact that Liranda allowed her to kill innocent people, the fact that Mika, a woman with very little ignis experience, was able to incinerate a whole town.

A short inhale was followed by a long exhale that sent ashes away from the breath. This was the moment—the mental lull after a horrible, horrible decision—that would decide whether her heart would break under the weight of regret. Would she collapse, or would she stand and embrace her role as a champion of Liranda and the Sorceress of Irstia? Could she frame the destruction around her as a small, terrible part of a larger picture not yet fully revealed?

Mika the sorceress slid a foot forward and stood, not once looking away from the spot where Page lay. She took in her surroundings and frowned. She regretted nothing save the deaths of Rosa, Antorio, and Lila.

"I am not crazy, Briarhart."

She stepped on his ashen remains, twisted her foot as if she squished a worthless bug, and walked to the statues in the distance. The statues of the pantheon stood in their usual spots, the same way they had on her adventurer's stone and now on her warrior's stone.

The first statue she visited was that of Liranda, which had a wicked smile and horns that glowed when looked at. The runes appeared around Mika, and she expelled essence on a spell that allowed her to summon lava without needing fire, along with a spell that increased her fire's potency.

She then visited the statue of Mooredoth. His chin was held high, and his fists were balled. Mooredoth's face gave a courageous look toward infinity. Mika expelled essence on a spell that allowed her to control a meteor.

Disgust filled Mika's heart when she reached the statue of Angelis. She refused to look at the face of the deity of vita, but she used her remaining essence to learn the spell that allowed her to change rain into drops of vita.

With her new spells, Mika moved westward toward the setting sun. She needed to leave before witnesses showed up and her face was plastered on posters throughout Irstia. Remembering the warrior's stone and the words her mother told her about serving ignis, Mika decided to find Ashlynn, escape Celeste, and somehow build an army to unite the region for Liranda.

*   *   *   *   *

Ron sat at a chair inside his living room. He leaned back and kicked his legs onto the table before taking a sip from his black ceramic mug. The taste of lavender and chamomile warmed his chest and made him relax. He smiled and looked at the flames that waved at him from inside the fireplace. The fire mesmerized him; its thick, cozy warmth further relaxed him. He closed his eyes and leaned his head back.

What a crazy year it'd been. The situation with Ashlynn, having to build the cells in the basement just for her, all the issues with trading, having to give the necromancers weapons every few months in exchange for safety, taking care of Mika, having to worry about guards coming when Ashlynn escaped ...

He took a sip of his tea. None of it mattered anymore. Tomorrow, the traders he hired would assist with the packing, and they would move to Velonde. There, he would join the Smiths' Guild, the largest in Irstia and second largest in the world. He would perfect his craft and be rich. He was happy to leave Celeste forever. He took another sip of his tea and smiled.

That's when the door to his home flew from its hinges, as guards burst across the threshold.

"Ronald Stannard!"

Ron jumped to his feet, but guards tackled him.

"By the elders in Di'Abribel," said a guard in full plate armor as he pulled out a scroll and held it in front of Ron, "an order has been drafted, approved, and signed commanding the lawful search of your home. Do not resist, or arrest will be immediate."

"I'm not resisting." Ron's words were smooth. He extended his hand open despite the spilled tea burning through the skin on his neck. "Do whatever you wish."

"Bind his arms."

Guards wrapped metal chains reinforced with black terra around Ron's wrists. He was sat on his chair.

The guard in full plate armor inched his face closer to Ron's, analyzing the healing burns.

"What happened here, Ronald?"

"I'm a blacksmith." He cleared his throat. "Accidents happen, you know."

The leader clenched and unclenched his fist. To him, Ronald was guilty before seeing any evidence. He pointed to the brown door. "Check the door."

Ron's eyes traveled to the brown door. Mika. Mika told the guards what happened. Or Ashlynn. Or both. His eyes followed the guards, and they opened the door.

"Red storm door," a guardswoman said.

The leader turned to Ron. "What will we find under the storm door, Ronald?"

"Just a tunnel."

"A tunnel?"

Ron swallowed and nodded.

Two guards cast lux on their descent. Ron continued eyeing the open red door, trying his best to jump out of the chair and run into the woods. The guards returned with their helmets off. The guardswoman shook her head.

The squad leader took off his helmet. He looked much younger than he acted and sounded, and his hair was the same type as Ron's. He cast lux and descended, coming out seconds after, and sitting on the table in front of Ron.

"You're building a tunnel," he stated in an accusatory tone.

"Been for about a year and a half now. Escape plan in case of, you know, necromancers."

The leader inched closer. "Why does it turn from cobblestone to dirt, as if the beginning was something else?"

Ron was glad his hands were bound. He couldn't pull at his collar or wipe his sweaty palms on his thighs to ease his discomfort. Because of this, though, he wasn't showing the guard his extreme amounts of anxiety and stress.

The squad leader repeated the question.

"I wanted to, you know," Ron used his shoulders to show expression, "make decent work of it. Once the attacks grew, I began to rush. Stopped using cobblestone after One Three Five."

A press of the leader's lips let Ron know he was convincing him.

"After the raid on Triumph, I stopped making weapons and doubled down on the tunnel. Few more weeks and it'll hit under the woods north of Cabria. Makes it easier to, you know, evade through woods instead of plains."

The guard was bouncing his leg; he kept his stare on Ron. The awkward silence made Ron want to keep talking, but he knew better. The more he said, the more he would dig his own tunnel toward his demise.

353

What seemed like minutes passed until the guard stood. He pulled Ron by his shirt; their faces were centimeters from each other.

"I know you're lying to me."

Fear ran through Ron's bones. Looking into this guard's eyes told Ron he was a deadly warrior who showed no mercy.

"No one believes Ashlynn, but I do." The guard pushed his forehead against Ron's. "And once the truth comes out, I'll crucify you myself. Any man that treats a woman like you did deserves nothing but death."

The guard pushed Ron, causing the homeowner to trip over his chair.

"Unbind him." Guards undid the chains on Ron. "Stand up, Ronald."

Ron stood. He didn't look the guard in the eyes, to avoid provoking him further.

The guard took off his gauntlets. "I disrespected you in your own home." He held a fighting stance. "We doing this so you can restore your honor?"

Ron held up his hands and spread his fingers. He shook his head.

"Sir, you're just doing your job. I'd be feeling the same way if a woman, you know, said another man did something bad to her."

This further angered the squad leader, but he picked up his gauntlets, put on his helmet, and passed the threshold to the front door.

"Fix your door, Ronald." His body faced away, but his helmet looked at Ron. "Hope your weapons and tunnel aren't built as bad as the door."

*　*　*　*　*

The doors to Ashlynn's room burst open. Her heart pounded against her chest at the surprising noise and rush of guards that surrounded her comfortable bed.

A guard grabbed her wrist and yanked her to the floor. Ashlynn's face scraped against the ground. A heavy knee was placed across her back, a leather boot pressed against her face.

"Ashlynn Sorip!" a female guard said. "You're under arrest for making a false report. Di'Abribeli rule seven dash seventeen dash one governs this law!"

Ashlynn couldn't believe her ears. Under arrest? She struggled to breathe past the heavy weight on her chest. "What do you mean?" Her arms were yanked back; she knew not to resist. "Is this about Ron? What did he tell you? Please, you have to tell me you found Mika! Please tell me Mika is safe!"

Her hands were cuffed, and she was pulled up via the cuffs onto her one leg and pushed toward the door.

"I can't walk on my own, you brainless idiot!" She looked at the girl. Her arms were crossed, and she leaned at the threshold of the door. "Where is Mika? Where is my sister?"

The guard uncrossed her arms and stood erect. "Another squad went to his house. No basement, no Mika, no halberd. You're under arrest for false reporting."

"This can't be! This can't be. Please, you have to go back! There's something wrong! Why would I lie? I'm not from here. I don't have any benefit of—"

The guard used tenebris to silence Ashlynn, so she cried obscenities into the minds of the whole squad until she was thrown into a cell of the Di'Abribeli jail.

$$* \quad * \quad * \quad * \quad *$$

Vivinia spun in the waters of Peak's Lake, following her beautiful siren mother, Sylisia. Her mother dove down, and the heroine followed. Sylisia pivoted to the side, and Vivinia followed. Her mother spun and headed directly at the heroine. Vivinia froze and covered her face. Sylisia stopped just in front of her.

"Gotcha!" she said, smiling at her daughter.

Vivinia crossed her eyes and held her tongue out. "This time."

Dolphin sounds came from above, telling all the sirens in the water that an army had entered the lake.

Vivinia and Sylisia looked at each other and smiled. They hadn't seen visitors in weeks! They were happy to test Vivinia's voice against humans. Although, by siren code, they weren't allowed to seduce females of an army, they would be happy to provide shelter, food, and entertainment to anyone who wandered into their home.

The heroine took the lead, and Sylisia followed, swimming to the surface. They both dove out of the water and landed on their human feet. They ran to a tree, picked off some leaves, and made garments that would hide the parts humans considered intimate. Several sirens ran toward them, handing them cordage baskets full of fruits and a basket filled with fresh, uncooked fish.

"Need help?" a siren with black hair and cyan eyes asked.

"No," Vivinia replied, "I think we'll be okay!"

The three sirens that brought food walked away. Vivinia and Sylisia smiled at each other and carried the baskets. They could see the army marching through the mountain pass. Their black uniforms told the sirens they were necromancers. They met halfway.

Sylisia spoke. "Hello! Welcome to Peak's Lake. It's an honor to have such a large army pass through here!" She extended a basket to the necromancer who rode on a black horse. "Would you like some food?"

Vivinia offered her baskets to another necromancer. He was older and rode on a spotted horse. The young siren did her best not to admire the females in the formation. Her tongue was moving on its own at the thought of human females.

"Could you excuse us for a moment?" the younger man on the horse asked. A recurve bow made of beautiful wood was slung across his back.

"Of course!" Sylisia closed her pink eyes and smiled. "Take your time!"

She turned to Vivinia, and they walked away, giving the two men and their army privacy.

"What do you think, Master Sergeant?" The older necromancer turned to his leader.

Master Sergeant Zain took a breath. He didn't look away from the two sirens. He watched them talk with each other. The siren with the blonde hair and pink eyes was happy; she laughed at whatever the younger siren, the one with brown hair and pink eyes told her.

"Although it pains me to do so," he said, looking at his second-in-command, "our orders are clear, Nirael."

Nirael looked at the sirens. The blonde siren kissed the brunette on the forehead. "They're beautiful creatures." He admired the two, not once blinking, but narrowing his eyes to get a better look. He raised his chin when he continued. "But I'll follow your orders and the orders of the Mistress unto death itself."

Master Sergeant Zain dismounted his new horse. Necromancers in Celeste were not able to maintain horses in the forest, so only army leaders had one. He stretched out his back and rotated his neck.

The sirens heard and knew to approach, both with giant smiles on their faces.

"Dear lady," Zain said, holding his arms out and looking around, "is it just you two here in this lake?"

Sylisia matched his expression. "No, the rest are in the lake itself. We don't stay out of the water too long."

"I see, I see." Zain adjusted the bow slung across his back. "You bring food. Do you mind if we eat?"

"Of course not! We prepared these just for your army. We will get more." Sylisia offered the baskets. Vivinia followed suit.

Zain accepted by waving toward Nirael.

Both sirens moved to him.

Sylisia held out her baskets, and Vivinia moved to the side.

She watched the man on the spotted horse look at the basket, but he seemed uninterested.

Does he not want any food?

Vivinia's thoughts were broken when she saw movement out of the corner of her eye.

She looked at Zain, as an arrow flew from his bow and pierced her mother's throat, leaving a massive hole in both sides of her neck.

Vivinia stopped breathing.

Sylisia gasped for air, gurgling pops escaped as she held her hands to her neck.

"Kill her!" Zain screamed.

Shouts followed.

Her reflexes allowed her to duck under Nirael's sword.

Vivinia dropped the baskets and ran to the shore. An explosion propelled her into the air. She tumbled.

She got up, looked back, and saw thousands of balls of mysterious black magic zooming toward her.

Vivinia flattened herself on the ground, releasing a scream. She crawled, then burst to her feet and jumped into the water, her heart beating faster than ever.

Her feet turned to fins, and she swam to the temple, releasing the squeaks and squeals that told everyone the army was attacking.

The eldest siren, Delarah, returned the squeals, telling everyone not to worry and to go into the temple. The traps inside would kill any outsider not crushed outright by the weight of the water.

The heroine made her way down; tears filled her eyes and mixed with the water. A lump formed in her throat. Balls of mori zoomed past, so she turned and zigzagged past the onslaught. After they stopped, she continued swimming down but didn't look away from the surface.

Black lines, the same color as the balls of mori, slithered into the water. They expanded, releasing a black liquid that mixed with the water.

Vivinia approached the liquid and touched it with her hand. She flinched back in horror. The liquid was like acid, it felt like touching a burning metal tool. The lingering pain did not fade, making her wish her hand would be chopped off.

They've poisoned the water ...

She called to the others, telling them to leave the water. Thousands upon thousands of sirens rushed out of the temple.

"Exit through the river and into the ocean!" Delarah communicated. They didn't know what to do against the acid, for their species had never been attacked by necromancers before.

Another siren communicated back. "The acid is starting to block the path to the ocean!"

"Get as many through there as you can! The rest, exit to the east and run toward Reach's coast!"

"We're surrounded by the acid!"

"Get to the surface! Every siren for themselves. You are charged with saving our species! Don't stop for anyone!" Delarah cried out, her squeals and squeaks desperate.

Delarah darted to Vivinia, tears filling her eyes. "Heroine, now is your time. You need to stop them from killing us. If one siren survives, our species lives."

Vivinia nodded, but she covered her face and began to cry.

"Don't cry, don't cry," Delarah said, taking Vivinia in her arms. "This is your moment. This is where you shine. You are the heroine."

"Okay … Okay. Okay, okay, okay." Vivinia closed her eyes, then darted to the surface, avoiding the noxious chemical that mixed with her pure, beautiful waters.

She shot out of the water with two balls of fire in her hand, launching them at the army of necromancers while she soared through the air. She landed on her human feet, dashed, and used her hands as a flamethrower to protect her kin.

Some necromancers changed their focus to her; others continued dumping acid.

Sirens began jumping out of the waters. When they ran, necromancers gave chase. The ones they captured were executed. The ones the necromancers couldn't catch were pursued into the mountains, into the trees, out of the lake, and toward the river.

Necromancers surrounded Vivinia. She encased herself in a ball of ignis that blocked all the necromancers' mori magic. She engulfed one in flames, the other she caused so much damage to the skin the necromancer had to retreat. Using her hands as flamethrowers, she spun in circles until she felt a sharp pain in her arm. Her focus waned, and the fire stopped.

She looked at her arm, chopped off at the forearm. Her lips trembled.

"She's the one that set the cathedral on fire!"

A slice to her abdomen cut open her stomach, causing her intestines to roll onto the grass. She fell to her knees and leaned over her entrails.

Why was this happening? What quarrel did a human army have with sirens? What cathedral were they talking about? She forced her eyes shut, and the shuffling of feet was the last thing she heard before a blade made a swift pass through her neck.

* * * * *

Thick, dark-gray clouds were trapped within the mountain skies of Peak's Lake. A bolt of lightning pierced the clouds and struck the ground within the mountains. Mika looked behind her at clear blue skies that went on for miles, confirming that something was wrong inside of her daughter's home.

Mika picked up her pace when she went through the valley of Peak's Lake. She adjusted the coat Rosa gave her. The temperature inside the lake had plummeted; it was much colder inside the lake than it was outside. A noticeable difference from her first time there. When she cleared the valley, she stood in shock at the sight inside of Peak's Lake.

The black clouds covered the sky, hiding the sun behind their thick blankets. The trees had faltered and dried. A single swing of an axe would chop any tree in half. The once-pink and fuchsia-colored flowers were brown and stiff. The water in the lake was pure black, and the bodies of sirens littered the ground. Miles upon miles of dead sirens lay in front of Mika.

"What happened?" she whispered, taking her first step after seeing the carnage.

She stepped over the body of a siren with light-brown hair, then jumped over the body of several others until she reached the black, gooey waters of Peak's Lake. Looking at the island in the middle of the water, she squinted and tried to notice any sort of movement.

Something moved behind her, and Mika spun around.

Her eye caught slight movement behind a tree. Mika sprinted toward it, summoned a flame, and jumped around the tree.

A woman with black hair and old leather clothes was huddled against the tree. She flinched every time the fire in Mika's hand popped.

Mika grabbed the woman by the hair and pulled her onto the ground. Mika held her dagger to the woman's neck. "What happened here?"

The woman didn't open her eyes. Her lips were curled into a painful frown. A whimper escaped her throat.

Mika pressed the edge of the dagger deeper onto her skin. "What happened here?"

The woman opened her eyes, revealing white pupils.

"Please ..." Her voice was weak, but when she moved her lips, Mika saw a mouth full of razor-sharp teeth.

Mika released her and sheathed her dagger. She applied vita to her neck and knelt next to the siren. The siren was weak, so Mika held her head on her lap.

"What happened?" Mika whispered.

The siren began to cry. "They attacked us." Her voice was low. Mika had to lean in to hear her. "They poisoned the water."

Mika shook her head. "Who are *they*? What did *they* look like?" Mika brushed the siren's long hair behind her ear. She wiped the sweat from the creature's brow.

"The army with the black robes ... they used mori."

Mika didn't respond. Rage began to build, but there was nothing Mika could do. She looked at the siren and tried her best not to show anything but compassion.

"Are you hurt?" Mika felt under the siren's shabby clothes. "What can I do to help you?"

The siren shut her eyes and shook her head. Her lips curled into a frown, and she inhaled past the tears. "Nothing."

"What do you mean, *nothing*? There has to be something."

The siren didn't respond.

"Talk to me, please."

The siren looked at Mika with her white pupils. "We can't survive without the magic of the waters. When we migrate, we take millions of vials to help us on our journey. The water is gone, and the water of the ocean is too far for me to harness its power."

"Then I'm carrying you to the ocean." Mika began to stand.

The siren stopped her, "No. Please ... it hurts to move. It really, really hurts to move ... and I can't survive in the ocean alone. The others are already past my vision."

Mika knelt and placed the siren's head on her lap again. "Your vision?"

The siren struggled to speak. "Sirens ... we can see each other past obstacles." She raised a weak hand toward the northern mountains of the lake. "A group there is dying."

Mika began to stand again. "Then I'm taking you to them." Mika doubted herself. It would be hard to find a group of sirens in the middle of a mountain.

"No ... stay with me ... please." Tears fell from the siren's eyes and into her ear. "Just please stay with me. They're dying too ... but they have each other ... I have no one."

Mika stopped. She exhaled and set the siren's head on her lap again.

For hours, the only sound in the air was the siren's repressed sobs and sniffles. Mika's knees and muscles hurt. Her legs cramped, and she lost circulation. She felt like her bones were spreading themselves out of her body, but she refused to move. She refused to make the siren hurt. Mika brushed the siren's hair and caressed her face whenever the sobs became louder.

The siren cleared her throat and opened her mouth, letting Mika know she was about to speak. "They won't survive in the ocean alone."

Mika felt like crying, and tears bubbled in her eyes. "What do you mean?"

The siren closed her eyes. "The jealous husbands, the pious followers of lux, the women we reject, the men who can't have us … We migrate because of humans. We've longed to conquer an island on the ocean, but the ocean is filled with the strongest creatures known to us. A lot of us die when we migrate through the seas. When the heroine was born, we saw hope. We saw hope of venturing the ocean and finding an island far in the seas. An island that humans would want to visit, an island that we could safeguard with traps, wonders, barriers in case they became aggressive." The siren shook her head. Her dry mouth made it hard for her to speak. "We were so close …"

Mika was about to speak, but the siren interrupted her. "I don't want to die."

What could Mika say to that? For once in a long time, Mika was bewildered, unable to think of the right words to say. She spoke without thinking.

"The ones in the ocean …" Mika looked to the south, toward the river that led to the ocean before looking back at the siren. "The ones in the ocean will survive. They will survive because they're at Gral's doorstep. They have to survive, and they will … because they have to."

The siren gave the words some thought before she touched Mika's face. She wiped the tears from Mika's cheek. "You're Vivinia's mother."

Mika shut her eyes and clenched her jaw. Vivinia must be her daughter's name. "I am …" She struggled to say the words. "I am the heroine's second mother." Sylisia's gorgeous face and happy smile flashed through her mind.

"She fought valiantly. Many escaped because of her sacrifice." The siren squished Mika's cheek and pointed further in the distance. "Please, lay her body to rest with the others."

Mika looked in the direction the siren pointed. In the distance, she saw a body hovering near the water.

The siren's voice faded. "They said they would attack Di'Abribel soon."

The siren closed her watery eyes and exhaled her final breath.

Mika slid the siren off her lap and brushed her hair, doing her best to make the siren look pretty. She brushed away the dirt on the siren's face and, before she stood, she applied vita to her knees and legs to ease the cramps. Mika made her way to the body in the distance.

As she approached, Mika noticed the body was not floating. It was, in fact, impaled on a spear that exited her neck. Her daughter's head was pierced at the tip of the spear; her severed arm hung from her mouth. Vivinia's intestines were circled around her body and the spear.

Mika stared into the weak, open eyes of her dead siren child. The word C A T H E D R A L was carved into her forehead—vengeance for what Mika did to the necromancer in the tunnel, and further vengeance for the lives Mika and the prisoners took in the cathedral.

She reached for Vivinia's head and closed her child's eyes before closing her own when she felt the stiff, cold, unnatural texture of her daughter's dead arm. She took a took a breath before opening her eyes and wriggling the severed limb from the open mouth.

Having to tiptoe, she pulled her daughter's head from the spear and placed it on top of the dead flowers. She lowered herself, wrenching her lips upon seeing her daughter's legs swollen and purple with the blood that pooled there. She carved the bottom portion of the spear with her dagger and placed it on the ground before removing the point of the spear and doing her best to slide it out of her daughter's body.

She inserted her child's intestines back in her stomach and placed the head near the neck. Mika leaned down and kissed her daughter's forehead.

I would've loved to have met you.

She held her forehead to her daughter's, closed her eyes, then stood. The most anger Mika had ever felt was at that moment. Powerful, controlled, and deadly anger. She summoned a flame that burned a powerful white.

Can you burn this place, including the bodies?

~ We can do whatever you want us to, Mother ...

Honor the life of the sirens. She dropped an ember next to her daughter.

Turn them and their home to ashes. White embers were tossed throughout the lake, catching fire against the dry foliage.

Cleanse the lake by boiling away the water. Mika launched a fireball far onto the other side of the lake. The sun seemed to carve past the clouds and amplify its rays into the lake, reflecting Mika's anger back at her.

She walked in silence out of the home of the now-endangered creatures. The growing wildfire inside would take months to quell, but it would be enough to bring the bodies of the sirens to rest and turn their once-beautiful home into a distant memory. A memory that would one day be rebuilt in their honor.

The fire grew, and so did Mika's fury and hatred for every one of Kathrine's necromancers. She reached for the warrior's stone and looked at all the shining symbols. Now, more than ever, she was determined to unite Celeste.

The moment I raise an army is the moment every one of Kathrine's necromancers will regret stepping foot inside this lake.

24. HOMECOMING

Mika took a deep breath, savoring the sweet smells of food that seeped over the walls of Di'Abribel. She could almost taste the frying chicken tenders. Her eyes remained closed, but she smiled. The smile grew until it revealed her teeth. She opened her eyes to see the stone walls of the city she called home had risen much higher and were much thicker than they were before she departed on her adventure. Every time one of the hundreds of archers garrisoning the top of the walls moved, water from the melting snow fell onto the ground, splashing into innocent puddles that muddied her boots.

The gates to Di'Abribel were closed, and a platoon of soldiers wielding spears formed a defensive wall in front of the gates. Should anyone break their defenses, a massive cauldron of boiling oil would drop on them from above.

"How may I assist you, madam?" A soldier with heavy plate mail armor and a spear approached Mika.

Mika shifted her focus onto the solider. "I am Mika Plum of Ye-vera. I reside here."

The solider looked her up and down, eyeing her scar. "Do you have any documents for proof? How long ago did you leave? Yever-ans who left are not permitted back into the city."

"I'm aware, but I live at 174 Poff, Tailor District. We left about six months ago, during the season of growth."

"Who is *we*? I don't see others with you." The soldier leaned closer to Mika. Past the darkness of the helmet, she could see a sparkle in his eye.

"I meant *we* because I had one more." Her emotions began to drop with sadness. "Addie. He died last week."

The soldier didn't say anything.

Mika shifted her body and lifted her coat to show her dagger as the only weapon. "I've been gone since the season of growth. I'm just a girl with a dagger and a single coat trying to get home. Please, let me find my rest. One seven four Poff. If they don't want me here, I'll leave with my belongings. Just … please try for me."

The soldier looked at the dagger, then looked at Mika's hair to check her mastery: none. This was common to do, since coloring one's hair to feign or hide mastery was punishable by death. He asked for her name and address again, turned to one of his soldiers, and had her verify the information.

"It'll be a while," he said when the soldier ran off into the city.

Mika cleared a spot of snow on the ground. She faced away from the walls and sat before lying down and using her empty backpack as a pillow. Now surrounded by guards, it had been the first time Mika was able to rest since the last night inside of Rosa's carriage.

Rosa and Lila …

Mika remembered hearing Lila's small voice and seeing her big eyes looking up at her in the Di'Abribeli market. She envisioned Rosa's pearly teeth and rosy cheeks when she gave them back the gold coin. She took a breath, imagining them now as a pile of ashes. A pile of ashes Mika turned them into.

I'm sorry you couldn't make it to Sytu. The only people she regretted killing in Triumph were those three people, the people she considered part of her circle.

Mika closed her eyes and remembered walking out of Di'Abribel after saying goodbye to Sandra.

Sandra … I wonder how she's doing. Does she think I'm dead? I was never able to write her.

The hairdresser's silver hair and stunning eyes popped into her mind. Her stern attitude, her mysterious room, her …

Mika drifted to sleep. She twitched and ground her teeth and mumbled to herself, easing the soldier's worries about her. Maybe this girl was just trying to get home after a rough adventure. The soldier called for someone to get blankets from the barracks near the walls, and he covered Mika with them. Hours passed until he received confirmation that Mika Plum of Yevera did reside in Di'Abribel.

"Miss Plum?" he whispered. "Miss Plum?"

Drool seeped from the corner of Mika's mouth.

He raised his voice. "Miss Plum."

Mika jumped to her feet. Her eyes wide, she brandished her dagger.

Seeing no threat in the young woman, the soldier remained calm, despite the weapon. "You're free to enter."

Mika's heart continued throbbing. She looked at the soldiers along the wall; all had readied their spears. The only calm one was their leader.

"Bad dream?" His voice was calm and happy, helping Mika relax.

Mika sighed and sheathed her dagger. "Always."

"Well," said the soldier, waving at his troops to relax and make a way for Mika, "hopefully, you'll sleep better now that you've made it home."

Mika stepped through the gates, lost in thought; she remembered everything that happened in her adventure. Thoughts helped her boring walk to the Tailor District and then to Poff Street seem quick.

Mika stood in front of her modest home that the government of Di'Abribel gave her after the destruction of Yevera. She reached into her backpack and pulled out a big bronze key. She inserted it into the keyhole, unlocked the door, and pushed it open. Nothing had changed inside her home, but Mika noticed it was spotless.

She stepped through the threshold and could see the white plume of her breath. The bitter cold inside the home made her shiver. It was much worse inside than it was outside. She called for a flame and threw it into the furnace. The flame grew on its own without the need for wood and began warming her house.

Making her way to the kitchen, Mika couldn't believe how eerie the home felt, how quiet it was. She placed her hands on the counter, trying to shake away the awkward feeling. There was no clanking, no panting, no running around and chasing flies ... because there was no Addie.

"That's why."

The house was quiet, mysterious, because the taps of Addie's nails on the wooden floor weren't there, his growls while looking at a bird outside were gone, the commotion from Addie's pent-up energy, his heavy panting ... all of it was gone, and she knew it would never come back. She closed her eyes and hung her head.

All this for a fucking boy. A worthless imbecile. I should've known. I should've listened to Sandra.

She raised her hand and smacked the counter; her cold hand ached. She gritted her teeth, and the flames in the fireplace pulsed in response.

But would I have found out about this if I'd have stayed? What about Ashlynn? Would she have died in Ron's basement? She'd still be in there.

Her eye caught a stack of letters on the opposite side of the counter. She hadn't left those there. Reaching for the letter at the top, Mika opened it and read its contents.

> Mika:
>
> I do not know where you are or what you are doing, I just hope you are safe. I heard about the necromancer attack on Triumph, and days later the mushroom cloud appeared for hours ... My ventus spell is not working on you. I am praying to the wind that you and Addie are safe. I am scared for you ...
>
> I shall keep coming by to clean.
>
> I miss you,
> Sandra Brooks

Mika placed the letter down. *Brooks.* She'd never learned Sandra's last name because the former adventurer had never opened up to her.

Mika picked a letter from the middle of the pile and opened it.

> Mika:
>
> Hoping the first day of the season of perish with Page was amazing. I am sure he is keeping you and your baby entertained. Does Addie like the falling leaves? You better not have found another hair stylist up there. I will kill you! (Kidding!)

You said you would write. I am mad at you! (Also kidding.)

I love you,
Sandra Brooks

With slow fingers, Mika opened the letter at the bottom of the pile.

Mika Plum of Yevera:
I missed you this week. The shop feels strange without your name in the appointments book. You should be close to Triumph by now, and excuse my intrusion, but I have decided to come clean the house until you return. I am sure you do not mind, but if you do, then you can do something about it when you come back. I do not know if you plan on staying there or moving Page here. Figured you did not want messes when you came back. You know, unlived-in homes are like unloved souls; they perish much faster than the others. It is strange, but I have never been able to express my feelings in person. It is always easier to talk through writing. I do not know why. Am I writing too much? I guess if I am, you can always stop and continue later.

Hope you tied your hair in a bun.

Speaking of, did you hear what happened in the market? The necromancers raided it in the middle of the night. Paladins, soldiers, and guards accounted for all the dead. I'm so happy you were not one of them. You must feel lucky knowing you avoided that massacre. Anyone who lived through that must be traumatized. These necromancers are trouble.

Best of wishes to you, Addie, and your future husband, Page.

Hope you are taking care of the flower,
Sandra Brooks

Mika looked at the rest of the letters but didn't open them. She put on a coat, ran out the door, locked it, and used her find spell.
"Ventus, Ashlynn Sorip." A strong, cold breeze blew in response.
Mika set off in a sprint.
I need to get Ashlynn and Sandra out of here before the rats attack.

Sliding to a stop, Mika looked at the black double doors of Di'Abribel's prison. The building wasn't big, showing every tourist that

Di'Abribel's crime rate was low, but the crimes that did happen were gruesome. Mika ran up the stairs and swung the door open. She stepped inside, let the door close on its own, and walked to the horseshoe-shaped desk. The wall behind the desk was plain and had no paintings on it.

A guard acknowledged her presence by looking at her, then returning his attention to a book.

"I'm here to see Ashlynn Sorip."

The guard looked at her, saw the serious expression on her face, sighed, and put his book down. "Regarding?"

"A..." Mika took a second, "death in the family."

The guard stared, then shook his head. He reached for a thick book on the desk and scrolled through the pages, back and forth, he didn't find what he was looking for. He grabbed another book and scrolled through those pages until he found Ashlynn's name.

"Relation?" He asked.

Mika asked with a confused look on her face. "To what?"

"What's your relation to her?" The guard had lost his patience if he ever had any.

Mika was about to lose her temper and burn the guard's face off his skull. She placed her hands on the desk and leaned forward.

"Sister," she hissed.

The guard laughed at her. He glared at her for a moment before he stood. "Ey! Got a visitor for fifteen!" He turned back to Mika. "Go wait over there." He pointed a dismissing finger at an empty cell in the corner.

To avoid the guard changing his mind about the visit, Mika remained quiet and walked to the cell. After a few minutes, another guard approached.

"You here for fifteen?" The young guard's voice was direct but unaggressive. He didn't seem to have an idea of how the other guard had treated her.

Mika spoke in her normal tone. "If that's Ashlynn Sorip, yes."

"Great." He looked at Mika's dagger. He could only see the bottom of the sheath. "Repeat what I tell you, without reaching for it."

Mika raised her eyebrow.

The guard waited.

"Without reaching for it," she repeated.

"Without reaching for it," he said slowly, "show me your blade."

Mika thought of her dagger. By instinct, she wanted to grab it and give it to the guard. The fact that she said *without reaching for it,* reminded her not to reach for it. She raised her coat and revealed the dagger.

"Turn around for me."

Mika complied.

"Interlace your fingers. Fully extend your hands on the wall. Hands still on the wall, walk backward."

Mika felt uneasy when the guard removed the dagger from its sheath.

"Keep your hands on the wall. Don't move. I'm going to search you for weapons."

After patting Mika down, he pointed deeper into the prison. "After you."

Mika walked through the cells, giving her a grim reminder of the prison in the cathedral. Reaching the last cell of the bottom floor, Mika looked through the bars and saw Ashlynn curled into a ball on her cot.

Poor girl must be used to sleeping like that.

The guard banged a wooden stick on the metal bars. "Fifteen! You have a visitor."

Ashlynn refused to move.

Mika called out, "Ashlynn!"

Ashlynn sat up, and her blankets slid off her body.

"Mika!" Ashlynn's voice was weak. "Mika you're alive!"

She began to cry. She stood and used a cane to approach Mika. She was losing weight again. Ashlynn reached her arms toward her sister, and Mika did the same. Mika's heart sank when their fingers touched, but she continued reaching further until her hands clasped Ashlynn's face.

"Why didn't you send help?" Mika joked.

Ashlynn's eyes widened. "I did … I did … I did—they, they told me they didn't find anything." Ashlynn coughed; it seemed like she had gagged. Her body released a long line of saliva from her throat.

"They called me a liar! They said they didn't find you and that Ron had a tunnel, not a prison! They called me a liar and arrested me because they think I'm trying to frame him because of his reputation! Only the lieutenant believes me! I've been here for weeks. Before this, they sent me to the shelter. I told them to check every day; every day I told them you needed help! They said his house was out of their territory, then I waited to get a ride to Di'Abribel! No one wanted to travel! When I got here, they took days to answer me, more days after I was questioned, and then more days before they arrested me! The elders said it had been too long to look through my memory because I could have fabricated the story in my mind! Where have you been? How did you get out? What happened to your hair? Is Addie okay?"

Not knowing what to answer or address first, Mika ignored Ashlynn. She could corroborate her story to the elders later, but she needed Ashlynn out of the prison. She turned to the guard.

"How much to pay for her sentence?" Mika asked the guard.

"Three months remain, so three diamond coins."

Three diamond coins? Committing a crime in Di'Abribel was no joke, and it wouldn't surprise her if the arrest was made just to prove a point.

"I'll be back," Mika told Ashlynn. She looked at the guard. "I'll be back with the coins."

Mika sprinted out of the prison and back home. She was tired from her walk, her adventure, but she needed to get Ashlynn out of the prison before the necromancers attacked, and she didn't know just how soon *soon* was.

She looked up at the heavens, the rising stars telling her that *soon* might just be when the sun finished setting.

25. LUX

The blanket covering Di'Abribel glowed yellow and orange, reflecting the fires that had started in and around the buildings of the city. The people of Di'Abribel didn't set their homes on fire to see; it was the necromancers' fiery catapults that incinerated the buildings of the city.

Hundreds of gangrels—dark, carriage-sized creatures of tenebris with massive batlike wings ending in spikes, silver claws, a rat-like tail, and a pair of footlong fangs—flocked above the tall buildings and dived into the streets. They snatched up their human prey and soared to the sky, gnawing away at their victims before releasing them to a free-falling death.

Leaning back on her heels, Mika screeched, "Aevum!"

The world, along with the gangrel diving toward her, slowed to a crawl. Having called out her spell so quick, with so much stress, she wasn't able to inhale. Her body already begged for air.

The gangrel's ash-black fur hid its features, but a smile was beginning to form behind its massive fangs. Its claws were extended and opened toward her, and the gangrel's open wings were slowing its descent for a more accurate kill.

Unsheathing her dagger, Mika fell to her knees, ducked her head, and pointed the dagger toward the gangrel, cutting into its fur as the creature soared over her, missing her shoulders by inches. Moving against each other, Mika cut down to its crotch. She inhaled when she flattened herself on the ground, causing the world to speed into reality.

373

Mika turned to her opponent. A line of missing fur was the only damage to the large creature.

The gangrel stood on its claws and extended its wings, releasing a screeching battle cry that flung black spit onto Mika's face. It took a step before sprinting toward her.

"Ignis!" Flames swooped from the buildings onto the gangrel.

The gangrel thrashed, the fire waned, and smoke rose. Fur fused into large clumps. A golden beam of lux cut through the creature of darkness, carving a steaming hole though its chest. The creature fell on its side, and an armored paladin ran to the creature and sank his sword into its heart.

"Are you okay?" A male paladin in white and gold robes clasped her hand.

With the paladin's assistance, Mika pulled herself up to her feet. "Yes, I'm fine." She brushed herself off, taking a breath to help her calm down. Two armored paladins and another in leather armor carrying a longbow approached.

"Sorceress," he said, looking down at Mika past his helmet. "Keep the fires from destroying the buildings."

Don't destroy the buildings.

~ Okay ...
~ We'll die if we don't ...

"Done."

The paladin squad leader turned to face them. "Let's move!"

After his first step, a gangrel swooped in and snatched him from the street.

"Lux!" The paladin helping Mika shot a beam of light in front of the rising gangrel, missing by several feet.

The paladin archer pushed Mika to the side, took aim, and fired. The arrow cut through the air with a bright light, missing the gangrel by yards.

The magician began casting another spell.

"Enough!" The other armored paladin, who carried no weapons, stamped his foot. "He's fucking gone! Enough!"

Mika and the paladins watched the leader inch away in the sky. A beam of light escaped him, cutting through the gangrel. The paladin fell to his death, and the gangrel fell in a death spiral above the paladin.

"This is why we don't help citizens!" The armored paladin smacked the magician across the top of his hood. He grabbed him by the shoulders and shook him with every word.

"No citizens to defend if there is no city!"

The armored paladin pushed his partner so hard the magician fell onto his butt. He turned around and placed his hands above his helmet. "I'm taking command. Mission remains the same."

The magician rose to his feet. He looked at Mika, then looked away.

The paladin squad's attire was tattered and dirty, and bloodstains covered the front of their armor. Their heavy breathing told they'd been engaged in melees since the gangrels showed up hours earlier as Mika was returning to the prison.

They're going to need help. She noticed the archer had just a few arrows left in his quiver. *I need to protect my city.*

"I'm going with you." Mika's gaze was confident when she looked at the armored paladin.

He turned around and shook his head. "Negative. You'll be a burden." He continued walking.

"Do *not* walk away from me."

The paladin spun around, summoned a lux broadsword, and took a stance against Mika.

Mika raised her chin and enflamed her hands. "I am not done talking to you, and you *will* listen to what I have to say."

The paladin's eyes traveled to her fiery hands, to his partners, then to her eyes.

"Marcus, look at her scar," the paladin archer whispered.

Marcus looked at Mika's scar.

"I think … I think she's the sorceress the escapees were talking about."

Marcus kept his eye on Mika until movement around his feet made him look down

"Damn it!" He raised his foot.

When Mika looked down, she saw the smoky black mist she saw months ago in the tavern. The same black mist that resurrects the dead and makes them fight against their will.

"We can't die; this'll turn us." Mika waved away some of the mist with her foot. She looked at Marcus and his team. "I'll cut out my own heart before I turn into an undead."

"Marcus, sir, she knows what she's talking about," the archer pleaded.

Mika stepped toward Marcus. "I'm going with you, whether you like it or not."

"Why?" Marcus stepped toward Mika and leaned into her; his helmet touched her forehead.

Mika's heart began to pump with adrenaline, and her legs felt like jelly; the feeling of a fight was kicking in.

"Because I can help the city." She leaned into his helmet with her forehead. "Carry on with your mission, instead of trying to act tough against a girl."

Marcus chuckled and poked Mika in the chest. "I don't give a damn about your gender." He pushed her away with his finger. "You better keep up. I ain't saving your little ass."

Mika adjusted her coat and watched Marcus walk away. The magician followed, and the archer approached Mika.

"I'm Ren. Magician is Earl." Ren gave Mika a short sword with a diamond, lux's jewel, in the pommel. "It's enchanted with lux."

Mika accepted the sword. Hefting it up and down, she tried to get used to its heavy weight. "I am Mika Plum of Yevera."

Ren sprinted to catch up with the group, and Mika followed. Marcus picked up the pace, and the squad moved, at a jog, through the empty streets of Di'Abribel. The streets, Mika figured, were empty because the mist had already resurrected the dead. That, or the citizens were barricaded in their homes … or carried away by gangrels. Or, what if—

A ghoul leaped out of a side street and clung on to Marcus.

Marcus roared and lifted her over his head, dashing her skull onto the stone street. "Fucking bastard!"

The undead woman was crying, but her arms reached for Marcus.

Ren kicked the ghoul across the face. Earl cut into her chest with a small axe, her heart beating under her ribs. Marcus ripped her ribs and squished her heart. The squirming stopped, and the men ensured she didn't move again.

Marcus stood and cleaned his bloody hand on Mika's coat. "Do something next time." Marcus pushed Mika away and continued his run toward the east.

Mika suppressed her anger and ran just behind Marcus. After a few minutes of jogging, the group reached the center of the housing district. The undead moved throughout the center of the district, screaming and crying every time the thought of hurting their fellow citizens crossed their minds.

Marcus raised a fist, signaling to stop. He scanned the area, and Mika scanned the crowd, reminding herself that the undead were still conscious and could feel *everything*.

I can't kill them with fire. They won't die and ... it's too cruel. She tightened her grip on her lux sword. *The Di'Abribeli are my people now.*

"There's too many," Marcus whispered. He waved the group behind a stall surrounded by crates then knelt behind the boxes. The group followed suit. Marcus peeked over the stall and shook his head.

"What do we do?" Earl peeked. He sighed, ducking further when he saw a flock of gangrels dive behind a building, their screeches echoing through the district.

"We cast a lux bomb." Marcus tapped his fingers on his knee at such a high rate it told Mika he was under stress.

Mika peeked over the stall.

"That'll alert every gangrel in Di'Abribel," Ren said, picking something off his bow. "And attract the aim of the catapults."

Mika focused on the district center. The golden statue of Angelis was broken; a metal ball nearby told Mika it was struck by a catapult. Undead surrounded the statue, swaying back and forth, their shoulders shuddering from their horrible cries and wails.

"Help me!" an undead man managed to gargle.

Mika shivered. The squad continued taking in the scene. Marcus's plan wasn't good; the reward was not greater than the risk.

Tall buildings surrounded the district center. The few buildings on fire had flames reaching out from the broken windows.

The doors to some buildings were open, others closed. Nothing on the roof, and Mika could see wood barricading windows on the upper levels. With a final look at the undead, Mika sighed.

"What if ..." Mika slid herself down and faced the group. "What if we go into one of the buildings, attract their attention, and fight them in a hallway, a few at a time."

Marcus was quick to reply. "No. Undead with offensive magic will annihilate us from the rear."

"They're citizens, not warriors," she said. "Most of them only know magic that betters their lives." She looked at Earl. "Plus I'm sure you paladins have anti-magic ... magic ... right?"

Marcus peeked over the stall and took a sweeping look at the center. "Which building you thinking of?"

Mika peeked over and slid closer to Marcus. "One without an open door." She pointed toward a building a short sprint away.

Marcus used a weak red beam that revealed a dot where he pointed. When he pointed it to the building she was talking about, Mika nodded.

"That one has a closed door and unbroken windows. No open doors or windows means no surprises from inside."

Marcus slid down and addressed the team, advising them of the plan he credited Mika with. Whether he credited her because he didn't want to be responsible for the failure or to show her respect, she didn't know.

"This doesn't mean I like you, sorceress." He balled his fist, cracking his knuckles in the process.

Mika stood. "Less talk, Marcus. More action."

The squad stood. Marcus flung a small lux orb away from their path of travel. The orb bounced on the ground, caught the attention of the ghouls, and exploded in a bright, loud *bang*.

"Go. Go!" Marcus pointed at the building, reminding Mika of her run with Stacy in the season of growth.

She sprinted ahead until Ren passed her.

He's fast.

He pulled further and further away, even when Mika ran harder.

Really fast.

Mika looked at the undead. Like dominoes, they turned to the sprinting squad.

"It's locked!" Ren jiggled the doorknob. When it didn't open, he slammed his shoulder into the door. "It's fucking locked!"

Mika held her hands close to her face. "Ignis!"

Fire from the buildings zoomed into her hands. She ran to the door and focused on the flames, just like she had done moments before killing Page.

"Hurry up! They're coming!"

The flames grew until they combined into a massive fireball. She pulled her arms back, Ren jumped out of the way, and she sent a fireball forward, exploding the door from the frame.

Earl ran inside, and Ren followed. Mika waited at the threshold for Marcus. His heavy armor caused his sprint to look like a jog. A ghoul grabbed his arm, but Marcus cast lux on his gauntlet and slammed it into the creature's face.

"Ignis!" Mika raised her hands, and a wall of fire extended toward Marcus, protecting him from the undead and giving him enough time to reach Mika.

"Still don't like you." Marcus shoulder-checked her on his way inside.

Mika ran inside.

Ren was at the base of the stairs with his bow ready to pull back and fire. "Stairs are clear."

Earl cast a lux barrier that blocked the undead from entering. The undead banged on the barrier with pitiful looks on their faces.

"Are you two ready?" Earl asked.

Marcus rolled his shoulders, stretched his neck, widened his stance, draped his arms to his side, and cast a lux shield and a long, pointed lux spear.

"I am," he said. "Not sure about the sorceress."

Mika felt like letting her ignis children feast on the smirking paladin, letting them burn him alive inside of his armor. But she restrained herself because, right now, he was more useful to her alive than dead. She stood next to Marcus and clenched her sword with both hands.

"That's not how you hold that," Marcus said, shaking his head. "It's one-handed!"

Mika glared at Marcus before releasing one hand and summoning a flame on it, bracing herself to fight the undead. When she didn't move, Earl released the barrier and allowed several undead to enter the hallway before recasting the barrier.

Marcus thrust the spear toward his enemies. Upon impact, the spear radiated searing light inside of the ghouls' chests, cutting through the heart even if Marcus missed it. Stab, block, stab, block, stab. Marcus was an animal when it came to fighting, so much so that Mika fizzled away her fire, straightened herself, and backed away from him. After more stabbing, more blocking, more barriers letting undead in, and endless cries of their once-human enemies, Marcus relaxed.

He rolled his shoulders and stretched his neck. He turned to his squad and took off his helmet. Chainmail was wrapped around glowing bandages on his head. Marcus moved the chainmail away and took off the bandages, revealing a scorched, blistered face without eyebrows. Marcus had been a victim of a burning and, Mika now knew, that is why he despised her.

"That was a good fucking plan. Guess you're useful for something." He chuckled, and one corner of his mouth rose in a snicker. "Still don't like you, though."

Mika refused to show emotion. She stared back at Marcus until he wiped sweat from his brow, infused the glowing bandages with more vita, and donned his helmet.

"Eastern walls are just minutes from here," he said.

Marcus waddled over the pile of defeated ghouls, peeked out, looked left, right, left, up, then ran out, waving for his team to follow.

Earl zoomed past Mika.

Ren stopped in front of her. "You're doing good, girl."

"Don't call me girl." She gave Ren a playful shove. "We're the same age, and I've been through more than you ever will." She leapt over the pile of bodies and set off in a sprint the second her boot touched the ground. "Keep up, Ren."

Marcus's voice was mocking and apathetic. "We need access to the roof of your shop."

An old lady was peeking out of the crack in the doorway. "No! No! You have no right! Paladins have no right to be in our homes! Get out! Get out!"

The squabble continued. Mika focused on massaging her fore-arm. Soreness from carrying the sword had set in.

Marcus's loud voice boomed and caught Mika's attention. He was blocking the door from closing with his plate mail boot.

"Look, you dried-up old bitch, we need access to your roof right now! We're in battle. I'm going to force myself in and beat your brain out your eyes if you don't let me in!"

"No! No!" The old lady pushed on the door to no avail. "Get out! Paladins are not welcome!"

Marcus donned his helmet.

"Darling! Darling, get the crossbow!" The lady screeched.

Marcus used his shoulder to break into the house. He grabbed the frail lady by the shoulders and tossed her against the wall.

She knocked her head on a wall shelf and slid to the ground, holding her wound and crying, "Honey …" she tried to scream, "Honey, they're in!"

"You're lucky you let me in, you—"

A bolt impaled Marcus's armor.

Marcus looked at the bolt, raised his arms to it, and fell to his knees. Marcus hung his head and draped his arms.

Before Mika could react, Marcus tensed up looked at the man who'd shot him. The skinny older gentleman stood with terrified eyes at the threshold of his bedroom door. Marcus stood and tore the bolt from his armor.

"Stupid old man!"

The old man dropped his crossbow and raised his hands, sheer terror manifested in his eyes.

Marcus grabbed his shoulder and shoved him to the ground. "Do you want to die by my hand or those of the necromancers?" Marcus slapped the man with the back of his gauntlet.

The old man closed his eyes and began to tremble so hard that Mika thought he was convulsing.

Ren and Earl ran up to Marcus. Marcus continued the scolding.

Mika knelt in front of the old lady. "Let me heal you."

The old lady's shoulders lowered, and she closed her eyes when she noticed Mika wasn't wearing paladin attire. With a shaking arm that caused her arm skin to jiggle, the lady moved her bloodied hand in front of her face. She began to weep when she saw blood.

"No, dear. No, I'm not okay."

A lump formed in Mika's throat.

"Here," she said, calling for vita after clearing her throat. "Let me help you."

Mika held her hand on the lady's head. The wound closed, and the blood stopped dripping. Mika passed her healing hands over the lady's limbs.

The light from the vita illuminated Mika's face, her scar the most prominent feature. The lady reached for Mika's cheek and passed her thumb over Mika's scar.

"Are you the one the survivors spoke of?" The lady's rough, leathery hands disturbed Mika, but she didn't let it show.

Mika looked the lady in the eyes, sighed, and looked away. "I am Mika Plum of Yevera." She passed her hands through the lady's stomach and down one of her legs. "I'm the sorceress who freed the prisoners from the Lost Forest."

"Mika Plum … you are so much prettier than I had imagined." The lady clasped Mika's face. "You saved my son. You saved my son, unlike these wasteful …" She adjusted herself and let out a painful grunt. "Unlike these wasteful, evil paladins."

"Mika!" Marcus bellowed. "We got the key to the roof!"

"We need to borrow your house," Mika whispered. "It'll be quick. I won't let them desecrate your home. I promise."

The lady nodded and wept into her hands. Mika stood and joined the squad in the bedroom. Earl ran up the stairs and unlocked the hatch to the roof. He peeked out, looked around, and vaulted onto the roof. Ren followed, and Marcus showed off by not touching the railing on his ascent. Mika was the last to emerge.

The roof was a large square surrounded by a waist-high wall on all sides. Covered by a brown leather tarp, the squad was hidden from the gangrels flying overhead. Next to the squad were the crumbling eastern walls of Di'Abribel. Claustrophobic sounds bounced from the archers at the top shooting their bows, the magicians in the towers casting magic, and the necromancers from below ramming the wooden doors with battering rams.

"Red smoke!" Earl pointed to the southwest. Smoke was rising from within the buildings. "The cavalry made it!"

Mika knew that a few hundred yards further from the smoke was a large field used to farm rabbits.

Marcus took off his helmet and squinted. He noticed the smoke and nodded. "I knew they'd make it. I fucking knew it."

Ren pulled out a blue stick from his belt pouch. "Sorceress, do you mind?" He extended the stick to Mika. The fuse needed to be lit.

"Ignis." Mika held the small flame to the fuse until it sparked and ignited.

"Where you want it?" Ren asked.

Marcus gave a dismissing wave and sat with his back against the wall. "Just toss that shit in the street."

Ren jogged to the edge of the overhead and tossed the stick into the empty street. Seconds later, the stick popped, and blue smoke began to rise, signaling to whoever was watching that Blue Team was in position.

Mika turned to Marcus and inhaled, but before she could ask, Marcus answered her question.

"Eastern walls have the fewest necromancers, but they'll make it in eventually. That's where we swoop in, kill as many as we can, and make way for Red Team." He pointed toward the red smoke with a bladed hand. "Paladins on cavalry will rush out of the city and flank the necromancers pushing against the northern walls."

Marcus looked to the west and stayed quiet. Past the bandages, Mika could see he was squinting and biting at the inside of his mouth.

"Just hoping Yellow Team made it. They'll use the sewers to sneak out the western walls behind the necromancers there."

Mika looked over the edge and analyzed the narrow street below. Three paladins and a sorceress against platoons of necromancers? Although paladins were fierce warriors, she knew no person could survive being outnumbered like they were.

She shook her head. "What's the plan? Just throw magic at them and hope they don't see us?"

"That's what I was thinking," Earl said. "How will we win with just us four?"

"Relax, children. Just cast your strongest magic or the one that would disperse them. I'm going to summon a hurricane that'll send them flying all over the place. If they don't die from being flung and thrown around the hurricane, they'll be weak. Necromancers are like rats: useless when they're alone."

"That's what I call them," Mika said trying to bond with Marcus, she inhaled to speak again, but Marcus spoke over her.

"Maybe our new *friend* can cast some fire into my hurricane so they can burn while they're twirling to their deaths. What you say, sorceress?"

Mika thought of the plan. Not only would that work, it would be *incredibly* satisfying to watch. Mika nodded.

Marcus smirked. "You two think of something to do."

Ren and Earl looked at each other—one gave scenarios while the other countered as to why it would be a bad idea.

Everyone finished talking, and a few minutes passed without anyone saying a word.

Mika cleared her throat and spoke over the growing din of the battle. "How many did Blue Team start with?"

Marcus sighed, tilted his head back onto the wall, and closed his eyes.

A loud explosion made Mika and Ren duck. Earl and Marcus seemed unaffected by the sound.

"Mika, Ren, you two got first watch."

Just after Marcus made the statement, his angry eyes relaxed, and he started to snore, his bandages moving into his mouth with every inhale, then out with every exhale.

How'd he go to sleep so quick in conditions like this?

Earl took off his pouch and used it as a pillow. He fell asleep within seconds.

Mika snapped her eyes at Ren; she raised her hands in question.

"Don't know when they'll breach. Could be minutes, could be hours, could be days." He took a seat over the wall, seemingly unworried about being spotted by gangrels. "Best we can do now is rest. Food'll be delivered by eagles every twelve hours."

Days? I don't have days!

Thoughts of Ashlynn worried Mika. She sat next to Ren on the wall, and the wordless wait allowed her mind to wander. Her heart raced when she continued thinking of Ashlynn. What was she doing right now? Ashlynn was safe inside the prison, but what if the necromancers broke through? What if the prison collapsed from catapult fire? Ashlynn's grave condition wouldn't allow her to survive an attack.

She began to think, and her mind turned blank. Minutes turned to hours.

A movement of Ren's leg made her look at him. He slid over the wall. "Our turn. Marcus! Earl!"

Marcus jumped to his feet. His eyes were wide, and he scanned the area. Once he realized nothing was wrong, he relaxed and nodded.

"Two hours?"

"Yeah." Ren removed his quiver and lay on his back, still holding on to his bow. The string had an arrow nocked.

Mika summoned a flame for warmth between her and Ren.

"Oh, *now* you use that." Marcus shook his head.

Though his voice sounded less demeaning than before, Mika ignored him, curled into the fetal position, and drifted to sleep within seconds.

It wasn't the screams or the sound of her name that woke Mika, but the sharp, agonizing pain that tore into the top of her shoulders. She opened her eyes to see herself hovering in the air. Marcus held her leg with one hand. He latched on to the wall with the other. Mika's hands went to the pain in her shoulders and clasped on to a gangrel's claws. Her eyes widened. Marcus was the only thing holding her down.

"Mika!" Marcus screamed. "Mika, use your magic!"

Mika felt her flesh tear away from her bones. "Ignis!" she squealed, but she couldn't focus. Tears filled her eyes.

A gangrel swept Ren away. Somehow, the tarp covering the squad was gone.

The door to the walls burst open and necromancers ran through.

Ren, still holding on to his bow, took aim at the gangrel that carried him away. He locked eyes with Mika, then aimed at Mika's gangrel.

The lux arrow cut through the air and dug itself into the eye of the gangrel that clung to her shoulders. Mika flopped to the ground.

She banged her elbows on the floor and lay motionless in a fit of sobbing. A boom exploded from below.

Marcus slid to his knees and applied vita to her shoulders. "The necromancers have broken through!" He picked Mika up when he realized her wounds wouldn't heal.

Mika screamed; painful, crying gasps escaped her mouth.

Flesh was missing from her shoulder; the gangrel had ripped away her skin and muscles. Her collarbone was pulverized. Mika collapsed.

Earl sent a beam into the crowd of necromancers.

Necromancers retaliated with a volley of mori missiles and ice spikes. One spike cut into Earl's chest before his top half exploded.

"The fate of the city lies with you!" Marcus slung Mika's arm over his neck, and he carried her to the edge of the roof. "Ventus!"

Wind whistled from all around Mika, forming into a growing hurricane in the streets below. The wind tore loose parts of her flesh and muscles.

"Cast the fire! Mika, cast the fire!"

Mika collapsed, but Marcus held her up. No adrenaline in her blood, the visual sensation made this the worst pain in her life.

"Ignis!" She tilted her hand toward the hurricane.

Her brain shook and trembled.

Marcus applied vita to ease the pain.

Closing her tear-filled eyes, she took a breath and squealed. "Ignis!"

Lava spewed from her hand, and the wind carried it into the hurricane.

The whistles and roars of the hurricane combined with the pops and gurgles of the continuous lava flowing from her hand.

"More!"

Mika, in agony, cried, "*Ignis!*" And the lava tripled.

As the hurricane grew, necromancers began being pulled by the wind into the fiery, burning winds. The hurricane grew and grew until Mika and Marcus were inside the swirling wall of wind and fire.

Marcus encased the two in a barrier, grasped the wall with one hand, and tightened his arm around Mika. He leaned toward the eastern walls and shouted, "Ventus!"

The hurricane obeyed, and it moved past them and over the walls, taking everything in its path. Shouts, roars, pops, gurgles, and howling winds filled the air. Bodies, weapons, equipment, and debris twirled around them in the magmatic hurricane that moved further and further away past the walls and toward the remains of Yevera.

The area quieted, and Marcus shot his arm in the air, releasing a beam of light. A distant horn sounded.

Mika collapsed, but Marcus held her up. "You're gonna see our victory before you die, sorceress."

Small, painful whimpers escaped Mika's throat. Struggling to keep her eyes open, she heard the rumbles and tremors of hundreds upon hundreds of horses. The clanking armor soon followed, and she saw shock cavalry paladins rushing out the eastern gates of Di'Abribel, leaving a trail of dust behind them.

Mika lost all energy, and Marcus sat her against the wall. She closed her tearful eyes. "Did we win?"

Marcus's breath entered her nostrils, his voice radiating in her ears. His mean, judgmental voice was different. This time, it was sweet and understanding. She could hear a smile when he spoke.

"Yeah ... but I still don't like you."

* * * * *

Mika's eyes fluttered open when the sunlight shone on her face. She looked at the ceiling of her home and opened her mouth to release a yawn that carried her morning breath and tears. She heard noises coming from the kitchen. Mika winced and moved her torn shoulder covered in wraps infused with vita and healing herbs. Mika stood, put on her sandals, and got ready for the day by brushing her teeth and brushing her now prettied, short hair. Janice was in the kitchen cooking food and Ashlynn smiled as Mika approached.

"Good morning, Janice." Mika went to her former coworker and placed her head on Janice's shoulder.

"How did you sleep?" Janice continued cooking but kissed Mika's head.

"Better," Mika responded without moving. She eyed the cauldron.

With a taste of the oatmeal from the cauldron, Janice used ventus to extinguish the flames.

387

Mika went to the table and hugged Ashlynn, who returned the hug and checked the bandages.

"Are you ready for your big day?" Ashlynn asked.

Janice served the food and took it to the two ladies.

"I'm always ready." Mika blew on the bowl and took a sip from a spoon without looking at the food.

A few hours after her meal, a paladin carriage arrived at her house and transported her to the amphitheater. There, thousands of citizens sat on the seats. In front of them, hundreds of paladins were in formation. In front of those, on the stadium, Mika sat with her hands clasped above her lap in a comfortable, golden white chair. To her left was Ren. His legs, now wooden pegs, extended in front of him. He too sat at attention the best he could despite his injuries. To Ren's left, Marcus sat at attention with a white bandage hiding his face. His chin was held high, his chest puffed out, palms flat on his thighs, and his boots were stuck firm onto the ground.

Eight empty chairs with armor, weapons, or gear were to the right of Mika. Each item on top of the chairs once belonged to a member of Blue Team—the heroes responsible for the victory of Di'Abribel. Blue Team was a team of Eradicators, one of the most elite groups in the Paladin army.

Master Paladin Axel, the leader of the paladin army in Celeste, gave a speech, explaining their mission in Celeste and honoring all the paladins, guards, soldiers, and citizens who gave their life during the raid. A quick memorial for each fallen member of Blue Team was given. Master Paladin Axel turned around, allowing Mika to see his athletic frame, lux-mastery hair, aqua highlights, and large ears. A younger paladin in robes followed him with a gold box.

Marcus stood at attention when Master Paladin Axel approached.

"Sergeant Marcus of Imbris, your display of leadership, courage, and tenacity in the battle of Di'Abribel showed the values held by the paladin order." Master Paladin Axel reached for a medal and hung it on Marcus's neck. He reached for another and hung that one from Marcus's neck as well. "The actions you took when those above you perished has shown your ability as a leader, and I am herby promoting you to the rank of Senior Sergeant in the Paladin Order, Region of Celeste, Continent of Irstia, and granting you a Medal of Courage."

Paladins in the distance shouted, "Lux!"

Beams of light rose to the blue, cloudless heavens. The crowd applauded.

Marcus saluted his superior. Axel returned the salute and moved in front of Ren. Marcus sat.

"Archer Ren of Velonde, you disregarded your own safety to save the citizen known as Sorceress Mika of Yevera. This citizen, you knew, would be instrumental in thwarting the necromancer attack on the city." He reached for a medal the shape and color of Rend's star.

"Your display of selflessness shows that being named after the deity of lux is truly deserving. The sacrificial actions you took allow me to bestow upon you Rend's Star, the highest decoration given to any paladin. Because of this, it is I who must salute you."

Master Paladin Axel knelt in front of Ren and saluted the young paladin. With tears in his eyes, Ren saluted back.

Paladins in the distance shot beams that rose to the heavens. The crowd cheered.

Master Paladin Axel approached Mika. He faced her, took a step back, and bowed.

Although she didn't have to, Mika stood out of respect for Master Paladin Axel, her squad, and the dead members of Blue Team.

"Sorceress Mika of Yevera, it is unknown what the fate of Marcus and Ren would have been without your superior strategies and your amazing gifts. As the Master of the Paladins in Celeste, I bestow upon you this gift." He gave Mika a key that radiated with the colors of the rainbow. "This key will grant passage and amenities through the region of Luxania and open any door in every building owned by the paladins. You are a welcome guest in our homes."

Paladins in the distance shot beams, and the crowd cheered, much louder for Mika than they did for the paladins.

"Thank you." Mika winced and touched her shoulder. She passed her hand over the bandages.

Master Paladin Axel turned to the citizens of Di'Abribel. "Our ceremony has concluded. Thank you for attending. Sorceress Mika asked that all citizens stay, for she has words she would like to share."

Master Paladin Axel left the amphitheater, and his paladins followed.

Marcus waved Mika goodbye. She could almost hear him thinking, *Still don't like you.*

Mika approached Ren and hugged him. "Thanks again."

"Stop saying thanks. Only did it because I think you're hot." He tightened his arms around the woman he saved.

"You're dumb, bestie," she laughed, rejecting the advance.

Ren's face reddened, "Ouch ..."

Mika winked. "Let me know if you ever need anything."

She turned to the crowd when he left. There, she saw the citizens of Di'Abribel.

Okay, now's the time.

"Tenebris," she whispered.

Using her emotion spell, she manifested a fear into her listeners' hearts. "The attack on our beautiful city is not the last."

People in the crowd shifted; whispers began to run through the citizens.

"While your families, your friends, your sons and daughters were dying, while they were being carried away and turned into an unliving abomination ... Talon, your beloved king, escaped the city through the sewers leading out of the western walls."

Anger.

She raised her voice. "His actions caused the needless death of paladins and countless innocent citizens."

The crowd began to shout; the angry looks on their faces told her the spell was working.

"Now, he comes back to the city as if nothing happened! Six days! Six days have passed and not a peep from the person who leads us!"

The guards and soldiers had the ability to stop Mika's insurrection, but none of them moved a muscle.

"The king has shown his true colors! Today, with my powers and your support, we will force King Talon to abdicate!"

Hope.

"Today, we will raise an army that will fight the black rats that have plagued this beautiful land, the rats that have murdered our children and stolen our livelihood!"

Courage.

"Today, we will rise as one, undivided nation! We will not be known as Di'Abribel, we will not be known as Yevera, we will not be known as Reach, nor Vicqua! Today," –and here she raised her unwounded arm and summoned a blue flame that melted the snow and warmed her citizens– "Today, we are united as Celeste, the region of ignis!"

Mika sent the flame to the King's palace, where it hovered high, showing everyone in Di'Abribel where they would march.

Excitement.

"Today, I, Mika Plum, Yeveran by birth, the Marked Sorceress, the Hero of Di'Abribel, crown myself as the Princess of the Di'Abribeli People."

The crowd boomed in agreement.

"March on to the King's Palace! Avenge our fallen brothers and sisters!"

Following the princess, the citizens of Di'Abribel stormed the palace with no resistance from the guards or soldiers. They found King Talon in his chambers, for no warning of the insurrection had been given to the hated king. After beating him, they bound his wife and his children, and exiled them from Di'Abribel and Celeste, placing the family in the back of a merchant caravan told to drop them off in the poorest city in Velonde with nothing but five silver coins.

The citizens were happy about the first female leader of their city, rejoiced in her willingness to fight the threat that plagued their lands, and loved her ability to fight on her own. Those who protested were surrounded by soldiers, bound, and publicly executed for their refusal to accept their new ruler. Mika ruled her obedient citizens with fairness and a stern hand, making her a feared but respected ruler. Weeks passed with no unrest.

"Ambassador?" Ashlynn shook her head. "I mean … if the princess wills it. You did ask that I be with you when you reach the top. I thought I would be doing something else, but honestly, it does seem like a good fit for me." Ashlynn rubbed her severed leg then stopped when a thought flashed in her mind. "Is it because I talk a lot? Did you do this on purpose?"

Alder approached the stairs to the throne. "I was summoned?"

"Yes, Alder." Mika smiled at her military advisor.

Alder approached and knelt in front of Mika, looking at the ground when she spoke.

"Will you be able to remember everything I tell you?" Before Alder could respond, Mika continued. "Do me a favor, look me in the eyes when I speak to you."

Alder raised his head and looked at Mika. "Yes, Princess. I'm able to remember everything."

Mika remembered the countless books she read under Ron's care; compiling their information, knowledge, and suggestions. "I want all information you have on Vicqua, the citizens, their military, finances, *everything*. Have scouts confirm accuracy of the maps; have them draw every portion of the city from a standing point of view. I need information on all passages, roads, fortifications. Everything.

"I don't care how you do it, but find out everything known about the queen. I want *everything* on her and her city. If you think it's unimportant, I don't care." Mika drove the point home. "I. Want. Everything. Furthermore, increase recruiting and increase training and discipline in the current forces."

She paused to let Alder digest the information, taking the chance to look at his black, combed-over hair.

"Bring me a list of everything we are spending resources on. Bring to me a list of trade agreements with Velonde, but double the request for dragonscale. I want a list of every expenditure, whether it's a diamond coin or pound of salt per day, I don't care. Take a list of every expense to my quarters by tomorrow morning."

Mika inhaled, pretending she needed time to take a breath and not to gather her thoughts.

"Encourage reproduction in the city; we need more citizens to increase our military numbers. Repair the Farmlands and give me best locations for towers." Mika blinked.

That's it ... right?

"I think so." Ashlynn replied in her mind.

Me too.

"Understood?"

392

Alder lowered his shoulders. He tried to sound nonconfrontational. "Yes, Princess, but … but I only handle military affairs. You'll have to go through Silvia for matters of trade and finances. Edward would be the go-to for growth and development …"

"I know this." She didn't know this, but she made it seem to her citizens that she never made a mistake. Mika had already gathered a group of loyal followers to use as scapegoats and blame them for mistakes made in the city. "I trust you'll relay the information."

"Of course, Princess." He waited to be dismissed.

"Thank you, Alder. Please see to the matters we spoke about."

Alder walked away.

"Mika, what do you have planned with Vicqua?" Ashlynn hid her chin from Mika and looked at Mika's eyes, then her mouth, then her own feet. "I'm tired of the fighting …"

Mika approached her sister and lifted her chin. Locking eyes with Ashlynn caused the princess to smile. "They're helping the necromancers, and the necromancers are our enemies! They're either with us or against us, and they've proven their loyalty." Mika hugged Ashlynn. "The fighting will stop once Kathrine pays for her crimes."

Ashlynn pulled away. "But what will you do with Vicqua?"

"I'll see once I get everything I requested." Mika sighed and smiled. "Let's go get our hair done. I know the best person in the city! Her name is Sandra, and she's anxious to meet you!" Mika called to a servant. "Please prepare a carriage for us. Also, I want Luke to be my permanent coachman."

The servant bowed. "Yes, Princess."

* * * * *

Ashlynn sat at the palace dinner table. It was the third week that Mika hadn't shown up for breakfast, lunch, or dinner. She wanted to tell Mika that Ron had been found in Velonde, extradited to Di'Abribel, and had agreed to make weapons for the Di'Abribeli army instead of being executed. Though the thought made Ashlynn furious, she knew Mika felt like she *owed* Ron something. Mika told Ashlynn everything, and she knew Mika felt that way because of all the knowledge she'd gleaned from Ron's books and conversations under his care. Ashlynn felt like Mika saw Ron as the father she never had.

Ashlynn put down her silverware, unable to finish the food. She had to come to terms with the fact that Ron's assistance with the war effort would be better than her seeing him die.

"Allies over enemies. Logic over emotion and feelings," Ashlynn told herself. This was a common phrase said by Mika after making questionable choices such as the killing of Vicquic citizens, public torture of Kathrine's necromancers, and espionage against her own people.

Mika was psychotic, but she genuinely loved Di'Abribel and everyone who supported her.

Janice approached. "Wine?"

Ashlynn shook her head. "No, thanks. Bad things always happen when alcohol is involved. How are the Toveys? Are the repairs to the home almost done? How do you manage working there and working here? I only had one job in my life and, honestly, working for someone else is not for me."

Janice looked at Ashlynn with a frown. "I've worked since I was a child, and I'll work until I perish. Please do not judge my life choices." Janice picked up Ashlynn's plate. "How is the princess?"

"I haven't seen her in weeks. She's usually out here trying to do something, asking questions about the city, the Farmlands ... but I haven't seen her ... I think she might be dead! Or hurt! Something is wrong with her, but I don't want to go into her quarters."

Janice began to walk away. "I would."

Ashlynn watched Janice walk away. When the door closed, she took a deep, deep inhale and rubbed her eyes. She wanted to whisper, *"shit,"* but the princess had told her she needed to watch her language, for she now held an important position of power.

"Poop."

Ashlynn trudged up the stairs with her cane, refusing help when asked. She made her way to the princess's room. Looking inside, she saw a gorgeous bed, a strong fire in the fireplace, and a clean room. Mika must be in the reading room ... again.

Ashlynn made her way through the palace and to the reading room. Outside the reading room was a silver table with covered plates of food. Lifting the covers, Ashlynn saw the food she ate for dinner. So, the rumors were true; the princess was skipping meals.

This was it. Ashlynn was too worried for Mika to be concerned about repercussions for disobeying Mika's order: *"Do not disturb me if my door is closed."*

Ashlynn grabbed the doorknob and opened the door. A horrible smell of old sweat, grimy clothes, and spoiled food entered her nostrils.

"Ugh!" Ashlynn almost puked. She opened the door further, and several papers on the floor flew away from the wind caused by the door.

One would not know the floor was made of wood because of the hundreds of papers littered throughout. Maps, notes, drawings, daggers impaled onto papers, and strings attached to other daggers that impaled other papers. On the table was half-eaten food. Some had drawn gnats; flies hovered over other pieces. She saw the back of Mika's head resting on a loveseat that faced the closed window.

Ashlynn thought Mika was dead. In case she wasn't, she took off her sandal, knowing she would have to step on the papers. She took a step in, and papers stuck to the bottom of her sweaty foot.

Mika was sleeping with her mouth open; she snored without moving her lips. Ashlynn could smell her unwashed mouth from feet away. Dirt and grime had mixed with sweat and made a black line on the crevices of Mika's neck and elbows.

"Mooredoth be blessed by the Eight!" She passed her hand through Mika's hair, trying to feel for a fever, and only meeting slimy sweat. "Mika!"

Ashlynn used telepathy to call Janice. Mika opened her tired eyes and looked at Ashlynn. Ashlynn began to pull her up, but Janice ran into the room. They both used ventus to carry the princess out of the room.

"We mustn't let disease get into her," said Janice. "She needs a bath."

"What are you doing, Mika?" Ashlynn had forgot her etiquette.

Mika's exhaustion blinded her to Ashlynn's scolding.

"There's no way into Vicqua …" Mika said, hovering through the air, into the halls, and toward the bath. "Necromancers will attack if we mount a siege … We're not strong enough."

Ashlynn didn't say anything.

"But I think I found a way in." Mika watched Janice fill the bathtub. "I think I found a way to take Vicqua."

Mika was lifted into the bathtub. Janice and Ashlynn bathed the princess, did her hair, brushed her teeth. They lifted her out, dried her, and took her to bed. Mika's refreshed look told Ashlynn and Janice she was glad to be clean, prettied, and resting.

Mika laughed when she snuggled the sheets. With eyes closed and ready to sleep, she smiled. "Ashlynn."

Ashlynn approached the princess.

"I'll sleep for a day or two. Have Luke prepare the carriage." She further snuggled the sheets, shaking herself down into the mattress. "He and I will be going to Vicqua without an escort."

26. SEDUCTION

Music from the birds floated into the queen's ears. The smell of flowers from the garden three stories down had seeped into the open window, and sunbeams reflected off her face and toward the painting. She dipped her brush into the yellow paint, patted it on the palette, inched her face closer, and made a thick line within the petal of the lily. Though she could use magic to make a better painting, she didn't want to. She loved feeling the weight of the brush pushing against the canvas. The door opened behind her, but she was so into her painting that she decided not to look back.

"Your Highness …" the rough, authoritative voice of one of her servants rang in her ears.

Queen Madeline painted the next petal, exhaling a sad sigh that ended with her lips and eyebrows churning downward in despair. She straightened herself and bladed her body halfway, enough for her head to turn and her cerulean-blue eyes to look at her servant, a middle-aged man with a bald head and close shave.

"Yes, Brandon?" When she spoke, she did not try to hide the sadness in her voice, no matter who was around.

Brandon tilted his head to admire the beautiful painting. He looked back at her. "The new ruler of Di'Abribel has arrived without a military escort. She fashions herself Mika Plum of Yevera, the Princess of Di'Abribel, and she would like to meet you."

Queen Madeline's eyes traveled to the ground. Just what she needed, another ruler interrupting her day to brag about themselves, show off, and bore her mind with trade agreements. She turned back to her painting. "I'll be there shortly."

"Yes, Your Highness," Brandon replied and walked to the door and turned back. "As always, it's a beautiful painting."

"Thank you," she said, eyeing her painting with a frown as the door closed.

The paintings are always beautiful.

If only people complimented the other things in her life, the things she *tried* to be good at, not the things she knew she was good at.

A few strokes here let her think about the attack in Di'Abribel a few months ago. It was, beyond a doubt, her fault the attack happened. She was, in some way, responsible for the destruction in Celeste by allowing the necromancers to feed reinforcements from Velonde and giving the army in the forest food, supplies, and equipment.

Some finishing strokes across the dark sky made her remember that she made the alliance for the greater good of Celeste, Vicqua, her citizens, and herself. Necromancers weren't intrinsically evil; they just had unusual ways of conquest. And necromancers, unlike paladins, didn't have purity trials after their conquests.

She set down her painting tools before stepping back.

They always care for the citizens they conquer ...

Doubts ran through her head, and her eyes traveled down her painting until they looked at the floor. More and more thoughts made the brush slip out of her hand, breaking her from her thoughts.

Always ...

She studied her painting: a black, moonless sky was covered by gray clouds. In a field of dying grass was a single flower, a yellow lily—also dying.

Madeline made a slow turn to the mirror. After checking her makeup and hair, she turned to the door and made her way down the stairs to the first floor. Another servant approached her.

"Highness!" Nathan spoke fast and it seemed like all his sentences ended with a surprised pitch. "The Di'Abribeli princess was escorted to the back! She was interested in seeing the flowers! We figured you'd be okay with that!"

Flowers? The princess wants to look at flowers? Almost all leaders who visit want to get straight to business. No banter, no wandering, just business.

"Yes." Madeline was nodding without knowing she was doing so. "Yes, of course, I'm okay with that."

Diverting her route to the rear of the palace, the queen opened the door onto a cold but sunny day. She looked down toward her garden.

Just outside a carriage painted scarlet red was a young woman with brown hair and a modest cold-weather dress that matched the color of the carriage. The princess of Di'Abribel was admiring the row of yellow lilies along the marble path.

The princess must've heard the queen approach because her head perked away from the flowers, and she spun around when the queen took an additional step. She stood a whole foot shorter than the queen, and the pink-and-white scar that ran from the princess's cheek to her ear was her most prominent feature. Or rather her most prominent feature until her eyes curved upward, and her lips followed, revealing the most perfect and beautiful smile the queen had ever seen.

"Queen Madeline!" The princess curtsied as a sign of submission, something no other ruler had done before. "It's an honor to meet you!" The princess's words were smooth and happy.

Madeline stared at the Di'Abribeli for a moment before scratching the back of her own head. "Princess, please, rise. Please, address me as something other than Queen. *Queen* places the sight of an elder in my mind. What shall I call you? You're so young …"

The princess rose and held her chin high. "I am Mika Plum!" Mika puffed her chest and gave a fun smile that raised her cheeks further. "—of Yevera." She placed her fists on her hips and emphasized her title. "The *Princess* of Di'Abribel!"

Silence.

Madeline didn't know what to do. Was the princess joking? Was she trying to be funny? She didn't sense an aggressive energy from her, just … a little acting? The Princess of Di'Abribel was born a Yeveran?

Mika exhaled. Her mood seemed to plummet. "Sorry …" –she whispered something under her breath– "I was trying to be funny." Mika shook her head with such vigor it made her hair follow her head's momentum.

"Oh!" Madeline tried to see the humor in Mika's actions and forced out a laugh. For some reason, Madeline was feeling a deep sense of sadness. "It was hilarious." Madeline took a step toward Mika. "It completely caught me by surprise is all!"

"I'm glad you think so." Mika widened her eyes and took a breath. "This princess thing is tough. I'm too young for this!" Mika locked eyes with Madeline. "I feel like I still want ..." Mika paused and whispered something. "I feel like I still want adventure. I don't want to be stuck in a palace all day, you know?"

The feeling of sadness was replaced by a feeling of excitement that seemed to boom with each of Madeline's heartbeats. "I understand."

Mika looked at Madeline with eyes that hungered for more information, eyes that waited for Madeline to keep talking.

After a swallow, Madeline spoke. "I assumed the role of queen at fifteen." Her gaze shifted to the lilies that were surviving the cold because of the magic within the garden. "I longed for adventure once. Not adventure, specifically. I wanted to build. Yes, I longed to be a builder." She was nodding, but she didn't notice she was. "When I was but a child, I constructed clay models, specifically bridges. Erecting a bridge over a body of water was the lifelong goal I held as a child."

Her eyes returned to Mika; she gave a half smile and shrugged. "Queenship called to me, forcing me to settle on the models. Models and paintings, specifically."

Madeline felt embarrassed for opening up to Mika, so quickly and to such a young woman ... Opening up to a ruler of another nation. Was magic controlling her emotions? She didn't have one of her escorts to block the magic, since she wasn't negotiating anything.

But she wouldn't know a spell with such power.

Mika stared back with wide eyes before she looked left and right. After taking one last look at the lilies, Mika smiled at Madeline. "Show me your models!"

"My models?"

"Yes!"

Madeline blinked and shook her head. "No ruler has ever inquired about my models ..."

"Well," said Mika. She moved her lips in a whisper. "Then that makes me the first!"

Excitement shot through Madeline again. "Okay ... okay, well, follow me!"

Queen Madeline guided Princess Mika through her palace, showing her all the clay models spread throughout the fortress. The princess was interested in each one, asking where the queen would place the bridge, structure, monument, or statue, what materials would be used, and how long she thought it would take to build. They stopped in the middle of a long hall with paintings inside golden engravings decorating the walls. All were painted by Madeline.

"Whoa!" The princess inched her face closer to the model of a handsome man wielding a heart. "The detail on this is amazing!" The princess, still leaning toward the model, looked at Madeline. "You literally gave him sweat glands and wrinkles!" She turned back to the model. "Who is he?"

"Taras Lancaster." Madeline's eyes narrowed in a frown. "Specifically, an imbecile of a man."

Mika straightened. "I've loved an imbecilic man before."

"Did you abandon him?"

"No," she said. "I killed him."

"You ... you killed him?"

"And his new wife and baby."

Madeline was taken aback, but the statement spiked her interest. "That is crazy ..."

Mika's eyes widened, and her knuckles cracked when she balled her fists. The candles on the walls seemed to grow, and Madeline sensed that she was seconds from being attacked, but she didn't know why. Mika's anger at the man must be powerful.

"I despise men," said Madeline.

A slow exhale left Mika's lips, and her face softened. She picked up Taras's model. "Prove it." Mika handed the model to Madeline.

The princess was so straightforward, so aggressive, young, and full of positive energy that it charmed Madeline. She grabbed the model of Taras, feeling the hard clay in her hand; it was the perfect condition to be thrown onto the ground and crushed underneath her feet.

Madeline looked at Mika; her smile was eager. Madeline raised the model in the air and slammed it on the ground, breaking it to pieces. She drove her heel into the model's face and rejoiced when it crushed underneath her feet.

Yes! Yes!

Mika jumped and landed a foot on the torso. "Fuck you, Taras!" She rotated her feet before kicking a loose piece across the floor.

Madeline recoiled. "I don't curse ..."

Mika stopped. "I can keep a secret."

When Madeline didn't respond, Mika kicked another piece, sending it through the air and onto the wall.

"Fuck you, Taras!" she repeated with a smile.

A laugh escaped Madeline's throat. "Fuck. Fuck you, Taras!" A swing of Madeline's foot sent pieces of the model across the floor.

Mika rejoiced. Madeline's mood matched hers, and Mika rushed to Madeline, offered her hand, and, when accepted, Mika spun the queen in circles. Mika used her free hand to expel aqua that turned into drops of vita, surrounding the two in a cascade of golden, healing water.

"Use your magic!" Mika yelled with a smile.

The queen smiled when she screamed, "Terra!" She held her hand in the air, and seeds shot out of her fingertips.

Being helped by the healing water, the seeds grew at incredible speeds in midair, turning into yellow lilies and blue morning glories that surrounded the two women in a floral shower.

Both ladies were dizzy by the end of their spinning and fell to the floor. Mika held vita to her head, and Madeline embraced the tilting and stretching of the walls.

"I think," Mika said, standing and brushing herself off, "it's time for me to go."

Madeline was upset, but she tried not to show it. "So soon?"

"I just wanted to introduce myself. I'm ..." Mika's eyebrows rose, her lips appeared to try to smile, but she couldn't force herself to. "Well, I'm lonely." Mika's teary eyes looked at Madeline. "I'd like to come back, if you let me."

I too am lonely ... I would like a friend. Madeline swallowed; she stayed silent for a moment to choose the right words and not scare off the princess. "That would be fabulous."

Mika's eyes widened, and her smile broadened.

Madeline smiled in agreement, and both women went to the rear gardens.

"See you in a couple of days?" Mika asked.

"Yes," she said. "Yes, I'll see you in a couple of days."

Doubt seeped into Madeline's head. What if the princess doesn't want to come back? Or gets too busy? What if she simply didn't want to be rude and was just saying she wanted to see her again so as not to embarrass her?

Mika stepped forward, raising her arms just a few inches. Madeline sensed Mika wanted to hug her but was too shy, too unsure if she should. Mika took a breath, curtsied, and made a brisk walk toward her carriage, petted both of her brown horses, and entered the cart. Mika turned and waved at Madeline.

Madeline waved back, bit her lips in a smile, and walked back inside. She rushed to the third floor with energy she never knew she had and bolted to her painting. She grabbed a brush, dipped it in red, and painted an eiclucronna, a flower with six petals and six stamens that protruded from the middle. The flower that symbolized friendship was painted next to the dying lily. Madeline didn't know why, but for some reason, her forty-one-year-old mind felt like that of a happy child who just made the best discovery of her life. She was excited at the potential of her new, and only, friendship.

Meanwhile, inside Mika's carriage, the princess eyed the rear of the palace. Her face straightened, and she brushed her hair with a diamond brush. Mika addressed the driver with her regular voice.

"Luke."

"Yes, Princess?"

"Make a pass through the western side of the palace. Make it seem like it's an accident, that we're lost or confused as to where to go."

"Yes, Princess. We're almost set to move."

Mika gave one last look at the palace walls, extending her gaze up to the third story, to the window of Queen Madeline's room.

Mika's eyes narrowed, and she adjusted her plan based on her new findings.

*   *   *   *   *

"You haven't been outside the county's walls in ten years?" Mika repeated.

She stopped painting and looked over the canvas and toward Queen Madeline. Mika's expression looked sinister when combined with the dark clouds and falling snow from the window behind Madeline.

The lady stared back, hiding the bottom portion of her face behind the canvas. "I have not traveled past Vicqua's walls, specifically, for ten years."

She regretted telling Mika this, for fear that Mika would make fun of her or judge her. She'd seen Mika six times now, and they had a flourishing friendship.

Mika set down her painting tools and stepped out from behind the canvas. "You *own* the Grand Waterfall! When was the last time you went there?"

"Several weeks prior to Father's passing and my assumption onto the throne."

"Oh, no …" Mika shook her head. "No. No, I'm taking you to the Grand Waterfall." She pointed at Madeline. "I'm taking you there, and we're going to explore the caves."

Madeline's ears perked; her eyes widened at the thought of adventure. She scanned Mika's serious face.

Mika shifted her weight on one leg and gave Madeline a sideways look. "Then, we're going to jump from the top." Mika returned to her painting.

"Jump from the …?"

"Jump from the top."

"First, traveling is expensive." Madeline's sadness returned when she said the sentence. "We must be frugal during these times. Second, the top of the waterfall is dangerous, surely …"

Mika dipped her brush and made long vertical strokes. "Traveling involves carriages, other people, soldiers, weapons, supplies." Mika stopped, looked over the canvas, and locked eyes with Madeline. "We are two fully grown, smart, independent women. We don't need any of that."

Doubt appeared on Madeline's face. The princess hadn't responded about the danger at the top of the waterfall.

Mika approached, offered her hand, and whispered, "Let's go on an adventure."

Madeline's heart answered before her brain could reject. "When?"

"When the snow stops and workers clear the roads."

"How shall I prepare?"

"I'll bring everything; just wear something for the ride and hike. We can't jump from the top wearing clothes; we won't be protected by the magic. You know how Kymarinou encourages sex and procreation." Mika rolled her eyes.

Madeline remembered about the deity of aqua, how his followers have higher birthrates, his landmarks are enlaced with aphrodisiacs, and how many of his creatures, like sirens, encourage reproduction. Her shoulders lowered, remembering the sirens. Thanks to her and the necromancers, they were either extinct or endangered.

Mika looked at the bookshelves that lined the walls, then back at Madeline. "Show me what clothes you have, and I'll find a matching outfit for the ride."

Madeline broke away from her thoughts and, after a quick discussion on what to wear, left to her wardrobe. She grabbed two different boots, a couple of pairs of pants, a few elegant shirts, and a big, round straw hat. When she returned to the bedroom, Mika was pulling at the books on the bookshelves.

"I've brought a few things—"

Mika jumped. Her face flushed with redness, and her eyes widened.

"Did I startle you?"

"Yes, I, uh ..." The princess cleared her throat. "I was just wondering why ..." Mika cleared her throat again. "Why all these books have the same engraving on the side."

Though Madeline wasn't convinced at Mika's response, she had no reason to doubt her friend. Mika had been through a rough adolescence and was fulfilling her curiosity. So long as Mika didn't find the lever that opened the bookshelf, Madeline knew there would be no suspicion from Mika.

"Madeline?" Mika asked.

Madeline pushed the thoughts away and felt pressure in her ears from clenching her jaw. She looked at Mika. "The symbol is my family crest." Madeline looked at the books on the shelves, not hiding the look of disgust. "And I write stories."

"You write *stories*?" Mika's voice bounced off the walls, her eyes widened, and she turned to the bookshelf. She reached for one but stopped and looked at Madeline. "Can I read one?"

Madeline twirled her necklace then rubbed her sternum. "Writing is not my expertise ..."

"I'll be the judge of that." Mika narrowed her eyes and smiled. "May I, Highness Madeline of Vicqua?"

Madeline inhaled and, with a shaky voice, replied, "You may."

Mika spun around, reached for a book high above her, and began to touch every book with a slow brush of her finger. The lever popped back into Madeline's mind the second Mika's hand reached the book that hid it. "All of them except that one ... please."

Mika stopped moving her hand. She brushed the yellow book, the only yellow book within the row of red, maroon, and brown books on the shelf. "This one is too personal?"

"Extremely. Please, respect my privacy ..."

Mika's fingers dripped down the yellow book, and she grabbed the red one below it. Opening the cover, Mika read aloud. "*The Dragon Priest.*" Mika looked at Madeline with sad eyes and a smile. "I love dragons."

Madeline granted Mika permission to lie on her bed. Heat on Madeline's reddening face caused sweat to seep out her forehead. She paced, hoping the princess wouldn't say anything negative about the short story. Mika continued reading, and Madeline walked to Mika's painting.

Mika's canvas had a background of red and orange flames. In the center of the painting, the face of a black shadow was screaming in agony. Was this painting because Mika herself was in pain ... or because she wanted to cause pain on others? Madeline tried to hide the worried look on her face.

"This is really good!" Mika exclaimed.

Madeline turned to see Mika adjusting herself; she had sat up and leaned her elbows on her thighs, her face inches from the pages.

"Which segment have you reached?" Madeline sat next to Mika, eyeing the writing through the corner of her eye.

Mika looked at Madeline, and a grin appeared. "He's about to collect the dragon flower." Her eyes widened, and she returned to the book.

She must read fast. She got up, picked up her clothes, and laid them out on the bed. After minutes turned to an hour, Mika shut the book with force and held it close to her heart.

"You need to publish this. Have the scribes make more!"

Madeline chuckled. "Its writing is incomparable to works of others."

"Untrue! This is amazing!" Mika looked at the ceiling and balled her fist. "When he sacrificed himself for the village of dragons! I can't believe that happened!"

"I try for happy endings." The feeling of excitement was growing inside Madeline.

"Happy endings are what people want! Everyone wants their happy ending!"

Madeline inhaled to speak, but Mika jumped on the bed, grabbed Madeline's head, and touched her forehead with hers. "If you don't have the scribes publish this, I will publish it for you."

Further excitement rushed through Madeline's body when she looked into Mika's huge, brown eyes. Madeline stepped back and held her composure; she tried to hide her smile, making her lips press together in a silly wrench.

"And so I will! I shall publish this!" She accepted the book from Mika.

"Yes!" Mika held her hand to high-five the queen.

After the high-five, the princess and queen picked an outfit. The queen rushed to her wardrobe, and, per Mika's request, she took the time looking for a necklace they could match with on their hike.

Mika heard the queen going through the wardrobe in the other room. She wasted no time, heading straight for the yellow book on the bookshelf. She reached up, pulled it, and tiptoed to look inside the hole. In the opening, there was a small lever that would unlock the bookshelf, allow passage through the palace, and lead her through the tunnels and to the northern walls of Vicqua. She put the book back in its place and counted its location: third shelf from the top, seventh book from the right. Mika scoffed after giving a look at all the books.

The Dragon Priest. She shook her head. *What a boring and stupid story. And that's not how a dragon flower works, Madeline.*

* * * * *

Madeline's jaw dropped, days later, when she saw Mika riding a horse and leading another. The horse Mika led was colored a smooth chestnut and its yellow mane was interlaced with lilies of varying colors.

"Your Highness ..." Mika jumped off her horse with ease. "Meet Lilly!" Mika approached the queen with Lilly's reins in her hand.

Madeline was in love with Lilly the second the horse looked into her eyes. The queen approached and touched the horse's face. "Good morning, Lilly ..."

"Di'Abribel's finest horse for Celeste's finest leader!" Mika stepped to the side and extended her hands to the saddle.

The queen adjusted her pants, placed her boot inside the stirrup, and swung her leg over, sitting on the horse with a smile on her face. An accidental tap from Madeline's heel made Lilly walk forward.

"Oh!" Madeline panicked; she reached for the rein, pulling it to the side and causing the horse to turn. Lilly smacked into Mika, and the princess fell onto her back.

"Mika!" the queen shrieked.

Mika rolled out of the way of the horse's hooves and hopped to her feet. The clenching of her jaw showed anger, but her blank face confused Madeline. Madeline let go of the reins, and the horse stopped rotating.

"It's okay! I'm okay!" The princess held her arms out like a T when she stepped in front of Lilly, making the horse stop moving forward.

Mika looked at Madeline and smiled. She raised her hand, made a fist, and rotated the back of her hand to the sky. "I like holding them," she said, referring to the reins, "like *this.* Reins hand maneuvers, free hand casts magic."

Madeline looked at the reins. With a careful reach, she grabbed and held the rein just at the front edge of the saddle. When she heard Mika mount her horse, she looked at her friend. "Have equines always interested you?"

The princess settled into her saddle, turned her horse around, and smirked at the queen. "Since I became a princess."

"That's only been a few months." Madeline turned her horse around in a slow, careful fashion. When she looked at the princess, the princess replied.

"I just need a few days to learn the basics! I dream or imagine myself practicing after that." The princess's smile grew. "Ready? Just hit her with your heels! Hard! It won't hurt!" Mika leaned forward. "If you need to, just scream! Like this!" Mika inhaled, extended her legs, and gave a loud "Kiya!" before slamming her heels into her brown horse. Her horse ran toward the gates of the palace, its hooves tapping on the cobblestone road.

"She's …" Madeline's eyes followed Mika. "Wild … Kiya!"

Madeline kicked the sides of her horse, and once it began to trot, Madeline bounced up and down on the saddle before she understood how to better ride it. Catching up to Mika, both rode out of the palace gates, through Vicqua, and out the southern walls toward the Grand Waterfall.

Di'Abribel looked tiny from the top of the Grand Waterfall. The mountains of Adventurer's Pass went farther and farther than Madeline had ever imagined, just miles and miles of brown, pointed peaks. From the top, it smelled like rain, and the freshness of the passing water bounced off every tree and rock. Magic kept the mountain at a bearable temperature and the water an endless, powerful flow. The sound was deafening because of the falling and slamming waters. Looking down, the fall to the bottom of the 3,700-foot drop was covered by white mist. When vertigo set in, Madeline leaned on a slim tree.

She tried to brush away the red sand that stuck to her skin because of their walks and crawls through the caves. She wanted to sit and rest her feet, she needed to stretch her legs, and she felt she could eat a whole chicken by herself. The hike was so, so long.

"I dare you to go first," Mika's voice was eager and carried a hint of cruelty.

Madeline took a breath, swallowed, and blinked her wide eyes before looking at Mika. "If the stories are not true, I will perish ..."

"The stories *are* true!" Mika's response was immediate. "Too many people have said they've done it for the stories *not* to be true. I've never heard anyone say their friend died after hitting the water!"

"Yes ..." Madeline shivered with the gust of wind. Both women were naked except for their boots. "Yes, but, additionally, there are those who never hit the waters. What if I hit a boulder instead?"

Mika clicked her tongue in thought. Her eyes scanned several portions of the rock that protruded toward the water like the walking plank of a ship.

Turning to Madeline, Mika replied, "Those were the cowards. The ones that were too scared to fully commit. They didn't give it their all, and because of that, they died. Like cowards."

Madeline recoiled. Though Mika's statement was blunt and harsh, she was right. Rocks protruded from the waterfall and, to jump into the blessed waters that wouldn't kill someone when they crashed into them, a person had to sprint on the rock and jump as far as they could.

"I am petrified. I do not want to do this."

Mika's shoulders dropped. She shook her head. "My mother told me, '*It's okay to be afraid, for those who act when they're afraid are the truly brave ones.*'" She looked at Madeline and shrugged her shoulders. "Adventure is not adventure without risk, and I didn't hike up here to be a coward!" Mika set off in a sprint toward the water; Madeline hadn't seen that she removed her boots.

"Mika!"

Mika looked back. "See you at the bottom!" Her words carried a slap of courage.

Madeline ran after Mika.

Mika picked up her speed to an uncatchable sprint, planted her foot on the rock, and soared into the air, tightening her arms to her chest before pointing the balls of her feet to the water.

"By Dwin ...!"

Madeline watched Mika disappear into the mist. Her heart pumped.

Madeline backed off from the rock and looked at the few trees around her. The sky shone bright above, and the sun was beating down on her like a blacksmith's forge. Madeline would need vita to cure her scorched skin, despite the season of endurance coming to an end.

She looked toward the trail and caves they'd hiked, remembering the hikers they had passed. They had a look of defeat because they hadn't had the courage to jump from the mountain after the grueling hike.

She walked to the rock and looked down. No Mika, just mist.

"I must be brave …" Her heart began to race.

"I must act and be brave …" Her breathing quickened to keep up with her heartbeat.

She closed her eyes and backed away from the rock. An exhale was followed by the unlacing of her boots.

"They did not commit their soul," she said recalling Mika's words. "And because of that, they perished like cravens."

She opened her eyes, kicked off her boots, turned around, and walked several steps. She faced the falling water. "See you at the bottom. See you at the bottom …" She took a step, then another, and then other allowed her to start a run. "See you at the bottom …"

She was at a sprint, the wind whistling in her ear.

"See you at the bottom!" She planted her foot and jumped, screaming when she propelled herself into the air.

Momentum tilted her forward, and she was at a face-first free fall toward the mist. Instinct forced her hands forward to break the impending fall. Air rushed into her face and eyes, forcing them to shut. The wind continued, and she felt her hair slap her back. She let out a wailing shriek before she felt glass shattering inside her hand. The sensation happened throughout her body, but it was gone quicker than it appeared.

The roaring of the falling water muffled, and Madeline felt the coldest water she had ever felt. When she opened her eyes, she saw Mika swimming toward her, moving her legs like a siren.

Mika's face was inches from Madeline's. Bubbles escaped Mika's mouth when she smiled.

Madeline realized she was not breathing. She was under water so cold her mind began to cloud. Her lungs started to hurt, and she needed air, so she fluttered her feet and swam to the top, taking a deep breath, the sound of which was lost to the deafening roar of falling water.

Madeline turned to see Mika rising from the water with an eager smile, and at that moment, Madeline realized she loved her best friend. She loved the Princess of Di'Abribel.

27. VICQUA

Mika looked at herself in the mirror, focusing on the big, brown eyes that rested inside her eye sockets. Looking below her eyes, she exhaled upon seeing the dark shadows there that told everyone she was a sleepless ruler. When she noticed movement of the door behind her, her eyes shifted to see Sandra walking in and closing the door.

Sandra walked toward Mika with a white mask in her hand. Her silver hair was put up into two buns. Sandra locked eyes with Mika through the mirror, and Mika stared back.

"Thank you for inviting me to this event." Despite Mika being a princess, Sandra spoke to her in the same apathetic, dismissing tone she did when Mika was her patron. Mika loved this about Sandra, for it showed that Sandra had always been true to Mika.

The two spoke in whispers so no one in the hallway of Madeline's palace would hear.

"I'm honored," said Sandra, "even though I know it is because you need my expertise." Sandra stepped behind her, adjusted Mika's head, and began working at her hair. Mika's hair had grown to her shoulder blades.

"Can't trust anyone else with the most important part of the plan!"

Watching Sandra through the mirror, Mika's eyes never looked away from Sandra's.

"What if she changes her mind?" Sandra asked.

"She won't. She's been talking about it nonstop since the invitations were sent."

Sandra pressed her lips together for a fraction of a second.

"Talk to me." Mika knew Sandra wanted to say something, but Sandra hesitated.

"As princess," said Mika in an ironic tone, "I allow you to offer me a suggestion." It was Mika's law that none of her citizens or subordinates offer suggestions unless she asked for advice.

Sandra looked at Mika through the mirror without a reply.

"Come on, just like old times. Just Mika Plum and Sandra Brooks in Miss Sandra's hair salon."

"Queen Madeline is a prude. She will not leave with anyone tonight. We need another way keep her out of the palace."

"Queen Madeline *is* a prude, and it's the exact reason why she *will* leave the palace with someone tonight." Mika sensed doubt emanating from Sandra. "Why do you think I decided to host a masquerade? The queen *wants* adventure, excitement, sex, fun, but she does not want to be seen doing it, doesn't want anyone to know she's a normal human being."

Excitement forced Mika out of her chair, and she turned to face Sandra with a smile. "You will approach the queen and make conversation. To show that her outfit works, to show she's unrecognizable, you *will* speak ill of the queen."

Sandra clenched her jaw. It was common knowledge that those who spoke ill of Queen Madeline were imprisoned and forced into hard labor at the mines within days of their infraction.

"Then," she said, "you will encourage her to leave the palace with a man so that our soldiers can transport the weapons and armor through the tunnels, into her bedroom, and distribute them to our sleepers."

Sandra wiped sweat from her brow, trying her best to make it seem like she was adjusting her hair.

"I need to finish your second braid."

Mika sat. Her voice changed to stern and commanding. "Thank you for the suggestion, but it won't be followed."

Mika looked at Sandra through the mirror, and Sandra met her gaze. Sandra backed up, and Mika looked at her pigtail braids in the mirror.

I look pretty, except for the damned bags under my eyes.

As if hearing Mika's thoughts, Sandra handed Mika a pure white mask; the only opening was for one of the eyes. Mika accepted the mask, put it on, and turned to Sandra when she heard the hairdresser inhale.

"I will not fail the princess." Sandra bowed.

Mika summoned a ball of fire.

"Sandra," she said, her words muffled behind her mask, "address me as Empress."

Hundreds of masked guests in colorful costumes danced together; others conversed, others used aqua to guide the drinks from their mugs into their mouths inside of the Vicquic palace ballroom. The sound inside the ballroom made it hard to think, and the beating of the drums felt like Mika had several heartbeats.

Standing with her hands clasped in front of her, Mika's eye was looking through the single hole of the mask at the other side of the room, the side where a woman in a blue dress and a pink mask with a massive hanging yellow feather stood. Queen Madeline's figure looked perfect in her dress, and her posture did not change from the norm.

Mika scanned the room for Sandra, scanning and scanning until Sandra's mask of emeralds stood out from behind a dancing couple. Sandra nodded at Mika, and Mika stretched her arms, pointing toward Madeline when she did so. Sandra's gaze followed, and she made her way toward the queen. When the two started talking, a man's sweet voice rang into Mika's ears.

"Pardon me, lady ..."

Mika turned her head to see a man in a gold outfit and black mask bowing and offering his gloved hand.

"Would you fancy a dance?"

"No, thank you." Mika looked back toward Madeline and Sandra, her voice was friendly and nice. "My dance partner will come back soon."

The man grabbed Mika's chin and turned it toward him. "Finders keep—"

Mika slapped his hand away. "Do *not* touch me." She pointed her finger up toward his mask.

His eyes glimmered, and he grabbed Mika's wrist and pulled her in. "Or else what?"

Mika broke free and slammed her palm onto the man's sternum, forcing him several steps back.

"Get it through that stupid little man-brain of yours that no means no!" She stepped toward him and used tenebris to infuse her words with terror. "Get away from me before I drench this floor with your blood."

The man stood in silence. His thumb was rubbing his fingers, showing his nervousness and anger. "Hmph." He turned and went toward the table filled with drinks.

Mika turned her attention back to Sandra and Madeline. When she saw that Madeline, a queen known for not indulging in alcohol, had taken a drink from Sandra, Mika knew her plan would work. The night continued, and Mika tried her best to dance and enjoy herself, but to her, enjoyment came from watching her plan unfold. Within the next couple of hours, Madeline and Sandra were speaking, drinking, and dancing with other men. Another hour passed, and Madeline's gestures were freer and more open.

Okay. Mika took a breath. *Let's go.*

Mika made her way out of the ballroom and through the hallway toward the back of the palace. She went up the first set of stairs, the second, and then the third.

"Brandon …" Mika removed her mask. "I need to rest in the queen's bedroom. I'm not feeling well."

Brandon was doing his rounds. He rushed to the door, unlocked it, and allowed Mika to enter. "Would you like tea infused with healing herbs?"

Mika closed an eye and applied vita to her head, pretending she was unable to stand.

"No. Please, just lock the door behind me." Mika stepped through the door and slumped on the bed.

"Yes, Princess. I will be making rounds. Please hang the flag on the doorknob if you require my assistance."

"Thank you, Brandon. Please, make your way out."

Mika heard the door lock and made herself comfortable on the queen's bed. She waited, putting her mind to matters that needed tending to in Di'Abribel to pass the time. When Madeline did not show up, Mika used her find spell, imagining the queen's face. A moderate breeze came from the south, telling Mika that Madeline had left the palace.

She made a calm walk to the window, opened the blinds, and pushed open the glass. She looked at the moonless sky that provided maximum darkness for her troops near the northern walls.

She stepped back— "Ignis." —and launched a fireball out the window and toward the heavens. She began to count when the ball of fire flickered away.

One ... Two ... Three ...

Ninety-seven ... ninety-eight ...

A flash of lux appeared in the distant trees, telling her the two squads of sixteen soldiers were in position.

Two seconds off, not bad. She walked toward the bookshelf, reached for the yellow book, but stopped, noticing it was not in the same location she first found it. This time, it was near the bottom of the shelf.

Mika clenched her jaw. She didn't want to take out every book. It wouldn't surprise her if there was a failsafe infused with magic or technology that would render the lever useless if certain books were pulled.

I can't believe that whore doesn't trust me.

Mika strained to remember the location of the book.

Third from the top and ... She forced her eyes shut, trying her best to remember the day months ago when she found the lever. *Seventh? Seventh from the right?* Mika wasn't sure, but she knew her mind was strong, and her subconscious wouldn't betray her.

Reaching for the seventh book from the right on the third shelf from the top, Mika stopped for a second before pulling it. When she tiptoed to look into the hole, she found the lever.

Hah!

She pulled it, hoping that no one heard the *clank* coming from the other side of the wall. She repositioned herself to move the bookshelf, and when she did so, the bookshelf moved sideways with ease. A dark hallway led to pitch darkness, but the second Mika entered, tenebris lined the walls and allowed Mika to see without strain.

Mika shook her head. She knew the necromancers had assisted in placing the magic in the tunnel. It felt the same way as the portions without torches in the cathedral.

Mika closed the bookshelf and rushed down and out of the tunnel, meeting her troops, all dressed in Vicquic clothing and carrying large bags filled with weapons and armor. The bags were infused with the shrinking magic Mika had used in her adventure.

"Who has the poison?" she asked and held her hand out to accept the flask.

"Just to reiterate," she said, conscious of her troops hanging on her every word, "if you are caught, surrender. Do not fight in their clothing, and do not dishonor Di'Abribel. If you are captured, we will free you in a few days when we execute the plan."

"Yes, Princess," all her troops whispered in unison.

Mika led the way through the long tunnels, only stopping to let the soldiers switch off carrying the bags. When she reached the bookshelf, she opened it, stepped through, closed it, and hung the flag on the doorknob. Over half an hour passed until Brandon knocked on the door.

"Brandon," Mika said through the door, "please have the cooks make me some chicken soup."

Mika knew the palace kitchen was the furthest location from Madeline's room, and she needed Brandon far away.

"Right away, Princess."

Three minutes passed, and Mika opened the bookshelf to let her troops line the walls with the bags.

"Trash room, go."

Three soldiers made their way out of the room and toward the first floor and under Madeline's room. They needed to be in the trash room in two minutes.

One hundred eighteen … one hundred nineteen …

"Start."

Mika's soldiers tossed the bags down the trash opening in Madeline's room. Once the last bag was thrown down, a soldier used lux to give the *Done* signal. An acknowledge signal followed from below.

Mika signaled toward the bookshelf, and her troops exited the palace, diverting away from the walls, toward the heart of Vicqua, and into a large home of a family killed by Di'Abribeli assassins days earlier. The home was cramped with hundreds of Di'Abribeli soldiers anxious to armor up and kill any Vicquic citizen or warrior.

After a relieved sigh, Mika lit scented candles to mask the smell of Di'Abribeli sweat and musk. Walking toward the window, Mika caught sight of Madeline's new painting. A yellow sun represented Madeline, a red sun represented Mika. Below their respective suns stood two cities, one Di'Abribel and the other Vicqua. Mika interpreted the painting as two friends, two rulers, caring for their cities.

Mika realized the reason the necromancers had finally stopped attacking Di'Abribel, her resources, and her traders.

Madeline was telling them of the coming alliance.

* * * * *

Mika sat at one end of the long, oval table. Half of the table was occupied with Di'Abribeli soldiers dressed and acting like royalty. The other half of the table was occupied by Vicquic lords, generals, and barons. At the far end of the table was an empty seat belonging to Queen Madeline. Looking at the various paintings on the walls, Mika recognized Madeline's style. Below each painting was a model, and at the table, there were golden candle holders that sat atop the long, white table mat.

The Vicquic royalty spoke to each other, and Mika's soldiers stayed quiet. They had not anticipated a time without the queen present. Mika's anxiety was through the roof, but she maintained her calm demeanor.

"A princess does not control anything," said one of the barons. "She's just a subject to a queen. Why not choose the title of empress, queen, or something similar?"

Mika gave the baron, an older man with a thick, gray beard and combed hair, a fake smile.

"Titles are subjective, sir. I may be a princess, but I hold more land and command more troops than you ever will."

The lords laughed, amplifying the baron's anger.

Mika's smile grew when she saw her soldiers trying to hide theirs.

A few moments of conversation passed until the queen stepped through the door.

"Apologies!" Madeline said with a smile. She'd been much happier after the night of the masquerade. She pulled her chair and sat.

When she looked at Mika, her eyes almost disappeared behind her smiling cheeks. "Good afternoon, Princess."

Mika stood, and her soldiers followed. Mika curtsied, and her soldiers kneeled. "Good afternoon, Your Highness."

Madeline's royalty bowed at Madeline, but only after Mika had initiated the respectful gesture.

"Please! Please, sit. Thank you. We're here today to bind Vicqua and Di'Abribel in an alliance, and to celebrate a wonderful friendship between our two great cities in this beautiful region!"

A waiter, one of Mika's soldiers who took over the last waiter's spot, approached with a tray of filled wine glasses. He was ordered to wear an outdated, formal, Di'Abribeli military uniform that would not be recognizable. The Di'Abribeli uniform would allow him to have justified kills through Mika's warrior stone.

He served Mika, rotating the cup after it was placed on the table, a sign that told Mika this cup was not poisoned. The waiter went up to all of Mika's soldiers and placed the cups in front of them and rotated them. He left, and Mika continued listening.

"... and, though I've made mistakes in ruling this city, this alliance shall be one of greatness, and most prosperous!"

Madeline sought the approval of her royalty. Half of them agreed; the other half questioned the need for the alliance.

The waiter returned, and he placed a glass of wine in front of the first baron, the one who attempted to insult Mika. He did not rotate the cup for him, nor any of the other royalty. The queen would not accept a glass of wine. She had to keep her royal persona. She was served water instead.

"Before we make the declaration—" Mika stood, knowing that once the declaration was made, she would be unjustified conquering Vicqua. "—I would like to make a toast!" Mika grabbed her glass of wine and held it in the air. "A toast to everlasting prosperity, friendship, and honor."

Her soldiers followed suit.

Madeline stood and held her glass of water in the air. Once she did so, the royalty held out their wine.

"For Celeste!" Mika grinned.

"For Celeste!" everyone repeated.

Everyone drank and took their seats. The potency of the poison was high, and just a sip would wreak havoc in a person's intestines within minutes.

Madeline continued speaking, and the waiter stepped in the room and began locking the doors from the inside. He reached for a closet and opened the door, taking out several brown bags filled with shrunken weapons and armor.

The queen's speech continued. Mika saw the slim general, the one with the fastest metabolism, holding his stomach, his face wrenched in pain. He bent over the table but tried to remain professional by keeping eyes on the speaker. The lords started feeling it next, and the massive sound of diarrhea exploded from the slim general.

He stood in a groan, then bent over when blood flew from his mouth and onto the general in front of him.

"By Dwin!" Madeline shrieked. "Call the healers! Someone, call the healers!"

He continued vomiting, and soon, the half of the Vicquic table was in a disgusting wrench of blood, vomit, and human secretion.

Mika's soldiers stood. Two ran to the queen and tackled her.

"What are you doing?" she yelled. "Let go of—"

An elbow met her nose, forcing a shriek.

Soldiers ran toward the bags of weapons and armor. Some ran out the doors with bags to meet the other soldiers waiting at key points in the palace.

Mika stood, using ventus and aqua to clean off the blood and feces from her path. She ignored the continued suffering of the royalty; her eyes were set on the queen.

"Mika!" Madeline's voice was filled with crying pain. "Mika, your lords are—"

She shrieked when one of the soldiers wrenched an arm up behind her back.

"Stop hurting her," Mika demanded.

The queen's face was mixed with blood and snot from her broken nose. Her blonde hair was in disarray, and tears were forming in her pretty blue eyes.

"Mika, what is happening?"

"I, Mika Plum of Yevera," she said, stepping toward Madeline, "the *Empress* of Celeste, sentence you and your citizens to death for the crimes committed against the region."

"What are you talking about?"

Mika's boot to Madeline's face sent the queen to her back.

"You and your *citizens* have chosen to ally yourself with the necromancers in the Lost Forest, allowing reinforcements from their Velonde chapter to pass through your city, with your knowledge. Those reinforcements attacked and killed Celestial citizens, including my mother, my son, and my daughter."

Madeline closed her eyes. "No …" she sobbed. "No … No … No, no, no …. Mika please—"

"Silence!" Mika's voice was firm but calm. "No mercy will be shown to you or to your citizens, for no mercy was shown to mine. Let the world know not to cross Celeste." Mika pulled Madeline's hair and exposed her neck. She clenched her dagger. One soldier sat on Madeline's legs; the other pulled her arms together over her head.

"Mika …" Madeline's words were hard to understand past her tears. "Mika, we're friends … Mika …"

"No, Madeline." Mika cut deep into Madeline's neck, forcing a squeal. "That was just part of a calculated plan."

Mika stood, and so did her soldiers. "Accept your easy death, Madeline. Do not heal your wound."

Madeline held her cut and slid her back to the wall. She looked at Mika with sad, painful eyes and a mouth that wouldn't stop shaking.

"I loved you …"

The queen's eyes rolled to the back of her head, and she slid along the wall and down to her side.

Mika took a second to look at her kill before she turned to her soldiers. "Keep moving with the plan. I've yet to hear horns or magic, so it's going smoothly so far. You, what's your name?" She pointed at the soldier with the graying, receding hairline and same-colored beard.

The other soldier proceeded with his orders and left the room.

"Nicholas Zarotis, edged-weapon commander." The man puffed out his chest and lifted his chin, proud of his rank and position.

"Nicholas, huh?" Quick breathing, sweat, and flashes of Mika's death rushed in her mind. She blinked and shook her head, hating herself for showing weakness.

She composed herself. "Once Vicquic soldiers have been defeated, gather all the citizens in the town square and advise them of their crime. Publicly execute all adult men and women who surrendered peacefully. Transport those who fought back to Di'Abribel and make a public display of torture for our citizens."

"Yes, Princess." Nicholas nodded.

"*Empress ...*" she said without rebuke. "Then castrate and enslave the teenagers. Brand and exile all children to Adventurer's Pass and the Freezing Mountains. All babies will be adopted and raised in Di'Abribel."

"Yes, Empress."

Mika took a second to think. "Nicholas ... this stays between you and me."

"I pledge my loyalty to my empress." Nicholas knelt.

"Tell the pregnant women they'll be spared because of their babies."

Nicholas knew Mika was choosing her words carefully, and so he did not speak.

"Keep track of who they are. Once all babies are over a year old, kill the mothers and adopt the babies into our customs."

Nicholas did not show a hint of doubt or remorse. "Your will be done, Empress."

Mika assisted Nicholas to his feet and raised her voice. "It's time for battle, Nicholas!" she said and enflamed his axe. "Anyone who raises a weapon against the *new* Celeste will face her wrath!"

* * * * *

Weeks passed after the brutal victory in Vicqua. News of the atrocities committed by the empress and her people spread throughout the region. It was clear that the Mad Empress would tolerate no opposition whatsoever.

Torture and experimentation without trial began against captured bandits and barbarians, contributing to the disappearance of raids within days, yet necromancer skirmishes doubled throughout the region. Those, too, slowed after necromancer reinforcements from the west were intercepted in Vicqua and north of Di'Abribel.

Mika might have basked longer in her bloody victories, but her thoughts were interrupted.

"Where are you taking me?" Ashlynn asked, tilting her head upward to look through the bottom of her blindfold. "I swear, Mika, if it's to show me something relating to death, dying, or something brutal, I will lose my—"

... *shit*. She shook her head, remembering she shouldn't curse.

"I didn't spend all these months avoiding tragedy just to come out and have it ruined by my sister."

The carriage stopped, and Mika opened the door, allowing the roars from the Grand Waterfall to fill her ears. She waited for Ashlynn to approach and helped her down the stairs. Luke untied a horse, placed a saddle on it, and both helped Ashlynn onto the stallion. Mika hopped on after, and she and Ashlynn rode up the trail, waving at passing citizens and tourists along the way.

Ashlynn talked and talked. Mika answered when she didn't drift away in thought. She smacked the sides of her horse with her heels to make it go faster in hopes that Ashlynn wouldn't realize where they were. Moving away from the trail, Mika's horse slowed and trudged through the soft grass. Mika ducked to avoid branches, and Ashlynn's senses helped her do the same.

"We're here." Mika hopped off the horse.

"Finally!" Ashlynn removed her blindfold, squinting when the rays of light attacked her eyes. She analyzed the trees that swayed with the powerful breeze, the water that churned in freefall from the top of the magical mountain, and her sister smiling at her.

"Why did I have to come here blindfolded? I've been to the Grand Waterfall before. I don't think I can jump from the top with one leg, though. I'll crash into the rocks."

Mika shook her head and pointed behind Ashlynn. "I'm fulfilling my promise."

"What promise? You haven't made me a promise to bring me here. Did you order the soldiers to bring Ron so I can tie him to a tree for the rest of his life? What promise, Mika?"

"Look up at the tree, and you'll see." Mika kept pointing behind Ashlynn.

Ashlynn turned to see a tree. She looked up and, within the leaves, she saw a single flame just smaller than an eagle.

When Ashlynn looked at it, the flame spread its wings and let out a cry that sounded like *zar*.

"Zarl!" Ashlynn jumped off the horse, seeming to have forgotten she was missing a leg, so she fell to the ground.

Mika ran over to help, but Ashlynn was at a quick hop toward the tree. "Zarl! Zarl, come here!" She held her arms toward her phoenix. "Zarl, please! It's your mother!"

Zarl twisted his head to look down at Ashlynn. When he recognized her, he screamed, *zar* and swooped down, alighting on Ashlynn's shoulder and placing his head on her cheek.

"Oh my, Zarly, oh my baby." Ashlynn pressed her cheek on Zarl's head. She grabbed him with gentle hands and held him to her nose. Her tears dripped onto his fire, causing the tears to fizzle away in a small wisp of smoke.

Ashlynn looked at Mika and whispered a thank you. Mika smiled and gave the two time alone, walking toward the falling water before sitting at the edge. She let her legs hang over, and they disappeared within the white mist. She sat and let her mind wander. After all these months, Mika thought, things were starting to fall into place.

She was able to sleep more; her citizens realized she wasn't avoiding them, she was just conquering cities in unconventional ways. She knew as long as her citizens were treated fairly, their families' property respected, they would not rebel against her. If they did rebel, her soldiers would intervene, for the soldiers had proven their loyalty, were well paid and fed, and were more disciplined than any neighboring army.

Celeste's wealth was growing, and the number of necromancers was declining. Still, the attacks and raids were as violent as ever. The growing village west of Triumph had been annihilated, and the town of Reach was being harassed every month. The necromancers were pure evil, she thought.

They kill children and elderly who don't fight.

Necromancers killed everything in their raids, they tainted lands, they left a permanent impact, and only a few of the cities they conquered became prosperous.

I'm good. I'm not evil. Celeste is good.

Mika understood their conquest, though. One day, like the necromancers, Celeste would invade Imbris and Velonde, but they would not kill those who chose not to fight. But she wasn't like the necromancers. The Empire of Celeste was just, and Vicqua was a one-time thing. Not only would Mika unite Celeste and Irstia under Liranda, but she would also bring peace and prosperity like there was in Sytu, and Mika would be the sole ruler.

Mika smiled, but her eyes snapped to the side of the mountain. A flame had flickered and caught her eye. Deep within the rocks, a small, red ember called to her. Mika followed the flame toward a cave. The flame never grew in size, and it withdrew as Mika approached.

She plugged her nose and blew. When pressure filled her ears, she took a breath and continued toward the flame and into the cave.

Using her night-vision spell, Mika navigated through the straight cave until she reached the end, at which point, the flame disappeared.

Before she had a chance to curse, Liranda's voice rang from behind her. "Oh, Mika."

Mika jumped. She spun around and fell to her knees in front of the deity of ignis. Mika's heart raced. Was she in trouble? Had she done something against Liranda's will? She knew not to speak unless given permission to or asked a question.

"Dear child, stand for me. Stand and let me see how much you've grown." Liranda placed her hand on Mika's head. When Mika stood, Liranda's hand traveled to Mika's shoulder.

"What you did in Vicqua was outstanding … a true act of pure treachery against the queen and wickedness against her people!"

Mika raised her chin, and Liranda allowed her to speak. "I hope they suffered worse than anyone the rats have killed."

Liranda's smile widened, revealing canines sharper than Ashlynn's. "Your actions have allowed me to gift you something." Liranda spun Mika around. "What will you name him?"

Mika's eyes grew, her mouth dropped, and she took steps without meaning to do so. In front of her stood a bright-red horse. Its fiery mane popped and swooshed every time the steed moved, forcing the cave to glow a beautiful, dancing yellow and red. The stallion looked at Mika, and both locked eyes.

Names rushed through Mika's mind with every step. When she stood next to the great beast, the Empress Mika drew her fingers through its burning mane. "Mythines."

"That's a beautiful name." Liranda teleported next to Mika and helped her onto the large horse.

"Whoa … thank you, Mother."

Mika patted the horse and leaned over to hug its neck, ignoring the pain on her stomach coming from the saddle's horn. During the hug, she set up a mental barrier. This beast, wonderous though it was, would not occupy the same place in her heart that Addie had.

"Sorceress Mika, what will your next course of action be in uniting this region?"

Still hugging Mythines, Mika looked into Liranda's black pupils. "The Reacans have crossbows that can pierce through necromancer armor. They have ships that can amplify magic and bombard far into Celeste. I will form an alliance with the town of Reach, making them a valuable ally in the last fight. Celeste will be united against the necromancers before I conquer her in your name."

"Perfect," Liranda purred. "When will that happen?"

"Preparations will begin today, the second I return to my palace." Mika backed up Mythines and moved him toward the mouth of the cave. "By your leave, Mother."

"Granted, Empress."

Mika remembered laughing when Vicquic soldiers were paraded in a cauldron filled with boiling water, rejoicing when she heard them scream and their flesh falling off their red skin. After a few steps, Mika couldn't help herself but ask one last question. One thing she needed to have clarification on.

"Mother …" The sorceress stopped the horse and looked at Liranda. "Is it normal that I didn't feel remorse when I killed the queen and watched the tortures?"

The question surprised Liranda. "No, darling, it's not normal."

Mika looked at the ground, then back up at the cave's mouth. Then she urged Mythines forward.

"Good," she said.

Maybe she wasn't like other people. Maybe she really was crazy, as so many had claimed in the past. Maybe she was too brutal to her enemies.

But she *liked* it.

She liked seeing the faces of those who realized they were moments from death, hearing the screams from those who burned and the cries of the surrendered who saw their families and friends being slaughtered like annoying pests.

Mika didn't care what others thought of her, be they peasants or rulers. Her only concerns were the soldiers she commanded, the citizens she cared for, those she counted as allies, and herself.

Everyone else could burn, and she would be glad to be the one doing it.

28. EMPRESS

Eyes forward and head bobbing up and down with every movement of Mythines, the empress rotated her shoulders to adjust her new battle outfit: scarlet leather armor with a plum-sized garnet—the jewel of ignis—in the middle of the chest. The armor rose past her neck and protected up her jaw to the bottom of the ear, leaving her scar visible for all to see. The flaming stallion grunted, and Mika smelled the feces it was leaving behind on the wide dirt road.

Looking back, she saw Celestial Protectors tread on the droppings without breaking stride.

Her Celestial Protectors showed no loss of stamina despite the double-sided battle axe each bore strapped to their back and the unrelenting heat—it was the season of celebration, after all—cooking them alive inside of their scarlet dragonscale armor. Each helmet had two black horns, paying tribute to Liranda. Celestial Protectors were the pride and joy of the Celestial military.

"Eft!" Commander Nicholas shouted, and left feet hit the ground.

"Rah!" Right feet hit the ground. Commands were cut short to add snap to the syllables.

Mika faced the front and used the fire that came from her stallion to make a giant ember above them, an ember that looked the same as Liranda's symbol. Dispersing the giant ember, it zoomed onto the axes of the Celestial Protectors, enflaming the blades, and leaving them a squealing-hot red. Empress Mika looked at Ambassador Sorip with a smile.

Ashlynn was slouched on her brown horse; she didn't like sitting upright like her empress. She turned her head to look at Mika and smiled, causing her short, black hair to bounce with the turn. Her bangs ended just above her eyebrows, and the back of her hair was to the middle of her neck.

Chirping and squealing from the back of Ashlynn's horse caught Mika's attention. She didn't turn to look, but she kept her ears to the direction.

Ashlynn turned around on the horse, easy for her to do with a missing leg. She reached into a satchel on her hip and pulled out a handful of seeds. Ashlynn spoke like a mother would to her newborn baby. "Are you hungry?"

She shook her head and inched it closer to Zarl. "Do you want food? Do you want a treat?"

Zarl chirped louder and opened his wings, hopping closer to Ashlynn. She opened her hand, and her phoenix ate.

Mika squinted and analyzed Reach. The heatwaves in the distance blurred the coastal town known for its strong navy. Although Reach was just hours away, Mika thought it would be best to rest before getting there. The troops would look more professional, be more alert, and give a better first impression that would, she hoped, spark an alliance between Celeste and the town that had conquered several islands off the coast.

Mika held up her fist.

"Ready!" Commander Nicholas's voice was rough and loud and snapped with every syllable.

Further behind the Celestial Protectors, Mika heard the commander of the archers and the commander of the cavalry ready their troops to halt.

"Halt!" all three commanders shouted at once.

The rippling thunder of sixty Celestial Protectors, one hundred sixty archers, and one hundred cavalry coming to a halt at the same time was satisfying.

Mika slowed Mythines to a stop. Silence filled the air, except for the crackling of the flames on the stallion's mane and the rhythmic hush of waves along the shore.

Nicholas removed his helmet and approached. "Empress?"

"Commander Nicholas, set up camp. We'll rest before we step foot inside Reach tomorrow afternoon. Make sure all gear is cleaned and shined tonight, except for the boots."

The highest military officer in Celeste bowed and put on his helmet. He met with the other two commanders and dispersed the orders given by the empress.

Mika hopped off Mythines.

Ashlynn placed Zarl on her shoulder. "Why not the boots?"

She slid off, converting her shield into a walking cane.

Mika passed her hand through her stallion's fiery mane. "A soldier with clean battle boots shows the world that he's afraid of going through shit."

Ashlynn felt rebellious. She lowered her voice so the soldiers couldn't hear. "So, why are *your* boots so clean?"

Mika's eyes dropped to her boots. They were pretty damned clean. She smiled at her sister, but her eyes narrowed. "When they have to go through shit, I'll be right there with them."

Ashlynn used her cane to walk. "Mmm-hmmm! I'll be waiting for that, and if you don't, I'm going to call you out on it! I mean, yeah, you've done stuff before, but empresses don't get dirty. You know, I was talking with a gentleman from Velonde a few weeks ago. Said he used to be a strong adventurer, but once he got rich and his life got easier?" Ashlynn closed her eyes and shook her head with vigor. "He said he got lazy, lost his adventurous side, got scared of every confrontation!"

Mika raised her eyebrow.

Ashlynn whispered in her ear. "That's gonna be you!" Ashlynn inhaled to keep talking.

"Well!" Mika cut off her rambling. "I'm just going to take you with me on our next battle so I can prove you wrong."

Ashlynn's face straightened. Her eyes widened.

Mika laughed. "Oh, who's scared now?" She gave Ashlynn a shove.

The imperial soldiers began moving around, setting up a camp that would maximize their effectiveness and thwart an attack. Claiming a large section behind a tree line, they set up defenses within the trees and around the camp. The archers gathered firewood, and the cavalry began to dismount and tend to their horses. The Celestial Protectors dropped their non-fighting gear in a line and, customary before taking off their armor, they began a vigorous, high-intensity exercise session.

This session consisted of sprints, wrestling matches, axe practice, and a man-down drag back to camp. The exercise was repeated five times for each man. The Celestial Protectors removed their helmets in unison. Despite their faces being drenched in sweat, none of them showed a hint of emotion. Only when Commander Nicholas gave the order to rest did they show their need for rest. Satisfied with the performance of her most prized soldiers, Mika turned to Mythines.

Removing his saddle, she guided him toward Ashlynn. Ashlynn had just finished brushing her horse's mane. Mika began cleaning the hooves of hers. She was glad the horse's mane was fire; she didn't have to brush it. When Mika was done, she and Ashlynn began setting up a tent. Because of Ashlynn's isolation and trauma during the past couple of years, it was impossible for her to sleep or be alone. Some found the platonic relationship of the empress and her ambassador strange, but neither Mika nor Ashlynn cared.

The small detachments of Empress Mika's army finished setting up camp, and it was time for one quarter of her army to eat. The junior soldiers sat in a massive circle. The sergeants in another, officers in another, and the three commanders in a separate one. Mika and Ashlynn ate together. In the Celestial Army, no intermingling existed between lower and higher ranks except for official business, assistance, or hardships.

By Mika's orders, every soldier ate the same food, and every commander ate the same rations as the soldiers. The only units that ate more were those who expended more energy, such as Celestial Protectors, scouts, and unmounted personnel. Today, this army ate rabbit from the massive Di'Abribeli farm and potatoes grown by shamans. The rabbits were big and meaty—the size of a medium dog.

The eating army began to talk independently, becoming louder and louder as each man and woman tried to talk above the person across from them. Laughs filled the air, burps, a clank of a sword dropping on armor, thuds of wood being thrown into firepits, the woosh of the fire when it began to grow. Mealtime was a time to relax, and all soldiers could speak freely and do whatever they wanted.

Although she didn't allow intermingling, Mika wanted to see the status of her military's spirit. She ordered all her warriors to form a huge circle. The soldiers were scared of the sergeants, sergeants scared of the officers, and officers scared of the commanders, causing the scene to quiet.

When Mika's smooth, calculated, deep voice sang in the ears of those around her, the crowd looked at her.

"Tell me ..." she squinted, trying to remember the name of a soldier across from her, "Horseman Oliver, you come from Azilia, don't you? What's the most interesting creature you've seen over there?"

Oliver looked at Mika, momentarily dumbstruck. Was the empress really talking to him? Asking him a personal question? He looked at the soldier next to him, a woman who also rode with him in the cavalry unit.

His colleague looked back at him. "Answer her!" she whispered.

"Well, I—" Oliver shut his eyes to think.

A lot of the cavalry units and some of the archers began to laugh at his awkwardness, further embarrassing the young soldier. The Celestial Protectors kept their composure.

"Silence!" The empress's voice boomed; the fires throughout the camp blued and grew with her voice. "I do not know why this is so funny." She gave a scolding look at the people who laughed the loudest and infused her words with pity. "This is how our enemy would treat us during times of peace."

She gave a sweeping look before infusing her words with honor. "You're all one team fighting, killing, and dying together, so you *will* respect each other, lest you wish to be exiled."

The empress adjusted her armor. Her voice calmed, and so did the fires. "Oliver, please, continue."

Oliver, still shy, cleared his throat. "We, uh," he looked at the Celestial Protectors. "Saw a, uh, group of traveling cyclopes being ambushed by trolls in the mountains near a town called Myanrun."

"Been there," Ashlynn popped into Mika's mind.

"Hush. Listen to his story."

433

"Tell us more about that fight."

Oliver shared the story, a fight between two groups of giants that shook the walls of the Myanrun. In the end, the animalistic trolls won over the more humanoid cyclopes. "It was nice of the trolls to spare the females and children."

"Thank you for sharing the story with us." Empress Mika smiled with closed eyes and tilted her head. She looked around. "Does anyone else have any stories of interesting creatures?"

"The New Lands has centaurs," said a horseman named Vincente, with a serious voice and an accent that reminded Mika of Rosa.

The group waited for him to finish the bite of his rabbit before he continued. Everyone loved hearing stories from the New Lands.

Vincente sucked the remaining meat off the rabbit's thigh. "They're as smart as humans." His voice was serious. "Four horse legs ending in hooves, two arms that allows them to wield weapons. The *horse* portion of them starts below their human abdomen."

Vincente cracked the rabbit's thighbone in half and used it to pick at his teeth.

"Are they friendly?" The shout came from a man.

Vincente continued picking. "They're diplomats." He looked at the bone then threw it behind him. "But have no fear of fighting."

Answering the questions, Mika and her soldiers learned the centaurs crafted their own armor and weapons, had social norms like humans, and hunted in packs. The only thing centaurs could not use was magic.

Vincente leaned back and placed his foot over his knee. "They'll spearhead the uprising of technology." He tried to start an interesting conversation.

"Wait a minute, wait a minute!" A young archer named Aaron stood, shaking his finger in the air. Instead of making the conversation serious and intellectual, he made it dumb. "The female centaurs, do they have a vagina like a human or like a horse?"

Vincente smirked but recoiled his head, telegraphing, *"What?"*

Chloe, a female archer with blonde hair braided into long pigtails, spoke with a loud, crass voice. "The fuck would it matter to you?" She laughed. "Your small dick can't work on a human. What makes you think you'll be able to please a horse lady that gets stallion cock every day?"

Aaron laughed along with the other soldiers.

Chloe's face straightened; her eyes widened. She snapped her head toward Vincente.

"So you're telling me them centaurs look like humans, talk and act like humans, but have parts the same size as horses." Her huge smile showed a crooked tooth and dull canines. She looked at all the women in the group. "Ladies! We need to take a trip to the New Lands and meet us some centaur studs."

Mika covered her face in embarrassment when the archer in front of her had a glimmer in her eyes. Her thoughts of having sex with a centaur made her miss all the questions, possible answers, and laughs that filled the air.

When the conversations of centaurs waned, a Celestial Protector named Robert with spiky hair told the story of harpies. Half human, half bird, the harpies were the ventus form of the siren. Although they didn't have sex with humans, they provided flights through the land in exchange for gold. Harpies reproduced by stealing bird eggs and infusing them with the gold, and the egg would grow throughout the months until a harpy would hatch with the same features as the stolen bird.

"What about you, Empress?" Nicholas asked.

Mika's eyes met one of the mountains of Peak's Lake and, after remembering Sylisia and Vivinia, Mika told the story about the sirens, telling her soldiers their fate, so far, was unknown.

The group spoke until it was time for the next group to eat. They finished talking, hugged each other, shook hands, bowed, and said their farewells.

Mika was proud she was able to bring the group closer together. It was, after all, the leader's responsibility to form the bond among the team.

"Ready to sleep, Ashlynn?" she asked.

Ashlynn nodded, and they went into their tent. Mika undressed and bent over to pick up the bag full of information about Reach. The swinging of the paladin key around her neck caught Ashlynn's attention.

"Do you ever take that off? I mean, it's pretty, but doesn't it get uncomfortable? Are you scared you're going to lose it? Well, I guess you can't lose it if it's around your neck. Oh, my goodness, what if someone chokes you to death with it? That would be so embarrassing!" Ashlynn shivered at the thought.

Straightening, Mika held on to the key. She looked at it and remembered Axel, the battle of Di'Abribel, and Triumph. No one, not even Ashlynn, knew what happened the moments after she was reunited with Page.

She flicked the key. "I earned it."

Ashlynn continued speaking with Mika, and Mika was happy to converse with her loving sister while she studied.

Once the stars appeared above the army, they strengthened the defensive position in the camp, ready for a necromancer attack. Mika and Ashlynn rested in their tent but kept their ears open for the sound of a horn that would alert the camp. Mika was thankful that none came. Half the camp slept until sunrise, and the rest slept when those awakened. By the afternoon, the Celestial Protectors donned their gear and began a painful set of exercises. Once they were done and the camp packed, Mika donned a pretty pink dress to look presentable for King Deon of Reach, and the detachment marched north toward the coastal town. Mika refused to look to the west to the mountains that held Peak's Lake.

"Captain Rashawn will be here shortly," Coastal Guard Daniel recognized Ashlynn.

Ashlynn bowed. "Thank you!" She noticed Daniel had lost weight and gained muscle since the last time she saw him.

Mika dismounted Mythines when Ashlynn told her Coastal Captain Rashawn was the man approaching.

"Good afternoon," he said, approaching with purpose. His voice sounded angry, but his mannerisms showed nothing but respect and coolness.

"Captain Rashawn, I am Mika Plum of Yevera, the *Empress* of Celeste." She accentuated the word *empress*.

"Oh, my goodness, why do you continue to say 'Of Yevera'?"

"Hold on, Ashlynn."

Captain Rashawn knelt. "It is an honor, madam."

"Thank you, Captain." Mika held her hand to Captain Rashawn. "Please, stand."

With rough and calloused hands, Captain Rashawn accepted the assist and stood in front of Empress Mika.

"I understand it was you who assisted Ambassador Ashlynn" – Mika extended her hand toward Ashlynn for a moment– "when she came to your town last year. For that, I'll be forever grateful. If you or your family ever need anything, please let me know."

"Thank you, Empress."

Ashlynn slid off her horse and stumbled to Captain Rashawn.

"Shawn!" She held her arms out and had a smile on her face.

Mika allowed Captain Rashawn to pass and hug Ashlynn.

"How you been, girl?" Captain Rashawn tightened his arms around Mika's ambassador.

Ashlynn accepted the hug and closed her eyes. She pressed her cheek against Rashawn's.

"Better, so much better! I've done so much! My hair has stopped falling out, my leg doesn't hurt anymore, I got a horse!" They pulled away from each other. "How are the boys and the lady?"

"Surviving. Boys still have nightmares, and the wife's been struggling to get as much leather out as possible."

The crashing of waves diverted Mika's attention. Past the damaged city walls were several ships swaying with gentle ease over the small waves caused by the pushing of the wind. Mika looked up to the ship's mast. The flag of Reach, a single golden anchor behind a purple square, looked back at Mika. Hopefully after today, those flags will be replaced with the flag of Celeste.

"Wake up," Ashlynn's voice bounced in her head. *"He asked if the soldiers are following us in!"*

Mika replied with complete trust in Ashlynn's words. "Yes, but they'll stay near the entrance." She turned to face Rashawn. "I don't want to seem like an invading force." Mika smiled.

They're not an invading force. Not unless the negotiations fail.

Captain Rashawn spoke with Coastal Guard Daniel. In the meantime, Ashlynn communicated with Mika.

"Okay, answer my question."

"What question?"

"I asked, why do you continue to say 'Of Yevera'?"

Mika locked eyes with Ashlynn. *"Because Yevera was my home, Ashlynn. It's where I was born, where I was raised. It's the only place I've felt like the people loved me and I loved them."* Mika watched Rashawn approach. *"I'll stop saying that when I find a place I feel I belong. Until then, I will continue to say, and continue to be called, Mika Plum of Yevera, the Empress of Celeste."*

Captain Rashawn spoke, drowning out Ashlynn's response.

"Your soldiers can rest within the walls. Please, follow me." He escorted Mika, Ashlynn, and Nicholas through the town. Empress Mika walked next to Commander Nicholas. He had removed his helmet to show respect to the citizens of Reach. Captain Rashawn led the way, and Ashlynn, because of her missing leg, rode her horse behind the trio.

"Do the talking, Ashlynn."

Ashlynn asked Rashawn about the first raid.

"Fucking necromancer scum," Rashawn spat at the ground. "They won the siege. Beyond a doubt, they won. King Deon was the first to get on a ship. Had his shit ready to go. Pushed the women and children out of the way until he was safe on the largest ship." He spit again and shook his head. His lips wrenched in anger. "Didn't even take his wife and kids with him. Left them in the streets carrying his riches." Rashawn continued to vent about King Deon as they passed through the market.

Ashlynn responded with "Wow" and "Really?" and "Mmm-hmmm," asking questions where appropriate.

Mika noticed a fisherman at his stall talking to another man.

"The repairs to your home done?" the man asked, passing his hand through his hair.

"Yeah," the other replied, his fists to his hips, "but Derrick needs help taking some debris out of his basement."

"King." There was disgust in the word when Rashawn said it. "Deon is a fucking coward, and most of the town agrees."

"So, you used the ships to escape the slaughter?" Ashlynn asked. "How many died?"

Rashawn didn't reply right away. "Three hundred and seventy-four. Most were guards; some were citizens who took up arms to defend the ships on the departure. Rest were the less wealthy. Mori missile hit the boarding ramps, and the ship had to leave them behind."

"The necromancers didn't attack the ships?" Mika asked after clearing her throat.

"Nah," Rashawn chuckled, "we've blessed the ships, so they amplify our magic when we're inside 'em. We sailed away to safety. Could go to one of our islands, but homes there have yet to be completed."

Those ships would be so useful. A navy would let us wreak havoc on the Lost Forest from afar.

"Spent two months at sea and our islands until the necromancers lost interest. Looted everything. Surprised they didn't raze the place." Rashawn guided the group through a narrow alleyway. Birds feasting on a fish fluttered away.

"I'm sure you're dying for revenge," said Mika, looking at Rashawn.

Rashawn sensed her gaze and returned it. "The most peaceful of citizens want to rip Deon's skin from his bones."

Mika smiled. "Well, maybe one day it'll happen."

Emerging from the alleyway, the group stepped onto the buzzing streets near the docks. People gave quick looks at the visitors, wondering who the young woman with the scar on her face was. Most seemed to recognize Ashlynn and waved at her when she passed. All the citizens, especially the children, admired the scarlet dragonscale armor of Commander Nicholas.

After a moderate uphill walk, the group reached the gate to the outer courtyard of the palace; the structure itself looked pristine and undamaged.

"Before you ask—" Rashawn unclipped a large key from his belt. "—yes, it was damaged, and yes, he ordered it to be the first thing repaired in the city." The gate opened without a sound.

The group stepped through and passed through the outer courtyard, which was adorned with a variety of flowers. The path was made of polished stone and flanked by bushy trees. Countless maids ran back and forth in the yard, pruning the trees, ensuring the flowers were trimmed, and double-checking the cleanliness of the stone path. When the group reached the stairs leading to the doors of the palace, King Deon burst out of the tall double doors.

"Welcome!" King Deon held his arms out. With humble eyes, he looked at the sky, giving the appearance that the sky was worshipping him. "I am King Deon." He lowered his arms and looked at the group. "I bless you with my presence."

His frame was thick, his muscles popped out of his shirt, but so did his belly. Built like a bear as he was, Mika could tell he preferred a melee weapon over a bow or magic. King Deon wore a gold turban with purple engravings, and the golden hoop earring he wore on one ear was almost hidden behind his thick, black beard that reached past his neck.

Mika curtsied. Commander Nicholas bowed.

"Good afternoon, King Deon, I am Mika Plum—"

"Please! No talking!" His voice was curt and high-handed.

Mika clenched her jaw because of his disrespectful interruption.

"Captain Rashawn," said the king, "don't you know better? Please, guide them to the back, where my women will serve us drinks and fruits! Go on now, hurry up!"

Captain Rashawn locked eyes with Mika. Mika almost recoiled from the fury plastered on Rashawn's face. With a *follow me* nod, Mika and her group followed Rashawn around the palace and to the back porch. Rashawn rushed to the balcony that extended past the edge of the hill. He placed his hands on the railing and stared away into the calm, blue ocean.

"Let me know when he's ready." Mika nodded at Ashlynn.

Ashlynn dismounted and held a peace sign to Mika before joining Commander Nicholas at a small glass table.

The breeze picked up speed around the balcony, caressing Mika's cheek and filling her nostrils with the salty smell of the ocean. She made her way toward Captain Rashawn, trying her best to be graceful with the noise she made. When she reached him, the only movement she noticed was the moving of his ear when he heard the sorcerer sigh.

She leaned her forearms onto the railing as she looked at the massive expanse of the ocean. Its waters ran further and further from her until they met with the winds of the sky, creating a horizontal line that divided the allied elements of aqua and ventus. A gust of wind brought the rustle of a flag to her ears. A seagull squawked, and a small shadow passed over her. Although the massive amounts of water and the strong breeze would render her magic unusable, she was at peace.

"I apologize for the king's behavior." Captain Rashawn kept his eyes straight ahead.

Mika looked at Rashawn. He refused to wipe the sweat that dripped from his forehead. He stood with one leg in front of the other, his palms gripped tight around the railing, the grip so tight Mika knew the wood was bending underneath his fingers.

Mika mocked his posture. It was the perfect time to plant a seed in Captain Rashawn's mind. She made her voice sound disappointed and used her emotions spell. "You'd make a much better ruler than he makes."

The twitch of Rashawn's fingers told Mika the spell cut deeper than she thought it would, that Rashawn had once thought about ruling over the citizens of Reach.

Mika let go of the railing and turned toward the chairs and tables. "It's a shame that he's still alive," she said, "preventing that."

Without another word, Mika walked away, leaving Rashawn to think about what she said.

Mika walked toward Ashlynn, dragged a chair, and sat within arm's length of her ambassador. They spoke with Commander Nicholas about the politics in Di'Abribel and Vicqua, the alliance between Celeste and Velonde, and by the time Captain Rashawn joined them, they spoke about the idea of magicians mounted on horses. Modeled on the mounted archers used by the Azilian armies, the magical cavalry would be fast, deadly, and able to provide support at mobile angles.

Maids brought drinks, fruits, and vegetables, but the trio refused to eat or drink anything except water.

"If our soldiers aren't sharing this with us," Mika's words toward the maid were sweet, "we won't have any either."

After hours of waiting, King Deon emerged from his palace. His appearance had not changed; Mika believed the wait was just for show, a power move to show that *he* was the one in charge.

441

King Deon approached Commander Nicholas and extended his hand.

Commander Nicholas stood to accept the handshake. "Nicholas, commander of the Celestial Protectors."

"Commander?" King Deon looked around. "I thought I was to speak to an emperor!"

"He's doing this on purpose, I know it! There's no way all this isn't planned, and no one is that stupid!" Ashlynn confirmed Mika's suspicions.

"The *Empress* of Celeste is behind you, King." Commander Nicholas's voice was calm.

King Deon spun around, he looked at Mika, then looked at Ashlynn. Although Ashlynn wore a skirt and no jewels, the King approached Ashlynn and addressed her.

"Empress!" He fell to his knees and passed his hand over Ashlynn's single leg. He went to reach for Ashlynn's other leg but sighed and shook his head once he *noticed* it was missing.

Mika locked eyes with Ashlynn.

"Don't let him get to you," Ashlynn must have noticed the rage in Mika's eyes. *"He's doing it on purpose."*

"King Deon, sir, I'm Ashlynn Sorip, two Ns. The empress is right there."

King Deon turned to Mika. "Empress! I apologize! I should have noticed by the jewels around your neck and your beautiful, pink, bright pink I should say, dress! What is your name, *Empress?*"

There was a suppressed, angry snarl at the last *empress* in the sentence.

"I am Mika Plum of Yevera." Mika's eyes were locked onto Deon's. "The Empress of Celeste." Mika was so flustered she didn't accentuate the word *Empress.*

King Deon raised his eyebrow and stroked his beard. "No need for such an introduction! I just need your name next time, Empress! What makes you the Empress of Celeste?"

"I rule over Di'Abribel, the Farmlands, Vicqua, the ruins of Yevera, and everything in between. Not only do I own the most land in this region, I plan on expanding Celeste with my allies. Therefore, I am the ruler and empress of Celeste."

King Deon pretended to be lost in thought. He shook his head and pretended to snap back to reality. "Please, do you mind? You're in my seat." He pointed at the chair in which Mika was sitting, a chair identical to the other chairs. "I've had it custom made for myself."

Still locking eyes with Deon, Mika slowly raised herself out of the seat. She moved away and watched the king plop himself on it. He relaxed on the chair and rested his head on his hand. Captain Rashawn stood at King Deon's side and crossed arms in front of his chest.

"Captain Rashawn must be King Deon's most trusted soldier." Ashlynn commented.

Mika heard Commander Nicholas stand. She moved to his chair and sat in it. Commander Nicholas knelt next to Mika, and they both faced the king.

"King Deon," said Ashlynn, "the mighty powers of Celeste are glad and relieved your beautiful town survived the raids of the necromancers. As I'm sure a person of your great intellect is aware, the necromancers have retreated to their forest after their several failures. We don't think this will be for long. We've come to form an alliance between our two great nations so we can take the fight to them."

Before the king could ask questions, Ashlynn continued doing what she does best, talking.

"What would this alliance bring you? Celeste will provide a squadron of our prime, elite units known as the Celestial Protectors. Battle-axe soldiers with understanding of ignis. They will follow your every command and protect the town against any and all enemies. Celeste shall also provide complete military access to the city of Di'Abribel, the rebuilt Farmlands, the Grand Waterfall, the county of Vicqua, and New Yevera once reconstruction is complete. Lastly!"

Ashlynn raised a finger and took a sip of water. "Lastly, Celeste will provide any goods from our trades with Imbris and Velonde, along with any riches and spoils claimed from our battles against our common enemies! All Celeste asks is command of your military at any time, including your amazing ships, and a tax rate of forty percent."

"Forty percent?" The king burst out of his chair.

Ashlynn remained calm; she held her hands up in innocence. "The taxes are to expedite the building of the military and furthering the war efforts. Once the necromancers have been vanquished, the tax rate will be dropped to five percent."

"Ludicrous!" King Deon covered his ears. He walked away from the table and toward the railing that overlooked the ocean. He turned around and approached. "Get out!" He pointed to the front of the palace. "Get out! Thinkin' you can come here and steal all my gold and resources? Thieves! Thieves, all of you!"

"King Deon," Mika's voice was stern, "I understand it's a lot to take in, but the necro—"

"Shut your mouth, you upjumped little whore!" King Deon held a finger inches from Mika's face.

> ~ *Burn him alive ...*
> ~ *Cut open his stomach ...*
> ~ *Display his entrails atop the palace ...*
> ~ *Burn him ...*

It had been months since Mika heard the ignis voices.

Commander Nicholas stood when her garnet began to glow. Mika held her arm in front of him, advising him to stand down.

The king plopped himself onto his chair and slumped. He held his forehead and closed his eyes. "You've disobeyed a lawful order, you're trespassing, and your *commander* has threatened me. Three crimes, enough for a public execution." He waved his finger at Mika. "Rashawn, arrest these criminals."

Captain Rashawn drew one of his swords.

Ashlynn jumped out of her chair and joined Mika's side. Mika could feel the anxiety seeping out of her soul.

"Mika?"

"Nicholas will go for Rashawn when I throw a fireball. We need to kill them without alerting the guards, or else we'll lose all Reacan soldiers. Their crossbowmen are invaluable to us, and we don't know how the ships work."

"Hurry up, Rashawn, I need to go bathe." The king sat straight, waiting for Rashawn to put on a murderous show for him.

Rashawn took a step toward the Celestials.

Mika conjured a flame behind her back.

Commander Nicholas donned his helmet and shifted his weight to propel himself forward.

Captain Rashawn's grip tightened around his sword. He stepped to the side and swung the sword across his body.

King Deon's head rolled off his neck.

The empress extinguished her flame and smiled. Commander Nicholas relaxed and leaned on Mika's seat. Ashlynn asked Mika if she saw what happened.

The severed head rolled over King Deon's belly and bounced on the ground before coming to a stop at Mika's feet.

"Empress Mika ..." Rashawn cleaned the small amount of blood from his blade before sheathing it. "May I approach and clean the mess in front of you?"

Mika's smile widened. "Of course, you may, Captain—or should I say, Lord Rashawn."

Lord Rashawn stepped toward Mika's feet and grabbed Deon's decapitated head. Rashawn looked at the head's face and blinked once, twice, three times. He turned Deon's face to Mika.

Mika held her fists in front of her chest and burst out laughing when she saw that Deon was still alive. The cut was so clean it didn't kill him. The empress crossed one leg over the other.

"What do you know?" Lord Rashawn plopped Deon's head on the table, threw Deon's body on the floor, and sat in the chair. "Bastard's still alive." He looked at Ashlynn. "Reach will accept your offer, only if complete command of the ships remains under our control. Do not worry, we shall consider all propositions made by you for the ships."

Mika laughed again when Deon's face wrenched in agony and sadness.

"Lord Rashawn ..." She saw the disturbed face on Rashawn when she showed her wicked smile. "The ships will remain under your control."

"Then let us have a ceremony so all citizens of Reach can recognize their new leader." Rashawn stood and knelt in front of the empress.

"Parade the head of Deon on a pike." Mika tapped the top of Deon's head until the dying king closed his eyes. "And have a horse drag his body through the streets. Do as you wish with his wife and children, but if they protest, kill them too. The ceremony will take place at sunset."

445

The citizens of Reach cheered when they saw Lord Rashawn on De-on's black horse. Rashawn held a pike with Deon's head impaled on its blade, and as ordered, the former king's body was dragged through every major street of Reach. At last, the cowardly king of Reach had been replaced. Better yet, he was killed by one of his own.

At sunset, all citizens of Reach gathered on the ships to watch Empress Mika give Lord Rashawn a flagstaff with the flag of Celeste. The flag had a red background; inside it was a yellow square with Liranda's black horns in the center.

Lord Rashawn handed Mika all of Reach's flags, folded so the anchor was at the front. With ventus, a Celestial Horseman hovered all the flags high in the air. Mika's words were loud, amplified by magic, and infused with pride.

"… and let all who witness this know that all Reacan citizens, now Celestials, will be allowed to keep their customs, traditions, and livelihoods while united under the flag of Celeste."

Mika lit the flags with ignis in a ceremonial burn. The horseman moved the ashes over the water, where they were laid to rest in the ocean. Some citizens cried, others stayed quiet, and others cheered. In the end, the mood was happy, for the citizens felt hopeful the nec-romancers could one day be defeated, and their ships would one day be the most powerful structures on the ocean.

* * * * *

In her dream, Mika stood atop the highest building in Irstia at the Imbric capital city of Edel. She looked around her. The stars shone bright in the dark sky, but the scene around her was like daylight. The largest moon shone bright, and so did the sun that had replaced the second moon. Recognizing the building from paintings and sto-ries, Mika found it strange that the view from the top of the building was the same as the view from the top of Mount Cabria.

Mika relished the sight, not recognizing the signs that might have told her she was dreaming. She stood over the small ledge, looked at the base of the mountain, and tipped herself forward, spreading her arms and smiling when she began to freefall. Passing through the rocks of the mountain, she fell through and passed inside the mountain until she landed in the waters, not once missing a breath while being submerged. She swam to the surface and realized she was inside a cove; the beach's sand on one side, and the exit to the ocean on the other.

"Margarita Cove," Mika whispered. The moment the words escaped her mouth, Sylisia, her siren partner, appeared next to her with the same smile that had made Mika fall in love with her almost one year ago.

Sylisia didn't speak, and her eyes looked blank, as though she were just a figure in a dream.

A dream ... Mika thought. She looked through the waters toward Sylisia's bottom half, noticing they were human legs instead of fins.

I must be dreaming, Mika told herself.

"Why would you be dreaming, silly?" asked Sylisia.

Mika shook her head, looked away from her dead partner, and submerged herself in the water. When she took a breath, her lungs filled with air, and the scene exploded when Mika concluded she was in a dream.

Mika stood on glowing lava, surrounded by smoke that almost hid the black inner walls of the volcano. Gurgles and pops surrounded Mika, and in front of her, she saw Liranda's horns within the smoke.

Mika made a slow descent to her knees. The dream's vividness was the greatest she had ever felt, much more *real* than in the waking world. Mika looked up when Liranda touched her head.

"Rise, child." Liranda held a staff with a fist-sized garnet set atop it. The garnet was surrounded by a red flame.

Mika stood, looking her deity in the eyes. "Can I hug you?"

She hadn't had the physical touch of anyone for a long time, and Ashlynn's touch had now become too common to notice.

"Oh, Mika ..." Liranda opened her arms, embracing her and rubbing her cheek against Mika's head. When the hug concluded, Liranda moved Mika away and spoke. "Being my only daughter means I have many, many gifts for you." Liranda handed Mika the staff with the fiery garnet.

Mika held the staff in her hands. The shaft fit perfectly in her small hands, and the engravings glowed the color of flowing lava when looked at.

"An ignis staff will amplify your fire and slow your exhaustion." Liranda stroked Mika's hair. When she did so, Mika could feel the horns that had grown above her eyebrows.

"Where will it be when I wake up?" Upon saying the words, Mika began to feel the weight of the blankets on her waking body.

Liranda stabilized the dream by releasing a flame from her finger. She looked at Mika. "In your quarters in Di'Abribel, darling. A succubus has taken human form and is on her way with it as we speak."

"But, Mother ..." Mika lowered her head in submission, trying to show she was not being confrontational. "I need to stay in Reach for a few months and ensure Rashawn and the Reacans keep their side of the bargain."

Liranda smiled. "You're so smart." The flames in the volcano became brighter. "Worry not, sweetie, a group of incubi and succubi will arrive to quell any with rebellious thoughts until you return with your staff."

Luring humans with their seductive looks, incubi and succubi absorbed their prey's souls and stole their victim's appearance and voice.

"I'd deliver it, but no human will have the right to touch it other than you."

Mika nodded, took a deep breath, and exhaled. "Yes, Mother."

Liranda kissed Mika's forehead, and the volcano erupted, enflaming Mika and the deity of ignis, forcing the sorcerer to wake up in her bed.

Too excited for her new weapon, Mika couldn't go back to sleep. She sat in front of the fire, staring into its mesmerizing rhythm until the sun shone on her face.

* * * * *

Mika and Ashlynn rode next to each other at the front of the army as it traveled south. The morning was cool, and the wind coming from the mountains of Peak's Lake only amplified the chills that made Mika shiver.

"I'm ... disturbed." Ashlynn looked at Mika with a sad, open mouth. "That was horrible what happened to Deon. I'm really, really upset about that. Not upset about what happened ... I'm upset about *how* it happened. I don't know how to explain it … ugh … I just literally saw his face all night in my dreams. He was really alive with his head chopped off!"

Mika looked at her sister. Her eyes were wide, and she was sitting erect—more erect than Mika was. Mika knew Ashlynn was pausing to gather her thoughts, so she didn't say anything.

Ashlynn closed her eyes. "I never thought stuff like that could happen. I'm guessing it's because the brain is what powers the body? Or something? I mean, it can go without oxygen for a few minutes, so that can explain it." Ashlynn shivered; whether it was from the cold or the thought, Mika didn't know. Ashlynn opened her eyes and faced forward. She wiped sweat from her brow and passed her hand through her hair.

"I really wouldn't want to die like that," she said. "Head chopped off and listening to my rivals talk about their plans to desecrate my body." Ashlynn shook her head and covered her face. Her exhale was shaky, and her voice carried the hint of a lump in her throat. "I don't want to see something like that again, Mika."

Zarl noticed her sadness and jumped on her shoulder. The phoenix rested his head on her cheek and began to sing.

Mika continued looking at her sister. Ashlynn had changed since she left the prison and became an ambassador. Unfortunately, she wasn't a warrior anymore.

"I understand your feelings." Mika faced forward. "And your feelings are normal. I'll try my best to make sure you don't have to see that sort of thing again."

Before Ashlynn could start a rambling session, Mika's forward scouts—two unarmored young men on horseback and without uniforms—sped toward them. Mika ordered her detachment to halt.

"Empress!" The boy with curly brown hair was out of breath. His partner looked behind them.

Mika couldn't remember either of their names. "What's wrong?"

"Two …" –he struggled to catch his breath– "two to three hundred necromancers are on the road, heading our direction from the south."

"Demeanor?" Mika's heartrate rose. Commander Nicholas approached.

The boy turned his face to the sky and took a deep breath. "I think they're just moving. No weapons drawn, walking, talking like nothing is going on. About two hundred magicians, around one hundred infantrymen. Light armor, small weapons."

"How far?"

"About an hour away."

Mika sensed eyes on her. She turned to Commander Nicholas. "Suggestions, Commander?"

Commander Nicholas looked back at the army. He looked at Mika and shook his head.

Mika turned her neck and looked out the corner of her eye. To the west were the mountains of Peak's Lake; an incline and a lot of boulders were scattered between her and the mountains. The terrain remained the same along the mountain for miles and miles. To the southeast, trees began to form, blocking the coast from view. Behind Mika, to the north, the town of Reach. The road heading south would lead her straight into the necromancers, whose numbers matched her detachment.

She could face the necromancers head on, but their magic would seep through her soldiers' armor. Most soldiers were recent recruits, and a lot of them had minimal combat experience. None of these Celestial Protectors had fought a *real* battle in their armor before. The empress could retreat to Reach, but that would waste half a day's travel. Worst of all, it would dispirit her troops.

Looking at the boulders along the mountain, Mika realized her army could hide among the boulders. Looking at the trees, her army could lay low and hide within the trees. The road was wide enough that the army wouldn't pass too close either. By the time she finished thinking, the commander of the archers and the commander of the cavalry were next to her.

Ambush ... Ambush. She communicated with Ashlynn. *"Ambush!"*

"Have the archers head up the hill and onto the boulders." Mika pointed to the boulders, then to the trees. "Protectors to the tree line. Have them lay low within the trees. Cavalry stays here."

"Once I cast magic, archers will engage with their arrows. After the first volley of arrows, the cavalry and Celestial Protectors will engage."

The commander of the archers smacked his fist to his palm. "Sounds like a plan, Empress." He ran his 160 archers toward the hill.

Nicholas called to his soldiers and pointed to the tree line. "Hurry up!" His voice roared above the clanking of armor. Celestial Protectors sprinted to the tree line. Thanks to their training, they would be there within minutes.

"Listen up, ladies and gentlemen, we're going to set up an ambush and kill some motherfucking necromancers. The empress has ordered the ..." The voice of the cavalry commander was drowned out by thudding hooves.

"Sorip, you're with me and the Protectors. Use your bow." Mika smacked her stallion's sides, and Mythines ran toward the trees.

Ashlynn followed. "This is crazy! Do you think we can really pull it off?"

The wind passing through Mika's ears made it hard to hear; she had to shout. "We'd better pull it off," she said, waiting until she passed the Celestial Protectors and was out of earshot. "Or else we're as dead as Deon!"

Mika slowed when she entered the cluster of trees. Ashlynn followed with her magic shield turned into a bow.

The two looked at each other, and Mika smiled. "Time for me to prove you wrong."

Ashlynn shook her head. Her wide eyes didn't look away from Mika. "You're something else." Ashlynn knew not to call Mika crazy.

They both faced the road, and Mika absorbed the flames from Mythines.

The Celestial Protectors lay on the ground with weapons drawn. Seconds turned to minutes. Five minutes. Ten. Twenty. At twenty-two minutes, an arrow whistled through the air and stuck into the ground, telling Mika the archers had gauged the distance and were in position.

Forty minutes.

The necromancers came into view at fifty-one minutes. They walked at a normal pace in columns, a regular marching formation.

Mika couldn't tell from that distance that they were necromancers, but she trusted her scouts. Her heartbeat began to quicken. *It's happening again!* She was leading an army against their sworn enemies. She hid behind the thick tree in front of her. Ashlynn continued peeking out. She seemed so scared. If Mika hadn't known Ashlynn before, she would have thought her a coward. Still, Mika loved Ashlynn more than anyone in her life.

The necromancers continued walking. Their black uniform was obvious, and infantry led the front of the group. In a few minutes, the necromancers would reach the arrow on the ground, about fifty yards away from Mika's position. The necromancers weren't in step, and they talked and laughed during their walk. Mika smiled when she realized her army was more disciplined than her enemy's. The group of more than two hundred necromancers marched about one hundred yards from her.

Mythines blew his nose, and Mika raised her hand in the air. "Ignis," she whispered. A massive ember appeared in the sky, high above the necromancers.

The empress raised her opposite hand. "Terra," she whispered. Stone boulders appeared inside the massive flame.

The necromancers stopped. The ones at the front looked at the arrow on the ground. The group in the middle looked up and jumped when they saw the massive ball of fire.

"Ignis-terra!" Mika's voice screeched out of the tree line.

Flaming boulders fell onto the necromancers who dispersed like cockroaches, as volleys of arrows began arcing onto the magicians.

"Ambush!" they screamed. "Ambush!"

A horn in the distance told Mika the cavalry was on its way just as Ashlynn fired her bow.

The Celestial Protectors shouted and sprinted behind Mythines toward the group of scattering necromancers. Wind filled Mika's ears as she galloped toward her enemy.

Necromancers retaliated, running away but casting minor magic spells, unable to complete a charge for their mori missiles. Mika dodged, ducked, and used a flame barrier to block the spells.

Celestial cavalry shouted before plowing through the infantry then into the magicians.

Mika used a flame to douse the necromancers. They screamed, ran, rolled on the ground to stop their flesh from searing off their bones.

The necromancer infantry recovered just in time to be met with another volley of arrows, followed by axes to the head by Celestial Protectors.

"Mercy!" a female necromancer screamed.

A Celestial horseman decapitated her and crushed the magician in front of her.

Empress Mika smiled when she heard the retreat order. Clanking of metal told her the Protectors had surrounded the infantry.

Charles, the commander of the cavalry, looked at the retreating army. "Ready for orders, Empress."

Mika summoned a blue wall of fire ahead of the retreating force.

Without another word, Mika's cavalry let loose with fierce battle cries and charged their horses toward the blocked-off magicians, trampling them and impaling the others with their swords.

Mika turned to the Celestial Protectors and imbued their weapons with ignis. Not a minute later, the battlefield quieted, and the imperial soldiers tended their wounds. Severed limbs and body parts were kicked out of the way, and wounded necromancers were brought in front of the empress.

Celestial Protectors kicked the backs of the necromancers' knees, forcing the seven captured to kneel in front of the empress and her stallion.

"Six horsemen, ten horses," Commander Nicholas spoke loudly, "and two Celestial Protectors died in this battle. These," he pulled back on the long hair of a female necromancer, "are their survivors."

The necromancer winced, then opened her eyes to give Mika a scornful look.

"You're not scared of me, are you?" Mika looked at the woman, likely the commander.

The necromancer's expression didn't change; she shut her lips and gathered spit in her mouth to launch at Mika, but Nicholas punched her across the face.

"Ambassador," Mika looked at Ashlynn, "go check for more survivors with a few cavalrymen. Bring all you find to me."

Ashlynn complied, knowing what was about to happen.

Mika dismounted. "I asked you a question!" She cocked her fist, enflamed it, and crashed it into the necromancer's face.

Blood dripped from the woman's nose.

Mika passed a look at every necromancer. "The fear you've placed on the people of Celeste will be unmatched by the *terror* I will place on the hearts of your fellow rats."

The empress squatted to the level of the commander and lifted her chin. "I'm sorry you didn't die." Mika gave the necromancer a sad look, then smiled. She rose and mounted her horse. "Dismember them. Legs first, then arms, then the head. Heal their wounds so they don't die right away."

Mika ignited the Celestial Protectors' axes. "Their bodies will be taken to the edge of the Lost Forest, lined up, and impaled to a stake, as was my daughter's."

The necromancers tried to squirm away. The Celestial Protectors held them in place.

"Kill them one by one. Make them watch."

Celestial Protectors held down the first necromancer. They took turns dismembering the necromancer per Mika's instructions. One by one, the necromancers were killed; their screams, shouts for mercy, and cries filled the air.

To keep her soldiers' spirits high during the torture, she used her tenebris magic of emotion.

She engraved anger in their hearts when she spoke. "They beg for mercy, yet this is what they do to your wives! To your husbands! To your children and your mothers! They beg for mercy when they are the ones who have invaded and destroyed our home. They do not wage a traditional war; they wage a war that causes our children nightmares, which causes your elders to wish they hadn't reproduced. They murder noncombatants."

The enraged shout of a Celestial Protector as he cleaved off a necromancer's arm told her the spell was working.

"You are not doing this for me, for yourself, or for those men and women you fight alongside of. You do this for those who have lost their lives in this needless war, a war that could've been prevented had Kathrine not decided to invade. We do not fight for land. We. Fight. For. Our. Home!"

The carnage continued until only the commander remained.

Mika jumped off Mythines and unsheathed her silver dagger. She ignited the necromancer.

The necromancer screamed. She moved from side to side, trying to free herself and stop the fire from burning her skin, from roasting her alive.

Mika mounted the necromancer's hips, leaned forward, and carved away at the necromancer's neck until she was decapitated.

Mika wrapped her fingers around the necromancer's hair and held the necromancer's face parallel to hers. Seeing the woman's eyes roll back in her skull, Mika tossed it at a Celestial Protector, and he swung his axe, carving the skull in half in midair. Upon doing so, the life essence of all the dead converged into a single green orb above the battlefield.

Amplified by the effects of Mika's warrior's stone, the orb grew and grew and, just before it appeared to burst, it seeped into all the men and women who took part in the battle. No memories came, so the victors didn't humanize their enemy, another benefit of the stone.

"Have some of the cavalry gather the dead. Rush them back to Di'Abribel for a proper burial." The empress mounted her horse and cleaned her hands on Mythines's coat.

"Take the armor off the dead horses and process them for their pelt and meat. Line them up for a ceremonial burning. They're our soldiers too, and we're giving them that respect. The rest of you, gather the torsos and heads of these rats—we're taking them to the Lost Forest."

The soldiers followed her orders.

The archers made it down the hill and formed up in rows a few yards away from Mika.

"Does anyone have a quill and paper?" she asked.

Chloe waved her hand in the air. "I do!" She was allowed to break formation, so she reached into a pocket and pulled out a leather notebook and quill. "I got you, ma'am."

"Thank you, Chloe!" Mika accepted the quill and paper. With a smile, she wrote:

Kathrine,
Make me a belt of skulls with these!
See you again soon,

Mika Plum, the Yeveran child you failed to kill.

29. DEFEAT

Misty gray clouds floated beneath the white sky, acting like a shield against the ball of fire humans called the sun. A powerful gust roared, carrying a free cloud that brought rain along with it. Both the raining cloud and the gust disappeared faster than they came.

Mythines stood with his hooves on the black, tainted ground. The Empress of Celeste sat on the saddle, looking at the wooden ruins of a home that once belonged to Michael and Cynthia Plum. Only pillars and the foundation stood, just like every other building in the town once known as Yevera.

The corruption set onto Yevera by the necromancers after their raid many years ago had blacked everything around like a rotten tooth. The reason Mika, her soldiers, and workers didn't succumb to the necromantic hallucinations that led to suicide was because of the healers who fought the mori magic with vita. After all these years, Mika understood why Yevera was never rebuilt. It was a long, expensive, and dangerous process. Once the mori magic was finally purged, though, the building of New Yevera would begin.

Mika looked at Commander Nicholas and several other commanders around her. They were quiet, looking here and there, adjusting their armor, easing cramps, studying the area, reading—*anything* to fight the boredom growing in their minds. Times like these made Mika regret ordering her army not to have interactive relationships with subordinates. She felt like talking to someone about her family, and Ashlynn was busy negotiating new trades with Sytu in Reach.

456

"Commander Nicholas," Mika turned her horse to face her most trusted soldier.

Nicholas closed his book and looked up at her. "Empress?"

"Make an account of all troops and equipment. Have the soldiers inspect their tents and weapons. We can't be caught off guard by the rain, wind, or rats."

Nicholas bowed, gathered the commanders, and spread the orders. Nicholas went his own way to assess his troops.

Mika looked to the north, to Mount Cabria. The tallest mountain in Celeste was covered in clouds.

A feeling of dread loomed over her, amplified by a dark sky that shrouded their main protection against the necromancers. Worse, if they were attacked within the next few hours once the rains started, her ignis magic would be rendered useless. Based on scouts sent throughout the forest, the necromancers knew an ignis user walked among the Celestials, but they didn't know this user was also the leader.

More than an hour passed until she was approached by Taylor, the commander of the Ladies of the Empress, an all-female platoon of ranged magicians. Taylor walked with a smile, and she adjusted her blonde hair with silver highlights, further revealing a set of crystal-blue eyes. Taylor bowed in front of the empress and then turned to throw a rock; using ventus to recall it, she threw it again.

"How are the Ladies?" Mika asked, not to inquire, but to fulfill her desire to socialize and cure boredom.

Taylor turned to Mika. Though the Ladies wore flexible robes to allow quick movement, Taylor wore crop-top leather armor, revealing the tattoo of a tiger's face on her abdomen. "They're struggling to stay pretty in these conditions." Taylor tilted her head and curved her full lips in a smile. "But they're doing well."

"It'll be over soon." Mika looked away from Taylor. She always felt physically insecure around a Lady. Because the Ladies' role was mostly for ceremonial and diplomatic matters, the requirements to be a Lady of the Empress were beauty, magical prowess, and charm. Taylor lacked none of those.

"How many girls enlisted after the parade?" asked Mika. "It seems every girl wants to be a Lady now."

Taylor dropped the rock. "Over five hundred! They all want to try out!"

Mika smiled. "I'm sure you'll find great candidates. Just remember the standards." Mika used her fingers after each point. "Beauty, magical prowess, and charm. In that order." The Ladies were brought to Yevera because they requested permission to participate, knowing a battle here would earn them a unique medal. Likewise, to become a Lady, mastery of an element was required, making their arcane spells instrumental in battle.

Nicholas waited for Mika and Taylor to finish their conversation. When it concluded, he spoke. "Report is ready, Empress."

Her butt and legs were tired from sitting in the saddle, so Mika swung her leg over and jumped off before stretching herself out. She nodded at Nicholas.

Nicholas read from a large paper. "Four hundred eighty archers in three platoons, four hundred forty clubmen in two platoons, two hundred twenty swordsmen in one, sixty Celestial Protectors in one, eight hundred shock cavalry in four, eighty Reacan crossbows in one." Nicholas took a breath. "Two hundred twenty mages in two, forty magical cavalry in one, thirty Ladies in one, and one hundred musicians. Reserve and defensive forces present and accounted for. Post briefings conducted." Nicholas folded the paper and placed it inside a satchel that hung from his armor. "Over three thousand men and women here, and all their equipment has been double-checked and accounted for."

"And those we placed as lookouts?" Mika tipped forward when a gust pushed her from behind.

Nicholas swallowed and shook his head. "No updates."

"It's been three hours." Mika's eyebrows furrowed; she heard Taylor briskly walk away. "Has a safety assessment been made?"

Nicholas's gaze fell. "The safety-assessment team was supposed to return twenty minutes ago."

Mika's fists tightened. She felt like yelling at Nicholas, but she elevated her voice enough to show her dissatisfaction. "What have you *done* about this?"

"I sent a squad of the magical cavalry to check—"

"Damn it, Nicholas." Mika spoke with her teeth clenched, and Mythines's fire grew with her anger. "How many times must I tell you, we are not a powerful army? We cannot win with force or expend our troops!" Mika turned to Mythines and clenched his skin. "They're nibbling away at our forces, and you're giving them the means to do so."

Nicholas's voice told Mika she was angering him. "Empress. Though I wish no disrespect, I am your second in command and seek improvement. What *should* I have done?"

Mika turned to Nicholas with a compressed mouth and widened nostrils. *What should he have done?* "You should have ..." She stared at Nicholas. *What would I have done?*

Mika's face relaxed; she looked to the burnt buildings behind Nicholas, the healer in the distance casting vita into the ground, then at her own feet. After a shake of her head, she looked at Nicholas. Stress, exhaustion, hunger, discomfort, sleep deprivation, and the recent news of the destroyed aqueduct had gotten the best of her. She realized her emotions were controlling her, so she retook command of them.

"I apologize. I overreacted." Mika grabbed Mythines's reins. "Let's go fix the problem."

Nicholas took a second to gather what just happened, then led the way to the northern sector of Yevera. A large scarlet tent had been erected. He, Mika, and the six other commanders stood around a large table.

Mika placed her palms flat on the table and leaned forward on the map. Several spots containing defensive posts were circled in red, along with the location of all platoons spread throughout Yevera and surrounding areas.

"It's obvious they're preparing for an attack during the last stages of the cleansing, when our stress levels are higher, our troops' motivation is lower, and we're all hungry and exhausted. The weather is just pure coincidence."

There were rumors circulating that Kymarinou had swayed the weather in an attempt to weaken Celeste, the region allied to his nemesis Liranda, and Mika was ordering major damage control on these rumors.

Studying the map, Mika looked past the northern hills of Yevera to a prairie that preceded a small forest. North of that forest was Mount Cabria. That forest curved to the east. If necromancers would come, they would do so from Mount Cabria or the forest to the east. Or both. Small platoons would test her defenses from the flanks, but not from the west because Di'Abribel would reinforce and sandwich the enemy against the western defense.

"The rats will come." Mika continued studying the map, cursing in her head when she heard the thunder rolling in and the rain begin its growing attack on the tent. "Gather the troops. Place them on emergency standby. Is General Hewelet still in Yevera?"

"Hewelet and his two platoons of paladins are in the western sector," Nicholas replied. "He refused to come to the table."

"Surprising!" Sarcasm was present in Cavalry Commander Charles.

"They're useless," said Taylor. "Paladins are absolutely useless."

"Stay focused. Move all troops to the northern sector." Mika stood; her voice boomed courage into her troops. "Disperse the orders immediately. They won't attack at night because the lux sun will make it brighter than it is now."

The commanders all left, and Nicholas was the last to exit.

Mika returned to the map, contemplating the inevitable battle in which she held no advantage. Seconds turned to minutes, and minutes turned to an hour when she heard a loud whistle followed by a howling explosion that shook the ground. The shockwave caused the tent to bend, and Mika stumbled.

Shouts came; Mika burst outside.

She heard another whistle, and one stone was followed by another infused with mori. They crashed into the ground yards away from Mika, destroying a camp of spearmen and sending Mika to her butt. The mist that raises the dead seeped out of the stone.

The healers focused on fighting the mist instead of cleansing Yevera.

"Empress!" Nicholas donned his helmet. "Catapult fire coming from the north!"

"Sound the horns! Gather the troops!" Mika clapped for Mythines. "Leave the reserve force to protect the healers!"

Nicholas turned to the musician commander, Bobby, who heard the orders and was running to gather his musicians.

"Call to arms! Call to arms!" Bobby unclipped a trumpet from his hip and sounded the horns.

Horns from platoons miles to the north followed in acknowledgment, and Mika reached for her magical staff strapped to Mythines's saddle.

More stones exploded around the destroyed town. The trumpets waned, and the drums began to roll louder than ever because of the sheer number of musicians.

"Forward!" Bobby shouted. "Hu!" The drums began to roll.

Nicholas ran up to Mika, screaming above the drums. "It's time!"

"It's time!" Mika repeated, and she rode Mythines in front of the musicians. The fifes began their happy, motivating melodies, the drums continued, and the trumpets sang, sending bouts of courage and patriotism through Mika. Another explosion came from behind, reminding her she was marching toward death. She was not eager for this battle.

Three platoons of archers and the Ladies of the Empress merged in front of Mika; two platoons of mages joined after, then over six hundred swordsmen and clubmen, and once Mika reached the front, the platoon of Celestial Protectors marched behind Mika and Nicholas.

Bobby shouted, his voice amplified by magic. "Get – in – step." Every syllable came with the placement of the right foot on the ground. "Right – 'eft – right!"

The drums continued, and the fifes played louder when stones began crashing into her army. The screams from her troops were soon replaced by footsteps running to close the formations. Mika did not look behind her, but she knew her army marched in step despite the artillery. Mika raised her staff and let out an explosion.

"Celeste!" All her troops shouted in unison, and she infused the rain with vita, healing her wounded soldiers as reward for maintaining their motivation.

A stone soared in the air and flew toward Mika before exploding yards in front of her, for she'd used a barrier to block the shockwave and debris.

She released another explosion from her staff when Mythines passed through the crater.

"Celeste!" Her army shouted, and she turned the raindrops to healing drops again.

Charles rode up to Mika; he didn't have time to speak before she issued orders.

She shouted above the drums, clanking equipment, and footsteps. "Two cavalry platoons to the northwest to flank the infantry." She pointed. "Two cavalry platoons to the east, flank around and target the catapults!"

Charles sped away.

Seven stones soared toward Mika's army, telling her there were at least seven catapults. She held her breath when they curved down.

Agonizing screeches were followed by curses, followed by more explosions. A Celestial Protector flew forward, sliding on the grass before taking his last breath. Nicholas stepped over his body as though he were rubble.

"They're going to be within the trees!" Mika told Nicholas, and he agreed.

Mika ordered her troops into an inverted L formation; melee units lined the north and east, protecting the magicians and archers who marched within the inverted L. The trees grew closer, and volleys of necromancer magic rushed from within.

Magicians in the rear cast barriers in front of the infantry and Protectors. The barriers held at first, then shattered, and the rest of the magic penetrated into her troops. Magical thunder extended from the clouds and boomed into the magicians.

Mika released an explosion from her staff.

"Celeste!"

They were almost within range.

Almost there ... She felt useless walking into battle, being able to do nothing when her soldiers were dying. The rain was at a downpour.

"Archers in range!" Taylor cried out.

"Fire at will!"

Archers fired; arrows covered the sky and curved toward the necromancers within the forest. Some arrows hit the trees. Some pierced the enemy.

"Magicians in range!"

"Fire!" Mika blew rain out of her mouth, cursing when she realized she forgot to don her helmet.

Magic of all affinities bolted from her army and toward the forest, causing explosions and debris to fly into the trees.

Catapults redirected fire toward Yevera, easing Mika's worry, but her worry grew further when she saw platoons of necromancer swordsmen, spearmen, and knights forming multiple rows along the tree line, protecting their archers and casters. Several platoons carried banners with mori and tenebris symbols, dispiriting Mika and her troops, reminding them that the necromancers fought for two allied deities.

Another volley of necromancer magic came, and Mika held up a barrier to her and Nicholas. Her troops' barriers shattered, and more of her soldiers fell.

A specter, a mori monster with the head of a skeleton and black rags, began to crawl out of the ground. The specter brandished a sharpened rake, growing and growing and growing until it was the size of a two-story house.

Mika set off an explosion.

"Celeste!" Her military continued marching despite the specter moving toward her army.

A beam of lux seared into the specter's chest. Paladins charged toward the specter, and the specter took the bait, focusing on the smaller platoons rather than plowing through her army.

Necromancer swordsmen and knights marched toward Celeste, and Celeste marched toward them.

"We are ..." Mika set off an explosion. "Celeste!"

"We are ..." All the commanders shouted with Mika.

Her troops' voices shook armor.

"Celeste!"

The drumrolls were at their most feverish, the eagerness showed on both armies, and when within sprinting range, both armies released a battle cry before crashing into each other, beginning their combat, and filling the air with shouts and clanking metal that dulled the sound of the fifes.

Mika rode to Magical Cavalry Captain Dain. "Meet with the crossbowmen!"

An inhuman scream escaped the specter, breaking Mika's focus. She turned to see paladins hanging from the spikes of its rake.

She turned back to Dain. "Meet with the crossbowmen! Protect them while they shoot the knights!" Without waiting for confirmation, she rode to Crossbow Commander Zyrell. "Move west, then north, and target the knights fighting the Protectors!"

Mika rode south and stood on Mythines's saddle to observe the battlefield. Her melee soldiers were in an inverted L shape with the north and east covered. Archers and mages fired upon the necromancers in the back, but her troops were also being fired upon by the necromancers within the trees. Hewelet's paladins were surrounding the specter, hacking away at its leg bones, trying their best not to be swept away by its massive rake and giant feet. Celestial shock cavalry plowed into the back of necromancer swordsmen but were met with lethal magical responses on their retreat. Half of the first cavalry charge died; horses with dead riders trampled necromancers and Celestials on their escape.

The musicians behind Mika beat the drums and played the fifes with worried looks on their faces. The downpour caused Mythines to be fireless. She cast a fireball, but it fizzled away.

Hundreds of gangrels descended from the clouds, their silver talons spread open during their dive.

"Divert fire! Divert fire!" Mika pointed at the gangrels.

Taylor, not knowing what to divert fire to, followed Mika's finger.

"Divert shots to the gangrels!" Her voice carried commanding stress.

The Ladies summoned a lux bow and shot it at the tenebris birds, the archers fired in a panic, and the magicians cast their fastest magic before the gangrels crashed into them, tearing their unarmored bodies to shreds.

Mika rode to a platoon of clubmen; their first row was engaged in a melee. "Get your rear rows to help the magicians!" She pointed behind her.

The rear row, veteran soldiers, turned and ran to the gangrels. When the first man reached the first gangrel, the creatures flocked away from the reach of Celestial maces.

The magicians and archers fired on the flock, killing a few until they were out of the effective range of their bows. They diverted fire back to the necromancers.

Gangrels curved around and attacked the crossbow platoon; without melee support, their numbers dwindled within seconds. The magical cavalry was routed, and Hewelet was lifeless next to the few remaining paladins. Finishing off the crossbowmen, the gangrels swept down on the rear of the westernmost platoon of clubmen.

A horn sounded, and necromancer axe infantry finished off the platoon of swordsmen on the northeast flank. The axe infantry circled around and flanked a platoon of Celestial clubmen before the rear rows turned on the Ladies.

The Ladies were routed, casting magic at their pursuers as best they could. Surviving Celestial mages pursued the necromancers pursuing the Ladies, and they all created distance from the fighting.

The rain prevented her from casting ignis. She had no support from the Reacan ships because of the rain and fog. Di'Abribel could not spare reinforcements. All Mika could do was heal some troops and watch the rest die. She remembered Liranda's words, *"For today, I bestow upon you just a fraction of a sorcerer's true power!"*

If only she had that power today.

"Please ... please help us, Mother," she prayed.

"Maces awaiting orders!" Nicholas shouted. He had moved to the eastern flank, and his soldiers had killed their necromancer counterparts.

"Attack the necromancers flanking our troops!"

Nicholas ordered the mace infantry to push against the necromancers, throwing all the formations into disarray. Troops were fighting troops from all sides, distinguishing themselves by their armor and their secret words. Mika had no sense of which platoon was which; she just saw soldiers in scarlet armor and soldiers in black armor slicing off each other's limbs, crushing each other's skulls with shields, and blowing the others apart with magic.

A Celestial Protector shouted, "Ready for orders!"

Mika pointed at the specter, hoping the battle axes of the Protectors would make better work of the monsters' bones.

465

As the second hour approached, the fighting began to wane, but the rain did not lessen. The necromancer infantry was defeated, but the catapults continued firing, and so did the archers and mages from within the trees. The drums continued to roll, the fifes played, and trumpets issued formation orders. The specter had been defeated, but so had all the paladins and three-quarters of the Celestial Protectors.

After forming up in a row, Mika determined there were fewer than one hundred of her troops alive. Remaining archers had run out of arrows, and the mages had reached exhaustion; their regeneration flasks once filled with green vegetable juice were empty. No word from the eastern cavalry told Mika they died executing their objective.

Mika looked around her, refusing to look at the ground where her dead soldiers lay. She swallowed, trying her best to keep her voice from showing the fear that ran through her legs. "Forward!"

Her commanders repeated, "Forward … march!"

The drums rolled, booming whenever their troops should be stepping on their right foot.

Her diminished army marched in step under the volley of magic that crashed into them, Mika doing her best to cast barriers.

Catapult fire silenced several of the musicians. Another stone followed, so she ordered the fast advance.

"Charge!" shouted the empress.

Her exhausted troops jogged into the trees, meeting with the excited archers who brandished hand axes. Though her infantry were better fighters, their exhaustion and diminished willpower sapped their strength. Celestials did their best to push through the forest, running after their taunting enemies, being ambushed by necromancers hiding within the trees.

The remaining musicians plus Mika, Nicholas, and Bobby were the only ones not within the trees.

"Nicholas?"

"Empress?"

"Come with me." She gathered her thoughts, trying to make sure her plan was the right one, "We're going into the trees to the east and flanking around. I don't think my magic will be affected from within."

Mika and Nicholas moved to the rear and entered the woods. The rain pelted on the branches and leaves, allowing just a couple of drops to seep through. Mika summoned a flame and held it to her face. Her choppy, terrified breaths made the flame move away from her, but it did not wither. Mythines's fire grew.

The empress inhaled through her nose, widening her nostrils to take in all the air she could. There could be anything behind the trees, under the ground, above the branches. Stalkers, the four-legged creatures she saw in the Lost Forest, could be camouflaged and ready to spit poison in her eyes, blinding her forever.

She caught Nicholas looking at her, so she did not lie about her feelings. "I'm scared, Nicholas."

Nicholas stretched out his back; he watched most of the musicians drop their instruments and flee the battlefield. The courageous ones grasped their daggers and joined the fighting.

The Celestial Protector Commander looked at his empress. "I was scared once."

Mika watched the fleeing musicians, not once blaming their actions. She looked at Nicholas.

"What did you do to help yourself?" She knew her eyes were widened, and she refused to blink in case something attacked when she did so.

"Nothing." Nicholas smiled underneath his helmet. "I stood there, and you apologized."

The joke calmed Mika, just enough for her to continue her plan.

She straightened herself on Mythines and faced forward, but her voice still shook. "Let's go."

Nicholas led the way, and Mika followed, making a slow walk through the woods that allowed both to catch their breath.

The fighting quieted.

No instruments were audible, but Mika's heart felt like it was doing the drumming. The clanking of armor was gone, but the chattering of her teeth made her think troops moved somewhere far in the distance. The shouts of pain were replaced by an agony inside Mika's heart, a discomfort that let her know she caused the deaths of over two thousand Celestials.

She had tuned out the sound of the pouring rain, so her body tensed every time a *swoosh* from the catapults passed overhead. She noticed only two stones fired now, not seven, telling her the cavalry reached their objective but had not completed it.

"We're the last ones alive," Nicholas whispered. "They might see Myth's fire."

Mika absorbed Mythines's flame. "How do you know they're dead?" She looked at Nicholas.

Nicholas was standing with his palm to the ground. "Using terra … this forest tells me all our soldiers are dead."

"Where are the rest of them?" Mika referred to the necromancers.

Nicholas shook his head. "Looking for survivors."

Mika's heart raced. Terror filled her mind as though she were in a nightmare. She begged and begged that she was in a dream, but when she plugged her nose and her ears filled with pressure, she let out a sob. She took a breath, held it … and released.

"I don't mean to be weak. I don't mean to be weak." She took another breath. "I apologize. Can you ask where they are?"

"One hundred and some yards that way." Nicholas pointed to the north. "Most of their army is there."

Mika remembered a terra spell that allowed her to call upon a meteor from space. The spell was powerful, so it would result in immediate collapse from exhaustion. Now that Nicholas and Mika were the last ones alive, she could use the spell without killing her own troops, but she didn't know where she was within the trees.

"I have an idea." Mika dismounted Mythines, sinking into the ground when her boots met the soft mud. She turned her horse and slapped him on the butt with a hand that communicated for him to go home. Mythines galloped out of the forest and toward Di'Abribel. She would be more mobile in the trees without him, and he wouldn't die from the meteor.

Mika walked north, and Nicholas followed with his battle axe resting on his shoulder.

A couple of yards in, Mika and Nicholas arrived at the first few bodies. Celestials lay dead within the trees.

Don't look down. Don't look down.

An accidental step on the stomach of an archer made her face churn, but she kept her eyes forward in case of danger. Several more yards were cleared, and she could see little movements between the trees further ahead. Movement underneath caught her eye, so she looked down to see what would be a memory that would be ingrained in her eyelids forever.

Lying on his back was a musician; his shirt had been torn off, exposing his chest. A massive laceration extended from one shoulder, across the chest, and to the armpit. His ribcage had been blown open by magic, revealing the musician's rapid beating heart and a peach lung inside his chest cavity. Every time the musician inhaled, the lung expanded and protruded from the opening. When he exhaled, the lung retreated into his chest.

"Nicholas—" Mika slid to her knees. The musician's eyes were open with a blank stare; blood seeped from his ear. He wasn't older than twelve. "Nicholas he's still alive."

Vita flickered from the musician's hand. His mind was trying to prevent his death.

"They're still looking for us." Nicholas crouched beside her. "They saw Myth running away."

"Nicholas …" Mika was out of breath. "You need to protect me while I heal this boy."

"Empress, I don't think—"

"Don't tell me what you think, Nicholas!" Mika hissed. "Look at him!"

Nicholas didn't turn around. He focused on the threats ahead of him.

"Damn it, Nicholas, I order you to look at him!"

Nicholas turned to the boy. He did not care about the boy. Victory, to Nicholas, was more important than any soldier in Celeste. He would sacrifice millions, and himself, to serve the Empress and reach Celeste's goals. He turned to face the necromancers.

The empress was in a deep state of emotional turmoil. Fear had forced logic from her mind. "He took up arms when the rest of his platoon fled. He sacrificed himself for Celeste without having any idea how to use his weapon!"

Mika's lips and chin were moving without her wanting to.

Tears appeared in her eyes, and she looked at the boy's distant stare. "I couldn't save my children, but I can save another mother's child." She looked at the back of Nicholas's helmet. "And you *will* protect me while I do so."

She closed one nostril and blew mucus out the other.

Nicholas took a moment to reply. "Yes, Empress." Nicholas used terra, and a stone boulder grew from the ground, concealing Mika.

Mika turned to the boy. A wound this complicated would take concentration and focus; she couldn't just cause the skin to fold into itself like a severed limb or a cut artery. She closed her eyes and whispered, "Vita." Her healing hand hovered over the wound.

"Ventus." She placed her ventus hand over the boy's mouth, giving him breathable air.

Using her healing hand, she began regrowing the ribcage, careful not to close it when the organs were expanding past the chest. She moved her wind hand to pull air and fluids from the chest cavity. After a minute of growing the bone, closing the wound, and extracting air and fluids, the experienced healer made the scar disappear, and her healing hand traveled to the head to ease the concussion. Mika drank the remaining liquid from her regeneration flask.

The procedure caused her to focus on something other than her failed battle, quelling her fears, and causing her confidence and logic to return. "Encase him in stone."

Nicholas enclosed the boy in a black stone barrier.

"After I faint," Mika said, "destroy those catapults. Come back for me and the boy. Do not fail Celeste, Commander."

"I will not fail, Empress."

Mika studied the area around her. The forest curved north of Mika's location, where the necromancers were waiting. There was a large tree next to Mika, much thicker and much taller than the rest. Looking up, she saw a cloud darker than the others, much fluffier too.

With a better understanding of what was around her, she turned to Nicholas. "Protect yourself."

Nicholas protected himself with a barrier made of stone.

Mika closed her eyes and called upon terra to grant her control of a meteor.

She opened her eyes, and her vision appeared in space; millions upon millions of stars were on one side, followed by the planet on the other. Her vision sped to a meteor that gravitated toward the atmosphere. It ignited.

"Ignis."

The fire grew in potency, and the meteor gained speed, traveling faster and faster until Mika recognized the continent of Irstia, then Celeste's eastern coast. She guided the meteor toward Mount Cabria, toward the darkest cloud, then toward the concave curve just north of the largest tree.

Mika's vision returned to her body, and she saw the beautiful white glow of the meteor exploding yards in front of her, incinerating the forest and causing a grand crater on the ground. The necromancers who survived scattered like rats, and Mika fell to the ground in exhaustion.

Nicholas undid his barrier, brandished his battle axe, and charged toward the enemy alone.

* * * * *

Bare feet walked on the gold-and-marble ceremonial altar. The feet were feminine, but big and old. One foot dragged, and the other walked with a wobble. The feet trembled, and the woman in a gray dress fell to her knees when her son's body was burned. Her son was a rider in the third platoon of the shock cavalry. He died minutes after Mika gave the order to head east and target the catapults. The woman covered her face, and several of her family members placed their hands on her shoulders.

Mika watched from the marble balcony of a building next to the altar and had been doing so since the burnings began the day after the *victory* of New Yevera three days earlier. Taylor, Nicholas, Mika, seventeen Ladies, twenty mages, and Joel, the dying musician Mika had saved, plus the musicians who fled were the only survivors on that rainy afternoon. Nicholas, Mika, and Joel would've died too had it not been for the Ladies and mages who returned to the battlefield after killing the pursuing necromancers.

"You need to fix your face ..." Ashlynn told her in a smooth voice. "It looks like you've seen the most disgusting thing in the world. Little disrespectful, if you ask me."

"That mother is crying the same way I did when Addie died."

Ashlynn took a moment to look at the woman. She'd been helped to her feet, but she continued her wails.

"I gave that man an order, and that order cost him his life. He died listening to me." Mika shook her head, and her eyes had traveled to the burning body. "I know I've killed without mercy or second thought, but these are my people." Mika looked at Ashlynn; tears made her eyes glimmer in the sun. "And I care about my people. I care about them like I've cared about Yevera, about Addie, Stacy ... you ..."

She grimaced from the pain she felt welling up inside of her. "I caused the death of my own. I killed my own people."

"I'm sure it's rough, having sent them to die, but—"

"No, you don't understand." The words had cut through Mika like a halberd swung at full force.

"Listen, Mika, they sacrificed themselves for something they believed in," Ashlynn said. "What would've happened if you told them to do something else? Wasn't he part of the platoon that disabled the catapults? If he hadn't done that, your troops would've taken more casualties when marching into the trees, and more healers would've died in Yevera."

Mika sighed and shook her head. Ashlynn wasn't wrong. Though Mika looked toward the next body placed in the altar, her mind was elsewhere.

"I can't think of anything I could've done different, based on what I knew at the time."

"That means you gave the right orders!" Ashlynn stood, leaning on her cane. "Our troops lived! We won the—"

"No." Mika snapped. "We lost our best troops during this battle. Troops we can't replenish quick enough. This battle was not a *win.*" Mika focused on one of Ashlynn's eyes, then the other, then back to the other. "I doomed Celeste by defending New Yevera."

"But New Yevera is a blessing!" Ashlynn threw her arms in the air, forcing Zarl to fall off and start flying. "Traders from here to Reach don't have to take a detour; lumber production will help our treasury, armament, and trade; we have a forward base to keep eyes on the necromancers; and best of all, your home has been rebuilt!"

Mika's face saddened when she saw a young woman and her two children watching the burning of her husband's body, a Celestial Protector. Mika put on a large hat, hoping people who saw her thought she was shielding her face from the sun's onslaught and not hiding her facial expressions.

"Mika…" Ashlynn clasped Mika's face and forced the empress to look at her. "I'll admit it. You lost the battle."

Worthlessness stabbed Mika's heart.

"And right now, you're feeling the twinge of defeat, the slash of embarrassment, and the burden of regret. You've lost troops before, but those battles were victories, so you didn't feel bad."

Ashlynn continued and squished Mika's cheeks. "You'll feel better soon, like you always have, and like you always will! It's your personality and who you are!" Ashlynn gave a friendly smile, her canines gleaming in the sunlight. "Fly on your wings of hope, Mika."

The crumbling world around Mika began to feel less heavy.

"Use a few weeks to take a vacation, Mika. The Imbric prince, king, and queen have been waiting for you to accept their invitation. Rest, recover, soothe your nerves, and you'll come back with new ideas and plans. Trust me. And don't give me that *I am Mika Plum of Yevera, the Empress of Celeste* nonsense. I am your friend and sister and can offer advice unsolicited."

A vacation did sound nice. She'd had little to no rest since she became a ruler, just days here and there with no real time to enjoy the pleasures of royalty. She'd never been to Imbris, and she knew their monuments, cities, and jewels were phenomenal.

"A month away from here would be nice." Her gaze drifted away from Ashlynn when she thought of all the matters that needed tending to. "I'll make a list of what needs to be done. Will you see to it?"

Ashlynn nodded with a smile and let go of her sister.

Mika jingled a bell, and seconds later, a servant walked to the balcony. "Yes, Empress?"

"Stephanie, send a letter to the Imbric king; tell him I accept his invitation. Have Luke pack my carriage. We can't spare troops, so Luke and I will travel alone."

"Yes, Empress."

"Thank you, Stephanie. I really appreciate you."

Stephanie looked down to hide her smile. "Thank you, Empress."

Mika began to walk away. Before she exited the balcony, she stopped, turned, and tilted her head up so she could see Ashlynn past the brim of her hat.

"I'll be back in a month. If you need me, send an eagle."

* * * * *

The empress returned thirty-four days later with a massive smile that only grew when her citizens cheered for her return. She exited the carriage and hugged Ashlynn at the gates of her palace.

"The bags under your eyes are not as purple!" Ashlynn said after moving a portion of clothing from Mika's shoulder to compare her tan.

"I'm excited to be back!" Mika returned Nicholas's salute. "What did I miss?"

Nicholas replied, "Nothing major."

The three walked together on the path flanked by trees that led to the front doors of the palace as Commander Nicholas updated her. "Skirmishes here and there," he said. "Reach has repaired their walls, Ronald has a new apprentice, aqueduct repair is steady, and our recruitment numbers are good."

"Ah," said Mika, holding up a finger, "speaking of recruitment, that won't be necessary anymore." Mika reached for a letter inside a satchel and handed it to him. "Nicholas, please publish these orders."

Nicholas's eyes widened when he read the letter.

"Is there a problem, Celestial Protector?" Mika asked, eager after seeing Nicholas's reaction.

Ashlynn spoke in Mika's head. *Mika, what does the letter say? What'd you think about when you were gone? Please don't let this be one of your cra—"* Ashlynn caught herself.

"Please don't let this be one of your brave ideas like you did with the mothers of the Vicquic newborns ..."

"To confirm accuracy," Nicholas cleared his throat and read the contents out loud, "Citizens of Celeste. The recent battle at New Yevera was far from a victory. Our elite men and women died defending a key strategic, economic, and cultural position in our great region.

The army of Celeste has been severed. Therefore, all men and women ages seven through sixty-nine *shall* report to the academy, where scholars will determine the best use of your abilities and place you in the Celestial army based on their findings. Factors affecting their decision will be available upon your request but are nonnegotiable."

Nicholas stretched his neck and continued. "A letter will be delivered to households on what day to report to the academy. Further instruction regarding training and practice will be issued after your assignment. Failure to comply will result in public execution. All travel out of Celeste has been canceled, and neighboring allies have been made aware of this order."

Nicholas folded the letter and looked at the smiling, wide-eyed woman in front of him. His empress, to whom he pledged his unwavering loyalty. Without so much as a hint of doubt in his voice, Nicholas raised his chin and finished the letter.

"Total war is necessary."

30. MORI

A large portrait of a man hung on the wall in front of the empress. He gave a serious, yet simple smirk that suggested he smiled only because he had to. His platinum-blond hair and golden-blond highlights were tied into a ponytail, and the wrinkles on his square, muscular face were the only indication of his old age. The man's white-and-gold uniform was spotless and covered with medals, telling the onlooker he was the paragon of the Paladin Order. *First Paladin Alphonse Lambert* was written in gold on a white placard that matched the decorated frame of the painting.

Empress Mika noticed she was leaning forward on the white-and-gold cushion chair, so she adjusted her necklace—the one that contained the paladin key—and sat back with her hands clasped at her lap and one leg draped over the other. She looked around her.

In front of her was a heavy metal desk that must have taken several men to carry into the room. A chair like hers, white and gold, faced her from behind the desk. On the wall and flanking the portrait of Paladin Alphonse were bookshelves with a diverse mix of books, decorations, equipment, and small paintings. Small orbs of lux were placed everywhere, their radiant golden-white light eradicating all shadows from the room. Still, the room did not hurt to be in, and the light was soothing to the eyes.

She heard his approach a moment before he opened the door and entered the room behind her. The door was closed. Steps came from her side, and Master Paladin Axel entered her field of view. He wore his ceremonial uniform, giving respect to the Empress of Celeste.

Mika locked eyes with Paladin Axel. He walked past her, returning her smile with stony disdain. Paladin Axel didn't look away from Mika as he sat in his chair. He placed his elbows on the metal desk and touched his fingers, holding them in front of his face. He glared at Mika.

Mika, who had trained herself not to show any emotion other than the ones she wanted to show, stared back with a smile that made her cheeks rise. "Thank you for meeting with me, Master Paladin Axel."

Paladin Axel inhaled, leaned forward, and placed one hand above the other on top of the desk. "Make your words quick."

Mika felt an itch on her neck, her body's way of feeling uncomfortable and threatened, but she refused to scratch at it. The urge to calm herself by playing with her necklace grew with every second. She didn't know why, but for the past several months, Axel and his army of paladins had shown nothing but disdain for Mika and her soldiers. Mika noticed her smile starting to wane, so she strained to keep it on her face.

"I'll get out of your way as soon as possible!" Trying to keep the peace, she smiled with closed eyes, then opened them wide and surprised. "Next week is the season of growth's solstice, the longest day of the year. The day when the necromancer magic will be the weakest."

Mika saw Axel's pupils move in thought. When they returned to Mika, she continued. "Celeste is ready to move upon the Lost Forest. Necromancer reinforcements have slowed, but they somehow continue to increase their numbers." Mika shook her head. She looked down and sighed. All on purpose and for show. Her acting was immaculate, and she knew Axel shielded himself against her emotions spell every time they met.

"If Celeste doesn't act now, the necromancers will complete rebuilding their army. Our scouts tell us we have just a few weeks before a coordinated attack on all the cities occurs."

A moment of silence.

"Get to the point, Plum." The master paladin leaned on one elbow and covered his mouth. He used the other arm to claim more territory on his desk.

"Celeste is requesting the assistance of the Paladin Order in the Last Fight." Mika grabbed a scroll, opened it, and slid it across the desk. "In return for your assistance, Celeste will give you all credit for the victory, all spoils, and a deed to the Lost Forest." Mika smirked. "This will look amazing to your superiors—though I'm sure they think highly of you already. All I ask is that Kathrine be taken alive. She must pay for the crimes she's committed against Celeste. I know your griffins have fully grown, and they will be instrumental in the battle."

Griffins were massive, winged creatures that could expel rays of lux from their mouths.

Paladin Axel exhaled and grabbed the scroll. He sat back and read the contents. Everything Mika had said was written as a contract to Paladin Axel and his army of paladins. He looked over the scroll and to Mika. She sat with a confident smile on her face. Axel ripped the scroll and tossed it. "Fuck you, Plum."

Mika's smile changed for a fraction of a second, but not enough for Axel to notice. "Master Paladin Axel, if you have a problem with me, then let's settle it now, once and for all."

She didn't know it, but the smile on her face was angering Axel.

"You are a disgrace to anyone who commands an army and rules a city." Paladin Axel wasn't yelling, but his voice was loud. "You execute those who refuse your sadistic ways, you enslave the women and the elderly—"

"It's not about sex or age," she said. "It's about allies or enemies. Logic over emotion and—"

Axel slapped his table so hard it caused the walls to shake. "You've sent children to fight and die in battle!" Axel's shout sent saliva flying toward Mika. "You're arming elders who have never held a sword in their life! Sending them to their deaths! You've made public displays of torture against your captives!"

"All captives were once combatants. Furthermore, Celeste's army will take years to build, years we don't have. They all agreed. Extreme circumstances require extreme measures."

"Extreme measures?" Axel stood, placing his palms on the table. He leaned forward and hissed his words. "Was the destruction of Triumph an extreme measure, *Sorceress*?"

Mika's face straightened; her eyes widened. The rage grew in Axel's face when he realized he was right. Mika finally eased the itch on her neck.

"Kymarinou blessed me with the dreams." Axel pointed at Mika. "I saw you burning Amirra's face, stabbing her husband through the temple, and destroying the town to prevent apprehension." He returned his hands to the desk and leaned further forward. "I should have you executed."

A dream? A dream? Mika knew the power dreams had, and now dreams worked against her. It didn't surprise Mika that Kymarinou would bestow the dream upon Axel. She remembered when the fire of her explosion settled, the view from the inside of a crater, the memories, *all* the memories from the citizens of the town, the memories of Rosa and Lila.

"Triumph was a mistake, Axel, but I don't regret anything I've done, there or here." She pressed her lips together; all her emotions were legitimate. "I am an empress and a grown woman. I own all the mistakes I've made and stand by everything I've done."

Axel and Mika stared at each other for what seemed like an eternity. Seconds turned to minutes until Axel sat on his chair and leaned back. He continued looking at Mika. Mika waited for him to say something. She wasn't afraid of Axel, but she was frozen, and her legs were shaking. The room felt so cold.

"The paladins I command will evacuate Celeste on the day of growth's solstice. We will not assist you, your soldiers, or your people any longer. You will perish along with your army."

Mika scoffed. She gathered her thoughts before she spoke. "*You're* a disgrace to your cause and your subordinates, Axel. You think because I've angered you and done as I see fit in *my* territory, that *you're* making the right decision? You paladins think you're so righteous, so *good* because you don't torture your enemies, yet history shows you've done everything I have." Mika stood erect and looked down on Axel.

"Everyone knows what happens during purity trials. It's not a secret anymore. You're not righteous, and you're the same as every other ruler in the world." Mika's hands dripped embers at the thought of

479

paladins killing their own citizens during purity trials, where someone's genetics decided if they lived or died.

Mika placed her hands on the desk and leaned toward Axel. "The ladder to victory has never been climbed without corruption or manipulation. I've done what I've done for my people; for victory, and you know this."

Axel didn't respond.

Mika stood, grabbed her paladin key, and yanked it from her neck. She tossed it across the table at Axel. "Necromancers have the most advanced ships in the world. When they unite Irstia, they'll sail to Luxania. Remember this conversation when the blanket covers your skies and your family is cut to shreds by walkers."

Mika headed toward the door. "Unlike your pathetic army, Celeste died holding her weapon." Mika turned the knob and slammed the door behind her.

* * * * *

A volley of magic rained from clear blue skies, taking a downward plunge toward Mika's army. The necromancers in the Lost Forest to the north wasted no time in firing off their magic the moment Mika's frontline troops were within range from the south. The musicians sent courage into the hearts of the assembled Celestials.

"Move!" Mika kicked the sides of Mythines and released blue flame from her staff, the signal for her troops to advance.

Magic fell into a platoon of crossbowmen, dispersing the formation from the mix of magical explosions of every affinity.

"Send the cavalry!" she ordered.

A horn from Celestial cavalry was followed by a horn near the Lost Forest.

"Request Reacan artillery!"

Still running, the crossbowman commander on horseback ignited a fuse that began spewing black smoke, signaling the ships of Reach to begin their bombardment.

More volleys of magic came from the forest, but not as many as the first; magicians and archers on horseback were causing damage at the necromancers' flanks. Mika slowed Mythines to match the speed of her sprinting army. She waited until the volley of magic was close and cast a massive ignis barrier that shattered into millions of pieces the moment the magic collided with it, protecting her troops but draining her energy, inching her ever closer to exhaustion.

Slowing her speed to take a gulp of her regeneration flask, she looked at her sprinting army. Tens of thousands of men, women, children, elderly, and soldiers ran in rows according to their specialty, all wearing scarlet uniforms and helmets with two horns. Mika kicked the sides of her horse. "Kiya!"

She could not lose.

Ashlynn followed on her own horse, shooting an arrow that curved into the leg of a necromancer.

"Archers in range!" she heard Taylor yell.

Ashlynn's voice screeched past the thundering rolls of the clanking armor, sprinting feet, and music.

"Fire!"

"Ignis!" Mika held her staff to the air; she lit the arrows of the archers, and they traced fiery arcs across the sky above the green plains between the Lost Forest and the Farmlands.

"Magicians in range!" the commander shouted.

"Just fucking fire! Fire at *fucking* will!"

Magical cavalry to the northwest was engaged in a fierce fight. Boulders from the catapults crashed into the western platoon of Celestial Protectors, breaking the formation and sending several of them onto their backs and stomachs.

"Get up!" they yelled at each other. "For Celeste!" The Celestial Protectors who didn't die sprinted back into formation.

Further ahead, platoons of necromancer spearmen, swordsmen, and knights lined themselves in front of their archers and catapults. Necromancer archers sent thousands upon thousands of arrows soaring through the air and into the imperial army.

"Get me some rain!" Mika shouted at a magician commander.

The commander held his hands to the sky. "Aqua!"

Rainclouds formed above Mika's army.

"Vita!"

Healing rain fell onto her troops and followed her frontline soldiers. When the rain fell onto the necromancers, Mika turned the drops to white embers.

Her army continued, and a horn sounded from behind. Celestial shock cavalry thundered past Mika's infantry and into the open flank of the necromancers.

Mika saw Kathrine at the rear; ghastly hands behind her flung magical balls of mori faster than all her catapults combined. Kathrine used terra spikes that rose from the ground and killed half the mounts of Celeste's shock cavalry. The men whose horses died joined a separate platoon that ran alongside the Celestial Protectors.

"That fucking bitch!" Mika hurried to the front of her army. "Move! Go, go, go!" She yanked the reins of Mythines, forcing him to stop. "Terra!"

Calling to the vastness of space, Mika summoned meteors traveling above the planet. They burned through the atmosphere and curved toward the necromancer catapults, causing massive explosions that also killed hundreds of archers. Despite her staff, she almost fainted from exhaustion.

"Fire!"

The western platoon of crossbowmen fired their bolts into the knights. A volley of arrows, followed by an array of magic, decimated necromancer spearmen. Celestial Protectors, swordsmen, axemen, and clubmen stepped on their bodies and went head-on with the necromancer knights and infantrymen. Shock cavalry passed Mika again, plowing into the archers through an opening.

Something isn't right. Mika drank from the regeneration flask. *Something isn't right.*

"Where are the ships?" Mika screamed.

She looked to the east, noticing no sign of smoke communicating a response to the signal. Catching a glimpse of friendly arrows overhead, she ignited them, along with the weapons of her Celestial Protectors.

Heavy magic use to the west was followed by deep horn and a cry of retreat from her magical cavalry. A platoon of magical cavalry was annihilated by a mori vortex that shredded the horses and horsemen before propelling their remains throughout the battlefield.

"Mika!" Ashlynn rode toward her at full speed. Her eyes were wide and sweat gleamed on her face. "Something is wrong to the east. I'll check and see what's happening!"

Mika rode toward the west as an explosion sent Celestial Protectors flying toward her, almost crashing into her and knocking her off Mythines. The necromancers who defeated the magical cavalry began curving into Celeste's western flank, closing in on the crossbow units.

Mika picked up the pace, encased herself in a fiery vortex, and galloped into the necromancers, carving their flesh with her fire. Emerging from behind them, Mika spun Mythines around and repeated the attack, but the necromancers moved out of the way, only to be met by walls of fire that shredded their skin. The necromancers refused to yield.

"Fall back! Fall back!" the crossbow commander yelled.

"No!" Mika shouted. "You fall back, we lose all the archers! Face your enemy like the warriors you are!"

None of the crossbowmen hesitated. They pulled out their short swords and began fighting the shielded infantry.

With the crossbowmen holding the line, Mika ordered the shock cavalry to move south, west, then north to flank. Mika rode toward the center of her army, where Ashlynn caught up with her.

"We need to retreat! We need to retreat right now!" Ashlynn's words were quick. "I went to the eastern flank, which is about seven platoons down, I mean I'm only estimating—"

"Get to the point, Sorip!"

Ashlynn removed her samurai helmet, closed her eyes. "Stalkers!" she shouted. "Stalkers! They came out of the forest and tore into our archers and mages! Like, ten platoons of necromancers, thousands of them came out and are curving around the eastern flank! How are there so many? How are there so fucking many? And the fucking cathedral is spewing the black blanket!" Ashlynn pointed to the cathedral. "We won't have a sun to protect us!"

A volley of friendly arrows and magic flew overhead when Mika looked at the darkening skies. A necromantic cluster of magic crashed into and pulverized half of the Ladies of the Empress.

Mika wanted to take off her helmet and pull out her hair, turn back time, spend more funds on equipment and training, undo everything that caused this failing attack to happen, but she took a breath and kept her cool. Her soldiers could be watching, and she needed to stay calm. She analyzed the battlefield for a vantage point. She trained her eyes on a hill to the southwest, about a mile away.

"Pass the word," she said. "Reposition all archers and magicians onto the hill. Once the melee starts, we'll have a high-ground advantage." She shut her eyes, inhaled, and exhaled so hard snot flew out of her nose and plastered itself on the inside of her helmet. "Sacrifice the melee units. They need to buy us time to reposition."

With a gaping mouth, Ashlynn swallowed. She nodded, spun her horse around, and galloped toward the easternmost platoon of dying Celestials as she donned her helmet.

Mika located Commander Nicholas's platoon in the center of the battlefield and sped toward him. Commander Nicholas was at the rear, shouting words past the clanking of armor, scraping of metal on metal, and the thuds of axes meeting exposed flesh.

"Commander Nicholas—" Mika dismounted her horse.

Nicholas ran to Mika. "Empress?"

She pulled him out of earshot of her troops. "How is it looking?"

"They baited us with the small numbers and are flanking from the east."

Mika already knew that, but how they managed to have such a large army, she did not.

"Commander, I need you to do something."

Nicholas remained quiet, but Mika could sense the stress emanating from within his armor.

"Hold your position." She clenched her jaw and swallowed. "Hold your position so our backline can move up the hill." She saw Nicholas's eyes scan the hill.

Nicholas nodded. He knew what her orders meant. He and his soldiers would die.

"Send them to the Abyss, Empress," he said and saluted Mika.

Mika reached for his helmet and moved the helmet's horns to her forehead. "I'll see you in the afterlife, Nicholas."

"I'll be waiting." Nicholas turned to his platoon and continued the shouting.

A lump formed in Mika's throat, slowing the mounting of her horse. With a heavy heart, she shot a red beam of fire from her magical staff—the signal for retreat. Her heart shattered when she saw the infantrymen being told to continue fighting. All eyes were on Mika's fire when she curved it into an arrow that pointed to the hill.

She rode at a light pace behind the slowest platoon of magicians, a platoon of elders, most of whom had never traveled out of their city. Their first time out of the walls would also be their last. The weakest elders, the ones too old to fight, and the youngest children, were the only ones who weren't brought into battle.

"We're almost there," she said, dismounting and running alongside the elders. "We're almost there ..."

Running up the hill with the elders, she passed a platoon of archers. All children, the youngest was seven years old. All the children cried. Most of their fathers and a few of their mothers were yards behind them, in a melee that would soon end with them dying. Mika felt the worst for them. These children would never grow and experience life like the elders did. These children would watch their parents die, and she knew, their last memory would be the sight of black armor crashing down on them.

They reached the hill.

"Position yourselves!" Mika mounted Mythines and faced the battlefield. She heard the remaining commanders mix the surviving Celestials into matching platoons.

Mika looked back, noticing her army was still large; she estimated over seventy thousand humans were lined in rows along the hill. Thousands more were in a fight with necromancers that were half their numbers but had three times their experience and training. The rest were dead on the grass below the hill. All citizens from Di'Abribel and Vicqua were pulled into this battle—and the battle was lost within an hour. Mika's lips wrenched when necromancers rounded on the Celestial soldiers, flanking them from the rear. The number of necromancers was shocking.

Where the fuck did they get reinforcements?

Mika pictured the map of Celeste and the nearby cities in the Velonde and Imbris regions. Through Adventurer's Pass? No. The valley was patrolled by Celestial and Velondian guards day and night.

The road that led to the Grand Waterfall? Too open. Reinforcements from there would have been slow, maybe ten per day, if that.

Southeast of Di'Abribel? New Yevera? Traders between Di'Abribel and Reach would have noticed. She thought of Peak's Lake.

Peak's Lake ... Peak's Lake! You fucking idiot!

Mika forced her eyes shut, remembering the river that flowed from the lake to the ocean. Ships from the necromancer base in Imbris probably transported reinforcements to the edge of the river, where they could move hidden within the trees and into the empty lake, exit from the west valley, and be only a day or two away from the Lost Forest. They knew Celeste would attack on this day. Kathrine was no idiot.

The number of necromancers did not surprise Mika, since interception of letters from the forest showed that Kathrine painted the Celestials to be bloodthirsty barbarians. Kathrine made it seem like her necromancers were ridding the world of evil.

"We should have known." Ashlynn had read her thoughts as she rode up to Mika.

Mika looked at her sister. *"But we didn't. And now we die because of it."*

The black blanket began covering the sun; a black mist poured from it and misted into the battlefield below.

"They're going to use our dead against us." Mika clenched her jaw when she saw a massive explosion destroy the platoon of crossbowmen she ordered to hold. The shock cavalry's flank had failed.

Ashlynn massaged her stump. *"Do you think the elders and the children will know to leave?"*

Mika sighed. She didn't respond, but she hoped that someone watching the battle's defeat would send word to all cities and order an exodus from Celeste.

"Empress!" Three men on horseback rushed to Mika. "Empress! Our ships are in a battle against necromancer ships from their base in Imbris!"

Of course. Why wouldn't that happen?

"Draw your weapons and fall in." Mika eyed the battlefield; only the distant echoes of dying Celestial men filled the night-looking sky.

"I think you should say something." Mika felt Ashlynn's stare. *"Speak your own words. Don't use your magic. Not today."*

Mika looked at Ashlynn, gave her a glare behind her helmet, then smiled. Mika knew Ashlynn couldn't see what she did, but she had done it anyway. The Empress of Celeste faced her army, and the music quieted.

Eyeing her stretching platoons of ranged troops, Mika was glad she couldn't see their faces. She would have a hard time looking them in the eyes and seeing their defeated expressions. What was amazing about her citizens was that, before the march, all Celestials painted a scar like Mika's across their face. Not only did they fear the empress, but they loved her also.

Still taking in the view of the army, she smiled when she saw Sandra looking at her from within a platoon of magicians. Sandra had no helmet, but her hair was tied in a tight bun. Knowing Sandra, Mika figured she tossed the helmet on purpose. Sandra, after all these years, finally gave Mika a smile, and she turned her face the second she did so.

Mika looked at a platoon of pavisers, recognizing Ron, the man who took away months of her life and almost killed her, by the halberd he used to cut off Ashlynn's leg. His heavy helmet hid his expressions, but she knew he was looking at her. Mika nodded at him, forgiving him for everything he did to her. Ron looked at his feet and nodded. Mika knew Ronald Stannard had started to cry.

Mika looked at Ashlynn; her samurai armor hid her face. Ashlynn and Mika stared past their visors into each other's eyes, and Mika knew Ashlynn was smiling at her. Ashlynn kept her promise of staying with Mika when she reached the top. Ashlynn, a Sytui, would die for a land that was not hers just because Mika was its leader.

Ashlynn gave a bob of her head, convincing Mika to give her speech.

The Sorceress Mika didn't use her emotion spell, but she amplified her voice with magic so everyone could hear. "All of you know what will happen in the next few minutes."

No one in the army moved.

"All of you have trained for this moment for the past two years, and all of you know how this is going to end. Today is not a day of defeat, nor is it a day of victory. Today is a day of release."

Some of her soldiers hung their heads. Others repositioned their feet. Others looked Mika in the eyes. Taylor held on to her daughter, kissing the head of the youngest Lady in Celeste.

"Today is a day where we, as Celestials, claim our independence from the hand that invaded and bound us. From the hand that cast us into a black hole of fear, from a hand that stole our children and stole our livelihood. The hand that has forced so many of us to die early."

The sun was covered, and Mika flung fires onto the battlefield so her soldiers could see their enemies.

"Today is the day we are released from this realm and enter the realm where our parents, our loved ones, our children, and our pets await us." She closed her eyes and smiled, thinking of Addie, Stacy, and Vivinia.

"Our soldiers have died." Ashlynn reported. *"Necromancers are advancing, and the dead are starting to move in front of them."*

Mika opened her eyes, straightened her face, and continued.

"The meaning of our lives is to create a world where those who come after us have a better chance of enjoying what we could not. We have made the path the best we could, and now we're ready to move on to the next part of our lives. Death is not the end of your story; it's only the new and better beginning. I shall visit all of you personally in the next realm, and I am forever grateful for the sacrifice you have made, not for me, not for you, but for this beautiful region we know as Celeste."

"Walkers from the flanks ..."

Mika ignored the approaching walkers. She gave her army—no, not her army, her children, her brothers, her sisters, her mothers, her fathers, her grandparents—a sweeping look. Whether it was her mind playing tricks on her or their actual spirits, she saw Cynthia, Stacy, Sylisia, Vivinia, Blake, Donald, Nicholas, a spirit that represented dead citizens, a spirit representing soldiers were also present, and, at the very front of all of them, Addie sat smiling with his tongue hanging from his mouth. All these were victims of the invaders that, today, would emerge victorious.

She remembered Ashlynn's words. *"Oh, my goodness, why do you continue to say Of Yevera?"*

The thought made Mika chuckle. *Not anymore,* Mika thought, she was not a Yeveran anymore. Now, she was a Celestial. She found her new family, she found her new home. She finally found a place where she felt she belonged and, in the afterlife, she would refer to herself not as Mika Plum of Yevera, but as Mika Plum of Celeste. And she would say that with a smile that would not be shaken by thoughts of this life.

Mika's smile widened. "Today, we die as a united family!" The empress raised her staff above her head. "Who are you?" An explosion escaped her staff.

"Celeste!" her army shouted, raising their weapons in the air.

"Who are you?" Her voice exploded through her army, vibrating within their armor.

"Celeste!" her army boomed.

Mika spun around, pointing her staff past the army of reanimated soldiers that she once called her own. "Ignis!"

A white beam of fire rushed through the air and cut through the armor of necromancer knights. Volleys of arrows and thunderclaps of magic from Celeste soared down the hill. Archers shot their arrows in rapid succession, pulling out their swords and running toward the enemy when their ammo expired.

Ashlynn shot her bow at the walkers ravaging the cavalry to the west. Magicians drank vials of juice and continued their magic. Mika sent a sweeping wall of fire to the necromancers in the rear, followed by rain of fire and volcanic eruptions from the ground.

Reanimated troops sprinted up the hill with Commander Nicholas at the vanguard. Mika prepared a lux spell, taking aim at Nicholas's heart. Nicholas used terra to unsettle her stallion's feet. Mythines bucked, sending Mika crashing onto her back. She stood, brandished her dagger, and sprinted toward her former commander.

"I am not afraid!" she screamed.

Commander Nicholas raised a battle axe with one hand.

Mika shouted. With a dash forward, she met Nicholas's fist, making her stumble. Nicholas kicked. She fell.

Nicholas stomped her sternum and rotated his hips, raising his battle axe above his head. "Empress …" Pain filled Nicholas's voice.

"Nicholas." She closed her eyes. Her ears exploded, and the black vision from her eyelids turned to white. The ringing in her ears didn't allow her to hear anything.

Finally, she thought, *I get to see my Addie ... my Vivinia ... my dragon ... Sylisia ...* She felt her cheeks touch the inside of the helmet when she smiled.

The whole world was white, and the ringing in her ears continued, making her want to tune it out or lose hearing altogether.

Her heartbeat slowed; so did her breathing. But she could still feel the grass tingling on the openings in her armor, its wetness seeping into her clothes.

She opened her eyes but continued seeing white. She knew they were open because she could feel herself blinking. She closed her eyes, and her eyelids made the area darker. She felt the girth of her wooden staff and the familiar grip of the silver dagger in her hands.

Was this the Abyss her mother talked about? Did she not please Liranda enough to be forgiven? Was this what it would be like for the coming years? The coming century? Her ears continued to ring a loud, metallic scraping that covered all other noise.

Using her knuckles, Mika felt the grass on the ground below her. She sheathed her dagger, feeling for her face where Nicholas's axe would have struck; her hand stopped when she felt the roughness of her leather helmet. She felt the horns on top. Maybe she was dreaming? Taking the helmet off, she plugged her nose and blew. Her ears filled with pressure, telling her she was awake. The metallic ringing continued, but her vision began to clear.

Within the white, she saw flickering little lights, little orbs, little stars that twinkled like the distant suns in the night sky that was, for some reason, white.

The ringing began to clear, but she didn't hear anything other than clanking armor, confused yells, screams, shouted commands. Mika opened her mouth to try to see better. For some reason, she thought that would help.

The white continued fading, and Mika saw a gray battlefield. Her reanimated soldiers were in front of her, all standing still with closed eyes. She looked at her army; they weren't in a column, in a row, or any sort of formation. They were in disarray, scrambling on the ground, reaching for something—trying to see with their hands. The necromancers at the bottom of the hill were having the same issue. Complete blindness.

Mika looked up. Underneath the tenebris blanket that covered the sun was a massive white orb of lux that eradicated every inch of darkness from the battlefield.

She heard a shuffle and laugh. Commander Nicholas was standing above her, laughing at the top of his lungs. "Long live Celeste!" He raised his axe with both hands and swung it over his head toward his Empress. "Long live the empr—"

A griffin swept down, crashing into Nicholas and expelling lux into his heart.

Paladins!

Another griffin dove in, releasing a massive squeal before using the same beam of light to sweep the battlefield.

"Paladins, Mika!"

Millions of eagles covered the lux sun and plunged into archers. Thousands of paladin horsemen plowed into magicians, crushing them underneath their hooves.

Thundering roars of men came before Mika saw paladins sprinting past Celestial citizens.

Mika watched the army of white and gold converge onto the army of black and gray. Paladins shot beams of light that pulverized necromancer armor. The drums rolled. The fifes played.

"Paladins are killing the walkers!"

Was this real? Were the paladins helping Celeste? Mika's breaths were uncontrollable; her army rushed into battle behind the paladins who were rushing into battle without any armor. Mika stood, stopping when a unicorn stepped in front of her.

Looking up, she saw Axel guiding Mythines by the reins. She walked up to Axel, ignoring the explosion that shook the ground. She latched onto Mythines's reins, but Axel didn't release them.

The look he gave her at that moment spoke louder than words could. *This is not over between us.*

Mika slapped his hand away, mounted Mythines, and kicked the horse's side. "Kiya!"

"Get that bitch, Mika!"

The wind whistled in her ears, kissing her cheeks. Clanking armor, scraping metal, and drums filled the air. Vicious shouts from the paladins bounced in her brain as they plunged their weapons into their mortal enemies.

Mythines was at a full gallop. Mika's eyes trained on Kathrine, who launched mori missiles with her ghastly hands, taking Celestials and paladins alike.

With tears in her eyes, Mika kicked Mythines again, forcing a cry out of her stallion.

"Protect the empress!"

Paladin horsemen surrounded her, protecting her from Kathrine's magic. They burst into pieces when meeting her mori missiles.

A mori missile zoomed over Mika's head. She clenched the horn of the saddle, let out a roar, and pivoted her horse.

"Aevum!"

She teleported herself behind Kathrine, plowing Mythines into her back.

Kathrine flew forward and slid face-first across the grass; her legs continued their momentum, arching themselves over her back like a scorpion's tail until the necromancer stopped sliding.

Mika slowed her horse to a walk. When she raised her staff, flames rushed upward toward the heavens in a roaring, fiery inferno that surrounded both leaders. She looked at Kathrine with eyes that hungered for vengeance.

With shaking limbs, Kathrine pushed herself off the ground. She wrapped her fingers around her sword and pulled it from its scabbard. Kathrine spun and shouted, her ghastly hands reached to attack Mika, but the ignis had grown hands of its own, holding the ghasts in place behind the necromancer.

Kathrine clenched her teeth, looked at the wall of fire, then at Mika, and it was then that realization struck—it was the leader of Celeste, not a mighty man or wise woman, who could control ignis. Kathrine grasped it was the empress, not the siren, who'd set fire to the cathedral. The same young woman, the same girl, who'd screamed at the top of her lungs when she was trapped inside a closet over six years ago, was now trapping Kathrine in a closet of fire.

Profuse sweating began, and her clothes incinerated. The necromancer gripped her sword with both hands when she realized the scorching heat made her unable to focus. Kathrine needed to know the name of the newest head she would hang on her belt.

Spit flew out of her drying mouth when she shouted her question. "Who are you?"

The empress further straightened herself on the horse, tilting her chin up and looking down at her next kill. She puffed her chest and flexed her abs and diaphragm, forcing her powerful voice to boom above the flames.

"I am Mika Plum, the *Empress* of Celeste."

Dedicated to Mika.

There was a point when I was about to delete this whole project. Then, one night, you appeared in my dream with tears in your eyes, begging me not to forget about you.

It was because of you that my wings of hope fluttered, and I was able to make your story to what it is now.

L.G. Benito

Celeste has been united, but what happened to the sirens who escaped the massacre? Find out in the heart-wrenching sequel!

Awaken: Fall of the Righteous